I0673236

First Edition

ISBN 0692045538

This is a work of fiction. Names, characters, businesses, places, events and incidents are either the products of the author's imagination or used in a fictitious manner. Any resemblance to actual persons, living or dead, or actual events is purely coincidental.

Cover by Shawn Jenks © 2017
Editing and Revisions by Amanda K. Hill
Follow @LennoxMcCaskill on Facebook, Instagram, and Twitter

This book is dedicated to everyone we lost in 2017 and their loved ones.

Fallen

By

Lennox McCaskill

Chapter 1

Shots From The Sky

"There is still little known about the mysterious deaths and disappearances that have plagued several areas along the Canada-U.S. border since January. Authorities have now quarantined a wide area near Lake Ontario and are working around the clock to find and hopefully end the cause of the deadly ailment dubbed, 'Toronto Reaper'. I'm Tonya Hajar, reporting live for CTV..."

"...the President in New York this afternoon. The speech is expected to focus heavily on the ongoing war in Afghanistan and the recession. However, we shouldn't be surprised to hear more about his plan to reform healthcare. We'll have a live look in just a few moments..."

~

The lens on the scope gleamed in the sunlight as she twisted it into place. She checked the give to be certain it was on tightly before fastening the muzzle onto the barrel of the gun until it too was secured.

Through the single eye hole of her gray mask she inspected the rifle, turning it over a few times and practicing her stance. She loaded then removed the ammunition clip several times rhythmically, listening to each click as though it were music. Her lethal instrument was lighter than she normally preferred, but the wind was minimal. It had turned out to be a very good morning to work. She rolled up the sleeve of her steel-colored outfit to check her watch. It was almost time and she was ready.

Placing the rifle under one arm, the long-legged assassin walked toward the edge of the roof and the rest of her tools. She glanced at the levels on the sound amplifier before peering out into the high-rise jungle that surrounded her.

Closing her eye for a moment, she let the sounds of the metropolis fill the space around her. Everything sounded so alive as the cars echoed all the way up the thirty-nine floors. It was her first time in New York. Shame she was only there for business.

The beginning of a muffled processional brought her back to task. She tapped the earpiece and then raised the volume on the amplifier once more. The masked woman shifted back to her spot and positioned the rifle on its mount, aiming it in between two tall, distant buildings.

Gazing through the scope, she searched for the stage. After a moment, she locked in on a set of red and white striped flags hanging over a blue carpeted platform. It seemed a very American scene. The woman aimed at each suited man's head as they took their seats behind the podium. A few seconds later, the assassin smiled as the target fell into her crosshairs.

She lightly brushed the trigger, letting the feel of it tease her finger as though it were part of some sort of foreplay. But she didn't pull it. Her instructions had been too specific.

Don't shoot until the President takes the podium.

Thankfully, it appeared she wasn't going to have to wait long. A rapturous roar greeted the American President as he walked onto the stage. She watched as he shook hands with each of the men in the row behind where he was to stand, before waving to the audience, and escorting his wife to her seat.

He looked like a king and wore a gracious smile like the one she had seen in pictures and broadcasts back home. She listened as he began his address. He had a regal voice and presence as he spoke, at least more than most of the men who'd unknowingly fallen into her scope.

The masked woman continued to follow his movements and thought about how easy it would be to end his life. She lightly caressed the trigger once more, but let out a resigned huff. It was so unbearably tempting. It was unfortunate that he was *not* her target. That meant he would live, at least for today.

As for the brown-haired senator seated slightly to his left...

The President moved his arms freely, opening up his body several times in the space of just a few seconds. He had no idea that her sniper rifle was currently trained on him.

The woman spent the next few minutes discerning any pattern to his shifts behind the podium. His tendency to turn around to the men seated behind him could make for a difficult shot. But then finding the right timing and angle for the strike was part of her favorite game. Oh, how she had truly missed playing it.

It took her longer than usual, but once she had his pattern the clock in her head began to count down. It had to happen in a matter of moments now. She just waited for him to make that key move just one...more...time...

BANG!

~

Katie shot into the summer sky like a bullet, closing her eyes as she sprang through the clouds. She opened them to the calm

3

that resided just below the vaulted ceiling of the world. She gave herself a few seconds to take it in before lowering the black rimmed goggles over her eyes. Once she tightened the strings of her hood she let out a deep breath. Then, as if freed by the sound of the starter's pistol, Katie dove back into the bustling pool that was Meridian.

"Okay, there's the interstate...and there's Placek Park," she began anxiously, trying to recall Troy's many attempts to help her navigate the city during their walks. "And if I'm facing Placek, I'm facing east..." Katie quickly spun around. "The Glasgow Building faces west...there it is!"

The blonde sped past her concrete placeholder and was soon soaring above a divided highway. The dry voice of the reporter she had just listened to replayed in her mind:

"We interrupt your daily broadcast to bring you this developing story. A routine traffic stop turned high speed chase along I-20 Westbound has taken a horrifying twist. We've now learned that the suspect, identified as former naval officer and truck driver Nathan Karl, is wanted in connection with the disappearance of his six-year-old daughter, Cynthia Jefferson. Her mother reported her missing on Monday and Jefferson is believed to be the child the officer, who initially pulled Karl over, reported seeing in the passenger seat..."

The story immediately brought back memories of Melody Riker, who she had pulled to safety from Bishop's destruction last year. Katie could only imagine how frightened this little girl must feel and couldn't stand by knowing that someone so innocent was in danger.

A few miles ahead Katie saw police cars blocking the road, leaving the right side of the interstate gridlocked. A line of cars were attempting to cut through the grassy median to go east, while a cluster of others remained in the hopeless standstill.

There were more flashing lights up beyond the blockade, only they belonged to the squadron of ambulances already tending Karl's trail of carnage. Some of the accidents looked minor, however the sight of twisted metal made her stomach churn.

She turned her eyes away, took a deep breath, and accelerated past.

The lurking memories from the accident that killed her mother were never far away, but the sound of whirling blades soon captured her full attention. A helicopter came into view just beyond the approaching exit bridge. As Katie closed in she noticed a familiar news channel logo displayed across the side.

That's Shay Donavon's channel...

Katie sped forward as though she had just made the turn on a relay. She aimed toward the driver's side, getting as close as she could without touching it. At the high speed the blonde was flying there was enough force around her to give the vessel a slight nudge as she passed. Katie glanced back, grinning slightly as it wobbled momentarily. The pilot looked to be the only one panicking as the reporter eagerly tapped her cameraman.

Anything to catch a glimpse of the 'reckless hooded woman'...

She hated that nickname more than any of the others she'd been referred by on the news. It seemed to be catching on more too since the pretentious Shay Donavon vomited it out of her mouth a month ago. Now it seemed like no matter what good she did, it was never enough. For every good thing she *thought* she was doing, there seemed to be more than a few headlines that only focused on the unlucky aftermath that sometimes accompanied her interventions.

'Flying Girl Ruins Bankrow Monument'

'Careless Under the Hood: $50K Worth of Damaged Vehicles'

They weren't fair. They were never fair. They often brushed over the actual good to hammer home the "real story". *Normal* people should be afraid of someone like her.

Katie looked on as the reporter smiled excitedly.

She doesn't look too scared to me...

The blonde shook her head before turning her attention back to the interstate. As she did, the large eighteen-wheeler came into view. It was moving fast but she almost overshot it and the half dozen howling police cars chasing it. Katie slowed and adjusted her trajectory until she was aligned with the top of the trailer.

As she approached the passenger window, her heart sank. In the side mirror she could see the flushed and tearful face of a young girl. Her frizzy red hair couldn't hide the expression that looked to be one of confused terror. She tried to see inside the rest of the cab when everything around her went dark. Suddenly, she felt like she was spinning. There was a thunderous crash that left her ears ringing until she heard the familiar desperate scream that had haunted her for years...

"Margaret!"

Katie gasped for air as she finally pushed her head above the currents of the cruel tides of her past. She could see a blue light fading from the corner of her eyes and just managed to catch a glimpse of the bracelet around her wrist before it too disappeared. The blonde quickly realized she'd stopped in mid-air and had lost ground on the procession below.

"Ugh!" she took a deep breath. "Great timing!"

Katie instinctively began humming the "Colossal Cleaners" jingle to keep from drifting away from reality again. She'd been using it as a trick for so long now that she barely remembered that the tune had come from a commercial. Her mind was clearer now and she needed to catch up. With a powerful kick in the air, Katie catapulted forward.

It didn't take more than a few seconds to gain ground and soon she was flying just inches behind the passenger window.

"Daddy, please stop!" she heard the desperate pleas of a child "I want to go home now. Please stop."

"You can't go home to that woman, Angel. She doesn't deserve you," a raised male voice returned. "Just trust me, okay?"

"Please, Daddy...Aaaaagh!" Cynthia Jefferson screamed as she finally noticed Katie outside her window.

"What in the hell is that?!" yelled Karl. He toggled between watching the road and casting a wide-eyed glare at Katie.

"Stop the truck!" the blonde shouted, momentarily shifting her attention to the tiny girl cowering in her seat.

"You're not taking her from me!" Karl shouted before reaching for a gun on the center console. "Get down, Angel."

"Daddy, no!"

BANG!

Katie had already pulled back before the shot was fired. She watched as the truck swerved slightly before correcting. The blonde groaned in frustration.

It hadn't been the first time someone had aimed a gun at her, but it had been the first since the Wiesenburg that someone had actually pulled the trigger. And now that Katie knew Karl had a gun, she couldn't risk the little girl being caught in the crossfire.

A barricade was taking shape ahead of them and at this speed it would only be a minute before they met.

He's not going to stop...

If the madness was to end, Katie was going to have to be the one to stop it. She knew what she had to do. She breathed deeply and got close enough to check the reflection of the girl one last time.

Jeez Katie, I can't believe you're about to do this...

She blew past the truck, flipped around, and landed between it and the barricade.

HONK! HONK!

Katie slowly began walking forward, humming her tune louder and louder with each step. Her heart was racing but she kept her focus on the little girl.

The truck's horn blared again before being drowned out by the frenetic thumping in Katie's ears. She stretched out her arms to brace herself for impact.

The truck slammed on the brakes too late, colliding head-on into the open palms of Katie.

As she felt the metal grill bend around her hands she winced, more from reflex than pain.

Katie waited a few moments before opening her eyes. She had hardly been moved. A relieved smile found its way to her face and the blonde slowly lowered her head to what was left of the warped front of the truck.

"DADDY!"

The smile vanished as she heard Cynthia shriek. She stepped back further to look into the cab, covering her mouth in horror as she saw the giant hole in the windshield of the driver's side. Suddenly she realized that in her haste to stop the truck and save the girl, Katie had only given a fleeting glance to check for the little girl's seatbelt. She never checked to see whether the driver was wearing one.

"Oh my God!" Katie said into her fingertips. She slowly turned toward the barricade behind her to see the still body of Nathan Karl crumpled onto the hood of one of the police cars.

As the girl inside the truck continued to scream, Katie held her breath.

No, no, no... What have I done?

"Hey, get an ambulance out here!" one of the officers shouted. "He's still alive."

The order was followed by a groan from Karl. She continued to watch as one of the officers pulled out a set of handcuffs, but soon the whimpering from inside the truck recaptured her attention.

Katie ran toward the passenger door and ripped it from its hinges. Cynthia was trembling underneath her seatbelt.

Thank God!

"It's okay Cynthia," Katie said assuredly, offering her hand. "It's over now and you're okay." The little girl seemed to watch her hand near with terrified eyes. Katie stopped before slowly retreating her arm back. "Your dad is okay too. Can I help you out of there?"

But the girl didn't have a chance to respond before the sound of several footsteps came clamoring into her ears. The blonde soon realized that on either side of the semi were a dozen police officers. She could hear their nervous hearts pounding.

"I was just trying to help," Katie mumbled softly. It was clear that her presence was putting everyone on edge. She flashed a quick smile at Cynthia Jefferson before stepping off of the road and shooting back into the sky.

Chapter 2

Lingering Pains

Wreings kept his eyes pointed toward the sky for a few moments. After a few deep breaths, the detective finally lowered his gaze onto the double doors of the church. He heard Cass' voice on the other side; it was vibrant and upbeat as she had tried to be on most days before their marriage ended. He didn't know how she did it or why it never seemed to work when he tried to do the same thing. But maybe that's why it didn't work out between them.

He began to reach for the door but paused when he heard something that distracted him. It sounded like a kid was playing on the side of the church. Wreings slid one foot backward down the stairs before turning and coming all the way back down. He walked along the cement path to the side of the church but no one was there.

The detective released a weary sigh and then glanced back toward the front of the white paneled building. He knew Cass probably didn't want to be in there any more than he did, but Wreings couldn't shake away enough of the bad feelings to go inside to be with her, not this time. Instead, he continued down the walkway until he had reached the spot in the garden he had never been able to forget.

It was the same point he always stopped on the day that he and Cass would meet there. Wreings stared across the treeless field for a few moments before letting his gaze drift out to the horizon. He recalled the few times they had come after daybreak. The sun would be just barely level with the towers of the city in the distance. It was a view that had brought him a smile on one or two occasions, though the expression had never lasted for more than a few seconds.

Before his mind could wander too far, a familiar scent passed under his nose. He immediately recognized the perfume. The realization was soon followed by the sound of delicate steps drawing closer on the concrete path. They stopped a foot away from where he stood.

Wreings kept his eyes moving out front, not lingering on any of the decorated plots around him. "Sorry, I'm late."

"That's okay," her rosy voice replied. "Traffic?"

Wreings nodded. "There was some kind of police chase or something, shut down half the interstate. I had to take the back way."

He listened to her take a couple of steps closer, but a few seconds passed before Cass finally spoke again.

"Are you...working today?" she asked.

He wanted the answer to be something else, anything else but the truth. However, his ex-wife knew better than anyone that Wreings had *never* taken this day off. Not since...

"Yeah," he replied with another deep sigh. He glanced back at the thick clouds overhead. He *needed* to work today. "I had planned to go in at 11:30 maybe 11:45."

"Oh, I was hoping we could get lunch..."

"Oh," Wreings began awkwardly. "Well...I could, ugh...push it back..."

"No, no," Cass halted his fumbling. "I don't want you to do that. I know that you...no, it's okay."

Wreings knew how she meant to finish her sentence, but didn't want to fall into the same trap he had during the last years of their marriage. Instead, he thought to change the subject. "How's Charlie?"

Cass laughed gently. "He's good. I think he misses you. Can you believe that?"

Wreings smiled for the first time that day as he imaged the clumsy German Shepard tearing through his clothes. They had only kept him whenever Cass' parents were off on one of their trips. Now it was just his ex-wife who did the sitting. "No, not really. He's probably waiting around to finally get his mitts on my coat."

"Because heaven forbid anything ever happen to that thing," Cass shot back sarcastically. "Though you're not wearing it today..."

"It's ninety degrees out," Wreings said defensively.

Cass tried to hide her continued laughter but she had never been very good at it. "How is Mick?"

It was probably a deliberate correlation for Cass to bring up his partner immediately after talking about the coat she hated.

"Good."

"Are he and that nurse still together?"

Wreings nodded.

"Good for him," Cass said. "Bad for my faith in the sense of medical practitioners."

"He's not a bad guy," Wreings returned.

"Maybe not compared to the people you deal with in your line of work..."

Wreings shook his head. "We're not really going to do this now, are we?"

He didn't need to look at her to know that Cass wanted to say something else. But if there was one thing they always agreed on, it was not to bring out the negative during these visits.

"How have you been?" she asked politely.

"I've been okay, most days," the detective replied. There was no use hiding something that Cass could probably see. She always knew when things were bothering him – it was like her sixth sense.

"Are you...is there someone that you...?"

Wreings drew a deep breath, closing his eyes as he released it back into the late summer air. He shook his head. "No."

"Tobias," she began in a familiar tone. "I don't want to worry about you."

"You don't have to," Wreings replied.

"Somebody does!" Cass snapped. "I thought that you would have reached out to someone after the divorce. Even if it's Mick. Tobias, you need to be talking to somebody."

The detective laughed. "So was the divorce supposed to finally make me better? Is all this just one big therapy session?"

"That's not what I meant, and you know that!" Cass replied. "I just want to make sure that you're okay. I still…" she stopped from saying 'I love you', but Wreings didn't need to hear it to know it.

"Right," Wreings replied. Silence lingered for a few moments afterward.

"What is that?"

The detective glanced down at the silk case in his hand and then shifted his gaze to the deep blue eyes peering at him. He hadn't seen Cass since the night she'd brought him the divorce papers. To his surprise her face was more welcoming than he had imagined it would be. Her thin lips were curled into a patient smile almost like she didn't necessarily need him to answer. Her straight blonde hair looked lighter in the sunlight.

Wreings handed the case to her and Cass let her purse slide to her elbow as she opened it.

"Oh wow," she began, pulling out a golden medallion by its short red strap. "Is this the Medal of Honor?"

"Yeah," the detective returned. He scratched behind his ear as he continued. "Well, it's a Medal of Valor. They gave it to me after everything that went down at the Wiesenburg…"

"I know how you *earned* this, Tobias," Cass said with a shake of her head. She delicately placed the medal back on the cushion and closed the case. Wreings could tell that she was about to cry and pulled out the handkerchief he brought with him every year. The sight released the tears and soon Cass had planted her head in the detective's chest. Wreings froze for a moment before letting his arms cradle her.

After what seemed like ages, Cass pushed herself away and wiped at her face with the blue cloth. "I'm sorry," she began. "You look so nice! I'm going to mess up your shirt and you've still got to go to work..."

"No, it's okay," Wreings returned assuredly.

"You should be the one to give it to him." Cass handed the case back and briefly adjusted his tie. She placed her palm against his left cheek before finally stepping away. After clearing her throat, she spoke again. "I've always been so proud of you, Tobias. He has too. You know that right?"

Wreings finally let his eyes fall to the stone cherub a few feet away from him. Its wings were spread with its face toward the heavens as it stood bashfully atop a two tiered pedestal. Wreings knew staring at it for too long was bound to make his face look as red as Cass'. But, he could never seem to keep himself from reading the inscription on the statue at least once every year.

Forever In Your Grace

Mitchell G. Wreings

A tear fell down his face but he quickly turned and wiped it away. Cass placed her hand on his shoulder and they didn't speak for a few moments. The detective imagined she was thinking what she often said, crying would be good for him. It was something that had helped her cope, but not something Wreings had ever understood. They had never grieved the same way and while he wished that hadn't driven them apart, it was a long way down on the list of things he wished had turned out differently.

"Give it to him," Cass prompted again.

Detective Wreings slowly approached the monument and knelt at its base. He placed the medal in between his old little league cap and a Hank Aaron baseball card. He then glanced at the frame leaning against the stone. In it was the only picture taken of the three of them together. Cass was still in bed, cradling the newborn in her arms while he leaned in gleefully overhead. Wreings hated it every year he saw it, but he picked it up and wiped away the time that had covered it since their last visit.

Cass placed both her knees in the grass next to Wreings. She adjusted her yellow dress before removing an envelope from her purse. Opening it slowly, she revealed a colorful card and turned it toward the grave.

"Happy birthday Mitchell…" she began shakily, just moments before the tears fell again. Cass quickly turned to Wreings. "I need a minute. Can you tell him how our team is doing?"

The detective nodded.

"Happy birthday, buddy. We got some really good players, but uh, I don't know what Cox is thinking," Wreings said with a slight laugh. "But hey, we're still in it. And you know the Phillies will run out of steam by the fall. Plus the rest of the division isn't anything special, so we could bring it all home this year, just like the year after you were born."

"Meridian will be there," Cass added, weakly chopping with her imaginary tomahawk. "Just like we always are."

She wiped her bright pink face with the handkerchief and leaned into Wreings' shoulder. After some slight hesitation, Cass wrapped her fingers entwined with his and began to read this year's poem to Mitchell she had written in the card.

"I smile whenever the wind picks up your name, my son..."

~

"It must have been hard for you," Slater began. "With your father's passing and all."

Denard Kline's first thought was that the comment was rhetorical. But he quickly reminded himself that Jameson Slater wasn't privy to his true feelings for Garrison Kline. Nor was anyone else for that matter.

"Yes," he replied, thinking of some eloquent compliment to give the late co-founder of Klymacks. He could barely stomach the falsehood. "I really didn't have much in the way of guidance and no other family. I suppose you could say the staff at Ivory Towers took me in. But it was never the same. There was so much we could have done together here...that we *did* accomplish right here in this building."

The Mayor's Director of Community Affairs stopped short of the end of the hallway. The natural light from the room behind beamed off the edges of her bright yellow dress. Slater wasn't smiling, but exuded a certain charm that had so far elevated the mood. A sliver of her brunette hair that had fallen from her ponytail, did nothing to blemish an otherwise perfect appearance.

It had been the first time that Denard Kline had seen her since the incident at the Phoenix Gala. Though the relocation of

Klymacks' R&D department to Meridian allowed him to keep in close contact with her under the guise of business, their brief interactions since February never seemed to satiate him.

Mr. Tilte had warned against losing focus at 'the first dame that flashed a pretty wink', and part of Kline knew to heed the mercenary's caution. After all, it was the woman's job to make high-profile investors in the city feel welcome and valued.

However, since discovering an apparent salvation from his prolonged death sentence, Kline found himself with a hitch in his otherwise carefully crafted plan, a straining need for companionship. It was something that he had lacked since he'd left Ivory Towers and Gregor.

Though Mayor Edison was the original chess piece he'd planned to maneuver on his return to Meridian, it was Jameson Slater who had first sat across from him at the bakery all those months ago. The only question Kline had now was where the bright Slater fit on the board.

"Well it sounds like y'all would have spent a lot of time together here," she replied, turning back toward the room behind her. "Is this where all the equipment is being delivered tomorrow?"

Kline nodded. "We generally have a number of workstations that fit into an area like this, but we thought the space might also lend itself to some of our emerging technologies and new projects."

"New projects?" Slater replied. "I'm still trying to wrap my head around your latest one."

"The 'unbreakable metal' is a popular innovation right now, but we're always in search of more," Kline began, walking past Slater and into the room.

"I'm not sure how you can top that."

Denard Kline flashed a coy smile at his guest as he thought about what Dr. Krouse was locked away working on secretly beneath them. "You'd be surprised."

"Clearly," replied Jameson Slater.

Before Kline could say anymore he felt a sharp sting in his shoulder. While it was uncomfortable, he managed to take it in stride. But then he felt an odd tingling in his chest as if someone was running cold fingers along his ribcage. He was shaking and quickly wiped underneath his nose. There was no blood. However, he could tell a relapse was oncoming.

"The space looks much bigger up close than in the floor plans," Slater continued. Her eyes were thankfully pointed toward the ceiling."

"It will look much different once the equipment arrives," Kline replied as he tried to regain control of his rogue body. "I'm sorry, what time was it that you said I had you until?"

Slater glanced at her watch and readjusted the loose strand of hair again. "I'm not quite sure. I'm waiting to hear whether my meeting with the non-profit repurposing the Thumper's building used to be will be rescheduled for later this afternoon."

By the time she returned her eyes back to him, the relapse had almost completely subsided. He flashed a smile while catching his breath.

"Are you alright?"

Kline nodded. "Yes, I just wanted to make sure that the Director of Community Affairs did not miss her own affairs to satisfy the whims of an eccentric businessman."

Slater let go a gentle laugh. "Now Mr. Kline if I recall, you said you don't consider yourself to be one of those."

"Very good memory," Kline replied.

"Thank you," she returned. "I also remember that you promised to discuss a possible community outreach program in the Upper Westside when..." Slater made a concerned face. She cut herself off to pull out a pack of tissues from her purse. "Hold on, it looks like you've got a little blood coming out of your nostril there."

Kline did his best to hide his displeasure as he took the wipe from the woman and patted underneath his nose. "I'm sorry, it must be the pollen here...I swear my allergies are never this bad in New York."

"Oh honey you don't have to say another word," Slater began, patting Kline on the shoulder. "When my sinuses get going, I'm just a mess. I can't tell you how much I'd pay for something that can do away with them all."

"Trust me," Kline said as he held the Kleenex to his nose. "I share your sentiments."

"Like I was saying, I'd really love to discuss a few community projects that I think Klymacks would love to help sponsor," Slater added as she returned the tissues to her purse.

"Dinner."

"What was that?" Slater said, seemingly confused by Kline's outburst.

He cleared his throat before speaking again. "We could discuss the projects over dinner tomorrow evening. If you're available."

"I'll have to check my calendar," she replied.

"Perfect," Kline returned.

"What was there?"

Kline refocused and followed Slater's pointer finger to the far wall where the burner had once sat. Though the machine had long been removed and destroyed, decades of heat and pressure had branded the spot where Mr. Tilte disposed of Dr. Phross and Byers.

He crumpled the bloody tissue in his hand as he stared at the 'ghost' of the burner. "Before it was purchased by Kline Technologies, this building used to be some sort of factory. I don't quite remember, but I do know that we kept the forge installed as it would have been more costly to...my father's relatively humble company at the time."

"Humble beginnings can..." a phone ringing cut Slater's Southernism short. She retrieved the buzzing device from her purse and after a glance at the screen she held up her finger to Kline. "Good afternoon, this is Jamie Slater," she began. "Yes, how are you doing? Oh, I'm fine..."

Denard Kline left her to continue her conversation, stepping back toward the privacy of the hall. Once he was out of sight, he opened his palm to look at the tissue. The dark red blots had brought back the harsh reality of his condition. The personal tour was over. He had done well to keep everyone that knew him at arm's length of his secrets. Though she was pleasant to be around, he needed to focus on the only thing that mattered: himself.

"I'm so sorry about that Mr. Kline," Slater began as she entered the hallway. "That was my appointment. It looks like we'll be having that meeting today after all."

"Duty calls."

Slater smiled and took a parting glance at the room. Kline let her pass before casting a look of his own. The painters already coming by later that morning would need to pay extra attention to that spot.

"So, how has your second visit to Meridian been?" Slater continued.

"Uneventful compared to the first," Kline replied, evoking a laugh from the woman in front of him.

"After what all happened in February, I would hope so. Well, do let me know if there's anything you need while you're in town," Jameson Slater replied. "I'll touch back with you about dinner."

"Of course."

Slater smiled politely before exiting through the door. Kline watched her enter her car and start the ignition before he felt a fierce stab at his side. He closed the door quickly as he fell to his knees. The ineffectiveness of the serum was showing the telltale signs that it was truly not the long-term solution to his condition.

Chapter 3

Lingering Fears

Well before they pulled into the long drive of Meridian Medical Center, there was an uncomfortable feeling festering inside Reagan. She had first put it off as some kind of nervous excitement like she had felt during the hospital matching process. However, the moment Aunt Laine pointed across the car toward the sole surviving building, Reagan knew her feeling was something different.

A chill ran up her spine as she saw the wide trailers and construction vehicles sitting behind the taped off area. The spot where the second tower used to be was now just a hole in the middle of a parking lot. The rebuilding initiative had only just begun, but it was hard for Reagan to imagine seeing anything return to the void.

But as the car rode toward the entrance, the exterior seemed to disappear. Soon, Reagan found herself standing in the hallway of the sixth floor. She felt something warm scratching at her and realized that Dr. Schroeder was breathing down her neck.

"It's going to start getting hard to pay for your sister's visits to the shrink," his voice echoed as he spoke his last words to her. "Your cavalier attitude could cost you your job. Don't forget that..."

KNOCK! KNOCK! KNOCK!

Reagan gasped as the tapping pulled her from her lapse. She quickly remembered where she was and looked to her window to see her aunt had her hand ready to open the door.

"Honey, we're here."

Reagan nodded and pushed the door open. Her aunt reached in but the young doctor waved her away.

"I'm okay," she said.

"Are you sure?" Laine asked. "I could go up there with you and..."

"No really," Reagan cut in, her hand firmly gripping the curved handle of the black cane. She unbuckled her seatbelt and turned toward the door. "I'm fine. You need to get back and Peter already said he can take me home."

With the cane in one hand and her other holding the top of the open door, she lifted herself from the seat and took her first steps back into the parking lot of Meridian Medical Center.

"Alright then," Laine replied, holding the far side of Reagan's face while planting a kiss on her cheek. "Good luck, though I'm sure you won't need it."

But the farewell hardly registered as the sight of the hospital captured her. She was still for a moment peering at the familiar emblem that was fitted on the entrance to the building. It seemed to loom overhead as though it were a raven watching her every move.

"You're ready," she muttered before slowly inching toward the entrance. Her heart was racing faster than her feet could move. There was a heat beating against her face. It grew hotter and hotter the closer she came to the building.

"Get a grip," Reagan added, closing her eyes. "The hardest part is almost over." She breathed in and out a few times before

25

focusing on the four glass doors a few feet away. "Just get through those doors."

She repeated the saying until the tip of her cane clanked against the tile of the hospital lobby.

It had only been nine months since she last stepped foot inside the hospital but there were enough subtle changes in the lobby to make it feel like a lifetime had passed.

The main seating area had been rearranged with the leather cushioned seats now facing one another instead of lined back-to-back. The light fixture that used to dangle in the middle of the room was no longer there. She thought she remembered hearing that it had fallen during the explosion. There was also a new face at the receptionist's desk to greet her.

"Hello there," the dark-haired, young woman began as Reagan approached. "Are you here to see a doctor or a patient?"

"I'm actually looking for the administration hall," she replied. "It used to be next door before…"

The receptionist waited a few seconds for Reagan to finish before offering an understanding smile. "Um, yes they moved admin over shortly after. You can find it on the fifteenth floor. Is there someone in particular that you're here to see?"

"Dr. Kondu," replied Reagan.

The woman suddenly looked as though she were face-to-face with a celebrity. "Oh, you must be Dr. Cattrell?"

Reagan nodded.

"We're so glad to have you back," she continued. "I'll call up to his office and let him know you're here."

"Thank you," Reagan replied as she turned toward the hallway. When she came to the elevators there was a large rendering of what MMC's campus was to look like after the completed construction. She stopped in front of the display and glanced over the images. The new tower was big, adding six more floors than its predecessor had, making it eighteen floors in all.

"The new Memorial Tower of Meridian Medical Center will honor those eighteen staff members we lost from the terrible attack in 2008..." she read. "...Immortalized in name and in spirit...Dr. Cheryl Fenton Memorial Hall...Bledsoe Memorial Wing..."

Reagan paused as she scanned over the familiar name of Virgil Schroeder who had the entire of the sixth floor dedicated to him. Seeing it angered her as she knew that if he had listened to Dr. Lutz, there may not have been so many deaths that day. But being as Dr. Schroeder had been the highest ranking staff member who died, it was hardly surprising to see him be the only victim given an entire floor in dedication.

She shook her head and kept scanning the images until she came across what she was looking for.

"The Veronica Lutz Intensive Care Unit," her words came out bittersweet as she remembered her mentor's reassuring hand slipping away from her once again. Reagan looked to her right and thought she could see the doctor running down the hall after Schroeder.

"Security!" the callous administrator's voice echoed in her ears.

A bright light flashed before her eyes and the white hallways of the sixth floor were soon entrenched in a crimson glow. Reagan gasped loudly as the heat struck her face, only for her to find herself trembling in the elevator lobby. She closed her eyes and breathed in deeply.

DING!

The elevator to her left opened bringing a much needed prompt for Reagan to move past the moment that haunted her. She stepped into the elevator just before the doors slid closed behind her. A few seconds passed before she realized that she hadn't selected her destination and she let out a sigh of frustration.

"You have to get through this," she said. "You're a doctor, not a patient. Get it to..."

Her vibrating phone caught her attention. She pulled it out to see that she had a missed call and voicemail from Katie to go along with a text message from earlier.

Good luck today! Call when you're out??? It had read. The voicemail was probably more of the same.

DING!

The elevator doors slid open revealing that Reagan still hadn't moved. A nurse dressed in blue scrubs and two elderly women quickly joined her in the compartment. She adjusted herself on her cane to give them room to squeeze in and briefly flashed a courteous smile at the nurse who made eye contact.

"Fourth floor please?" the man asked.

"Seventh too," one of the elderly women added. Reagan nodded and pushed in all three destinations.

The doors closed once more and this time the elevator began its ascent, stopping to let out the nurse and then the women before continuing toward the administration floor. Reagan watched as the digital numbers ticked away, drawing closer to her meeting with Dr. Kondu. She hoped she could pull herself together long enough to get through what was likely a pre-screening. She had been waiting for this moment since the feeling came back in her legs. It was very much the first step in getting past the horrific moment that had stunted her career.

The elevator slowed and soon opened its doors to the tenth floor. Reagan walked out into the lobby and searched the walls for the direction of the correct room. Once she found it, she began reassuring herself, recalling a number of her past accomplishments as she walked down the hall. Dr. Kondu's office was just a few doors away.

Reagan felt much calmer than she had in the lobby and went to reply to her sister's text. She had her thumb positioned on the keypad but didn't move it, and after a few seconds of hesitation Reagan slid the phone back into her purse and continued down the hall.

~

BUZZ! BUZZ!

As she sat on a ledge high above Meridian, Katie hoped that her sister had actually replied this time. But when she glanced at her phone to see who texted her, she saw that it had actually been Troy.

29

"U still interested in shakes after work?" he had asked.

A smile flashed briefly on the blonde's face as she responded with a "Duh" and a smiley face but quickly faded after the message was sent. Katie returned to the messages between her and Reagan and scrolled through them.

There were large chunks of texts, most of them belonging exclusively to her as if she were having her own conversation. There were a couple of one word replies from her sister sprinkled in here and there, but for the most part Reagan hadn't initiated or really participated in any conversation for months.

What is your deal, Rae?

A message from Troy popped up on her screen and the blonde quickly replied before placing the phone down on the inside of the ledge. The last thing she needed was her phone vibrating over the side. It was the fourth one she'd had in nine months so she'd made a concerted effort to be more careful.

She leaned against the wall of the building and stared off. Traffic was still backed up, which was no surprise since they had to shut down part of the interstate from all the damage done by Nathan Karl.

"That looks awful," she muttered, shaking her head. The blonde's eyes then moved across the rest of the city until stopping on a set of large cranes. Seeing the reconstruction efforts underway at Meridian Medical Center only made her ponder the situation between her and her sister more.

Katie couldn't help but think back to the Gala, when Reagan seemed to recognize her in the stairwell. Though she later claimed not to remember anything from just before getting hit in the head, the way Reagan carried on around Katie was strange.

Their visits were much shorter than before, usually because there was some kind of physical therapy her sister needed to attend. But it seemed to happen so frequently that Katie thought the sessions were made up. Most times it seemed as though her sister was reading some sort of script.

Then when Reagan was able to fully move her legs, things completely changed. Her sister grew more distant, seemingly preferring isolation to her company. Most of the time she claimed she simply wanted to be more aggressive with her physical therapy, which made sense given her sister's ultra-determined nature. However, Katie got the sense that there was much more to it, especially after the one and only time they'd spoken about the night at the Wiesenburg...

"You're sure nothing is bothering you?" Katie remembered asking as she helped her sister to a chair in her bedroom.

Reagan shook her head. "I'm just exhausted. I had my first session in the pool this morning and I didn't realize how intense the water could be. I'm sure that I don't have to tell you though..."

"Yeah, swimming was no joke..." Katie replied laughing awkwardly. "...But it's more than just today. You've been acting, I don't know, different lately."

"I'm fine," Reagan quickly replied. "I told you it's just the rehab and trying to get back to a place where I can finish my residency at MMC."

"I understand that," Katie returned. "I just wanted to make sure..."

"Make sure of what?" Reagan shot back.

The outburst came with a look that Katie had seen before. Reagan's eyes were wide and focused entirely away from the blonde's gaze.

"Reagan, it's been a month," she began. "And you haven't said one word about what happened back at...you know."

"I barely even remember what happened, Katie," her sister sighed. "Everything was so crazy...And you know as soon as that creep hit me on the stairs I blacked out. The next thing I remember is waking up in an ambulance with Peter."

The rebuttal echoed in her head. Reagan had a way of sounding formal when she spoke. It was usually because her words sounded like they came from a grown up. But her sister's line sounded more rehearsed than confident. That hadn't stopped part of Katie from wanting to believe Reagan, but she knew her sister was lying. She was just unsure of whether it was out of confusion or fear – though she hoped it wasn't the latter.

A strong gust of wind pulled Katie's mind back to her perch above Meridian. She glanced at the sky overhead which already showed a hint of the weekend's clouds coming in. Rain made flying much harder.

Katie picked up her phone and adjusted her hood before leaping high into the open space above the graying clouds. From where she hovered she could see clear across the sky at the sun. It was a much needed therapeutic view, unabated by the growing complexity of the world around her. She let out a sigh and tried

32

to relax as she always seemed to have to remind herself to do lately. But it was nearly impossible for her mind not to dwell on the things that were bothering her.

In a summer that had been particularly lonely so far for Katie it was also one that was very challenging. Beside her sister ignoring her, Troy's internship at the museum took up most of his time during the week, and Nancy had only just gotten back in town on Monday after spend two months in Europe working with her mother. With the exploits of The Flying Girl being talked about and analyzed by seemingly everybody, she found herself constantly battling a neuroticism that she was sure normal people never did.

Nancy knew her secret and was usually able to talk her down. But between the time difference and schedule, they had barely had time to say 'hello' to each other, let alone vent about what Meridian's hooded woman got into that day. After the first month of her friend's absence, Katie contemplated telling Troy *everything*. Though she immediately knew it was a bad idea, it was one that had a way of popping back up whenever the two were actually together.

Which, like with everyone else, hadn't been often.

Whether it was the early mornings or traveling inter-state to view other museum's collections, the guy she had spent so much time with in the spring had practically become a ghost. She supposed it was fortunate that Troy's internship had been more intensive than either realized a job at a museum could ever be. It was easier to don the hood and goggles when she needed to. She could actually count the number of times she had to stand him up with an excuse. However each time did leave her feeling more guilty than heroic.

The blonde closed her eyes and breathed to keep from getting any more worked up than she already sensed she was getting. *Alright, seriously this time Katie, try to let it all go...*

Meditation had never been her thing, especially since she sucked at it. Still Dr. Mack had always talked it up as a good way to destress and she had been much quicker to lean on the therapist's advice now that she was no longer a weekly patient.

Katie tried concentrating and found herself counting each beat of her heart. Soon she could feel the force brushing against her arms and legs as it "held" her safely above Meridian. She took another deep breath and let herself fall further into it.

The feeling was warm and comforting. It reminded her of the only time Nancy talked her into soaking in a bubble bath. Had it not been for the narrowness of the tub, she'd probably have done it more often but the feeling she had now was beginning to feel like a fantastic alternative.

Slowly the blonde's mind drifted away from the worries that had stalked her for seemingly forever. Her ears began to fill with a humming sound that she couldn't identify at first. As it got louder she began to realize that the tune was close to the rhythm of the "Colossal Cleaners" jingle. She started humming along until she realized that the voice of the partner to her duet was one that she recognized.

Almost immediately after the realization, Katie felt the force around her tighten its grip on her. Within seconds her arms and legs were completely bound. Meanwhile, the voice humming broke off into a much louder, menacing ode. Katie's eyes shot open but what she saw around her wasn't the afternoon sky. Her surroundings had completely changed and she was now standing over the familiar scene of Bishop's house smoldering in flames.

She couldn't move as the force refused to relinquish its grasp and the cries she wanted to let out fell mute upon her lips. Katie could only watch as the fire spread through the rest of the remains.

Suddenly, a fiery hand shot up from the pyro.

The humming had all but disappeared, replaced instead with a shrill scream that was nearly deafening. The heat beat against Katie's face but she was unable to turn her head.

The emblazed figure limped heavily as it approached. Katie's heartbeat was galloping now and squirmed desperately to break free from the force.

Please, please let me go! Please! LET ME GO!

Katie gasped and shot forward, only to feel her body falling through the clouds. She quickly managed to catch herself before dropping into view of the skyline. Her eyes searched for signs of the fiery man but she was no longer in the woods. It was then that she noticed the fading blue light of the bracelet and realized that she had let herself slip into another one of its "tricks".

As she breathed in and out frantically, she focused on the images that she had seen before the light completely vanished. But once it was gone, like always she could only remember a very small fragment. She shook her hands in frustration.

"Ugh!" Katie groaned. "This is so…UGH!"

The blonde took a deep breath and tried to shake of the defeated feeling that tended to accompany those episodes. The uncertainty in her life was annoying enough. But just when she thought she could take a break, the mysterious bracelet found a way to remind her that there were no breaks for her.

She wasn't normal, and that was never going to change.

Chapter 4

Haunted

Wreings thought it odd for the station to be this busy so close to noon. The way badges were filing through the halls, it looked like he had walked in during the middle of a shift change. He tried picking up on some of the conversations but could only catch bits and pieces with all of the other commotion.

He spotted Donnelly talking to Officer Varney by the Captain's office. His partner shook his head with a familiar look of disgust before the thin, blond officer standing next to him shrugged.

"What's up, Detective?" greeted Varney once Wreings had made it to the desks. "Crazy shit, right?"

"What's going on around here?" Wreings glanced back at the crowded break room.

The officer seemed confused by the question, "Are you kidding? Where have you…?" There was a scratch of feedback from Varney's radio that cut him short.

"218 please be advised of a possible 10-37 on the corner of 5th Street and Rigmeer, over…"

"Copy that," he sighed into his radio. He patted Wreings on the shoulder and passed a short wave to Donnelly before heading toward the door. "218 on the way."

Once Varney had disappeared, Wreings turned to his partner. "Did I miss something?"

Donnelly shook his head and laughed. "No V, you're just in time. They put two fresh pots on in the kitchen about a minute ago."

Wreings took a quick glance at the busy space behind him. "We might be down to one pot by the time I get back there. Seriously Don, what's going on around here? They announce another 'early retirement' or what?"

Donnelly shot him a look of disbelief similar to the one Varney had given him. "You really haven't heard? Someone shot the President, V."

His partner's statement shook him and the entire complexion of what was happening around him changed. He suddenly realized that the crowd by the break room were all facing the direction of the station's TV. "Is he...?"

"You didn't hear about any of this?" Donnelly interjected.

Wreings' continued to look around the station until landing back on his partner. "No, I was..." The image of the stone cherub had been etched in his mind since he'd left Cass this morning. Every day had been hard and it only worsened after the divorce. But the week after the Fourth of July had been the hardest week to concentrate since he'd lost Mitchell. The detective quickly closed his eyes and pushed the bad memories away. "...I didn't catch the news this morning."

Donnelly looked at Wreings curiously, but didn't press. "Right... Well from what I've heard it looks like he'll be okay. The bullet went right through him, just a couple inches from a lung or something."

"That's lucky," Wreings sighed as he finally took his seat. "They catch the guy who did it yet?"

"They've been looking all morning. They think it was a sniper," Donnelly said. "Couldn't have been a very good one. Had a clear target to aim at and missed. Ended up hitting some guy behind him."

"So someone did die?"

Donnelly nodded. "Not that I've heard. Hit some senator, I can't remember his name."

Wreings nodded as his partner turned back to his computer. He began the process of removing his tie and unbuttoning the neck of his shirt. He instantly felt as though he could breathe a little better. "I can't believe someone already tried to kill him."

Donnelly scoffed. "You serious, V? You know how many racist bastards there are in this country, hell in this state? First black guy in office, probably triggered half of them. Anyway, LJ was up here this morning looking for you."

"Yeah?" Wreings replied. He had only rolled up one sleeve when the examiner's name was mentioned. He immediately stopped and focused on Donnelly, ignoring the grin on his face.

"She dropped off some report you asked about and asked if you were okay since you didn't show this morning," his partner continued, throwing a plain folder on his desk.

Wreings sighed guiltily, "Yeah, I meant to tell her I wouldn't be in this morning."

"Don't worry, I told her you probably weren't used to having a functioning phone," Donnelly replied. "I figured that was believable."

"Thanks."

His partner shrugged and pointed at the folder. "If that's for the Arden case, you won't need it. Our perp signed a confession this morning."

"No kidding?" Wreings returned distractedly as he opened the folder and began looking through the pages. "I figured he'd confess eventually after we told him we'd found the gun he used. I wish we had that kind of break with those bank robbers."

The unsolved murders of Hix and Jones left a bad taste in his mouth. With everything that had happened at the Wiesenburg and Thumpers plus the DA and FBI breathing down their necks, the murders never really got the attention that Wreings knew they deserved.

The crime scenes had been staged and the way the coins turned up was too convenient for his liking. But it appeared that he was nearly alone in thinking that as the crime was quickly tacked on to Gol's lengthy list of transgressions.

"So is that more homework then?" Donnelly asked.

"You could say that," Wreings replied, continuing to flip through the file. As his eyes scrolled over the last page, the detective pressed his thumb against his forehead. "Hey, you remember that jumper from last week?"

"That guy who took a nose dive from the twenty-fourth floor of his apartment?" Donnelly returned. "What about him?"

The detective glanced around to make sure no one was in earshot of their conversation. "His name was Tim Berton and he was on that list of people connected to the arms dealing."

Donnelly nodded. "Yeah I remember. What about him?"

"According to this report, he had small traces of marijuana in his system but was otherwise clean," Wreings finished.

"And that means...?"

"I don't know. It could mean he wasn't doped up when he jumped like they said on the news," Wreings returned. "But it's weird. According to his girlfriend he called her sounding scared as hell. She thought he was just on drugs remember?"

"What's any of that got to do with us?" his partner questioned. "Don't tell me we're getting into that bullshit again..."

Wreings shook his head. "No, it's just...Everyone assumed that Berton was on PCP or one of the other synthetic drugs he had at his apartment, but he was sober – for him anyway."

Donnelly shrugged. "Again, what does that have to do with us?"

Wreings cautiously glanced at the Captain's office before reaching in his desk drawer for a small slip of paper. He walked it over to his partner's desk.

"What's this?" asked Donnelly.

"That's the list I was using to track the leads we had during our...unofficial investigation," Wreings replied.

"So?"

"So every single one of these people is now dead," Wreings continued, tapping his finger against the list. "All within the last eight months, and all with questionable deaths."

"What's questionable about some drugged up punk jumping from a roof?" Donnelly quipped. "I've probably heard about at least twelve of those already this year."

The detective shook his head. "Nothing if he was actually drugged up. A small trace of pot wouldn't do it for this guy. Remy from Narcotics didn't think so either."

"Narcs are the only badges more suspicious than you, V," his partner snapped. "It's not like he was clean either. Small trace or not, Berton was using since high school. The longer you're on that stuff the more it messes with your head. All it takes is a bad batch."

"But it's not just him. Remember Cameron Kelley? He was found with a bullet to the brain," Wreings said.

"And they found the Russian prick who shot him..."

"They found the gun stashed in his room. As far as I've heard, he's still claiming he hadn't ever seen it. No prints either," the detective replied quickly, moving his finger down the list. "And then there are the other two runners. One died in a car crash the week after the Wiesenburg and the other overdosed on pain pills a few days later."

Donnelly sighed and looked at Wreings with disbelief in his eyes. "You're a real suspicious son of a bitch, V. You know that?"

"There's just too many coincidences with this case."

"It's not a case – it's not *our* case!" Donnelly returned. "First of all, I wouldn't bet two quarters that what a *known* Russian mobster says is actually true. Second, bad shit happens enough to good people. Maybe this is the universe's way of saying 'kiss my ass' to the bad ones. And some people have it coming, just look what happened to that jackass protestor. You remember that guy, the one your girl saved from falling off the Emerson building? Runs his mouth about The Flying Girl and Meridian owing him for his own stupidity and then falls through a building because of his own stupidity."

Wreings remembered hearing about the fate of Clyde Tesser on the news. The city helped pay his medical bills but that apparently hadn't been enough. He kept yelling to anyone who would listen that the city wasn't safe and that he'd prove it. Two weeks later he was found dead at the base of a condemned building whose roof had collapsed. Turned out he was right.

"I swear V, we've gone over this at least once a week since March," Donnelly paused before picking up his chair and setting it just in front of Wreings' desk. "Alright, let's say that your whack-a-doo theory is right. How the hell can we investigate any of it? Every single case of suicide, accidental death, or murder has been solved or closed and not because of lazy badges, but because there hasn't been any other evidence to warrant an investigation!"

His partner's words seemed to echo the themes from his conversation with Captain Glades last November. "I'm not blaming any other cops. There's no way they could make the connection. You're the only one besides me to see the list."

"Come on, V. It's not like these were regular guys. Most of them were in deep with drugs or something illegal that was bound to get them killed anyway."

Wreings shook his head. "But Don, it's not just that they're dead, it's the way they're dying."

"Look if what happened to all of these guys really is connected, then it's likely through some Final Destination bullshit that I don't want any part of," Donnelly said. "And you shouldn't either. Sometimes you just got to take things at face value. Forget about the Kelley kid and this Berton guy. Didn't we have enough of a headache with Hix and Jones..."

"Oh come on, Don! You can't tell me that Jones' murder scene wasn't staged," Wreings quickly cut in. "And his body just happening to be found outside of Thumpers..."

"Of course, V. The whole thing stunk. But as slimy as Gol is, why couldn't it have been him that had both guys killed to cover up his operation?" Donnelly returned. "We know that both of those assholes were on the surveillance tapes we took from Thumpers and they had the coins. Hell, one of the girls working the back said she saw Hix there the night before Jones was killed."

Wreings sighed. "But why would Gol go through the trouble of having them killed but leave the underground casino tokens where they could be found?"

"I don't know," his partner paused to let a couple of badges walk by before turning back to Wreings. "My opinion, Gol was a cocky son of a bitch who got away with everything in this town, including murder. Do you know why? Because he owned Meridian, he owned the judges, council members, probably even some cops too. If someone set him and every corrupt piece of shit that had been holding us by the balls up then good for them."

"What makes you think whoever set him up wasn't out to take his place?" Wreings said.

Donnelly shook his head. "If your imaginary person exists then let them try. It'll be a lot harder to pull that shit Gol did again. The Feds are practically living in Meridian. But forget that, it's not like we can take a timeout to deal with hypotheticals. We may have got a confession this morning but it's not like easy cases are just falling into our laps. You got to stop chasing shadows or you'll drive yourself and me crazy."

"It's hard to chase shadows when you're stuck sitting in the dark," Wreings replied.

His partner finally laughed and slapped the detective on the shoulder. "Alright Buddha. You keep saying things like that and you *will* drive me crazy."

He walked back to his desk and picked up the keys to his coupe.

"Where you heading?" Wreings asked.

"Getting lunch with Nadine," he replied as he checked his phone. "If she can ever pick a place. You want me to bring you back something?"

The detective shook his head. "Thanks but I ate a late breakfast. Did you already start on the paperwork for Arden?"

"Hell no," Donnelly scoffed. "I figured I'd give you something to do since you missed me milking the confession from him."

Wreings tried to hold back a smile. His partner's bravado was always well timed. "Shame I missed it. Probably won't get another chance to see one of those for another five years."

Donnelly responded by rubbing his eye with his middle finger and then turning toward the hallway to the parking deck.

Once he had gone, Wreings pulled his cellphone from his pocket. He turned it back on and immediately felt it vibrate wildly in an assault of notifications for messages he had missed. There were missed calls from Cass' mom, his brother, and both of his parents – all the people who usually reached out on Mitchell's birthday. As he scrolled through he came across a pair of texts from LJ.

"I have a present for you!" read the first, with the second sent an hour later reading, *"Are you coming in late this morning?"*

Lately, he and LJ had spent most mornings together before his shift but Wreings hadn't thought to tell her about his absence today. The truth was that he didn't want to have to talk about it, he never wanted to talk about Mitchell. But the closer he and the medical examiner became, the less sure he was of whether there was any point.

No matter how many years passed by, the pain of losing his son continued to bear down on him. Anytime he had a moment to himself, he would hear the sound of Mitchell's heartbeat fading.

His partner was right, investing in the loose connections and thin leads of cases could absolutely drive any other man crazy. But he decided a long time ago that he'd rather chase ghosts than be haunted by them.

The detective shut his eyes and exhaled before turning toward his computer. He knew he shouldn't think any more about it if he could help it. Luckily, between the case load and figuring out an apology for LJ, it appeared he was going to have plenty of distractions to get him through this day.

Chapter 5

Unexpected Encounters

"Hold on one second," Katie returned, moving the phone to fit between her cheek and shoulder as she adjusted her bag.

"Where are you?" her friend asked.

"On campus," replied the blonde. "I had to return a couple of books to the library. I almost forgot after what happened this morning."

"Back to Reagan," Nancy refocused their conversation. "It's not like you were there when it happened."

"I know, I know," Katie returned with a sigh as she hurried through the courtyard. "But I've had this feeling that I can't explain. Like, remember what I said after all that stuff happened at the Plaza?"

"You mean where you thought you could feel him inside your head?"

Katie nodded as if her friend could see her. "Yeah something like that. It's just a feeling, I don't know how to explain it. I just feel like guilt or something. But lately...well, I guess for a while it's felt like everything he did was somehow my fault too."

"It's not." Nancy replied emphatically.

"It's just how I feel," Katie said simply, keeping her eyes on the archway leading to the road. "I know it doesn't make sense but I just feel like I need to say something to her."

"Well it bloody well shouldn't be 'I'm sorry'," her friend shot back. "Katie, there was *nothing* you could do about the explosion."

"I know…"

"And even if she doesn't know, it was you who saved her and all those people at the hotel," Nancy continued adamantly.

"I know…" Katie repeated.

"I feel like I've told you this a thousand times now," her friend lowered her volume as the sound of other voices approached. "Look, you're not a danger, you're not Bishop. And if you ask me, Reagan should be the one apologizing to you."

Katie wondered whether to tell her friend about the recurring visions she'd been having…

"Katie?"

"Yeah, sorry," the blonde replied, casting the thought from her mind.

"You need to stop blaming yourself for everything that happened," Nancy continued. "Do you know what people say about you in France?"

"No?"

"They call you l'ange masqué."

Katie waited to take another bite. "What does that mean?"

"They're basically calling you a cloaked angel," Nancy replied. "I guess that's on account of you wearing the hood and goggles."

"Oh wow…" Katie said.

"Much better than anything they call you over here."

"I would love to live somewhere else," the blonde began. "Anywhere else as long as I could actually *live* while I'm there, you know? And it'd be great not to have people afraid of me."

"I wish you would have come to visit. You would have loved France. It would have been a quick trip for you, wouldn't it?" Nancy returned.

"Ha," the blonde replied. "I don't think I can fly that fast."

"I remember you being pretty speedy when you saved that idiot from falling..."

"Funny, all I remember is breaking his arm," Katie quickly replied.

Nancy sighed. "You saved his life, didn't you?"

"Sorry, but for once I wish I could save someone without hurting them," returned the blonde.

"Right, so are we just not going to count your sister?" Nancy returned.

Um, did you not hear about the guy I put in a coma...? "Let's just stop talking about it," Katie replied.

"No, Katie...you can talk down about yourself all you want," she persisted. "It won't change the fact that you're a hero – a real live hero. What's gotten into you?" Nancy continued. "You're not usually like this."

The blonde glanced down at her wrist but knew before her eyes landed that there wouldn't be anything to see. The bracelet, for all its emotion warping habits, was not responsible for her surge of negativity, not this time. She could blame it on the news or the mistakes she's made. But in truth, it was the power itself that weighed on her, especially since she still didn't know where it came from or how she even got it.

"Things have just been hard lately," Katie returned. "With Reagan, and with my powers...You know it drives me crazy when I don't know where I stand."

"I understand, but you're currently driving yourself crazy thinking about it, aren't you?" Nancy returned. "Katie, sometimes you just have to get away from the drama. I think tonight will be good for you."

"What's tonight?" asked the blonde.

"Seriously, Katie? The party?"

"Ugh, you're supposed to remind me of these things. I already made plans with Troy," Katie groaned. "What time is your party?"

"It's supposed to be at eight," her friend replied.

Katie was almost through the courtyard now. "Troy is actually in town. Besides, you know I'm not really good with parties."

"Oh, well yeah a date would be fun..." Nancy trailed off.

"I'm sorry, is everything alright?" Katie asked.

"Yeah, yeah," her friend quickly lifted her tone. "There was just something important that I wanted to tell you."

"Wait, what is it?" Katie quickly returned.

"I'd rather not say it over the phone, especially since I'm at work," Nancy replied as another influx of voices and music came through the phone. "Actually, I have to go now. My two o'clock is here."

"Nancy! You can't do that!"

"I'm sorry, Love. I've got to go but stop stressing out about everything," her friend replied. "That includes this whole thing with Reagan. Okay?"

And with that Nancy was gone, leaving Katie with nothing but her own curiosities. She wondered what it was that Nancy could have to tell her.

Suddenly, Katie heard a loud crash. She turned quickly to see a man had fallen to the ground, a number of books strewn in front of him. His casual attire and aviators made her think of the frat boys she'd seen wandering around campus last year.

"I'm so sorry, I didn't see you there!" His apology confused Katie until she realized that he must have run into her. She hardly felt a thing, but she chalked it up to her tunnel vision leaving MSU's campus.

"Are you okay?" she replied as he picked up the two books he had dropped.

He nodded and regained his feet before taking the books from Katie. He tipped his cap and carried on in the direction he'd been going. The blonde likewise kept moving hurriedly until she had left the always busy campus behind her.

She had just stepped onto the lawn of Placek Park when she felt a strong vibration. After a quick check of her phone, she realized that it was coming from inside of her bag.

"What the heck?" she muttered as she began searching for the vibrating culprit.

Finally, Katie pulled a small, black box from the pouch. It was the size of a box of cards but had no special markings. After a second in her hand, the vibrating stopped and a thin white light made a lap around the side of the box before shooting across the top and stopping at the point Katie had placed her thumb. She moved it to see the outline of her thumbprint remained.

"Can you hear me?" a muffled voice asked suddenly.

Startled, Katie dropped the box.

"Ms. Cattrell, please pick up the VT," the voice continued.

"The what?"

"The voice transmitter, the rectangular box sitting at your feet," the voice replied impatiently. "And please be quick about it as the following conversation is one I'm sure you don't want broadcasted around your current audience."

Katie looked around at the populated spaces of the park. No one seemed to be looking in her direction, but she knew that whoever she was talking to was at least within her line of sight. She carefully reached down and picked up the box.

"Hold it like a phone, please," the voice continued. "The volume will adjust based on its proximity to your ear."

The blonde followed the instructions reluctantly. "Who are you?"

"You can call me Trevor if that eases you," he replied.

If it eases me? Who the hell are you, creep? "That's not patronizing at all...Trevor."

"My apologies, Ms. Cattrell..."

"Stop calling me that!" Katie snapped. "You don't know me and I don't know you so..."

"Actually, we just met," Trevor shot back. "In the courtyard of your school."

The frat boy! Katie ran her eyes around the park in search of the cap and bookbag. "You're the guy who ran into me?"

"Yes, and I know more about you than you think, Margaret Katherine Cattrell."

A chill gripped her heart as she heard her full name exit the box. "How did you...?"

"We confirmed your alias several weeks ago," he continued. "Now please listen as what I'm about to tell you is very important."

My alias? How does he know...?

"Who are you?" Katie asked. "What do you want?"

"To be forthright, we need your help and there are a lot of lives at stake."

We? "I'm listening," the blonde replied.

"A few months ago, we were alerted to a series of peculiar deaths concentrated around the border cities of the United States and Canada," Trevor began. "Because of the nature of the bodies, it was initially feared that the region had been exposed to some sort of chemical attack. However, those deaths were not caused by a what, but instead by a who," he finished.

"Okay, what the hell are you talking about?" Katie replied. "You're being really cryptic."

"I apologize, but this is a very sensitive matter," returned Trevor. "We've managed to keep it contained. However, with more people dying, some members of the Canadian press are beginning to seek the truth themselves. I can't give you specifics until you've agreed to help."

Katie searched the people on their phones. "You picked a pretty bad place to discuss this 'sensitive matter'."

"We didn't know how you would react if confronted," Trevor replied. "We certainly didn't want you flying away…"

Who is this creep? "I really don't know what you're talking about."

"Ms. Cattrell, we've learned that the people who keep the best secrets are the ones who have a secret to protect themselves," he began. "There is no reason to fear us. I trust you'll keep ours if we keep yours?"

Katie walked by a couple frat guy types but neither were on their phones. "Why me?"

"We thought your expertise might be required. The who I spoke of earlier has a number of super-human abilities that our forces have yet to match."

Wait, what?! "Super-human abilities?" Katie asked as images of Bishop's pyro flashed in front of her eyes.

"That's all I can tell you without confirmation that you'll help," the man said.

Katie closed her eyes and took a deep breath. The thought of someone out there who might be like her...

She hoped it would all go away, that when she opened her eyes she'd find herself being woken up by Nancy after falling asleep watching a movie or something. There would be no powers, no mysterious phone calls, *no* super-humans...

"Ms. Cattrell?" Trevor's voice barged in and tugged Katie back to this unfortunate reality.

She opened her eyes and released a wary breath. "I think you have the wrong person, mister. It was nice talking to..."

"We can tell you where it comes from," Trevor interjected.

Katie's mouth hung open as the meaning behind the words stung her heart.

"The powers," confirmed the voice. "Yours, Theodore Bishop's, others potentially like you."

Others?

"Judging by your silence, I assume that something I said may have peaked your interest?"

"Who are you?" returned Katie

"I am Trevor," he replied coyly. "And it's who we're after that really matters. Our time is short. In your bag, in the same pocket you found the transmitter you'll also find a business card." Katie searched for the card as Trevor continued. "Use it to contact me once you've made your decision."

"It's blank," Katie said as she pulled out the card. "There's nothing on it."

"Run your thumb over the face of the card for the number," Trevor replied.

Katie shook her head. "Wait, all of this is crazy. How do I know what you're saying, anything that you're saying is the truth?"

"Judging by your exploits, I assume that you are an extreme thrill-seeker, have a high level of compassion for strangers, or feel a duty-bound obligation to help others. Any of those would be a more likely catalyst for your aide than trust in my words," replied Trevor.

"And the others...?" Katie began. "Like me and Bishop?"

"At six o'clock this evening, you should do a search for the 'Toronto Reaper'. View the fifth entry on the ninth page of the search results." There was a brief pause by Trevor. "The site will look fake, but read the top story. Carefully."

"Reaper?" Katie muttered. "Look, Trevor I'm not going to do anything unless you *actually* answer my question. Are there more people with my powers?"

There was no response for a few moments and Katie almost repeated herself. The man on the other end cleared his throat before finally responding. "I promise that I will be able to answer your questions should you decide to assist in our efforts. What I can tell you now is that there are more dangers in this world than you can possibly imagine…"

~

Digging her nails into the large banana nut muffin, she put the tiny sample she pulled off into her mouth. As the first part of the crust hit her tongue, she smiled. It tasted even better than it had looked in the boulangerie display.

As she chewed, she peered at the television she'd been watching through the shop's window. The grim faces of reporters were still on screen, a red banner scrolled beneath them with words written in white: "New York on High Alert". How uninspiring of a headline. She had seen three similarly worded updates on the few news stations she'd watched on the television in her room. Did American's really lack that much imagination?

She expected there to be more anger, maybe a pointed finger at one of the various countries that hated America. The world had been teetering on a needle for most of her life, it shouldn't need much to topple over. But it appeared for the moment, that the authorities and media outlets here were more concerned about finding the shooter, or "ghost" as she had heard in one sensational report.

She turned her eyes to the people walking past her on the street. The police were never going to find this would be assassin, and her instructions were to ensure that no evidence would ever surface. No one would know who the real intended target was.

It was truly a pity. She yearned for a confrontation.

The woman glanced back over to the shop's glass and looked at her reflection. Her pale legs and arms were the first thing to catch her attention. She hardly liked showing that much skin, but it was still summer in America. Still, the black dress and heels she was wearing did make her feel as though she blended in...

"Hi, there.'

A fair-haired man stepped into the reflection. His grey suit fit relatively tightly to his form. The shoes, watch, and cufflinks oozed of a pretentious status she had often seen in her targets. But while his smile and intentions were curious, he did not seem a threat. She continued to eat her muffin.

It was obvious by his inflection that he meant to address her, but she didn't turn in the hopes he would simply leave.

"Is this seat taken?" the suited man continued.

Through her sunglasses, she peered at the other tables placed outside on the corner. They were all full, save the empty seat across from her. She did not respond to the man's question directly, instead she pushed her iron-rod chair away from the table.

"Wait, wait," the man insisted, putting his hand dangerously close to her arm. "I wasn't trying to kick you out. I'm in between meetings and it's like a zoo out here. I saw this chair free and...if I'm bothering you then I can just try some place else."

His awkward hovering around the table was drawing more attention than she wanted. The assassin adjusted her large-lensed glasses before shifting the chair back to the table.

"Thanks," the man replied as if she had addressed him directly.

He stuck out his hand as he sat down. "Hi, I'm…" his phone stopped short his introduction. "I'm sorry, just one second."

As the man reached in his jacket to retrieve his phone, she crossed her left leg over her right, giving her easier access to the blade strapped around her thigh. Just in case.

"Yeah, yeah, I'm taking my lunch now," the man said to whoever he was speaking with. "They're in my office. No, I'll be back after lunch." He put the phone away and again extended his hand. "Bryan."

How American.

She decided to offer a slight smile back but nothing more, and quickly returned her focus to the television inside the shop. It was as much to conceal the left side of her face as it was to check the status of her mission.

"It's crazy, isn't it?" the man continued as if she had invited him into a conversation.

She sighed but nodded.

"You know, I should be completely honest," Bryan began. The declaration confused her since she hadn't questioned the suited man's integrity out loud. She turned her head toward him slightly as he continued. "I hope it doesn't sound weird. I really am in between meetings but I noticed you before I ever saw the empty chair. What's your name?"

She had heard about how American males hunted their female counterparts. The assassin much preferred to be the one behind the scope. This Bryan looked to be expecting some sort of flattered response from her. The arrogance was all over his face.

She stared at him for a moment before uncrossing her legs. The woman slowly raised her foot out toward his calf. His eyes widened and his mouth twisted into a perverted grin as she ran up his leg with her toes.

"Whoa!" he laughed. "Um, I wasn't expected that…"

She grabbed hold of the bottom of his chair with her foot and quickly pulled him closer to the table. Bryan's interest was growing, she could feel it against her toes. He glanced around the table as if trying to see who was watching.

"Action over talking?" he said. "I can get with that, Gorgeous."

The assassin held in a groan as she walked her fingers across the table. She motioned for him to lean in. The fool was too eager to oblige. Bryan cleared his throat and moved closer to her face.

It had only taken her a minute to think of three ways to kill him discretely at the table, but this was proving to be one of the rare occasions when leaving an unknowing prey alive would be just as fulfilling.

When Bryan was halfway over the table, the woman moved her straight, jet black hair behind her ears. Then she lowered her dark sunglasses. Bryan's expression drastically shifted as he caught a glimpse of her unshielded left eye. The scarred tissue that surrounded the darkened socket was probably not what this naïve hunter had fantasized about moments earlier.

Bryan shot up and haphazardly adjusted the expectation that had swelled in his pants. "I need to go...I...I need to get to that meeting..." He quickly scampered off down the sidewalk, glancing back with a mixture of disbelief and disgust.

She realigned her sunglasses using the shop window and then returned to looking at the news. The headline now read: "Senator Succumbs to Injury".

The assassin smiled and took the final bite from the muffin. It tasted much sweeter now that she knew the job was done.

Chapter 6

Instability

"We've received word that the President's condition is stable and..."

"...Still searching for the shooter. Authorities have yet to give any indication as to whether they have any leads but it's believed that the single shot came from one of the various buildings overlooking today's event..."

"...But we regret to inform you that the senator who was inadvertently struck by the bullet that hit the President has died. Senator Chase Gilbert, who was in his second term as..."

~

Kline's muscles still ached but the rest of the pain had finally dwindled. The fact that discomfort had lingered for so long certainly was a cause for concern, one that Dr. Krouse would need to provide answers for.

"Mr. Kline?" the voice of his assistant recaptured his attention.

The big man inched forward in his chair toward the conference speaker on the desk. "My apologies, JB," Kline returned. "It sounds like you're still doing an excellent job in my stead."

"Thank you sir," JB replied enthusiastically. "We've completed the proposal for the new initiatives as you requested, but Ms. Lymacks has yet to accept a meeting with us."

Denard Kline clenched a fist. The "other half" of Klymacks' controlling interest had stubbornly refused to even acknowledge any of his department's proposals. It was likely retribution for the relocation of the R&D department to Meridian without her divine blessing. But staying close to this city had become integral to his plans and it was easy to get the rest of the board to agree since the Mayor of Meridian had already promised incentives. But Kathleen hated having her hand forced.

Still, while he had expected some pushback, this months-long power play by his counterpart had become an unwanted nuisance.

"Don't worry yourself with her," he replied. "When she comes to see the facility tomorrow, I'll be sure to 'remind' her of the needs of this department."

Before JB could reply, Kline's cellphone started ringing. He pulled the device close and glanced at the screen. The number was cloaked. That could only be one person. "Actually JB, I must apologize again. I have a pressing matter that I need to attend to."

"Oh, not to worry, Mr. Kline," returned his assistant. "Shall I send you the itemized list for the delivery tomorrow?"

"That would be fine," Kline said before shutting off the speaker. He quickly clicked over to his phone. "Is it quiet where you are?"

"You've lost the plot, mate," began an agitated Tilte. "You've done some crazy things before but this one takes the cake."

"I must warn you, Mr. Tilte," Kline abruptly cut him off. He took a deep breath while opening and closing his hands gingerly. "I have far less tolerance for your belligerence right now. So I recommend you choose your words for the rest of this conversation with care. Now, *is it quiet where you are?*"

"Yes, you already know it is," Tilte replied. There was a brief groan of resentment on the other end before Kline heard a calmer response. "Why didn't you tell me that you were going to go through with it?"

"Go through with…?"

"Turn on the tele lately?" Tilte replied.

Kline smiled. The mercenary's quip was as good as a confirmation. "So she succeeded."

"And that's another thing," Tilte again raged. "You didn't tell me that you were going to use *her* to do it. She shot the bloody president!"

"She meant to!" Kline replied. He leapt from his chair as the mercenary's insolence broke his patience. There was silence on the other end and after a few steadying breaths, Kline raised the phone back to his ear. "Is that all?"

"We were practically in the clear," Tilte sighed. "But now every bloke in this country will be trying to find who tried to kill the President."

"Which is *exactly* what I wanted," snapped Denard Kline. "If she had shot Senator Gilbert unimpeded, it would've been obvious who the target was."

"Look, if you wanted to kill that senator, I could have easily done him in with his car last year. I had it planned before, remember?" the mercenary continued. "The bloke probably still drives himself places on the weekend. All you needed to do was sign off and it was done. Bringing her in to do a job is only going to muck things up like bringing Bullet in did."

Kline ignored the mention of his unfortunate miscalculation. "The last time Senator Gilbert was in the news, he was accusing Klymacks of dealing advanced technologies to dangerous foreign powers. If he had died then, who do you think would top the list of likely suspects?"

"But there wouldn't have been any suspects, mate," replied Tilte. "You talk up her talents...The bitch is good with a gun and a knife but have you forgotten what I'm good at?"

"Yes, but unlike the rest of the targets, I think any mysterious death would have been thoroughly investigated at the time," Kline returned. "As for today, Senator Gilbert appears to be just an unfortunate casualty of the failed assassination attempt on the 44th President of the United States. His name won't even warrant a headline."

"But they're not going to stop searching for the shooter," Tilte returned adamantly. "Do you think the Secret Service is just going to let this go one day? Not. Bloody. Likely."

"On the contrary, I think it's going to leave quite the impression on them," Kline countered.

"What are you going on about?"

"Everything is going according to plan. Just consider your ignorance of Gilbert's assassination a way to ensure that your focus remains on the tasks I've given you, Mr. Tilte," returned Denard Kline.

There was a distinctly sarcastic laugh on the other end. "So I'm supposed to feel better now?"

"Don't be naïve," Kline replied incredulously. "Senator Gilbert's ill-fated crusade against the so-called 'domestic assistance of terrorism' was no more than a personal attack on Klymacks. He even had the audacity to question my innovations! To question the integrity of Garrison Kline is one thing but to question my intelligence is a sin with no reprieve. I couldn't imagine a better punishment than a public execution."

"Be careful not to let your feelings get in the way of business," Tilte countered. "Especially since I'm the one doing the dirty work."

"You're being very well compensated," Kline returned.

Tilte scoffed. "Money won't do me no good if I'm in jail or dead, mate."

"No, I suppose it wouldn't."

"I don't like this," the mercenary continued. "I don't like any of this. You told me you needed me to be where you couldn't. You said you didn't need any loose ends."

"And I don't like loose ends," Kline returned sharply. "Mr. Tilte, *you* should be careful not to let your feelings get in the way of your job. I've been playing this game a long time..."

"Oh cut it with that chess bollocks," snapped Tilte. "You brought me here to be your go between for you and the operation until your little side project was done. Once you and the scientist are through, that's supposed to be it. But first there was Bullet, then it was the Majority, and now you have this one-eyed nutter on the payroll? You're better off sending her back across the ocean at the first chance. Now that pretty little cyclops might be a hell of a shot, but she's not like Bullet. She's a killer and got an itchy trigger finger that one. I can smell the crazy on her."

"She poses less of a headache to me than you do at this very moment," the big man returned. The pain had begun to grow once more and Kline was getting very impatient. It was time to pay a visit to Dr. Krouse.

"You're forgetting which one of us has spent more time with her sort," the mercenary continued. "Hell, you've only been walking out in the real world for a year or two…"

"Our arrangement works better when you simply do as you're told," Kline replied. "Every risk I've taken has been a necessary one and one that I've calculated, weighed, and planned counter measures for."

"Right, that's why I got a hit list that's longer than me standing straight up," Tilte cut back. "You must have planned for Bishop to put Bullet in the news too then, eh?"

"No one could have foreseen the emergence of Theodore Bishop. No one!" Kline gritted through his teeth. He soon had the scent of blood in his nostrils for the second time that morning. This time however, the sensation seemed to calm him. He touched his finger to his nose and gazed at the dark plasma while he tried to lessen his anger. It was childish to let a lackey have such an effect on his emotions.

"All I know is, what was supposed to be an easy hit on some thieving woman and old man turned into a literal flaming disaster. It brought the Feds in months earlier than they should have," Tilte replied.

"Maybe, but what inevitably transpired at that house that night gave us something greater..." began Kline.

"Oh, don't even bring that one up with me," Tilte began. "This obsession with the blonde has really cocked up the original plan."

"The power she harnesses...that power will be the key to my salvation. Waiting on Krouse and Phross to perfect the serum quickly became Plan B after the Beta tests."

"Still haven't heard how you plan to catch her, or the one that got away, mate."

"Yes well, I've got a plan for that too," Kline replied. "But for now, just focus on your job."

"Like that's been a piece of piss," Tilte sneered. "Don't think I enjoy risking my neck night-in and night-out just for you to go and draw more attention to what we've got going on. You're plans aren't all that complex. You know everything may look good for you now, but if you're not careful, someone's going to ask one more question than you'll be able to answer. And who knows, it may even be the bird from the Mayor's office. I'd hate to see the day when you're forced to put her on my list..."

The image of a gun being pointed at Slater's head incensed Kline. "Thank you for such...poignant advice, Mr. Tilte," he replied as calmly as he could. He adjusted the already perfect knot of his tie and tried to hold the rest of the venom from leaving his mouth. "But again, we're arguing as if there still isn't work to do."

Tilte sighed. "Right."

A sharp pain radiated through his lower back. "Now, I need to pay a visit to the good doctor." Kline replied before ending the call.

He turned toward the shelf behind his desk and pressed the face of his watch. The left end of the case separated from the wall just enough for him to fit his fingers behind. Kline groaned painfully as he pulled the frame aside to uncover the elevator doors that resided behind them.

Two metal doors slid open and the big man hobbled inside. He quickly balanced himself on the railing to catch his breath. A fervent beeping began, prompting Kline to reach for the keypad. He quickly typed in the security password to halt the irritating buzzing. Within a few seconds, the cab began to shift and soon Kline could feel the descent beneath the factory. He leaned against the walls and closed his eyes and tried to ignore the burning in his muscles.

DING!

The doors slid open revealing a wide, dimly lit space. Kline's eyes moved immediately toward the intercom on his right.

"Krouse!" he shouted as he held his hand against the button.

There was static on the other end for a few seconds before the doctor's voice came through the speaker. "I was wondering when I was going to be graced with your presence."

"Have the tests come back yet?" asked the big man.

"I told you when they'd be ready..."

"I need them sooner, Dr. Krouse," Kline snapped.

"Did you have another flare up?"

Kline shot a disgruntled stare into the speaker. "These so-called flare ups of yours are coming far more frequently and are lasting far too long."

Krouse showed little semblance of sympathy. "I told you that may one day be the case. When we ran the beta test..."

"My serum is nothing like the beta version!"

"Yes, your serum is more refined but as long as the unstable technology is in your system it will continue to degenerate your cells," Krouse returned. "Mr. Kline, you already know all of this..."

Kline smacked his hand against the wall and quickly recoiled from the stinging pain. "But it wasn't supposed to happen this quickly!"

The big man looked up to see the face of Dr. Merlin Krouse staring back at him. He clicked off his communicator and put his hands behind his back. Though his expression was stoic, Kline sensed the scientist was enjoying seeing him like this.

"Well perhaps it's your emotions. It would make sense that increased adrenaline and heightened hormones would cause the components to work through your blood stream faster. None of the test subjects lasted long enough for us to study whether varying emotional environments altered the efficacy of the serum. It's a shame that you incinerated Dr. Phross. His body could have explained a great deal."

"Leaving traces of *your* failures wasn't an option, Dr. Krouse," Kline replied, glancing into the empty hallway. "And you don't have time for any extra projects."

"My *failures* are what have kept you alive this long," the scientist returned mockingly. "Anyway, your *project* is almost complete, as is my captivity in this hell hole."

"Hell hole?" Kline laughed sarcastically. "I know I have so many memories from *my* stay here. Don't you? Did you know I actually kept count of each day you and Garrison Kline kept me down here? It amounted to 1,456 days, somewhere close to four years..."

"That was not my decision..."

"But you were complicit!" Kline snarled as he took a giant step toward the scientist. Krouse stepped back but Kline kept up his approach until their faces were inches apart. "Four years of testing, and another thirteen years locked away at Ivory Towers or at that wretched orphanage. You helped him take those years away from me. Dr. Krouse, your complaints of these accommodations are not only infuriating but dangerous given your current situation."

Krouse looked away from the intense stare Kline was giving him. "My only job was to keep you alive," he said. "I had nothing to do with where you were kept."

"Kept? Like some stray you kick dirt at as you walk by?" Kline was incensed. "I am the reason Kline Technologies enjoyed even moderate success. It's my brain that helped increase Garrison Kline's failing stock. It was me! You actually thinking that you've help me live this long is pure ignorance. My *life* has never been and the only thing I look forward to is breaking the biological bonds that have kept me chained to this agonizing purgatory you and that backstabbing man put me in. I should kill you now for..."

He stopped as he suddenly realized the reason for the researcher's silence. His large hands were tightly gripping the neck of Dr. Krouse. Kline quickly let go, watching the gasping Krouse sink to the floor.

"Perhaps my emotions have managed to get the best of me in recent months," he continued. "But I assure you, I am well within my right to demand more from you. Now I've given you a secluded space to work and I've supplied you with sufficient help to build the machine and plenty of autonomy to oversee its completion. I need the tests results by tomorrow."

"I've given you multiple tests already," Krouse finally coughed out. "There is still no way to be absolutely sure that the energy signature you gave me is enough to power the nanites indefinitely. We need to have a real sample of the subject in the cultivation chamber to know for certain. We..."

Kline had already begun to walk back toward the elevator platform when he stopped momentarily to hear out the rest of Krouse's words. They never came, but they didn't need to.

They needed The Flying Girl. They needed her power.

Chapter 7

Monsters and Demons

She breathed in deeply and then out again as she finally got comfortable with the floating brace under her arms.

"Alright Dr. Cattrell, let's go ahead and start this set. Are you ready?"

Reagan nodded before lifting her right leg out of the water. She tried to lower it slowly as Irvin often reminded her.

"One!" her trainer began. "Now the left. Come on, let's put that power back in your legs. Okay good! Let's go for two…"

She knew she was supposed to do ten on each side but the padded weights around her ankles were already burning her muscles. Irvin kept enough distance between his hands and her calves to guide, but not aide the descent. Reagan groaned as she lifted the other leg.

"You've got this Dr. Cattrell," cheered the trainer. "You're already a quarter of the way there."

"That's it?" Reagan asked.

Irvin shrugged. "It's closer than when you started isn't it? Six! How are you feeling?"

"My legs are killing me," Reagan's words came out raggedly in between each breath.

"What about your back? Seven…!"

She didn't know how to answer that question yet. There was a certain degree of discomfort but it had been something she'd gotten used to since the nerves had begun to heal. "I'm good. Just keep counting."

"Yes ma'am," Irving laughed. "Eight! Other side..."

Reagan closed her eyes and gritted her teeth as she strained for the final two reps.

"That's ten!"

Reagan immediately relaxed and tried to catch her breath. Once she was done, Irvin submerged himself and unstrapped the weights. When he came back up, he gave her a thumbs up.

"Great job. Now let's get you right-side up again," he added.

"Ugh, can't I just float here for a second?" she asked hopefully.

"Resting? That's not like you, Cat."

Reagan spun her around so fast that she lost her position on the float. She splashed clumsily before finally finding her balance. She wiped the water from her eyes to see that a scrub-clad Peter Sava was smiling at her by the door.

"Peter," Reagan greeted before flashing a slightly embarrassed smile back. "You're early."

Ever since receiving his compliments at the hotel, Reagan had become acutely aware of how she might look whenever her friend was around. The one-piece swimsuit was beyond unflattering. The red of the suit clashed with her hair and the wet latex stuck to her body in *all* the wrong places. It was the dumbest and most superficial thing she had ever found herself caring about, but she just couldn't help it. None of this usually bothered her but Aunt Laine had to work after taking the morning off, leaving the always-willing Dr. Sava to be her ride back home. "We have a few minutes left, there's probably more comfortable places to sit in the lobby."

Dr. Sava did a quick sweep around the room before pointing to an empty bench in the far corner. "No, it's fine. There's a spot over there." He then turned his pointed finger to Irvin. "If it's okay with you..."

"Irvin. And it's not a problem here. Dr. Cattrell has one more exercise to do for our session."

"Heh, early?" Dr. Sava began triumphantly as he trotted to the bench. "I think you meant to say that I had perfect timing, Cat."

Reagan shook her head and muttered under her breath. "Yeah, that's *exactly* what I meant."

"You need an extra minute to recover?" her trainer asked, sounding suddenly concerned. "Your face looks flush..."

"No, it's fine," Reagan quickly interrupted. "Let's just go ahead and...whatever we're supposed to be doing, let's just do it."

Irvin nodded before swimming to the edge of the pool and bringing back a blue medicine ball. Once he handed it to Reagan, he positioned a small step from behind them to just in front of her feet. "Alright then, time for stairs."

"Great..." replied Reagan.

"Three sets of twelve, six on each side."

Reagan nodded. She lifted the ball above her head and took a peek in Sava's direction. To her relief his eyes were focused on his phone.

"Okay," she exhaled before finally taking the first step.

~

"Okay," Katie exhaled before continuing. "So what do we do?"

Nancy finished mixing the punch before glancing up toward the blonde. "Did you look at the site?"

"No, he said to look in another hour," Katie replied. "Nancy, he knew my name. It's like they're the CIA or something. I mean, what if they're watching us right…"

"Katie, stop it."

"But what if it's true?" the blonde returned as she buried her face in her palms. "Nancy, there could be people out there that know about my powers."

Her friend put the ladle down in the bowl and walked into the living room. She stopped in front of the blonde and draped her arms around her. Katie thought she might say one of her trademark positive expressions to ease her anxiety but to her surprise Nancy remained silent.

Please say something, anything…

After a few long seconds, her friend exhaled. "I don't think we are in any danger."

The words didn't really comfort Katie, even though it was what she wanted to hear. "How can you say that?"

Nancy leaned away, allowing Katie to see the faint traces of worry on her face.

"Well, I think this is all very elaborate if they are just wanting to capture you," she replied.

Yeah, I guess that makes sense...

"There may actually be someone out there who could tell me about my powers..." Katie muttered distractedly. "What do you think I should do?"

"I don't know," Nancy shook her head. "I don't really like this cloak and dagger. It just doesn't feel right."

"But if it is all true then I can finally find out why I'm like this," Katie said. "Maybe they'll know how I can get rid of..."

"No Katie!" Nancy stopped the blonde's thought short as she reached for her arm. "If what they said is true, that means that there's some kind of monster out there..."

"Monster?" Katie said hesitantly before glancing back at her friend. Nancy looked confused for a moment, which angered the blonde. "You mean another person like me?"

Nancy's eyes widened and she shook her head vigorously. "No! Love, no! That's not what I said..."

"You didn't have to!" Katie snapped, stepping away from Nancy. She felt the hairs on her neck stand up. "People with powers - my powers - are always doing bad things."

"That's not true at all Katie," her friend returned. "That's not true at all. Think about how many people you've saved in less than a year..."

"Stop it, Nance! Just stop!"

After a few seconds of silence, Katie began to feel her heart pounding against her rib cage and every inch of her tingled as though she had returned from going numb. The blonde glanced at the faint trace of the bracelet around her wrist. It had hijacked her emotions, with Nancy yet again being the recipient of her fury. Katie closed her eyes and took a deep breath as she fought away the tears.

~

Reagan hung onto the rails, her lower body still in the pool while she continued to catch her breath. It had taken much longer this time to do her cool down lap. She wanted nothing more than to be lying in bed, but the young doctor was in too much pain to even move from where she was.

"Sore?" asked Irvin.

Reagan shrugged. "No more than usual."

"What are you doing in between sessions?" he asked.

"There's a stationary bike and free weights at our gym," Reagan replied. "Nothing crazy."

Her trainer nodded. "Nothing crazy, huh?"

Reagan turned toward Irvin. "I'm just trying to stick to the rehabilitation plan."

"If you're following the plan you shouldn't be in this much pain," Irvin replied. "You've barely been able to get through the last three sessions and as far as I can tell that's not due to any relapse, at least none that I can see..."

"I'm fine, just sore," returned the young doctor.

"Look, the rehab process is hard," her trainer continued. "It's good that you're pushing yourself. But, you may want to try and dial back the amount of exercise you're doing in between sessions. You need to give your muscles time to repair, okay?"

"Thank you," Reagan replied, preoccupied with finding a towel to cover up with. One was eventually handed to her by Dr. Sava.

"Relax? You must not know Cat," he said to Irvin, reaching out to shake the trainer's hand. "Peter Sava."

"Irvin Montoya. You're a doctor too I take it?"

Sava nodded. "Bags under the eyes give it away?"

Irvin laughed before climbing out of the pool. He turned to Reagan. "Just remember to breathe every now and then, Dr. Cattrell."

~

"Did it happen again?" Nancy asked softly.

Katie nodded, her eyes still closed as she pictured the blue glow from the bracelet. The image faded as she felt Nancy's hand begin to rub her back.

"Just breathe, okay?" her friend added. "Just breathe."

The blonde pulled in everything that she could fit into her lungs and then let it release slowly like sand slipping through her fingers. "I'm sorry," she began. "I don't know why it's always you that I'm a bitch to."

Her friend laughed for the first time in what seemed like an eternity. "I feel like Ramona just said that to me."

Katie gave a wide grin of her own. She opened her eyes and wiped away the rogue tear that had managed to escape. She looked at her friend's open arms and slid into them without hesitancy. "I missed you so bad this summer."

"I missed you too, Love," Nancy replied.

The embrace lasted a few moments more before Katie stepped away again and turned toward the balcony. The fading sky had almost sunk into night and she could see her troubled reflection clearly in the glass. "I need to know, Nance."

"It's too dangerous, even for you," Nancy replied after a heavy sigh.

"*I'm* too dangerous," Katie returned. "Look what happened to the city last year. Look at what *just* happened..."

"That was Bishop's fault, Katie!"

"But I was there too!" the blonde spun back around. "And I told you, I'm not so sure Bishop meant everything he did. For the little while that I had his thoughts...he was hurting, Nance. All the bad stuff...it was like he was unbalanced or something. That could be me!"

Nancy shook her head. "You shouldn't be punished for things you haven't done, Katie. I've said that a thousand times."

"Someone almost died today because of me," Katie said abruptly. "That man, whether he was good, bad, or whatever, he could have died *because of me*."

"You saved that sweet little girl," Nancy replied. "Just like you saved Melody last year."

"But it feels like for every Melody Riker there's like five blocks of destruction. I don't even remember how many people have been injured or how many…"

"Stop, please! You have to stop doing this, Katie," Nancy pressed. "You're. Not. The. Problem."

"But these powers are," Katie replied. "Every time I think I've got a better handle on them I'll do something like what happened just now, or hit something too hard, or…I don't know. But I *need* to know…"

~

"So you're not going to tell me?" Sava asked as he picked up Reagan's bag.

Reagan winced. Her body was aching more than it usually did but she did her best to ignore it. She picked up the pace with each step, letting the sound of the cane's rubber base motivate her to go faster.

She glanced confusedly at Sava, "Tell you what?"

"How things with Dr. Kondu went…"

"Oh, sorry," Reagan returned. "So there is no final decision yet but he said that all the reports he's gotten from the doctors and therapists have been 'excellent'."

"Hey, that's better than where you thought you'd be what, six or seven months ago?" Sava returned. "And at the rate you're going, you'll be medically cleared in no time.

Reagan shrugged. "Yeah, I guess."

"Are you okay, Cat?"

"Yeah, I'm fine," Reagan sighed as she forced a smile for her friend. "Thanks for waiting, Peter."

"No problem. That Irvin guy seems like a cool guy," he said. "A little soft on you though if you ask me. You should be doing at least ten sets of stairs."

Reagan's smile was genuine this time. She had a feeling it wouldn't take long for Peter Sava's charm to crack her hardened exterior once again. "He's the soft one? Did you miss all that back there?"

"He was just concerned," Sava replied. "You looked like you were having a hard time."

"Oh...thank you," returned Reagan sarcastically.

Sava quickly assessed his previous comment. "I meant that I saw you wince more than a few times, mostly when the trainer wasn't looking."

"I'm fine, Peter," Reagan replied. "I was just a little sore today, that's all."

"Well you're limping a little bit," added Sava.

"Am I? I'll keep that in mind. You don't have to go back in tonight do you?"

"Nah, I'm off until Friday morning."

"A whole day and a half," Reagan began. "What will you even do with yourself?""

"Work basically," Sava replied, "I'll be studying all day for the boards tomorrow."

"I do not miss the studying..."

"What about you?" Sava asked.

"Tomorrow, I don't know," began the young doctor. "Depending on how my body feels, maybe I'll take Irvin's advice and just relax. As for tonight, I have a date with my DVD collection."

"With popcorn?" Sava hinted.

Reagan laughed. "Are trying to ask if you can come over?"

~

"I'm asking that you wait," began Nancy hurriedly. "Think about this before you make any rash decision."

"I don't think this would be a rash decision. This is literally about finding out where my powers come from," Katie returned.

"But it is rash, Katie. You don't even know who this Trevor works for or what sort of crazy person it is they're after."

The blonde glanced at her room. "It's almost six isn't it?"

Nancy folded her arms and followed Katie's eyes. "In ten minutes..."

Katie could hear the frustration in her reply.

What is her deal?

"I don't get it," began the blonde. "Don't you want to know what's happening to me?"

Nancy shook her head before walking back to the kitchen. "I do, but I don't."

What...?

"I don't know," her friend continued. "I want to know that you're safe, that your powers aren't hurting you. But at the same time I don't really care where they came from...at least not enough for you to fight another Bishop!"

"But that's just it, Nance," returned Katie. "How do I know that I won't become another Bishop?"

Nancy was about to say something back but instead passed an unusually accusatory gaze at the blonde. "What aren't you telling me?"

"About what?" Katie replied defensively.

"Something happened, didn't it?"

~

"That's not going to happen, Peter," Reagan replied. "I don't do scary movies."

"Oh come on Cat," protested Dr. Sava. "Horror movies provide valuable insight into the youth of today's culture. Their educational AND fun."

Reagan shot him a disbelieving gaze. "If you could be any more ridiculous, please feel free to go on..."

"Whatever, I am just saying relax and have some fun," he said.

"Maybe when I'm working double-shifts again," Reagan replied. "I've got too much going on in my life right now."

Sava nodded slowly. "Like what? Did something happen with your sister or something? I thought everything was good between you two?"

"As good as it can be," Reagan replied. "Look, I'm almost a year behind, Peter. And I might not get to go back immediately once I am cleared."

Sava opened the door to the locker rooms. "Have faith, young one..."

Reagan stopped just short of the door. "Oh stop it. Peter, I'm serious. I think the hospital is waiting to see how I hold up. It takes a long time for people who've suffered from this type of paralysis to really get back to where they were. And even then they can suffer setbacks and regressions and..."

"Whoa, whoa, Cat!" Sava slowed the pace of their conversation. "Relax. You've been killing it so far."

His words did little to relax her. "But what if my body can't hold up? I only just started using this stupid thing a month ago!" returned Reagan, holding up the cane. "I need to know if can do it before I even bother getting someone else's hopes up."

Sava laughed as Reagan shook her cane. "You look like some hooligan just stole the bread you were using to feed the pigeons in the park..."

Reagan tried not to laugh at Sava's quip but the 'fake old lady' voice her friend used proved too much. "I hate you sometimes."

"But you still come back," he aimed his finger wag at her.

"I do," Reagan shrugged. "But seriously Peter, I was so tired after today at MMC and I'm already sore after that last session."

"No, you're sore because you've been doing double what you're supposed to be doing," Sava said.

Reagan's felt a tiny pinch in her chest as Sava's tone shifted to a more concerned one. "I told you, it's not like I've been doing it all the time."

"No, just when you get worried," her friend replied. "Which kind of seems like all the time lately."

"I have to see how much I can take."

"Do you hear yourself? You're scared that your body might fall apart yet you're pushing yourself to the point that *your body might fall apart*," Sava replied. "Cat, you have to slow down. You're just getting your strength back. I mean, at the very least you could just follow the rehabilitation program you're on."

Reagan swiftly ended the conversation. "I need to get dressed. I might be another fifteen minutes, is that okay?"

Her friend sighed and pretended to look contemplative. "Only if you agree to one of the movies being the original *Halloween...*"

"Don't push your luck," Reagan grinned and took her bag before walking through the doorway. She waited until she heard the door close to prop her hand against her back and continue gingerly down the hallway. This was more than just soreness, but she couldn't let anyone else see her struggling to move, not even Sava.

By the time she got halfway through the locker room, she needed a break. Reagan rested her cane against the sink and lifted her bag onto the counter. As she leaned forward over the faucet she raised her shoulders to stretch out her back. Reagan only managed the position for a few seconds before she felt the spasms.

Her arms trembled as she continued holding herself up. She clenched her jaw and closed her eyes, taking in deep breaths of air to keep from screaming out.

After a few more agonizing seconds, the spasms eased. Reagan exhaled once more before looking into the mirror at her reflection's watery eyes. Without any more hesitation, she turned on the water, unzipped her bag, pulled out the orange pill bottle, and quickly unscrewed the lid.

~

The serious look on Nancy's face was one that she had rarely seen. But as she and Katie continued their awkward standoff, the blonde knew she couldn't hide the truth from her friend any longer.

"I've been..." she began. "I've been seeing things I guess."

Surprisingly, Nancy's expression softened. "More memories?"

"No," Katie replied. "Well, I actually can't tell what they are, only that they're different. Nothing ever really comes through clearly but I'll like, zone out and see..."

"See what?"

"All kinds of things. Mostly fire. That's the easiest way to explain it," said Katie.

Nancy furrowed her brows and turned toward Katie's room. It was then that the blonde realized that she herself was staring in that direction.

"Is that all...?" Nancy asked timidly.

Katie could feel her skin tingling as she thought about the stone she had locked away in her underwear drawer.

You have to tell her now, Katie...

She raised her hand and twirled her wrist. "So my invisible 'super bracelet'...well, Bishop had one too. And when he died, it fell off and warped into this rock-thing. I didn't want to leave it there so I kind of took it and have been keeping it in my room..."

It was hard to read Nancy's face. Her eyes were wide open but her mouth was sewn shut. Though the blonde desperately wanted to be interrupted, it looked like she was going to have to keep going.

Just have to pull off the Band-Aid...

"...And ever since then, I've been having those visions, or whatever." As the blonde continued, she felt the tears welling up in her eyes. "And sometimes I'll hear things that aren't there or see things that...I should have told you sooner but I was so afraid of...I don't know, Nancy. I don't know!"

Before a tear could fall, Nancy had already pulled Katie into her grasp.

"It's okay, it's okay," she tried to reassure her. "I'm not mad at you. Well, that's not true. Why didn't you tell me?"

Katie shook her head, "I didn't want you to be afraid of me the way everyone was afraid of him."

"You're not Theodore Bishop!" Nancy said emphatically. "You're a hero Katie, and you're brave. Always have been. The powers didn't change a thing about *you*. So you're strong. Very strong, and can do things that no one else in the world can. That makes you special, doesn't it?"

"And dangerous," Katie countered.

"*Special,* Katie. And I don't care what any of those stupid people say about you. You're an easy target and they just dramatize everything so people will tune in over and over again."

"It's hard to exaggerate what I've done, Nance," Katie replied. "And you didn't see that girl's face. She was scared of me!"

"I think she was just scared, Love. And you keep leaving out the part about you saving another little girl," Nancy said. "You're helping people, Katie."

"But am I helping that many people?" the blonde countered. "Because it really doesn't seem like it sometimes. They haven't rebuilt the buildings by the park. And that guy from the hotel; I put him in a coma..."

"You were protecting your sister!" Nancy returned. "He was a bloody terrorist anyway."

"But I lost control, Nancy," Katie said. "When I saw him standing over Reagan, I...I don't know."

Nancy put her hand on Katie's. "You were protecting your sister," her words were deliberate. "For every scummy bad guy on one side there's a thankful person on the other - a Melody Riker, a Reagan Cattrell. I know it doesn't always seem that way on the news, but that's only because that kind of negativity sells. Ramona says it all the time. People would get bored if all they heard was the good in the world."

"I hope that's not true," Katie said.

Nancy shrugged. "It seems like it lately. But trust me Katie, I know you; I trust you."

Katie wanted to smile at her friend's words, but caught a glimpse of Nancy's purse from the corner of her eye. "You really trust me?"

"Implicitly," her friend replied, gripping Katie's hand.

The blonde slowly took her eyes away from the counter. She tried to keep her mind off the news and the brand new Taser she had seen in her friend's purse the other night. She tried to keep out every comparison she could think of between herself and Theodore Bishop.

In the end, her attempts failed. It was still there. The blonde shrugged her friend off and glanced back at her room. "I have changed Nancy and I need to know why. I need to know what's happening to me."

Nancy looked as though she wanted to argue but held it in. Instead, she simply nodded. "Well then, maybe it's your turn to put in a favor."

Chapter 8

Hedging Bets

Wreings looked up to see Donnelly putting on his suit jacket.

"Is it six already?" he asked as his partner pushed in his chair.

Donnelly nodded and glanced at his watch. "About eight minutes past. How's it going with the Arden case paperwork?"

"Almost done," replied the detective with a weary look at his computer screen. "I thought you would have finished all this earlier this morning."

"I bet you would have liked that," Donnelly replied with his usual sarcasm. "You miss the close of a case, you pick up the paperwork. We call that a partnership, V."

"Right," Wreings shook his head. Though he had done the write-ups for their past three cases, Wreings appreciated something that kept him from dwelling on his son's birthday.

Donnelly grinned and picked up his car keys. "You coming out tonight?"

"Tonight? What's tonight?"

"Hudson's retirement. Remember? A bunch of guys from the station are heading to The Pen in about thirty minutes"

"That's right!" sighed Wreings, pressing his thumb against his forehead. He must be really out of it to have forgotten the planned celebration for Hudson.

The economy had gotten worse and the MPD wasn't immune. So Hudson and a handful of badges on the wrong side of forty-five were given "permission" to take an early retirement. The news had caught them by surprise and set Detective Tejeda off. She had a huge blowup in the Captain's office a couple weeks ago. It wasn't Glades' fault but she took the brunt of the criticism around the station.

"I think I'm going to sit this one out," Wreings continued. "You go on without me."

"Nah, V," Donnelly shook his head. "You're coming and don't give me that 'busy' crap, I know you ain't got nothing else to do. Come on V, it's going to lame but who cares? I heard Tejeda was buying a round of shots for any cop that shows up. Plus, Shane will cover my tab if I can get you to actually come out for once."

Wreings shook his head. "So I'm your prop bet?"

"Nadine ain't cheap," Donnelly returned. "Got to catch my breaks somewhere. Anyway, it's not a bet if you know you'll win."

"Really?" Wreings said before turning back to the computer. "You know something I don't?"

Donnelly smiled. "You know who said she'd be there."

Wreings' fingers stopped typing. By 'you know who', Donnelly meant LJ.

"I forgot to tell you that I also told her you'd be there when she stopped by this morning," Donnelly added with a wink.

"I thought you were leaving," Wreings muttered. His partner smiled.

"So you're coming then?"

Wreings turned back toward Donnelly. "I didn't say I was."

"You didn't have to," Donnelly returned, pointing to his eye. "I don't have to be a detective to know that look."

Wreings watched as his partner walked past him and out the front of the station.

"Damn it, Don," the detective sighed. He quickly reached for his phone and searched for the text LJ had sent him that morning. He wasn't sure what he was going to say, but he didn't want her waiting on him. Today was just not a good...

Suddenly, a message flashed across his screen.

"Can we meet?"

The question wasn't as surprising as who the message had come from...

"Wreings!"

The detective spun around to see the Captain standing at the door to her office. She motioned for him to join her inside. He took another quick glance at the text message before tucking his phone away and walking over.

Once inside, he saw that he and Glades weren't alone. Instead there was a tall man in a tailored black suit and blue tie leaning against the wall. He was clean shaven like Donnelly, but with darker hair and a set of round glasses on his nose.

"I'd like for you to meet Agent Salvador Roberts," Glades began formally. "He's here with the FBI."

"How are you doing?" Wreings greeted the agent and gripped his waiting hand firmly.

"I can't complain, Detective," he returned. "I've heard a lot about you. And your partner."

"Yeah," Wreings glanced back at the Captain. "Donnelly just walked out, but he probably hasn't left yet if you want me to..."

"Oh, there's no need to bother your partner, Detective," Agent Roberts cut in. "Please, have a seat."

"I don't mind standing," Wreings replied resolutely. He couldn't help but wonder whether his secret investigation into the arms trade had finally been discovered. The look on Glades' face didn't help shake the unease he was feeling either. "I'm surprised the Bureau isn't sick and tired of Meridian by now."

Agent Roberts smiled slightly. He slid one hand into his suit jacket pocket and began to use the other as an embellishment for his words. "Funny, with all that's happened here and to you personally, I'm surprised that it's you who is not sick of this place."

"The city has its moments," Wreings returned. "But there's been nothing that has happened here that hasn't happened anywhere else."

The smile the agent wore quickly turned into a smirk. "I don't know. I'd say there were maybe one or two *tiny* exceptions..." he eventually replied.

"Could we get on with this?" Captain Glades cut in, her tone sharp and aimed at Roberts. Wreings was glad she was on his side.

"I apologize," Agent Roberts responded with a bow of his head. His thick accent made the action all the more formal. "Of course. I know my colleagues and I have detained you all day, Ms. Glades. But if you'll allow me a few more moments…"

"What's all this about?" Wreings asked.

"Are you familiar with the name Clarence Oswalt?" asked Roberts.

"Yeah, that name definitely rings a few bells." There was still a six foot, four inch tall hole in the wall of the Wiesenburg stairwell matching Oswalt's frame. "He was one of the survivors from The Majority, right?"

"Yes. Actually, he was one of the founders. According to our sources, he was one of Byers' first recruits along with Eric Bronson and Alexa Luger," Agent Roberts stepped away from the wall and began moving around the office as he continued. "With the latter two dead, the FBI considers Oswalt our most valuable asset with regards to The Majority. It's possible that he may know of future targets, recruitment, and of course, the possible whereabouts of Byers himself."

"Provided he wakes up," Wreings said. "He's still comatose from getting thrown through a wall."

"For now," returned the agent. "His condition has improved and we're told there is a potential, albeit slight, for him to regain consciousness."

"Didn't two other guys survive?" Wreings asked. He was careful not to sound as immersed in the investigation as he really was.

"David Quinton and Kelly Nelson," Roberts returned. "Unfortunately, neither was involved with the terrorist organization for very long. We gathered all that we could but even so, their contribution was woefully short of our needs."

That wasn't too hard to believe. Wreings remembered hearing profiles of The Majority terrorists on the news. Nelson, a former construction worker, had apparently only learned how to use a gun after being let go from his job at a shipping yard the day before Christmas. Quinton was a veteran like Byers and Bronson, but Wreings had figured he didn't do much but follow any orders given. He was diagnosed with PTSD after he was sent home from Afghanistan and couldn't get a job.

"What does any of this have to do with me?" Wreings asked.

Roberts cleared his throat before continuing. "Approximately two weeks ago, we found Quinton hung to death in his cell. Six days ago, Nelson was found the same way."

"They all seemed willing to die for the cause back at the Wiesenburg," Wreings shrugged.

"Oh no, Detective," Roberts shook his head. "I don't believe they killed themselves,"

"Why's that?" questioned Wreings.

"Because both men were *killed* by the same person."

This time the detective couldn't keep the curiosity from his face. "What?"

"We almost didn't see it," continued Agent Roberts. "And like you said The Majority were terrorists. Extremists. Committing suicide while they were in custody was one of the first concerns we had. But you see, not everybody fits into such an easy box. Quinton, yes he most certainly did, but Nelson...his psych eval didn't match that assessment. So my team looked closer at their deaths and found that both of the nooses used were tied by a southpaw. Nelson was right handed."

While Wreings had no intention of saying it out loud to the already overconfident Roberts, his story sounded a lot like good detective work. "That's really interesting and all, but you still haven't told me why you are telling me all this."

"Yes, let's please cut to the chase." Glades interrupted impatiently.

Agent Roberts glanced at her with a peculiar look of disappointment but then quickly returned his attention back to Wreings. "The FBI is transferring Oswalt from the hospital to one of our secure facilities. The Meridian Police Department has graciously offered to provide a handful of spare officers to help during the transition. But...I still hope that further reinforcements could be possible."

The detective couldn't keep himself from laughing. "I don't think me being there is..."

"No, please don't misunderstand, Detective Wreings," Roberts quickly stepped in. "While your fabled heroics from the Wiesenburg Hotel were very impressive, it's not yours that I'm interested in."

Wreings looked on curiously as the agent pointed toward the ceiling. It was only after he heard the Captain's sigh that he realized that Agent Roberts was pointing to the sky.

"I'm not sure what you mean," replied Wreings.

"The fact that someone managed to infiltrate the *two* separate facilities we used to hold Quinton and Nelson, undetected, opens the possibility that someone with exceptional skills has intimate knowledge of our plans and procedures. That gives them an advantage that I don't particularly care for. Oswalt's knowledge is integral to our efforts to track down Byers. I'd like to have some form of advantage of our own."

Suddenly, Wreings felt a tension in the air as Roberts stared hard at him. He tried his best not to let it show but he quickly noticed that the Captain had turned a questioning gaze toward him as well.

"With all due respect to you Agent Roberts," began the detective. His fingers tapped the phone inside his pocket nervously but Wreings made sure his voice was steady as he spoke. "If you think I have some in with the girl then you're wasting your time."

"Detective Wreings, since *she* first appeared last November, the list of people who have had direct contact with The Flying Girl has remained a small one," Roberts returned. "And that contact has been incidental at best. But in your extraordinary case, you actually had a conversation..."

"Agent Roberts," Glades stood up from her desk as she cut in. "Detective Wreings is right, we're wasting a lot of time here. Unless..."

"If you'll just let me finish Ms. Glades..."

"It's *Captain*! And I've let you carry this on long enough," Glades returned angrily, shooting daggers at the agent. "My detective has already said the same thing to multiple reporters. He doesn't know The Flying Girl, no matter how much every tabloid junkie wants him to."

Agent Roberts seemed expectant of Captain Glades' response. Wreings wondered what the two had discussed before he had come in.

"I apologize, Captain," he began after a sigh. "It's just that I find it hard to believe that a man who is held in such high regard for his "uncanny" perceptiveness can be the same man that failed to register enough visual data about The Flying Girl, as you all seem so fondly to call her, to even generate a sketch."

That wasn't the most subtle way to call someone a liar, but it was nothing that Wreings hadn't gotten used to hearing over the past several months. "It was a rough night. She had on a hood and goggles, and to be honest, I was more worried about the hostages." He'd almost grown weary of repeating himself.

Roberts nodded his head as if he understood, though Wreings could tell he was still *very* suspicious. "Of course. Well, apparently I have been wasting everyone's time this evening."

"I don't think I've ever heard that line from the Bureau before," returned Glades.

"We usually know what we're talking about, *Captain*," said Agent Roberts pointedly. "Detective Wreings..."

"Yes sir?"

"The transfer happens to be taking place in the B Service Tunnel under Meridian Metro General," he said. "11:30 AM. Perhaps we'll have some luck tomorrow."

With that, the agent walked out the door.

Wreings heard the Captain breathe out deeply. She fell back into her chair. He couldn't tell whether it was a gesture of relief or frustration.

"You spent all day with that guy?" the detective quipped.

"Four of them at one point..." Glades replied. She shook her head as she leaned forward. "They want her...they want her real bad, Tobias. And you know, I'm not really sure whether they're afraid she's going to level a whole city or if they want to use her as the ultimate deterrent themselves. Isn't that sad?"

"Sounds like we're back to stocking up for war."

Glades nodded. "Like we ever stopped?" The Captain shrugged before exhaling one more time. "Did you know she's contributed to eighteen arrests since that night at the Wiesenburg? Nineteen if you count that kidnapping she stopped this morning. Now, I don't care what Shay Donovan or any asshole on TV thinks, that's damn valuable."

Though his verbal response was casual, Wreings emphatically agreed. "Yeah, she's alright."

"Of course..." Glades continued with a skeptical gaze. "Of those arrests, seventeen of them were handled by this precinct; three of them involving perps *you* and Detective Donnelly were tracking."

Detective Wreings glanced at the Captain innocently. "I didn't know that."

"Neither did I, until Roberts told me," replied Glades. The look she gave Wreings was the same one she had given him the moment she handed the weapons trade files to him. She had defended him vigorously but the detective had a feeling it had likely been out of loyalty to her own and respect than genuine belief in his side of the story.

"Am I under some kind of investigation?" Wreings asked.

Glades shook her head. "No, but you're definitely on that prick's radar. They've been combing through dispatch recordings...anything that can lead them to a link between someone at this station and blondie. Just remember that."

"I'll keep that in mind," Wreings replied, with a look toward the door.

"Tobias," Captain Glades called out before he could reach the knob.

"Yeah, Captain?"

She waited for a few seconds before continuing. "You doing okay...today? I'm sure this mess is one of the last things you needed."

"Today..." Wreings turned back toward Glades, but kept his eyes pointed to the exit. "...Today I actually appreciate the mess, Captain."

Chapter 9

After Dark

Reagan looked up from the couch to see that Sava had begun to put away the groceries in her tiny kitchen.

"Hey, I am not a complete invalid, you know," she began.

Her friend held the refrigerator door open, passing her a glance before setting her almond milk inside. "I mean, you said that you were barely able to move your legs and honestly, I thought you had fallen asleep," he said. "Besides, I'm pretty much done now."

The first statement was definitely true. Reagan's arms and legs had felt like jelly and by the time they had returned to her apartment she could barely stand. She leaned forward slowly to see that the second part of Sava's statement was also true. Only one bag remained on the counter.

"Oh I'm sorry, I guess I wasn't paying attention," Reagan retuned wearily. "Thank you."

"It's all good," Sava replied. "I zone out on my mom about two minutes into every call. Three minutes tops."

"You're awful," Reagan managed a laugh before peeking at her phone on the round coffee table. She could tell that she still wasn't thinking that clearly, since the first thought that popped into her mind was to call her sister. It had been hours since Katie's message and she was likely fuming at the lack of response.

"Where does this go?" asked Sava, holding up a wrapped loaf of French bread.

Reagan pushed the thoughts aside, pointing to the space between the refrigerator and the toaster. "You can leave it right there."

Sava tossed the loaf to its spot and crumpled the empty grocery bag in his hand. "Are you okay, Cat?"

"Oh yeah, yeah, of course," replied Reagan instinctively. She pulled her eyes away from her phone once again and quickly refocused them on Sava. "I think the day is just finally catching up to me."

Sava nodded as he sat down beside her. "I figured that you were tired and all but, I don't know. You practically agreed to everything I told you I'd get at the grocery store."

"What? Didn't I give you a list?" Reagan asked.

Her friend gave a slight grin.

"Peter!"

"Hey, if I'm going be subbing in while 'Leggy' Laine gets her groove back then shouldn't I get some kind of payment?" Sava returned. "And it was nothing egregious. Just some Cheetos and Hot Pockets."

"That sounds so disgusting," Reagan shook her head before sinking back into the cushion behind her.

"But you see what I'm saying? You wouldn't have even realized if I hadn't told you. You're out of it, Cat."

Reagan winced as she moved to lie down on the couch. She nearly fell off but managed to grab hold of the armrest. Sava reached in to steady her.

"I'm okay," she assured. "I promise. My body is just tired and still a little off-balance I guess."

"Okay," he replied skeptically. "So I guess tomorrow you'll be taking it easy then?"

"Jesus, Peter. Could you just give it a break?" Reagan snapped.

Her friend raised his hands and backed away slowly. "Okay, okay, I get it. Don't try to be a doctor to the doctor. Got it."

Reagan sighed and reached for her friend's hand. "I don't mean to keep...I'm sorry, Peter."

He shrugged and offered a smile in return. "I get it, Cat. With all the PT you've had to do to get to where you are now, I can't imagine how tough it's been."

Reagan imagined that her physical struggles were very much there for anyone to see, especially someone as close to her as Sava. But those had only been a portion of what was bothering her.

"It's not just the rehab, Peter. It's..." She turned herself on the couch to face her friend. Reagan paused as she realized that she was about to put voice to something she wasn't sure she should say.

"What is it?" Sava asked.

For the first time all evening, Dr. Sava looked at her with anticipation as though she were seconds away from revealing the long lost secrets of her mind. Reagan glanced at her phone once more before closing her eyes. She patted her friend's hand and then carefully leaned away.

"It's nothing," she finally said. "Just some family stuff that I need to figure out how to deal with.

Sava nodded. "Your sister?"

"Yeah."

"What does she got going on now?" her friend asked.

"Honestly, I wouldn't even know where to start," replied Reagan.

"Do you want to...talk about it?" Sava asked.

But the young doctor shook her head in reply. "Let's just watch these movies. Put the scary one on first, please..."

Dr. Sava laughed. "Sure."

"My computer might still be in my bedroom," Reagan added.

"You need to invest in an *actual* TV," Sava said as he began walking in that direction.

"Never knew I needed one until...well, this," returned the young doctor. She waited until Sava had disappeared down the hallway to pick up her phone and quickly searched for the last message from her sister.

~

Katie landed softly on the roof. It looked deserted but she quickly stepped behind a large exhaust port and out of view. She leaned against it as her eyes shifted toward the door of the stairwell.

Ten minutes passed before she saw the handle move. She shuffled further back and watched cautiously as the door opened. Light from the stairwell lit the ground, but for a few nervous seconds, the blonde saw no one exit. Then a lone shadow appeared and out came the familiar shape of Detective Wreings.

She caught a glimpse of his face as he turned to close the door. It was much like it had been when he first showed up at her apartment door a month after the Wiesenburg. She could never tell whether he looked more tired or stressed.

"Hey, you here?" he said in a whisper.

"You're usually the first one here," Katie said as she stepped out from behind the port.

"I'm usually the one setting this up," the detective replied.

"Did you find anything?"

Wreings shook his head. "No. But that guy said we wouldn't find anything else anywhere though and you didn't give me much time."

"What about the website?" Katie asked.

"No IP address, no idea where or when it was created," Wreings began. "If it existed then it was only there long enough for you to see it. All traces of it are gone now. Oh and that number you gave me, it's a non-working number, not registered to anyone."

"Damn it!" Katie groaned and looked up into the questioning eyes of the detective. "I'm not crazy. This guy is real."

Katie reached inside her bag and pulled out the box she had gotten from Trevor. Detective Wreings took it from her and moved into the light.

"What's this?" he asked.

"I don't know," began Katie. "It's like some kind of high-tech walkie-talkie. This guy Trevor gave it to me after we ran into each other at school."

"I don't get it?"

"He was following me," said the blonde. "I don't know for how long but he slid that in my bag and then started talking to me with it. He knows who I am, what I can do…"

She could see the detective's eyes widen. "He knows about your powers?"

Katie nodded and then pulled out the card. "He gave me this too."

Detective Wreings looked over it. "There's nothing here."

"The number is embedded in the card. You have to run your fingers over it."

"Did you call the number?" he asked.

"No, I was a little freaked out," Katie replied.

"Okay, so back up," the detective returned. "What exactly happened? What did he say to you?"

Katie breathed in before beginning. "He said that he…well, the people he works for need my help. There is this thing in Canada that is killing people and…"

"Whoa, what kind of thing?"

"I'm getting there!" Katie continued. "I think it's another superhuman. Anyway, Trevor said I could find out more information about it on this website. But when I went there, I found all of these awful pictures of..." she had to pause as the horrific images popped back into her mind. "Pictures of dead people who were killed by some contamination issue from the water of Lake Ontario."

"Yeah, I think I heard about that," Wreings replied. "They quarantined a bunch of places along the border, right?"

"That's what it said, but according to this site, the deaths are actually being caused by the Toronto Reaper..."

The detective shook his head. "That Reaper thing was a hoax," he began. "They debunked it months ago."

"Look, I don't know what's happening or if any of this is really true. But I do know that there are people out there that know who I am besides you and Nancy! I'd at least like to know who they are too. Is there anything else you can do?"

Wreings seemed to hesitate for a moment before doing that weird thing Katie noticed he did whenever he was thinking. "What did the guy look like?"

"I don't know, I really wasn't paying attention at the time," Katie returned. "He was white, maybe a little tanner than me. About my height, maybe? I don't know I just keep picturing this fratty-looking guy."

The detective sighed. "I guess that's a start..."

He pulled out his phone and typed the description in. "Alright," Wreings slid his phone back into his coat pocket. "I'll look into it. In the meantime, I'd try to keep a low profile. Maybe hold off on the hood for a day or two."

"But this guy didn't come at her," Katie shot back. "He came at me!"

"It's not for them…"

"What are you talking about?"

Detective Wreings glanced toward the lit up Meridian skyline. "I had a little run in with the FBI today. Apparently, they are making getting their hands on you a very high priority."

"Do you think that's who this is?" Katie asked anxiously.

"I don't know," Wreings replied. "But I doubt it. And all this cloak and dagger stuff sounds more like the NSA or CIA than the Bureau. Besides, it wouldn't make sense for them to get you to go to Canada if they were trying to catch you down here."

"What do you mean?"

"One of their guys, Agent Roberts, he made it seem like they wanted you here tomorrow. They're moving Oswalt. He's apparently going to come out of it."

"What does that have to do with me?"

"Roberts asked me if I could put it in your ear to show up at the pick-up point," continued Detective Wreings. "The other two Majority members were killed in custody. They probably figure they can scare whoever off if you're around."

"What did you say?"

"What do you think I said?" the detective began. "Same thing I've been saying to every reporter, talk show host, and whoever the hell else has asked if I know The Flying Girl."

"What about tomorrow?"

"Don't show up tomorrow," Wreings quickly added. "The Bureau isn't going to be traveling lightly and there's going to be some of us out there too."

Katie thought for a moment on the detective's advice, unsure how to respond. There were a few moments of mutual silence before Kate finally asked the question she'd had ever since the detective mentioned the name...

"Oswalt," she said timidly. Katie saw the opening in the stairwell wall the man's body made. "Is...responsive?"

Wreings flip-flopped his hand. "Maybe. The FBI seems to think so," replied the detective, pausing for a moment before letting out a sigh. "Look, I don't think I ever told you but, you did the right thing back at the hotel. You did what any good cop would have done."

Katie laughed sarcastically, "Because any good cop would have thrown a man through a wall and straight into a coma."

"If they could," he returned. "I've known plenty of badges who have had to make that same tough call. And when the decision is to hurt the bad guy to save a civilian, it's the one that ten out of ten cops would make."

"I'm not a cop," Katie returned in frustration. "I'm *'an unchecked power, doling out punishments at a whim with total disregard for who gets caught in the crossfire.'* Or haven't you heard?"

"Who said that?" he asked.

"Shay Donavon," Katie replied in disgust.

Detective Wreings shook his head. "You've got to block that kind of stuff out."

Katie sighed. "I'm trying, it just seems like it's everywhere lately."

"You're an easy target, just like us," Wreings returned. "With all the stuff that's gone on around here for the past few years, the department couldn't have a bigger target on our backs. The homeless disappearances, corruption from city officials, the dozens of excessive force complaints we get a year…sometimes it sounds like we're *not* the good guys."

"Well at least you have a medal to show for it," Katie replied. "Everyone still thinks I killed the one on the roof."

"That's the story the other guy gave them. According to his account, you intervened before she could shoot him," Wreings replied. "And until I can find out the identity of the other guy on the roof…"

"Ugggggggh!" Katie howled in frustration. "He's lying!"

"Look, for what it's worth, I believe you, but it wasn't my investigation," Wreings returned. "And you can't exactly come forward as a witness, not with the Bureau and whoever else out there looking for you."

"Couldn't you say something?" Katie questioned.

But the detective shook his head. "Enough people already think I'm buddy-buddy with you as it is. It's the same reason why I couldn't tell anyone that the bomb from the hotel wasn't real. Then they'd know that we talk."

"Why do you think he's lying?" Katie asked wearily.

"I'd guess he's hiding something," Detective Wreings began. "The Majority took him to that roof for a reason and it's either embarrassing or unsavory, like half the wealthy business owners in this country. With all the rumors that went around about his dad and Klymacks, I'd bet there's more than a few skeletons in those closets."

"He was creepy," Katie jumped in.

"Yeah, there was definitely something about him that rubbed me the wrong way," he added.

Katie opened her mouth to speak but felt her phone vibrating her hip. She quickly pulled it out to see that her sister had messaged her. "Okay...?"

"What's the matter?" asked the detective.

"Nothing, it's just..." Katie paused and reread the message. "Reagan. My sister. She just sent me a...it's nothing, but I need to be getting back."

"Yeah, I need to get going too," he said. "And look...the job doesn't always seem worth it, but you're doing good work out there, and helped us put away a few bad guys too. Just cut out all the other noise, alright?"

She took a deep breath as she pulled away above the city but hovered for a moment to consider the detective's advice. Then she tightened her hood and sped up into sky.

Chapter 10

Evening Plans

"I told you getting those amateurs involved was going to make a mess for us," began Mr. Tilte.

Kline formed an annoyed expression as if the mercenary could actually see him through the phone. "Your 'I told you so' isn't necessary. We are not in a crisis, just a heightened state of vigilance. The plan hasn't changed."

"Hasn't changed?" Tilte replied. "Everything's changed, mate! They're moving Oswalt in the morning to another one of those Federal facilities. Do you know how hard it was to get into one of those?"

"We will not be waiting that long," Kline returned as he opened the email from his assistant on his laptop. "You're going to have to go to work tonight."

"What are you going on about?"

Kline's eyes scrolled down the screen. "Tomorrow's transport of equipment and prototypes from Klymacks' R&D. There's a device on one of the trucks that could prove very useful."

"What's it do?" Tilte asked.

"Let's just say it could render any opposition hopeless," Kline returned.

"What time's it going to be here?" asked Tilte.

"In the morning..." began Kline before he trailed off. Up until now the only real threats he'd encountered on the board were miniscule ones, pawns that could be easily dealt with in one or two moves. But the game had escalated and if he didn't get his next move right then he would find himself cornered.

The FBI had been more than happy to let the locals hold onto Oswalt during his prolonged slumber. Their sudden action meant they either believed that the terrorist was due to wake up or the deaths of Nelson and Quinton had them questioning their security.

If the latter, it meant that Tilte's hand in the deaths of one or both of the other two captives had been discovered. That would mean that they needed to act quickly, as the mercenary's task would only increase in risk and difficulty, and there wasn't any more time to waste on The Majority. The real concern would be if Oswalt was showing signs of life. The mere possibility infuriated Kline.

With so many pieces in flux, Kline thought over his next move carefully. After a few seconds, he knew that his prior strategy was no longer applicable. Sacrifices needed to be made much sooner than he would have preferred. But then, that was the nature of the game.

"...Unfortunately, we can't wait that long," Kline continued, turning his gaze out the window as the town car began to move again. "There is a truck stop about three hours north of the city. Based on the itinerary I had JB outline for them, they should be there to break anytime between ten o'clock and midnight. Once they're asleep, you should have no problem breaking into..."

"Hold on now," began Tilte amusedly. "You want me to break into your trucks, and steal one of your gadgets, and then use it to kill Oswalt? You've lost it, mate!"

Kline almost snapped back at the mercenary's chide but held it in as he knew the raised barrier separating him from his driver could only block out so much sound. Instead, he reminded himself of what Krouse had told him. "Trust me, my sanity is far from being the question. Now, I am going to send you the coordinates, make of the trucks, and identification code for the shipping container the device is in. Make the break in look professional, but intentional."

There was a brief moment of silence on the other line before Tilte grumbled something unintelligible. He exhaled and replied, "Right. What about tomorrow at the hospital? Wasn't planning to get in through a parking garage."

"Leave that to me," Kline replied. He looked ahead to see the marquee of the restaurant coming up on his right. "Notify me once you've acquired what we need."

He ended the call and tapped the power button on his laptop three times.

"Smart Lock Initiated. Shut Down Commencing."

Kline made sure the screen had cleared before closing the computer and sliding it back into his bag. As the car slowed, the big man took a deep breath and closed his eyes.

"Every decision is crucial at this stage, Mr. Kline," the familiar voice called to him.

When he opened his eyes he saw himself as a young boy again, the white knight in his hand, a focused Gregor across from him. The old man's eyes were pointed downward, but not at any one particular piece.

"And not just yours," continued Gregor. "But mine as well. You have to decide my next move for me."

"But how would I do that?" he asked naively.

"Make a move that leaves me no other option. A sacrifice, perhaps," Gregor returned.

The sudden stop of movement pulled Kline back out of the memory. He sighed as he opened his door. "Yes, I think you're right."

The driver pulled the door the rest of the way open and smiled as he greeted him.

"Thank you," Kline returned with a courteous smile of his own. He picked up his bag as he stepped out and checked his watch. "And ten minutes early as well. You're very good at this, Antonio."

"Thank you, Mr. Kline," replied the driver. "Would you like for me to wait out front?"

"Nonsense," the big man replied. "It's already past seven and I can't imagine you've eaten dinner yet. Have a seat at the bar and order what you'd like, except for alcohol of course. I'll cover it."

"Sir, I..."

"You can," Kline halted his reply. "You've got me to my reservation early and I appreciate punctuality."

~

"I don't know if a bar is a good idea," Wreings said as Donnelly greeted him with open arms and a beer.

"I never said it would be," his partner replied, a sly grin on his face. "But it beats just sitting around doing paperwork, right?"

Detective Wreings shrugged. "I guess we'll see."

He glanced around at the black and white photos that adorned the walls of The Pen, most of which featured heroic stories of local cops. It would have been generous to say that he had frequented the establishment a handful of times. In fact, Wreings could only recall stepping inside just once during his eleven years on the force. But he had heard enough around the station to know about the cop-friendly bar. It was loud, especially on Thursday nights when it had cops from all of the dozen precincts in the city.

"Did the whole station turn up here tonight?" Wreings asked.

Donnelly raised his beer to his lips, speaking through the lid before cocking his head back to take another sip. "The guy's ancient, V."

"Fifty-three isn't that old, Don," Wreings countered, letting his partner finish the swig before continuing. "But yeah, I guess when you've been a cop for thirty years you might end up knowing some people."

Donnelly held up his empty bottle, aiming the bottom of it at Wreings. "Want me to get you one?"

"Nah, I'm good for now," Wreings replied. "Maybe later."

"Right," Donnelly scoffed before heading toward the crowded bar. As his partner signaled for the bartender, Wreings tried to decide whether he was actually going to stay or not. He turned back toward the entrance only to see the surprised face of Officer Annabel Hopkins there to greet him.

"Sir?" she said with a smile. "I didn't expect to see you here."

Wreings offered a slight smile back, though he knew his chances of getting away dwindled the longer he stayed. "I didn't either. Donnelly only reminded me about it before he left."

"Him I expected to see," Hopkins laughed grew as she awkwardly patted the knot of his tie. "But look at you, I think this is the first time I've seen you wearing one of these."

"Yeah," Wreings said, eager to avoid going into that particular conversation. He quickly looked over the young officer, who looked as though she were still wearing the bottom half of her uniform. She had her brown leather jacket draped over her shoulders, with a deep blue tanktop underneath. "You going in tonight?"

"No, I just got off," Hopkins replied. "I can't actually stay too long. I'm supposed to report in with the FBI in the morning."

That caught the detective's ear. "You're on the Oswalt detail?"

Hopkins nodded. "We've got a briefing and security check at six in the morning. You'd think we were transporting Hannibal Lector or something. Have you seen Detective Hudson?"

Wreings turned to survey what he could in the bar. He spotted a number of older-looking men huddled around a table in the back. Detective Tejeda was laughing with one of them. "I'd say he's straight back that way," he pointed.

"Thank you, sir," Hopkins replied before attempting to squeeze through the bodies toward the back of the bar.

"Hey V," Donnelly, who had rolled up the sleeves of his dress shirt, waved for him to come over. A stool had just opened up next to him at the bar. Detective Wreings sighed. He just couldn't get away. He stood by his partner for a few seconds before Donnelly nodded toward the seat.

"You going to grab some Kevlar or what?" asked Donnelly.

The question confused Wreings until he took a closer look at the seats. What he originally thought were leather cushions on the bar stools weren't leather at all. "These are vests?"

Donnelly took a huge swig from a new bottle of beer and nodded. "Better covering your ass than your chest," he replied afterward. "Come on, V. You're standing around like you'll be snitching to Internal Affairs in the morning."

Wreings shook his head at his partner's barb and finally sat down at the bar next to him. Donnelly smiled and slapped Wreings on the back before signaling the bartender back over.

"Hey Blue," he held up his bottle to the thin, clean-shaven man at the other end of the counter. "Can I get one for my buddy, Mr. Phoenix over here?"

"I told you I'm good, Don," Wreings returned. But his partner waved away his protest.

"Just one, V," he pleaded. "For me. This is probably going to be the last time I'll get to do this."

Before Wreings could say more, Blue had already popped the bottle cap into the trash and placed the beer in front of him.

"Detective Wear-ings?" Blue asked politely.

"*Ver-ings,*" returned the detective.

"It's German," Donnelly added. "The 'W' is like a 'V', and the whole mess sounds like one syllable..."

"I think he's got it, Don," Wreings cut in.

Blue laughed at Detective Donnelly before turning back to Wreings. "So what was she like?"

"Who..." Wreings stopped himself as he caught on to who the now wide-eyed bartender was referring to. "Oh, she's um, she's not like what they say on TV."

"So she's really good people?"

Detective Wreings pictured the blonde cradling Dr. Cattrell in the stairwell. He nodded. "Yeah, she's good people."

Blue grinned as if Wreings had restored the young bartender's faith in a lifelong hero. "That's cool, man. Hey, order what you want. It's on the house." Donnelly threw his arms up, but Blue just laughed. "You still got to pay, Mick."

Wreings couldn't help but smile as his partner grunted but wondered about Donnelly's earlier statement. "What did you mean about this being the last time you'd be out like this?"

Donnelly shook his head and then took another sip of his beer. "It's nothing, just some stuff with Nadine."

"Oh," Wreings said. "Did you need to...?"

"Nope," Donnelly quickly replied.

Wreings took the hint. But as the detective took the first sip of his beer, he noticed a strange subdued look on Donnelly.

"Eh, I don't know," his partner suddenly said. "Me and Nadine, we just...eh, you know what...nevermind. It's nothing, V."

"Good evening, Detectives!"

Wreings almost choked on his next sip as LJ's voice surprised him from behind.

"LJ," he coughed out as he looked up at the radiant medical examiner. Her hair was pulled up into a bun revealing the shimmery earrings that looked like miniature dreamcatchers. They dangled just above the thin straps of her flowery blouse.

Donnelly took another sip from his beer and stood up from the stool. "Hey LJ, have a seat," he said.

"Oh, no that's okay..." she began before Donnelly held up his hand.

"No, I insist. I was supposed to play Sergeant Olivera in pool before this guy showed up," Donnelly said, giving Wreings another pat on the shoulder. "You need a drink?"

"I'm not sure," LJ started with an awkward smile.

Donnelly grinned and slowly began backing away from them. "Well, right here is where you want to be sitting. The Pen is covering his tab and seeing as how it's you, I'm sure V won't mind getting you something, or a few somethings."

The medical examiner slid onto the seat next to Wreings as Donnelly walked into the crowd.

"Is Detective Donnelly okay? He seems a bit melancholy," she said.

"Yeah," Wreings nodded, suddenly curious as to what it was his partner was trying to say. "I don't know what's going with him."

"How are you?"

As Wreings turned to LJ, his eyes made contact with hers. "Me? Yeah, I'm fine. Can I get you anything?"

"What is that that you have?" she pointed to his drink.

Wreings glanced over the teal label. "Hashbarger, not a bad taste if you like beer."

"Strong German name," LJ joked. "I think I'd like to try it."

"Sure thing," Wreings replied as he tried to get the attention of the now hustling Blue behind the bar.

"So everything is okay?" LJ continued. "When you didn't meet me downstairs, I stopped by your desk. Detective Donnelly mentioned that you weren't coming in until the afternoon."

"Yeah, I..." The detective paused as Blue finally caught his signal, giving Wreings a reprieve from answering LJ's question. The bartender raised his head and prepped another bottle of beer, this time placing it in front of LJ. The entire transaction had been brief, too brief for Wreings to think of anything else to say but the truth. "I had to meet Cass."

LJ's smile wavered. It was sudden and very slight, but Wreings could sense the shift in mood. Cass' name hadn't come up often in their conversations, almost as if she didn't exist in their world.

"I'm sorry I didn't get your messages or say something earlier," Wreings continued.

LJ's eyes turned away from the detective for the first time since Donnelly left. "Oh, there's no need to apologize, Detective. I suppose I had just gotten used to the routine and hadn't known you to take any time off unless it was enforced." She took a surprisingly long swig from her Hashbarger before a smile finally returned to her face. "I'm just glad nothing was wrong. How is she?"

Wreings couldn't tell if there was something else behind the question but he simply nodded. "She's doing okay. And look, I really am sorry..."

"It's okay," LJ started quickly. The look on her face showed she was eager to change the subject. "Did you have a chance to go through the report I left for you this morning?"

"I could only glance at it. We had a lot of paperwork to catch up on," Wreings replied. "I had actually planned to go over it tonight, whenever I was done with all of this."

"Well I left my commentary for you in places I saw discrepancies," LJ returned. "I hope you don't mind."

Wreings smiled. "I think I'd be worse off without your commentary, LJ. I've hit a wall with this stuff so far."

"Well, in that case you're very welcome, Detective Wreings," LJ said. She took a few more sips from her beer before leaning in close to the detective. She began with a quick glance to either side. "Perhaps if you told me more about this case you're working on, I could be of further assistance?"

LJ wore an excited look that Wreings had begun to see more and more often, especially when he talked to her about any open case. In the mornings when they met outside the morgue, she'd often ask the detective to go over some of the things from his and Donnelly's cases. It appeared now that she was addicted.

"I don't know, LJ..." he began before the gleam in her eyes distracted him. Her smile widened as he laughed and shook his head. "I don't know about this one. My gut is saying there's more to this, but everything about this death, everything official anyway, chalks it up to a suicide..."

"How interesting," LJ's face did little to hide her intrigue. She downed the rest of the beer and placed the empty bottle on the counter in one swift motion.

Wreings stared at her with surprise, drawing a look of concern from the medical examiner.

"Did I drink it too fast?" she asked.

"No, no, no," Wreings replied assuredly. "I just didn't take you for much of a beer drinker."

"I didn't know I was," LJ said as she turned the ingredient label to her face. "That was my first one. But I think I like the sweetness of it. Do all beers taste like this?"

Wreings found himself once again in wonderment of LJ. No matter how often they spoke or even the subject matter, she always projected an innocence and lighthearted view of the world. He needed that, especially on days like today. "I mean I'm not an expert," he began. "But I've had my fair share. What do you normally drink?"

"I don't normally. The drink I had at the Gala was maybe the third one that I've ever had. Truthfully, I'm afraid I'm a bit of a novice when it comes to alcohol consumption," LJ replied. "I had a cocktail at my cousin's graduation and a glass of wine at my college roommate's wedding shower. But...you shouldn't ask the name of either."

"Yeah, I figured that'd be more your speed," Wreings replied.

"And what speed is that, Detective?" LJ said, narrowing her eyes.

"You know...cocktails, wine. Beer isn't really a..." Wreings couldn't tell if she were actually offended or not. "I meant that those are the kinds of drinks that are served at...*fancier* places than...I just didn't take you for someone who'd go to...a bar, I guess."

"Should I leave?"

"What? No! LJ that's not what I'm saying," Wreings was suddenly flustered. "I just...you're always dressed so nice when I see you...outside of work I mean...not that you don't..."

LJ's laughter stopped his attempted recovery and Wreings realized he had been the victim of a rare joke by the examiner.

"I apologize," she began. "I didn't mean to let you go on. I don't think I've ever seen you so befuddled."

"You're good," Wreings smiled. "You're real good, LJ."

She lightly gripped Wreings' knee before turning toward Blue. "Do I just signal him if I would like another drink?"

Wreings finished his beer and waved her arm down, replacing it with his own. "Here, I'll get you another."

"Why thank you Detective," LJ replied. "I shall enjoy another Hashbarger while you tell me of this 'dangerous case' you're working on."

The detective shook his head in amusement. She wasn't going to give up and lately, she had been a hard one to say no to.

The two shared another laugh as Blue brought over another pair of beers. Though he knew the happiness could only be temporary, Wreings was suddenly glad he'd come to The Pen. There didn't appear to be any lingering hostility held by LJ and the moment of light she provided him was enough to drown out the darkness of his past.

Chapter 11

Invisible Scars

The sky overhead was devoid of any stars, only the cloud covered moon provided assurance that she wasn't just looking into endless darkness. Katie glanced at the girls laughing in the living room, each held one of the assortment of alcoholic drinks that now lined the kitchen counters. Their faces were all bright, their expressions carefree. It looked so easy for them to relax and let loose. That must have been nice. The conversation with Detective Wreings had done little to ease the weight of the day.

"Are you okay, Love?"

Katie hadn't even noticed Nancy step out onto the balcony.

"Sure," Katie replied.

Nancy's steps were meticulous, likely trying to avoid falling over. That made sense seeing as how she and the three girls from the shop were already tipsy by the time Katie had returned an hour ago. Her friend had looked at her apologetically when she arrived as if to say 'I couldn't help it'. But it hadn't been Nancy's lack of sobriety that initially bothered Katie.

Nancy had waited until just before Katie was about to leave to reveal that she and Jimmy were no more. The exact words may have been 'I'm done with that asshole!' It was meant to cheer Katie up, but it surprisingly had a different effect. While she was very happy her friend had finally liberated herself from him, the blonde kept thinking about her own unfortunate relationship with the bracelet.

"Katie?"

The blonde quickly shook away her thoughts and turned her focus back to Nancy. "Sorry, what did you say?"

"Now that we finally have a minute, how was your chat this evening?" she asked.

"All kinds of fantastic," Katie offered a hollow smile. "Found out the FBI is looking for me too."

"Oh dear," Nancy sighed. Her roommate was now carefully leaning on the railing. Katie turned to join her.

"He said he can look further into the number from the card and stuff," Katie continued. "But I have a bad feeling about everything still."

"Well at least he's looking into it. That's good right?"

Katie nodded. "Yeah I guess. He says I'm doing good work out there and not to get my head down, or whatever."

"He's a charmer, that one." The liquor on her breath smelt strong and her accent was much thicker.

And she's drunk... "He sure is."

"Not as charming as Mr. Jerome of course..." Nancy continued, passing what Katie interpreted to be a playful smile toward her.

"Oh my God, Nancy!" Katie returned. "That's so gross."

"What? I think he's a very attractive man," her roommate continued. She wobbled as she stepped away from the railing and quickly gripped it to steady herself.

"Yeah, he's cute I guess. But he's old," replied the blonde. "He's like older than Reagan."

The retort seemed to sober Nancy slightly and she turned her gaze off into the distance. Katie thought it strange at first, before dismissing it as normal drunken behavior. Still, she attempted to lighten her tone as she continued talking to Nancy.

"Besides, I'm not the *newly* eligible bachelorette in Meridian," she replied with a nudge.

Nancy's smile briefly returned. "I think it'd do me some good to stay that way. At least for now."

"Yeah?" Katie replied.

"I hate feeling like…" Nancy continued. "Like I've just been so stupid for so long. Jimmy and me lasted much longer than I should have allowed."

The blonde could see her friend was intent on talking, so she just nodded along every so often until the Brit turned back toward her.

"Are you happy?" Nancy's question seemed to pop out of nowhere.

Katie was unsure if the conversation was still on relationships or just in general. "With Troy? Yeah, most times at least."

"What do you mean?" Nancy asked.

You should have just kept it to a 'yes' or a 'no'…

Katie sighed and turned to face her friend. "It's been hard, pretending to be…well, pretending to be someone I'm not sure I am."

"Nonsense," Nancy replied. "Powers or not, you're still *you* on the inside."

"I don't want to talk about this," Katie wearily returned.

"I think you should tell him, Katie," Nancy said.

"Nancy, I can't," Katie returned. "I can't. I just can't. It is hard, but there are moments, small moments sometimes that make it all seem...I don't know?"

Her friend didn't respond, instead she looked on encouragingly as Katie continued.

"I mean, like the other night we went to that drive-in where you can see two movies for really cheap. We brought lawn chairs and ate really bad food. The movies were really cheesy but it was so much fun. And we were far enough outside of downtown that there were actually stars out. Nancy, I cried. I cried in the middle of *Night at the Museum 2*. Not because I missed my parents or because I was afraid. I cried because it was perfect!"

"Oh, Katie," Nancy said as she clumsily hugged the blonde.

"And I know those moments won't happen as often when school starts back, but I don't want to risk them going away completely," Katie said. "If Troy ever looked at me the way Reagan does, or even worse, treated me the way she does..."

"I think he'd understand," Nancy replied.

No one understands. You don't even understand, Nance...

"I'm not so sure."

"Katie," Nancy quickly glanced at the girls inside. They were all deep in conversation, so her roommate pressed on. "I don't think people are as afraid of you as you think they are. Didn't Reagan ask to see you tomorrow to talk?"

"Yeah, but who knows what that's about," Katie said. "And even you're afraid of me."

Her friend looked offended. "I am not!"

"A little bit at least," the blonde turned her eyes away from her friend. "Nevermind."

"No Katie," Nancy continued. "Why would you say that?"

"Because..." Katie paused as she peered at the flushed cheeks of her friend. Nancy had been drinking for too long to have any important argument. It was better to just let it go.

"Because why?" it appeared that Nancy had other ideas.

The blonde stepped away from her and over to the other side of the balcony. "Before you left, I saw something in your purse. I wasn't snooping or anything like that...You had asked me to order in but your wallet wasn't on the counter...Anyway, I didn't know what it was at first, but then I realized...you bought a Taser."

Nancy's jaw hung open but Katie couldn't tell whether she was ashamed or just confused.

I can't believe I just... "I didn't say anything," Katie continued. "I didn't know what to say. Electricity is what killed Bishop, it's hurt me before and...I don't know. I couldn't believe it at first, but then I couldn't blame you either..."

"It's not for you," Nancy softly replied. She cleared her throat and placed her glass on the railing. Her eyes had already started to water. "It was *never* for you."

"What?"

"It doesn't matter," Nancy said with an uncomfortable looking smile. She wiped under her eyes and turned away. "The point is Katie, I feel safer around you than I do anyone else."

"Nancy?" the blonde stepped toward her friend who was now avoiding her gaze. "Do you have it just to have it? Or did you actually get it for..."

"I told you it doesn't matter," Nancy returned. "Not anymore, anyway."

Jimmy?! The blonde read between the lines very quickly. "Oh my God! Why didn't you tell me? Did he hurt you? Are..."

"Shhhh!" Nancy quickly put a finger over her lips and glanced at her friends in the living room. They hadn't seemed to notice over the music playing.

"No Nancy, this is not okay!" Katie continued with an adamant whisper. "Why didn't you tell me? I would totally kick his ass if he hurt you!"

"I didn't say anything for the same reason you didn't tell me about the other bracelet," Nancy returned, placing her hand on the blonde's shoulder.

"Damn it, Nance! That's not fair!"

"I didn't really know how and I was scared," her friend continued. "I've been scared for a long time. The trip to Europe, it did a lot for me. You've done a lot for me too, Katie. I talked to my mum about things that I've never talked to anyone about before, even you."

Katie didn't know how to respond. So she stood dumbfounded as her friend picked up her glass and walked back toward the door.

"I'm sorry that I didn't, that I *haven't* told you everything," Nancy said softly. "But I'd like to, if you're still willing to listen?" She inhaled deeply and then returned her eyes to Katie's.

"Yeah, I'd like that," Katie replied.

"I'm okay, really," Nancy said once more.

Katie breathed as her anger gave way to concern for her friend.

How did I not know? Why didn't she tell me?

"Nancy, I had no idea," Katie said.

"That's because I didn't want you to," Nancy returned. "Like I said, Jimmy and me should have ended years ago. It wasn't your fault Katie. It certainly wasn't mine, but it just took me some time and a trip back home for me to see that."

Nancy placed her hand on the handle, but instead of opening it, she glanced back with a reassuring smile. "I've seen monsters, Love. You're not a thing like any of them."

There were so many things Katie was thinking and wanted to say but she couldn't narrow any of it down. Part of her thought she must have been an awful friend not to have seen even the slightest fear behind her friend's smile.

"Thanks, I...I..."

"Oh, someone is calling you."

Nancy pointed to the bright light shining through Katie's jeans.

"Your lover or 'Commissioner Gordon'?" Nancy joked.

"It's Troy," Katie replied. "But I'll call him back…"

"You'll do no such thing," her friend returned, attempting to make a straight face. "The poor boy's been working all day."

She walked back over and leaned in to kiss Katie on the cheek before heading back inside.

Katie couldn't help but smile. "I love you."

"Well, hello to you too," Troy's voice replied through the speaker. The blonde quickly realized that she had already pressed the 'accept call' button.

"No, not you," Katie said. "I mean, not that I…um…I was talking to Nancy."

"Hmmmm…"

"Stop it," a flustered Katie returned. She continued watching Nancy who had rejoined her friends. Within seconds they were all dancing to the music. Nancy's face appeared full of joy, as if what she had just revealed to Katie had been just a blip on her radar.

How does she do that?

"Katie?"

"Oh, sorry," the blonde returned her attention to the phone. "What were you saying?"

"I asked if you wanted me to pick you up. I can get off a little early," Troy replied. "Your text didn't make it sound like you were too thrilled to be there."

"No...well, yes and no," Katie began. "I mean everyone else is having fun and the girls from Nancy's shop are really nice. It's just been kind of a rough day."

"Well then say no more," Troy replied. "I'll be walking to my car as soon as I take care of a few things over here. Soon, my fair lady, your chariot will arrive."

Katie laughed. "Maybe we can finish the rest of those movies tonight?"

"That's what I was thinking," Troy returned. "Still up for a detour for shakes at Somethin' Special first? I'm starving."

"Mmmhmmm, I could go for a shake..." Katie said. "Detour approved!"

~

Notification of the detour only added to her satisfaction. She reread it one more time to make sure she had translated the coded message correctly.

Flight plans changed. I need you to come to Meridian. Further instructions when you land. Terminal 7. 12:45.

Though it appeared that her employer seemed as equally erratic as he was meticulous, the assassin relished the opportunity to extend her stay in America.

She glanced at the terminal sign above her head and quickly spun around. Domestic flights were to her right. Now that she did not have to worry about the international procedures, the assassin had plenty of time to do something that she actually preferred: people watching.

The airport was crawling with fascinating fashions, even more so than in the streets.

There was a different feeling now than when she had first landed at the John F. Kennedy airport. The "attempt on the President's life" had predictably raised the tension all around and she had already passed a number of police and federal agents walking through the halls.

She analyzed her reflection along the glass overlooking the runways. While she still felt exposed without her eyepatch, the assassin knew that it would have stuck out. Instead, the tinted sunglasses concealed the scars over her missing eye. Letting her dark hair down underneath the black baseball hat had been a clever way to hide from the security cameras. The black sweater and long jeans may not have been in season, but they were a far cry from being conspicuous.

And so far, her cloak of normality had seemed to work. It'd been relatively easy for her to blend in. That seemed to be the beauty and the danger of New York. One could never identify the predator from the pack.

Hopefully, this Meridian was more of the same.

Chapter 12

Convenient Coincidences

"So what if…" LJ started gently. She paused and glanced cautiously down the empty sidewalk, giggling after realizing that they were still just a few feet away from the bar.

"I think you've had one too many, LJ," Wreings laughed.

The examiner wagged her finger. "I don't think so, Detective. If you take the alcoholic content of the six drinks I had and divide that number into my body weight," LJ grinned and poked her finger into Wreings' shoulder. "Which I will not disclose at this time. Then you'll see that I've maintained a level of sobriety just under the threshold of inebriation."

"Yeah," Wreings shook his head. "What you said right there is something kids used to trick others so they'd plow through drinks in college."

"What do you mean?"

"Some big guys get wasted from a couple of beers while this tiny, tiny girl can put away shot after shot," Wreings returned. "You're drunk when you're drunk and there's not some math equation that can tell you when. Especially if you're not used to drinking."

LJ looked mortified. "No, there has to be a science to it!"

Wreings shook his head. "Tejeda is like what, a buck forty? I promise you, she's probably just now getting a buzz and I saw her putting down shots left and right."

"How interesting…"

"Where did you get that from?" asked the detective.

"Jess and I discussed it yesterday," she replied. "He heard it from...ohhhhhh."

Detective Wreings looked on curiously for a moment before he realized what LJ had probably just realized. "Don said something to him, didn't he?"

LJ nodded before they both burst into laughter.

"Alright," the detective continued. "Never *ever* listen to a thing my partner tells you."

"Why would he make up something like that?" LJ asked.

"He probably thought it'd be hilarious to get Jess drunk," Wreings replied. "He's kind of twisted like that."

LJ shook her head. "Detective Donnelly is very clever. Using science of all things."

"Yeah, sometimes he's an evil genius," Wreings replied.

"So am I drunk?" the examiner questioned. "I am drunk. So I am drunk."

Wreings tried to respectfully contain himself. "It's uh, it's looking that way."

"Are you drunk?"

"I had a buzz for a while," replied the detective. "But it's wearing off."

LJ gave him a playfully sad look before unexpectedly wrapping her arm around his. "Would it be too much to ask then for you to escort me home? I'm just a few blocks away."

The detective cleared his throat as he immediately felt her warmth drift into his body. "Yeah, sure. I didn't know you lived close to here."

"Right on the edge of Midtown on Bartleby Street, by the Monicelli's Pizzeria."

"Yeah I think I know where that is," said Wreings.

"Wonderful, we can keep talking about your case then," LJ said as they began down the sidewalk. "Oh, yes, I was saying something about that before we started talking to Detective Hudson...Oh, I'm going to miss him.

"Yeah," Wreings returned. "It's a shame how it happened. But he gets to keep his pension, he'll get benefits in a year..."

"But he was such an honest man," LJ cut in. "What's happening is ageism."

"It's the economy," Wreings sighed. "But you're right. Hudson was a hell of a cop. He could keep Tejeda toned down too."

LJ suddenly spun in front of him. "Coincidences!" she exclaimed as she began stumbling backwards.

"What?" Wreings managed to catch hold of the examiner's arms before she backpedaled off the sidewalk.

"We were talking about everything seeming like a coincidence," continued LJ. "But you were saying that you don't believe in coincidences."

Wreings realized the examiner had jumped back into their initial conversation. He nodded in reply. "In a way, especially after what they found out about Franks."

"That he was dirty!"

"Right," the detective returned. "Franks was supposedly doing business with Gol and most of the gambling stuff at Thumpers came through the shipping yards. The unofficial word right now is that Franks was the one transporting the weapons through the docks..."

"So he was part of the arms trade?" LJ cut in.

"And now he's dead," Wreings nodded. "Just like everyone else involved. And Bishop only killed half of them. Every other known associate of Bullet or Franks...all dead, one by one."

"That is suspicious," the examiner said slowly. "So do you think all of the deaths have been perpetrated by someone else?"

"Honestly, I don't know how that'd be possible," Wreings said. "They may already have the guy who killed Cameron Kelley, and this Burton easily could've killed himself. But I don't know. I just can't shake this feeling that I'm missing something. Something that can connect one to another, you know?"

LJ nodded against his arm. "But some of it could be coincidence, couldn't it?"

The detective sighed and peered off down the dimly lit sidewalk. "When bad stuff happens, it's not by chance. There has to be a reason..." he muttered.

"What did you say?" LJ glanced up at him.

Wreings took another breath in. The buzz had completely gone now. "It's not a hard sell to believe that what happens to one crook is independent of another. But corruption...corruption is like the roots under a tree. You and me, we don't see them. The roots I mean. What we see is the pine or crape myrtle or whatever the thing is supposed to be, right? So under the surface, all this other stuff is going on but you don't see it unless you try to dig it up. Thing is, the longer that tree's been planted, the harder it is to dig up, you know?"

The detective paused as he noticed the hazel eyes of LJ looking up at him. "What?"

She shook her head. "Nothing, that's just a very thought-provoking analogy. It's very apt to compare crime and corruption to an intricate root system."

"Yeah, thanks," Wreings replied.

"But Lenny Franks was killed by The Majority," LJ began. "That has to be a coincidence."

Wreings recalled the conversation he had just had with The Flying Girl. "You know I wouldn't be surprised if we didn't have all the facts on that."

"What do you mean?" LJ asked.

The detective wanted to tell her what he knew, but thought better of it. "Just a feeling."

LJ nestled further into his side. "You seem very in tune with your feelings this evening, Detective."

Wreings was uncertain on how to proceed. LJ had always been cautious at showing the feelings she had for him. But after a few hours at The Pen she had turned into a very affectionate drunk.

She began to yawn before quickly covering her mouth. "Excuse me!" she apologized. "Though I hope you're incorrect about there being someone or various someones plotting something so nefarious, I believe you should be rewarded in your quest for the truth."

"You make it sound like I'm some kind of knight or something," Wreings laughed.

"But you are," LJ replied, pointing to the brick building a few yards in front of them. "Here we are!"

They stopped at the base of the stairs and Wreings immediately got a feeling of déjà vu. Decorative bronze railings rode the sides all the way up to a single glass door. Above it the unmistakable rounded awning stretched the length of the steps. It was like looking at the entrance to the country club Cass' parents were members of.

"You live at the Bastien Abbey?" surprise layered Wreings' words. They were some of the most high-end condos in Midtown.

"I do," the examiner answered excitedly. "And you really are."

"Really are what?" returned the detective.

He steadied her as she began walking up the stairs. Once she had reached the top, she smiled and patted his chest.

"Like a knight," she replied. "You're brave, chivalrous — as this walk can attest. You're fearless, truthful, and...and honorable..." She almost fell as she swiped her keycard on the pad by the door. But Wreings was there to catch her once again. He picked up the card she dropped and opened the door.

"Maybe I'll walk you up too," Wreings said as he followed her inside.

"That would be an excellent idea, Detective," LJ nodded. She grabbed his hand and led him to the set of elevators across the wide hallway. There was a light-haired woman standing behind the concierge desk. "Hello Miranda," called out LJ.

The woman waved and seemed to eye Wreings up. "Nice night to be out, huh, Dr. Jimenez?"

"Such a beautiful night!" LJ replied before Wreings could utter a word. "So many wonderful and new experiences. I think I am drunk!"

Miranda laughed cautiously. "Looks like it. And this gentlemen with you...?"

"Detective Wreings. I just wanted to make sure she got home safely," he flashed his badge. Though it felt a little silly, he appreciated the thoroughness of the Abbey's concierge.

"Tobias Wreings, the Knight of Meridian!" LJ suddenly exclaimed.

Miranda raised an eyebrow and shook her head, but she pressed the 'up' button and walked back to the desk. "I'll set the elevator for the twelfth floor."

"Thank you!" LJ waved as the doors slid open. "Have a good night!"

"You too, doctor," Miranda returned.

The doors closed and the elevator began to move. LJ leaned her head into the chest of Wreings. The next thing he knew, her arms had wrapped around his waist. Still unsure of whether to return the embrace, all he could think to do was smile awkwardly as she looked up at him.

"In shining armor…" she said after another, longer yawn.

"I don't even have body armor," the detective replied, finally bringing an arm across the back of LJ's shoulders.

"Oh, I found it very interesting that The Pen recycled vest for use on their seats," the examiner returned. "And they were actually comfortable!"

Wreings nodded. "Yeah, they were. Funny, they are really uncomfortable to wear."

"And not as safe," LJ continued. "There are so many varieties of ammunition that can penetrate the threading. They really provide a false sense of security."

"Yeah, Don's not a fan either."

DING!

They stepped off the elevator and the examiner took a few seconds to gain her bearings. She glanced to her left and then to the right. Finally, she nodded and pointed to the fourth door down the hallway.

Once they were at the door, Wreings took the keycard and slid it into the slot over the knob. When he opened the door, LJ gave him a saddened glance.

"I suppose this is where we must part company," she said.

Wreings could feel his heart racing. "LJ, I'm sorry I…"

But before he could speak anymore, the examiner's finger had pressed against his mouth.

Everything about her body language signaled that she could lean in for a kiss at any moment, and part of him really wished she would. But he knew that wouldn't be right, not *today*, maybe not any day.

As she took a step toward him, Wreings took her hand into his and lowered it to their sides. "I need to get back home, LJ."

She looked confused for a moment but managed to muster a smile. "Yes, of course..." the examiner turned toward her apartment but stopped short of stepping through the doorway. "Please be safe on your trek back, Detective."

"Will do," Wreings returned. "Good night, LJ."

"Good night."

~

"I trust you've had a good morning?" Kline began after glancing at the time on his watch.

"What's in the box?" the gruff voice replied through the phone.

"A frequency manipulator," Kline stated. The big man stood up from his bed and wandered toward the curtains. Pulling them aside, he gazed out at the Meridian dawn. "It can alter the audible and inaudible soundwaves around you by..."

"Let's keep the science out of it," Tilte cut him off. "How is this going to make things easier for me, especially considering all the shit you already had me do?"

Kline didn't appreciate being interrupted by the mercenary yet again, but there was no real time to adequately correct his behavior. "Open the box."

"Looks like an earpiece or something. What's it do?"

"Have you ever had an ear infection?" Kline began. "Or lost hearing in one ear? Or had any number of the hearing ailments one can experience? The ear plays an integral part to maintaining our balance, coordination, and perception. The device you hold creates an additional frequency that interferes with that, altering the existing frequencies that..."

"So it'll make 'em dizzy then?" Tilte again brushed away Kline's explanation.

The big man held in his anger, though he could feel his patience wearing thin. "It does much more than that, Mr. Tilte. Once activated, anyone who isn't also receiving the normalizing frequency won't be able to stand. For them, things that are close are no longer within reach. Up becomes down and within seconds they'll be experiencing an extreme form of vertigo. But, if dizzy is all your simple mind requires to understand it then by all means..."

"So what about the other thing you said? The normalizing frequency?" Tilte continued. "Your toys don't come with many instructions."

"The wearer receives that through the earpiece to cancel out the disruption," Kline returned. "There's a switch on the back that allows you to select the level of disruption. The farther right you turn it, the greater the vertigo experienced by anyone within a short radius. The small button next to that activates the normalizing frequency. You'll want that on before activating the disrupter."

"Could have used this months ago," Tilte grumbled.

"Well you have it now," Kline replied as his phone began vibrating. He glanced at his phone screen to see it was his assistant, JB.

"Seems like a pretty weapon-like thing for people who supposedly don't make weapons to have lying around," the mercenary quipped.

"It was meant to replace the hearing aid," Kline replied. "However, an error was made with the amplifier and it quickly became obvious the prototype couldn't function as intended. The project was put on hold after the merger. The important thing is that it will work for you. Now you have what you need so I trust I'll be hearing about Oswalt's demise on the news?"

"Right," returned Tilte. "When should I call you?"

"I'll call you."

With that, Kline ended the call and switched over to the waiting JB.

"Good morning, JB," he greeted. "I was just about to get ready to head back to the new facility."

"Good morning to you as well, Mr. Kline. I am sorry for calling so early but the shipment has encountered...some issues earlier this morning," his assistant began.

Kline grinned at his reflection in the balcony window. "What kind of issues?"

Chapter 13

The Divide

Reagan's hand hovered over the knob for a few seconds. She'd been nervous since the first knock, but there were so many feelings swirling around inside that the young doctor wasn't sure whether any of this was a good idea.

KNOCK! KNOCK!

"Rae?"

It was too late now. Reagan took a deep breath before finally opening the door. Katie's fist was up as if she had been ready to knock again.

"Hi," Reagan greeted.

"Hey Rae," Katie replied as she swiftly walked into the apartment. If standing in the narrow hallways had shaken her, she did a decent job of hiding it. "I got your text. Is everything okay?"

"Yes, I'm fine," Reagan answered as she closed the door. She delicately turned to face her sister, wincing a little from the soreness in her body. "How are you?"

Katie seemed confused. "Um, I'm okay too, I guess. Your text was kind of…"

"Yeah, I guess I probably should have said something more in that text," replied the young doctor. "I was just out of it last night and…well, thank you for coming."

"Of course," Katie replied.

"Did you go out last night?"

The way she blurted her question was awkward but Katie didn't seemed too weirded out. Her sister put her bag down on the counter and glanced back at Reagan before wandering into the living room. "No. Well kind of, I guess. I hung out with Troy."

Reagan smiled. "Oh, that sounds nice."

~

She sounds so weird...

Katie watched as her sister stepped gingerly, cane in tow, into the living room. She looked to be favoring one side. "Are you still feeling okay?"

Reagan nodded as she sat in the gray chair across from the couch. "I'm just sore from my session last night."

"Oh, how was your interview?" the blonde asked.

"It was okay."

"Okay as in a 'you're doing great, see you this Fall' kind-of-thing?" Katie pressed.

"More like a 'we'll get back to you' kind-of-thing," Reagan replied.

"So there's a chance?"

Reagan tilted her head to one side and then the other. "We'll see."

Katie wanted desperately to get a more positive reaction from Reagan, but she quickly became distracted when her eyes fell upon a brown coat hanging on the back of a chair. It looked too big to belong to Reagan. "Did you have company last night?"

Reagan followed Katie's eyes toward the counter and the chair. "Oh, Peter left that here. He picked me up from physical therapy last night."

"Oh," Katie began intrigued. "Did Aunt Lane have a date?"

Reagan rolled her eyes and both sisters finally shared a laugh.

"At first I thought it was really gross," Katie continued.

Reagan nodded. "Oh it is definitely very gross. But..."

"She seems happier," Katie finished, her eyes turning back toward the coat. Katie slowly sunk into the couch across from her sister and recalled the unbridled concern of Dr. Sava when he didn't know where Reagan was at the Wiesenburg. "Peter seems like a really great guy. Are you two...?"

"It's not like that." Reagan's quick reply was probably meant to sound assured, but Katie thought it sounded more like she was also trying to convince herself of that. "We're friends, just friends. Anyway, I'm sorry I didn't respond to any of your texts. My mind's been really all over the place lately."

Lately? "Yeah, I get that..." Katie said. "But you had me worried."

"I told you, I'm sorry," Reagan returned, offering the slightest of smiles. "Things have been difficult these last few months. I kind of just needed some space and time to think I guess."

The way her sister was carrying on wasn't like the direct and sure Reagan Katie knew. Though that Reagan tended to be an overbearing know-it-all, she at least said what she was thinking. Katie didn't care for whoever this was sitting in front of her. "Do you mean space from me?"

Reagan opened her mouth as though she were going to speak but instead let it hang open while she tapped the cane on her lap. Katie took the silence as a 'yes'.

"Reagan?" she said cautiously.

"This isn't easy, Katie."

"Well, considering I don't know what *it* is…" the blonde shot back. Reagan breathed in as if she were trying to gain more air to speak or something.

Oh my God, JUST SAY IT!

"You know, don't you?" The words slipped out of Katie's mouth before her fears could pull them back in. The few seconds of silence that immediately followed left an uncomfortable tingling in her spine.

Reagan finally looked at her. The expression on her face showed a strange calmness, almost as if she were relieved that the question had been asked.

"Yeah, I do," she nodded. "I didn't believe it at first. I thought it had to be some kind of dream or something. I remember that man standing over me and then he was gone, and you were there. In the jacket Dad gave you. And every time I see her on the TV…it's you."

"Yeah," Katie said. "Is that why you've been so weird lately?"

"I didn't know what to say," Reagan replied. "I still don't. Part of me still doesn't want to believe that night even happened. But...Katie, how long have you been like this?"

There was a distinct feeling of uncomfortableness swimming around inside of Katie. "It seems like it's been forever now, but since last November when um, Bishop did all those things."

~

Reagan shuddered at that name. Theodore Bishop was and always would be the last name she ever wanted to hear. Unfortunately he seemed to be a person whose notoriety she couldn't escape.

"I can't remember how I got them," her sister continued. "I don't even know what all I can and can't do, but I was trying to figure that part out. I guess I still am..."

"You don't know how you got them?" Reagan asked.

Katie shook her head. "I don't remember anything from that night, just flashes, but nothing concrete. The only thing I really know is that I was at the Hot Abacas concert before the powers, and somehow wound up in my bedroom the next morning, breaking everything."

"And you just decided to fly into burning buildings?" Reagan said. "And start smashing terrorists through walls?"

Katie's already dim smile waned even more. "Well I really didn't ever decide to. It just kind of happened."

Reagan realized that she was getting upset. She had at least hoped Katie had known something about what she was doing but it was apparent that her sister was even *more* irresponsible than she had feared. "Right, well don't you think you should be trying to figure out how to get rid of them so you can...?"

"So I can what?" pressed her sister.

"So you can be normal again?"

Katie scoffed. "Well in a perfect world, I could switch being a freak on and off."

"I didn't mean it like that, Katie," Reagan continued. "I just meant that you don't have to do what you're doing. There are plenty of police out there that can save people."

"Trust me, I hear that every single time I turn on the news," Katie said. "But there are people out there that even they can't deal with. Like those guys who shot up the hotel, or someone like Bishop that..."

The name again triggered horrific images for Reagan. The sound of the hospital explosion drowned out her sister's words and the young doctor felt sweat forming across her forehead. All Reagan could see in her head was the image of Dr. Lutz's face being engulfed in a fiery blaze. She pressed her eyelids closed to get the fire to stop burning her brain. "Can we just not talk about him?!"

"Are you okay?" Katie asked.

Reagan glanced into her sister's eyes. "It's nothing."

Katie finally shifted away on the couch. "That didn't sound like nothing?" her sister continued. "Reagan, why are you being like this? What is your problem with me?"

"Katie..."

"I'm serious!" Katie cut her off. "You're always telling me I'm not doing enough or whatever. Now that I actually am kind of doing something, you're calling me a freak!"

"I'm not saying you're a freak, Katie!" Reagan defended.

"Then what are you saying?" her sister returned. "What the hell are you...?"

"You're too dangerous!" Reagan blurted out the words before her mind even registered what she said. But as soon as it hit her ears she realized how it sounded. She buried her face in her hands and then slowly brought her fingers together around the back of her neck. "I...I didn't mean it like that. Katie..."

"You're afraid of me too?"

Reagan shook her head. "No, no, no, you need to listen..."

"I don't want to listen to you," Katie said as sadness creeped into her voice.

"Katie please, you weren't there when it happened," Reagan pleaded. "One minute, everything was okay. Then it was like he just lost control."

~

Reagan's words tipped an anger inside of Katie that she hadn't felt in quite some time. Her sister basically just compared her to Theodore Bishop, someone whose name apparently bothered her when mentioned. The look her sister wore now reminded Katie of the moment Detective Wreings first saw her in the stairway of the Wiesenburg. His gun was drawn then. But at least that made sense.

Katie looked away. "I'm not like him Reagan."

"I'm not saying that you are, but..." her sister began. "What if something happens?"

"Like if I get angry?" Katie said as she quickly rose from the couch, causing Reagan to flinch. That only increased Katie's anger. "Oh come on, Reagan! Do you really think I would ever hurt you?"

"Of course I don't. It's just been really, really hard for me Katie after everything that happened, everything that's still going on. Katie, I saw you throw a man through a wall! He's in a coma. And then there's the guy this morning and the woman on the roof..."

"That wasn't me," Katie snapped back. "Everyone thinks it was me but I didn't do that! I didn't kill anyone! I could never do that, Reagan."

"What?"

Katie groaned in frustration. "Look, everything that you're seeing on the news right now is bullshit. Complete bullshit! And HELLO! I threw that creep through the wall because he was about to *kill* you Reagan!"

"I know, I just..." Reagan began. "I don't know why I brought up that stuff up. When you mentioned his...that name, I just...my mind has been all over the place. Honestly, I'm more worried about you."

~

Reagan knew there was another fight coming, but at this point it was unavoidable. "Do you know one of the first things I remember the nurses talking about that night after my surgery?" she continued. "Apparently, some woman had literally flown into a burning building after the man who blew up MMC," Reagan continued. "I was still on medicine so I thought I'd just imagined it. But then when I found out it was real...all of it was real, I remember thinking how crazy it all sounded."

"Yeah well, try being me," Katie replied sarcastically.

"It's too much like Dad," Reagan replied.

Katie shot an uncertain look toward her. "What's he have to do with this?"

"He has everything to do with this," the young doctor replied. "He didn't think, he just...There are consequences in real life and people can get hurt if you make the wrong decision. You could get hurt."

Katie rolled her eyes. "Do you think I don't know that? I'm reminded about it every single time I save someone. And thank you so much for not only comparing me to someone you're scared shitless of, but also to someone who you've told me you hate. I'm so glad I rushed over here for that..."

"Katie..."

"No Reagan," Katie halted her sister's words but couldn't seem to block the tears anymore. "It's kind of funny I guess. I didn't know there were still things in this world that could really hurt me."

With that her sister marched to the counter, picked up her bag, and walked out the door.

The fight was over and Reagan was left as she was after so many conversations with Katie. Alone and regretful.

~

Katie wiped her face as she fought to keep from being overrun by sadness. When she reached the stairwell, she wished she could've slammed the door behind her. But in her current mood she likely would've brought the whole wall down with it.

There was a moment during their argument that Katie felt as though she had done something wrong to her sister. But all she had done over the past year was be there for her! What was even more infuriating was that Katie wanted to know where her powers came from too, probably a whole lot more than her sister did. And while they didn't have to agree on what kind of man their father was, it really bothered Katie that all Reagan ever saw in him was the negatives.

It appeared to be as she originally feared. Reagan wasn't going to be in her corner for anything. She would probably never see Katie as anything more than that scared little girl who used to cower in her bedroom, unable to have a functional life in the so called "real world".

After a few moments, she decided that she needed to go back and continue hashing it out with her sister. But when she turned back toward the door another thought suddenly entered her mind.

Katie reached inside her bag and pulled out the white card she had gotten the day before. She looked over the indented numbers and one-by-one typed them into the keypad of her phone. Her thumb hovered over the green button for almost a minute before she finally pressed it in. The next few moments felt like ages to Katie. But when somebody finally did answer, it was a familiar voice.

"I was beginning to think you wouldn't call," greeted Trevor.

"You said you could help me," Katie began through a sniffle. "Help me figure out my powers and where they came from?"

"I did. But are you willing to help us?"

Katie could feel her sister's hesitation as though Reagan was shaking her head no right in front of her. That was probably why the decision was so easy to make. "What do you need me to do?"

Chapter 14

Nothing to Report

"What do you mean?" Wreings asked.

"What do you think I mean?" Donnelly returned. "You two share a few drinks...she's clearly wasted...you walk her home...come on V, I already feel like a creep for asking."

The detective sighed as he tightened his belt. "Doesn't sound like it's stopping you."

"That's cause I got to ask!" his partner said enthusiastically.

"I told you Don, I overslept."

"Overslept my ass," Donnelly shot down. "Is she there right now or something?"

Wreings turned on speaker and left his phone on the bed while he walked to the bathroom. "She's not here, Don," he said. The detective splashed on his face and then ran his wet fingers through his hair before heading back to his partner.

"You're breaking up or something," Donnelly returned. "What'd you say?"

"I said, she's not here," Wreings restated. "Seriously, I just overslept, nothing wild about that."

There was a disappointed sigh on the other end before Donnelly grumbled something.

"I can barely understand you," the detective said.

"I was saying I can barely believe you went to sleep at all," his partner replied. "Just stop and pick up something on the way in. Burger or anything, I'm starving."

"Alright, I'll get you something," Wreings returned. "What do you...Hey, hold on. I think I got another call coming in. Hello?"

"Christ, V," Donnelly laughed. "What are you, sixty? Learn how to use your phone..."

"Shut up, Don," Wreings said before finally getting the call to switch. "Hey, is everything okay?"

"Well hello to you too," the rosy voice of Cass greeted.

Wreings cleared his throat. "Sorry, it's just I wasn't expecting... you know..."

"I know," his ex-wife replied with a slight laugh. "I thought you'd be too busy at work again to answer your phone."

"Oh, I'm not in yet."

"Are you okay?" Cass' tone carried genuine worry. Wreings quickly moved to ease it.

"Yeah, yeah," he began assuredly. "I just overslept."

"Overslept or didn't sleep?" she returned.

Wreings didn't want to go down that road. "Look Cass, I got Don on the other line..."

"I'm sorry," she cut back. "I shouldn't have said that. It's just...I wanted to know how everything went last night."

"Everything...?"

"Being alone," Cass replied. "Yesterday would have been the first time that...I just wanted to see how you were, if you had any, um...trouble last night."

Wreings glanced at the clock on the nightstand and exhaled deeply. The concern in Cass had only grown since their conversation started. He rubbed his forehead before sinking onto the edge of the bed.

He closed his eyes and released a breath. "Stop worrying about me, Cass."

"It's not that easy, Tobias," she replied gently. "I'm sorry if I'm being ridiculous. But last night wasn't the easiest for me either and I had it on my heart to call you."

"Yeah, I get it," Wreings nodded. "And thanks, for...I appreciate it. But look, I still got..."

"It's okay, you get back to it," Cass began. "I don't want to be the one keeping another good guy off the streets."

"Thanks," replied the detective. "And if you need to...Do you need to talk, or something?"

There was silence for a few long moments.

"You still there?" said Wreings.

"Yes, sorry," his ex-wife replied, her voice broken somewhat. "I'd like to talk."

That's what Wreings thought she'd say. "Sure, well I'll give you a call after work. Maybe around ten-thirty, eleven?"

"I'll be up either way," she replied. "Be safe, Tobias."

"You too."

Wreings ended the call but saw that his partner had already hung up as well. He dialed him back but it eventually went to Donnelly's voicemail.

KNOCK! KNOCK!

"Housekeeping?" a soft voice called out from the hall.

"Hold on." The detective finished fastening the second to last button on his collar and opened the door. A small, gray-haired woman stood next to a cart on the other side, a startled expression on her face.

"I apologize, Officer," she began slowly. "I didn't realize you'd still be home. It's a Thursday, isn't it?"

"Yes, Ms. Debra," replied Wreings, picking up his gun and coat from the chair. "It's Thursday. I'll be out of your way here in a second."

She squeezed his arm and offered a polite smile. "That's quite alright. I haven't seen you in a while. How are you these days?"

"I can't complain, ma'am," the detective replied. "And yourself?"

"I've been wonderful," Ms. Debra returned. "Tell that charming brother of yours hello for me."

Wreings smiled slightly as he knew she had a hard time keeping things straight. The absent-minded housekeeper meant Donnelly as she'd never met his actual brother. But the detective never had the heart to correct her. "Sure thing. You have a good day, okay?"

"You too, Officer."

Wreings waved and left the door cracked for the housekeeper. He began down the hall, securing his gun in his holster. As he turned toward the staircase he heard his phone loudly ringing.

"Now you want to ring," he grumbled before bringing the phone to his ear. "Good thing you called back. I was thinking of getting you a veggie burger."

"Skip the lunch." The serious voice of Donnelly immediately concerned him. Wreings shot through the door and began quickly moving down the stairs

"What happened?"

"You need to meet me at Meridian Metro," his partner returned. "It's bad, V."

~

"How bad is it?" Kline asked the foreman as he walked back toward the building. The stocky man flipped through the pages on his clipboard and offered a nonchalant shake of his head.

"Just went through our third check. As far as I can tell, nothing is missing from either of those two shipments." The foreman pointed at the two freight trucks to their left. The driver of each was lowering the door to their cargo.

Kline nodded and pointed to the final truck, whose driver was approaching them. "But the third?"

"We've got one item that is still unaccounted for," replied the foreman. "An item AA4421. The itinerary says it was a hearing enhancement device. It was locked inside the carrier of the cab."

"But it's missing now..." Kline began. "Could it have been misplaced inside?"

The foreman glanced at the driver before turning back to Kline. His expression was one of certainty. "Well sir, the lock on the case was snapped and a few of the other boxes inside looked like they had been cut open, like someone was looking for something..."

"So it was stolen?" Kline said coldly. He turned his eyes toward the driver who immediately removed his hat.

"I'm sorry, Mr. Kline," he began. "The boys and I locked everything up last night. Entered the security code y'all gave us and everything. Someone must have bypassed that and cut through that lock system without setting off any alarms. Heck, I didn't know 'til I heard that case door swinging in the back. Pulled over, saw someone had gotten in, and called Mr. JB right away. I'm really sorry, sir. I..."

"There was nothing more you could have done," Kline started assuredly. Tilte's infiltration skills occasionally still impressed him. "It appears this thief knew exactly what he was doing. Mr. Grieves, what item did you say was missing?"

"AA4421," replied the foreman, peeking back at the clipboard before handing it over to Kline. "It's listed under the Legacy Inventory section."

"Thank you," Kline returned. "Your men can start unloading the shipments of the other two trucks."

Mr. Grieves nodded and signaled to the group of men waiting by the side of the building. "Let's move those two over to the lift gate entrance and start unloading," he shouted.

"As for the breached cargo..." Kline trailed off as he contemplated his next words. "I suppose we can't touch it until the police arrive."

"No one has called the police sir," Grieves returned.

Kline handed him the clipboard and turned back toward the building. "Well, now would be the time to do so, Mr. Grieves."

"Yes, sir!"

Denard Kline listened as the men behind him scurried off. The engines of the trucks started humming and soon he was filled with a nervous exuberance.

The board was wide open now and the subsequent moves were more crucial than they had ever been. Above all else, he needed to be calm. The game had been accelerated and there was little doubt that now that the end was in sight...

The vibration of his cellphone pulled his mind back. He grinned slightly as he saw who was calling him.

"Kathleen," he began casually. "How was your flight?"

"It was uneventful," replied Kathleen Lymacks, her voice oozing with the mask of pleasantness Kline had come to expect. "Which I understand is the opposite of how your morning has been?"

The veiled attack was likewise expected. "It is being dealt with. None of our current projects were tampered with."

"You sound so sure..."

"Most of the delivery's contents are either the various machines needed to execute our processes or are useless without the procedural files that are encrypted in our database," Kline returned. "So I am sure that our valued company secrets are not in danger. The only thing stolen was a device that never made it past testing during the dwindling life of Kline Technologies, before the merger."

"Was it valuable to us?" Lymacks replied. She must have been walking through the terminals at the airport as there were voices around her.

"To Klymacks? It would hardly be worth anything without a considerable investment of resources to continue development. But there are other devices that have already capitalized on the intended functionality on the market, so it'd hardly be worth it based on where we are now. Still, its value ultimately lies in the eye of the beholder and I don't think whoever stole it wanted the device to modify it," said Kline as he approached the door to the building. "There were a number of interested parties who wanted to pay considerably for it as is."

"Please, Denard. Your screw ups hardly warrant the gloating," sighed Lymacks. "And I find it hard to believe that one of our rivals would risk this unless it was worth it to them."

Kline walked along the corridor. In the open space in front of him, the workers had already begun transferring the delivery into the facility. "I would agree with you if the device worked as it was intended."

"What do you mean?" questioned Lymacks.

"All you need to know is that the stolen device does have a more militaristic use," returned the big man.

"All I need to know?" for a moment, the oft-perky voice on the other end sprang with an irritated edge. "You know Denard, I was really looking forward to this visit. I think you and I have a number of things that we need to clear up."

"Of course," Kline replied. "However, I do believe a more private setting for both of us would be better."

"Yes, I suppose it would," resigned Lymacks. "I'll be meeting with Mayor Edison and the heads of some of Meridian's companies over the next two days."

"So you won't be visiting the revitalized facility?"

"Anxious to show off your new play pen?" she began. "No Denard, as it turns out, I won't be available this afternoon."

Kline glanced at his watch. It was now a quarter until noon and he was anxious for updates. "Well, I'm afraid that I still have my own important things here to attend to. So perhaps we'll continue our talk whenever you find time?"

"Denard," Lymacks returned to her typical tone. "I know you think you've earned some sort of autonomy during this relocation, but do keep me informed of this situation."

"Of course," Kline replied before ending the call. The last words of Lymacks were clearly meant as a warning for him. Since he'd facilitated his departments move back to Meridian he had garnered a large amount of praise from their shareholders and partners. It was the sort of praise that had once been given to a much younger Kathleen Lymacks.

It was obvious now that she took the threat Kline posed seriously, which was more an annoyance than a problem. Still, he needed to offer a semblance of assurance whenever they managed to have their discussion as there wasn't time to engage in a power struggle with Lymacks.

There was still much more important matters to attend to.

Chapter 15

Introductions

Katie held on tightly to the strap of her bag, humming the "Colossal" tune as she nervously looked at her surroundings. The gray buildings around her seemed to dull the daylight overhead. They were spaced out, separated by a combination of gravel and cement pathways that looked like intersecting roads from up above. The sign at the front said this place was a water waste treatment facility, but it looked more like a ghost town.

This place is so creepy.

Part of her knew she had made a questionable decision, but she had no intention of going. She had flown all the way to Canada for answers and wasn't leaving without them.

The faint sound of a motor caught her attention and within a few seconds a black jeep appeared from behind a small set of fenced in silos. She took a couple of steps back as the vehicle started to slow down a few yards away from her.

The blonde could feel herself fidgeting anxiously. The windshield was tinted so she couldn't see whoever was inside looking at her. A few more seconds passed by before she finally saw the driver's side door open.

A white-haired man in a blue jumpsuit stepped out, holding something with thick handles and what looked like a short, plastic antenna. It reminded her of one of those remote controllers for a little kid's car. He kept a straight face under a pair of aviators.

He slowly stepped away from the car and toward Katie. As he came closer, the device beeped rapidly.

"Who are you?" Katie asked, taking another step back.

But the man ignored her question and silently kept walking her way.

Okay, asshole...

"Hey!"

This time Katie yelled and took a giant step forward. "Who are you?" The man finally stopped and made a move for the side of his waist. That's when Katie noticed the handle of what was likely a gun sticking out.

"Where's Trevor?" the blonde finally demanded.

The man glanced back toward the jeep before tapping his ear. "Yeah, it's her," he said dryly.

"*Bein entendu!*" a static-laden voice replied. The words sounded vaguely familiar but the blonde couldn't quite place them.

Katie heard footsteps marching toward them. Confused, she bounced her eyes around until she saw three similarly dressed men emerge from behind different buildings.

Two of the men were aiming their guns at her as they approached. A shorter, unarmed man waved for them to stay in place. Katie immediately recognized him.

"That was fast," greeted a straight-faced Trevor. He signaled for the other men to lower their weapons. They turned their guns away but hardly looked relaxed. "Over fifteen hundred kilometers in, what, just under two hours? That's impressive, Ms. Cattrell."

She didn't know how long it had taken to get back home, pack, and write Nancy a note explaining her decision to leave but the man standing before her shouldn't have either.

"You're such a great host," Katie replied, glancing at the men around her holding guns.

Trevor followed her eyes but then waved his hands like it was no big deal. He peeked at whatever the white-haired man was showing him on the controller. "You never know who it is you're inviting to dinner."

"Well, you look like you're prepared. So can you finally tell me who you are?"

Trevor turned toward his entourage and pointed toward the jeep. "Vous allez." The men nodded and walked toward the jeep.

French, that's it! Katie thought she recognized the language as what she'd often heard in the background of the phone calls she had with Nancy that summer.

"Are you French?" she shot out.

"You have a good ear," replied Trevor.

"And a good memory, you haven't answered any of my questions yet," she returned. "Who are you? Why are we meeting here?"

Without the hat and bookbag, she could tell now that Trevor was much older than she had first thought. He had faint traces of gray in his hair and the sides of his eyes carried wrinkles. He folded his arms, seemingly considering whether to finally answer Katie's questions or continue to avoid them. "Let me walk you to our command center. It's just this way."

He had already began walking when she decided to begrudgingly follow.

"You know I thought you'd be a bit more willing to actually tell me *something* since I came," she said. "I don't know how you expect me to trust you."

"As I said, trust wasn't a prerequisite for your part in this mission," Trevor replied casually.

"Really? I'm so glad to hear that," Katie returned sarcastically.

Trevor finally laughed, though Katie suspected it was just as sarcastic as her response. "You could walk into any church and find hundreds of people worshipping a man not one of them has empirical evidence of having ever existed, yet each of them would refute the notion that he isn't real."

Cynical much… "So…"

"Have a little faith," Trevor returned.

"Oh, I get it," Katie began. "So you can't tell me who you are…Then just tell me about my powers?"

Trevor kept his eyes straight ahead. "In due time Ms. Cattrell. First, there is the matter of the Reaper we need to discuss."

"Yeah," Katie quickly jumped back. "That website you had me look at was really messed up. It had all these crazy things and…I don't know, it was really hard to believe."

"That was the idea," Trevor replied. "The domain used to belong to a Canadian blogger. Before our involvement here, there were a string of unexplained deaths along the border. When those deaths began happening around Toronto, there was briefly a rumor of a hooded figure nearby. Naturally, stories of a Toronto Reaper sprouted up. It took some effort to change the narrative to an ailment rather than a person."

"How?" Katie asked.

"We have resources," he returned before pointing to a larger building behind another fenced in collection of silos. "Our outpost is inside."

Katie surveyed the rest of the area around it. "What is this place? The sign said it was a..."

"A waste water treatment facility," Trevor finished. "Lake Ontario is some kilometers east."

Katie noticed the same emblem was on Trevor's jumpsuit and the sign. "But you guys aren't really doing that here."

"No. While the 'contamination' is being investigated this facility's day-to-day workers have been displaced to other facilities by the Great Lakes while we operate out of this one," he replied.

"Jeez, who are you people?"

"Ms. Cattrell, I hope you have surmised by now that my identity and affiliation are neither pertinent to your involvement nor am I permitted to disclose them."

"So you're not the boss," Katie quipped, drawing what she believed was a scowl from Trevor.

Two can play this game!

They were only a few feet away from the building now and Katie saw the black jeep, along with three others parked along the side wall. There were two more men standing sentry by a door. Both were tall and clean shaven like the others. The one on the right reached for the handle and opened the door for them. Katie hesitated for a moment before following Trevor inside.

To her surprise, the building was much bigger on the inside. She was standing on an elevated platform with a long steel staircase leading down into a wide open space that was filled with people. Some of them wore lab coats, some were dressed like Trevor, and a few others wore what looked like regular clothes. There were also other men and women walking around dressed in padded military-esque clothing. Cords seemed to be covering the floor, leading to a hub of laptops, computer screens and one large monitor.

"This way," Trevor's voice called out from another set of stairs. The call immediately drew everyone's attention. The people sitting in chairs spun around while everyone else halted their conversations. All eyes were trained squarely on her.

As she moved toward Trevor the uneasiness that had somewhat lessened on their walk to the building had come back in full swing. She didn't like the staring and found herself questioning if they, like Trevor, also knew who she was.

"Does everyone here know who I am?" she manage to squeak out to Trevor.

But before he could answer, a stern female voice suddenly shouted out. "As you were!"

In an instant, the staring ceased. In fact, it looked like everyone was now avoiding looking at her. Katie quickly searched the room below for the woman who had made that call. She soon realized that it belonged to the one scaling the stairs beneath her. As she neared the top, Trevor straightened his stance.

"Who's that?" Katie asked.

"*She's* the boss," he whispered back.

The woman grabbed the railing and lifted herself up and over the final two steps in one motion. Her uniform was an all-black version of the military ones she'd seen worn around the facility. She had a short pixie cut, a young face, and hazel eyes like Trevor. The woman's dark complexion didn't hide a long scar that ran down the right side of her neck.

The woman gave Katie a quick glance up and down before letting out an impatient sigh. "Where's the rest of her?"

"Excuse me?" Katie shot back. The woman looked like she was a few inches *shorter* than her.

"Have you told her yet?" the woman ignored Katie and turned to Trevor. The blonde thought her accent sounded a lot like Nancy's, but lacked her friend's joy.

He shook his head. "We hadn't made it that far."

"Finish briefing her up here." The woman passed a skeptical glance at Katie before descending back down the steps.

"Alright then," Trevor began. "We…"

"Whoa, whoa," Katie cut in. "What the hell was all that about?"

"Like all of us, the Commander is eager to complete this mission," Trevor replied. "We've been tracking him for weeks now."

Katie tried to ease her temper as she continued to stare at the so-called Commander as she mixed back in with the others downstairs. "Him…The Toronto Reaper?"

Trevor nodded. "The first victims were found in New York at the end of last year actually. But a journalist from this region coined the name before we were able to intercept and halt that spread of information. He hasn't even made it as far as Toronto yet. We have men stationed along Etibicoke Creek to keep him from making it any farther."

"So he's trapped somewhere in the woods?" Katie asked.

"We believe he's somewhere in the park adjacent to our current location," replied Trevor. "It's been evacuated, as has the neighboring town."

"Well then I don't get it," started the blonde. "If you can do all this stuff you say you can, why do you need me?"

"We've attempted to capture the target on two previous occasions," returned Trevor. "Each attempt taught us something new, however those lessons unfortunately accompanied failures. Now we believe we have a way to subdue him permanently. The only problem is that none of us have the physical attributes to be successful in executing it."

"On that website, it said that the victims were…in bad shape," Katie said as she recalled the grotesque descriptions she had read. "So all of that is real?"

"Superficially, the descriptions you read are indeed true," Trevor began. "However, what is actually happening to the people he's come into contact with is actually much more extraordinary and unfortunately, much more horrifying." He paused a moment as if he meant to build on Katie's uncomfortableness. "You see, we initially thought that these people were being exposed to some sort of new chemical weapon because the composition of the bodies had changed so drastically. But then we discovered the truth."

"Which is...?"

"By touch," Trevor replied. "Contact with the skin of the target somehow allows for a unique transfer of certain bodily fluids and hormones as well as one's...energy, if you were. So for our solution to work, someone has to actually be able to get close to him."

Transfer of energy? The thought initially frightened her. That sounded a lot like what happened when she and Bishop had grabbed each other's bracelets under the Emerson building.

The more Trevor described the Reaper, the more afraid she was of finding out more about herself. "So any time someone touches him he basically sucks the life out of them, like a vampire?"

"If that helps with your understanding," Trevor replied. "Though I admit that your analogy is an apt one. And much like the mythical creature, he grows weak in between feedings. Though it's a rough estimate, we believe that it takes between eighteen and twenty-six hours for the power boon to subside..."

"The what?"

Trevor looked calmly at Katie. "While the energy transfer leaves the 'provider' dead, it appears the 'receiver' is temporarily given heightened strength, reflexes, and endurance."

"Oh, so not only does his touch kill you, but it also makes him superhuman," Katie quipped.

What have you gotten yourself into Katie?

"Relatively speaking. What would be considered super strength to me may not even register with you," Trevor said.

Katie didn't know what to say. In five minutes, the world that she knew was already crazy had just taken an even bigger plunge off the deep end. There had been part of her that couldn't imagine anything on that website actually being real. The Reaper sounded too much like one of the villains from the corny superhero movies Troy and everyone else was borderline obsessed with.

Her decision to come was made more in anger, but she now realized that Nancy may have been right. If she was going to learn more about herself, she was going to have to overcome a real-life monster to do so.

Chapter 16

Casualties

"We are still waiting on confirmation but early reports suggest that there are several police officers among the casualties..."

"...And while we don't know the motive behind this attack nor do we know how many victims there are, we have confirmed the presence of Federal agents at Meridian Metro. You may remember the hospital as the one that housed Majority member Clarence Oswalt..."

"...With reports that a number of people in the hospital were affected by what witnesses have described as an 'ear piercing'..."

~

It had been a little over nine months since Detective Wreings had found himself staring up at the roof of a pop up tent, a survivor of Theodore Bishop's destructive outburst at Meridian Medical Center. Now as the sounds of shuffling feet and quivering voices reverberated in the service tunnel, he couldn't shake the eerie feeling of déjà vu.

He stood over the body of Clarence Oswalt, outstretched and lifeless on the hospital gurney. His expressionless face looked exactly the same as when Wreings had seen him the month after the Phoenix Gala. The major difference though was that this image of Oswalt wasn't comatose but instead marred by the bullet hole that'd been planted between his eyes.

"Alright, he's all yours, I guess," said the detective, stepping aside to let his colleagues begin bagging the body.

The detective shook his head before turning his attention to the three occupied white sheets a few feet away. "Son-of-a-bitch," he muttered angrily. The death of the former terrorist was frustrating, but the bloodshed of two badges and a federal agent took things to a different level. Just a glance at the other faces in the tunnel told the same story. No one liked seeing cops killed on the job.

Especially ones they knew.

"Hey V," Donnelly waved him over from the side of an open ambulance. There were a couple of EMTs standing at either side of the door. They were hovering over someone. Wreings could tell it was a cop by the pants and shoes. He couldn't see the top half but the look on Donnelly's face didn't look encouraging.

He jogged toward his partner and nearly stopped in his tracks when he realized that the cop being attended to was Hopkins. She was lying flat on a gurney and he could see a lot of blood. Wreings continued on, slowly approaching the ambulance. It wasn't until he saw the young officer sit up that he felt some relief.

"How you doing Hopkins?" he began, looking her over. Her uniform top was off as the medical staff continued tending to the stab wound in her right shoulder.

She grimaced and offered a slight wave to the detective.

"I've been better Sir," she replied. Her eyes drifted away from the conversation. "But I'm alive. Luckily."

Wreings followed her gaze to the sheets covering the fallen.

"Officer Carey," Hopkins continued, a tear trickling down her left cheek. "Officer McTigue. They were good cops and great people."

"We're going to get the bastard who did this!" Donnelly said, slamming his hand so hard on the van that it startled one of the EMTs. He waved a silent apology and then looked over in the direction of Agent Roberts, who was in a heated conversation on the phone. "Goddamn Feds. We're just foot soldiers to them. Why the hell couldn't they move the slab themselves?"

"I don't like them anymore than you do but they aren't the ones who did this." Wreings said, trying to calm his partner. He turned back to Hopkins. "Look, I know you just…"

"It's okay Sir,'" she jumped in, nodding her head. "This is a crime scene. I'm a witness. You two are the acting detectives. Whatever y'all need to know, I'm ready to help."

Wreings followed the path of another falling tear down Hopkins' face. "If you need a few minutes…"

Hopkins shook her head, wiped the tears from her cheeks, and straightened her back. "No, I'm good now. They say this cut is only superficial, it barely even hurts."

"You're all done Officer," said one of the EMTs.

"Thank you, thank you both for patching me up. Would one of you mind passing me back my top?"

"There's a lot of blood on your uniform," one of them responded.

"Well, a blanket or something," Hopkins said. "I'm kind of feeling exposed here in just a sports bra."

They nodded and one quickly jumped in the back of the van to retrieve a large blue sheet. Officer Hopkins said a 'thank you' and turned her attention back to Wreings and Donnelly.

"So what happened here?" Wreings finally asked.

"When we got here, Agent Roberts put Officers Carey and McTigue down here while Officer Estes and I went with him upstairs to get Oswalt," Hopkins began with a surprising clarity to her voice. "Everything seemed routine upstairs. We took him back through the service elevator and came back down here, ready to load him up. "

"But McTigue and Carey had already been shot?" Donnelly cut in.

Hopkins nodded. "I immediately drew my firearm, but Agent Roberts told me to get back on the elevator with Oswalt. I think he told Officer Estes to cover him, but that's when it all went..."

"Went what?" Donnelly asked.

"There was this sound, like a ringing in my ears," Hopkins suddenly looked as though she were struggling to recall. "I remember getting dizzy and not being able to stand. I thought I could hear Roberts and Estes calling but I don't know. I definitely heard a gun go off next...I swear it's like I was falling the whole time."

Wreings looked quizzically at his partner. "Didn't Estes say something about a noise?"

Donnelly nodded. "Yeah. Pretty much the same thing."

"Do you remember seeing anybody, Hopkins?" Wreings questioned the seated officer.

She shook her head. "Not clearly. There was someone next to me. Male. I thought it was one of the other two at first. Then he said something. It sounded like he might have had an accent."

"What kind of accent?" Wreings asked.

"I don't know, British maybe…"

"What did he say?" asked Donnelly.

"I don't know," she replied. "Wait, just give me a second."

Wreings could tell she was frustrated. "Hey, Hopkins it's alright…"

"No," she insisted, closing her eyes. "*Time…*"

"What?" the detective returned.

"He said '*Time's up Oz,*'" Hopkins said triumphantly. "That's what he said."

Donnelly shrugged. "He's got a nickname for him? Like he knew him? Was this before he shot him or after?"

"Before."

"Byers?" questioned Wreings.

Wreings shook her head. "I don't know about Byers. Remember, the shooter sounded like he had an accent."

Hopkins closed her eyes again as she spoke. "Then the noise stopped."

"It just stopped?"

She nodded and turned toward Detective Wreings. "Yes sir. And the weird thing is, it's like he didn't seem to realize it. I was still a little cloudy but I saw him standing over the gurney so I kicked it at him."

Wreings couldn't help but grin, prompting a slight one in return from the young officer. "And you got his mask?"

"He fell on top of me and I reached for the first thing I could. But I couldn't make out his face. My eyes were still blurry, but I think I remember feeling a beard. We tussled for a minute before he threw me against the elevator door and stabbed me," Hopkins replied. "I must have knocked the gun down when I hit him because I thought I saw him reach for something on the ground. But Agent Roberts fired at him and scared him off."

"He missed?" Donnelly shook his head. "Clear shot with the asshole looking the other way and he missed?"

"I could barely see straight and I was right next to him," Hopkins' voice was full of frustration. "I should have had him."

"She's right, Detective Donnelly."

They all turned to see the stone-faced FBI agent approaching the ambulance.

"Whatever weapon this attacker was using," he continued. "It was clearly designed to debilitate us to the point of near uselessness."

Roberts walked past Wreings, giving him a look that was clearly meant to imply blame. "Whoever we are dealing with is very sophisticated."

"Any ideas as to who that is?" Wreings asked.

Roberts offered little more than a sneer before turning away from them. "No."

Donnelly glanced at Wreings and shook his head. "I thought you had two more agents around here somewhere, what happened to them?"

"One was watching the transport at the entrance to the tunnel. The other met the same unfortunate fate as your two officers," replied Agent Roberts.

Wreings nodded. "Where is the one now? We need to talk to him."

"He saw nothing," Roberts replied quickly.

"Nothing?" Donnelly repeated in disbelief. "He was standing at the entrance and didn't see anyone coming or going? I'm pretty sure this place only has one entrance and one exit. You sure your boy wasn't sleeping on the job?"

"I assure you, Detective Donnelly," Roberts began as he turned back to face them. "My *men* were alert and where they were supposed to be. I also doubt that the attacker came in through the proverbial 'front door'."

Donnelly was about to reply when his phone went off. "Give me a minute," he said as he stepped away from the ambulance.

Roberts glanced over Hopkins before turning his full attention to Wreings. "Detective, could I have a word?"

Wreings nodded and followed the agent to the only place that wasn't occupied by forensics, cops, or hospital staff.

"Yeah?" he asked.

"Could this have been avoided?" Roberts asked pointedly.

The detective couldn't believe the question. "You're not serious, are you?"

"Hey!" Donnelly called out, drawing both the detective and Roberts' attention. "Security's got a video. Looks like we got the bastard's face!"

~

"Is it possible that they didn't see your face?" Kline asked calmly. He locked the door to his office and walked back toward the glass.

Tilte had barely let him speak since he first answered the phone and his angry associate went quickly back to ranting.

"You didn't hear me?" he shouted. "There were bloody cameras everywhere! As soon as that bitch ripped off my mask, any one of them could have got me! Of course they saw my bloody face!"

"Then that would be an issue," Kline said casually.

"Of course it would!" Tilte said indignantly. "And why the hell do you sound like that? Southern Charm promise to give you a show?"

Kline's smile faded. Tilte's continual poking of his affinity for Meridian's Director of Community Affairs had long grown tiresome. "Why shouldn't I sound like this? Oswalt is *dead* after all, as is the rest of The Majority and Senator Gilbert. There are no longer any lingering strands that can be connected to me, Klymacks, or Garrison Kline…save you and Dr. Krouse, of course. All of the troublesome pawns have been disposed of…"

"Congratulations," Tilte said sarcastically. "Oh, and you're welcome. Now I need you to get me out of here!"

"Your mood certainly leaves something to be desired, Mr. Tilte," Kline returned. "We still control the game..."

"Will you stop with the bloody games?!" Tilte fired back. "Look, I'm going back to the hotel, getting my things, and getting out of this city."

"Times have changed over the last twenty-four hours, Mr. Tilte," Kline began. "Have you already forgotten our national emergency? The President has been shot, remember? Add in the FBI's current involvement with this issue and you're likely to find every feasible exit heavily guarded. Even you would likely find yourself in custody before dinner, and I can't have that."

"Well I'm not waiting around here," replied the increasingly impatient Tilte. "I've been living in this hotel for months. As soon as they put my face on the TV..."

"Yes, your current accommodations are no longer an option," Kline said thoughtfully. "There's Bullet's safe house, I suppose."

"On the Lower Westside? You've got to be joking, mate," the man laughed incredulously. "You think I'm going to blend in out there?"

Kline continued to watch the workers arrange the equipment from his perch above the main floor. Perhaps inspired by his current mood, but he imagined the foreman Mr. Grieves like a conductor arranging the symphony of forklifts and hand trucks. He hadn't planned for the mercenary's identity to be compromised during Oswalt's execution, but the turn of events worked even better for his plan.

"Your candor is tiring, Mr. Tilte," he returned.

"Sorry if I'm not as thrilled as you are, it's been a hell of a morning cleaning up another of your messes," Tilte replied.

"You seem to be fixating your blame on *my* so-called messes," Kline quickly returned. "But it was you who thought it was wise to shoot two police officers and a federal agent."

"I wasn't taking any chances with five of them. And it was a good thing too!" Tilte snapped back. "The bloody earpiece of yours stopped working. That's the only reason that other cop got the jump on me!"

"I assure you Mr. Tilte," Kline replied wearily. "If it indeed stopped working, it's likely the result of user error."

"User-error my ass," Tilte responded.

"This bickering is going to get us nowhere," Kline refocused the conversation. It was Tilte's turn to be guided to his spot on the board. "I think I may know of a way for you to get out of Meridian."

"I'm listening."

"There should be a boat coming in. It's carrying some of the larger machinery for the new factory."

"You mean at Franks' shipyard?" Tilte asked. "It had better be a late shipment. The docks are at least two hours away from here."

"It comes in tomorrow evening. You could take a bus to Savannah from the All Points MUTS station. I can secure your passage to the ports from there but it is up to you to pirate yourself aboard the ship. It would be returning to New York and then heading to one of our subsidiaries off the coast of Spain."

"I don't mind that. But I'm not real interested in waiting a whole day," Tilte returned. "Besides, aren't the FBI still investigating Franks out there?"

"Not physically. It is my understanding that the agency is spending most of its man power reviewing Franks' financial records and communications at their headquarters," Kline replied. "Either way, escaping by boat remains the path of least resistance for your refuge."

"You're a class act, you know that?" Tilte quipped. "Just send me the details."

Denard Kline ended the call before proceeding to dial the number for the foreman.

"Mr. Kline," he answered. "Is everything alright?"

"Yes, Mr. Grieves. I just wanted to ask whether the police were still here collecting statements on the stolen equipment?"

"Oh no, sir," Greaves replied. "I'm sorry they left about ten minutes ago. I thought you didn't want to be disturbed."

Kline smiled and turned toward his open computer. He watched as the breaking news symbol flashed across the screen. The headline below it read: *'Possible Sound Weapon Used?'*

"That's alright," he began. "I just saw something that I think needs their attention."

Chapter 17

Face-To-Face

The gym was almost empty as it usually was on a weekday afternoon. A woman was stretching on one of the blue mats by the window. The older man she always seemed to run into was using a set of free weights in the corner, but all of the cardio machines Reagan used were free.

As was typical of the days following a physical therapy session, each step Reagan took needed extra concentration. The muscles in her legs seemed to battle against the strain of weariness. Ignoring the pain that afternoon had been especially difficult since her fight with Katie.

Reagan had only wanted to convey her concerns to her sister, but had seemed to deepen the only recently mended divide between the two of them. And while she knew she'd made valid points, she regretted not being able to find much needed common ground with Katie.

Reagan hoped that refocusing her mind on her regimen would provide her with a much needed sense of control again.

She walked slowly toward the group of stationary bikes facing the mirrors. She had recently made it a personal challenge to spend most of her gym session without the aid of her cane, though she always brought it just in case. Once she had one hand on the seat cushion, she placed her cane on the ground and slid onto the bike.

"Phew," Reagan breathed. She fitted her feet onto the pedals and gingerly leaned over to tighten the straps. "Come on, let's get going."

It was a difficult lead in but once Reagan started turning the wheels she felt some relief. The movements became smoother after a few minutes and soon she able to hold the pace she wanted.

This was exactly what she needed. Physically, at least.

Even with a fresh wave of enthusiasm pushing her now, Reagan still couldn't keep her mind away from the fight with her sister. She turned on the monitor that was attached to the bike in hopes that someone had left on a mundane sitcom that could distract her long enough to keep her exercise high.

But as the screen lit up, Reagan saw that the news had been left on.

"And we continue to follow the progress of President..."

Reagan's eyes burned through the subtitles as her finger continued pressing the channel toggle.

"...With the Secret Service on high alert after yesterday's attempted..."

Reagan was in no mood to watch cable news, but it appeared that the attempted assassination was on every channel. She held her finger on the down arrow until she saw the number for one of the local stations. But to her surprise there was a news story on there as well.

"Really, it's on every..." her pedaling slowed as the image on the screen immediately caught her attention. "No...that's Metro..."

The camera angle on the broadcast obscured the sign over the entrance but Reagan recognized the building and the parking lot of Meridian Metro General. There was a 'Live' indication at the bottom of the screen, attached to a banner that read 'Hospital Shooter At Large'.

"We've not yet confirmed the number of casualties from today's shooting at Meridian Metro General. What we do know is that a masked man indeed opened fire in the service tunnel underneath the hospital. While it may be too early to speculate, it is important to note that this is the same hospital currently holding Clarence Oswalt, member of the anti-elite terrorist group known as The Majority. There are also reports of some kind of sonic weapon being used, though that has yet to be confirmed..."

Oswalt. That name sent a sting to her neck and she could feel the spot on her forehead where he'd struck her with his rifle begin to throb. She started the controlled breathing exercises she used to help Katie with. She put her finger on the channel toggle but couldn't push the button in. Her eyes were helplessly glued on the captions that continued to scroll across the bottom of the screen.

"Whitnee, it's just crazy to think that this could very well be the third terrorist attack in Meridian within the past year...

The broadcast had cut away from the live footage and there were now two reporters side-by-side on a split screen. They both wore varying degrees of grim expressions across their faces. The words clearly belonged to the male on the left, who had a studio décor behind him. The woman, who was standing behind an ambulance, nodded.

"Well it's becoming a frightening trend, not the least because of the nature of these attacks. This isn't New York or DC, this is Meridian and we simply haven't experienced this level of

sustained terrorism. In fact, we have to go back to the mid 90's for the last time there was a terrorist threat in the city."

"Yes, the Meridian Central Park bombing during the Olympics..."

Reagan finally dug her finger into the power button. She tried to stand but felt very weak. Her stomach was turning, her hands were shaking.

She closed her eyes and tried to gain control of herself, but the images were coming too fast.

"Get a grip, Reagan. Get a grip..."

The young doctor refused to panic out in public. She needed to take back control.

But any chance of that ended when Reagan opened her eyes.

"Ahhhhhhhh!" she screamed as the dark, crazed eyes of Theodore Bishop stared back at her. She fell from the bike but quickly recovered to shuffle herself away on the floor.

"Oh my God, are you alright?"

Reagan turned to see the other woman who'd been occupying the gym kneeling at her side. The man was standing behind her, a very concerned look on his face. When Reagan looked back the menacing visage of Bishop had gone and she was left instead with her own look of confusion and fear.

~

Katie looked on with confusion as she watched the huddled group beneath her. She didn't like knowing so little, especially being so far away from home. She felt like she was in over her head. There was a man, or something that used to be a man, out there killing anyone who touched him. What she had hoped was going to be a necessary, albeit strange, journey to find out more about her powers had turned into something much scarier and much more dangerous.

But what made her feel even more anxious was the fact that her phone didn't seem to be working. Katie had tried to send texts to both Nancy and the detective but none of the messages had gone through.

One of the lab coats suddenly stepped onto the platform and Katie awkwardly shoved her phone inside her jacket pocket. Once she was alone again, she pushed out a breath filled with frustration.

Get a grip, Katie!

She stepped away from the railing. "Relax...relax...," she began rhythmically. "C-O-L-O-S-S-A-L...hmm, hmm, hmmmmm..."

As she hummed, those at the table were getting louder. Katie peeked back over the side of the platform to see what was going on.

The Commander was doing most of the talking, dragging her pointer finger across an outstretched map. It looked like something out of an old war movie. She had placed small colored chips in various places and pointed to several of those around her. There were a few comments from Trevor and the white haired man sprinkled in, but for the most part, the rest of the people around the table were silent.

They were soldiers, that much was obvious. Their posture, the silent nodding, their build...everything about them reminded her of the soldiers she had seen on TV and in movies. As for who they all worked for, that was still a mystery. The ones who had actual uniforms on displayed no familiar emblems or flags. And none of them seemed to come from the same place. Trevor was French, or maybe French-Canadian, but the Commander was British. She heard another who sounded as though they may have been from Africa, and even a lady who sounded a lot like her Aunt Laine.

Maybe they're from the UN or something? Is there an army for that?

Trying to figure out the identity of her 'hosts' was frustrating, but it did keep her distracted from the reality of what was happening around her. That and trying to figure out what was happening between her and her sister. She had shouldered much of the blame for their deteriorated relationship. She was the troubled one, the one with all the issues. However, this last argument seemed to have more to do with Reagan's issues than her own. She could tell her sister was still in some degree of physical pain but the blonde thought there might be something else going on.

Dr. Mack had always told her that people reacted to catastrophic moments differently. Katie remembered being very angry and confrontational in the early days after her mother's death. After what had happened to her sister over the past year, the blonde wondered if something similar was happening to...

"Alright, you have your orders," the Commander suddenly exclaimed. "Let's end this today."

"And the girl?" Trevor said as the others marched out.

The Commander turned her cutting gaze toward Katie. "Use your discretion, Lieutenant. But I've given you your answer."

"Understood, Commander."

Trevor signaled to three men and they began ascending the stairs. Once he was back in front of Katie he pulled out a pair of black gloves from his pocket. "Take these."

"Gloves?" she asked before taking them from Trevor.

"Having your skin exposed would not be wise," he replied.

Katie stood confused for a moment. "Are you going to tell me what we're doing? Are we going after the Reaper?"

"That name gets more ridiculous with every additional utterance, Ms. Cattrell," Trevor said, motioning for the soldiers to head outside. "But yes, we intend to capture the target on this little venture."

Katie glanced down at all the people typing furiously on their computers. Her eyes met with those of the Commander's, who had apparently been staring at her since ending the meeting.

"What did she say to you?" asked the blonde.

"About you?" returned Trevor. He followed her eyes toward the Commander. "Just to use you as I see fit."

That doesn't sound comforting.

"How?" the words slipped out of Katie's mouth.

Trevor, who had already turned toward the doors, glanced back at her. "I'll show you."

As the blonde began to follow she pointed a blatantly sarcastic smile toward the Commander. "Psycho," she muttered before finally catching up to the men outside. They had begun to pack the back of two jeeps with large briefcases.

"What are those?" Katie asked.

"A deconstructed containment unit we designed to hold him. We need to keep it close for when he's caught."

The blonde nodded and watched as Trevor picked up a black, round case. "Here," he said, tossing it to her.

Katie opened the box carefully. Inside there were eight thin darts, filled with a clear liquid. "What are these, tranquilizers?"

"Something like that," Trevor said. "There's enough sedative in one of those darts to put someone like me to sleep for an entire day. Getting one of those in our target will likely give us a few hours without struggle. That is still plenty of time to prep the containment unit."

"So you're really going to trap him?"

"You sound relieved," Trevor replied, helping one of the soldiers with their gloves before putting on his own. "You didn't believe us?"

"I don't know," Katie shrugged. "I guess I just didn't like the idea that we were going hunting or something."

"Of course," Trevor replied.

"But if you have these, then why do you need me?" the blonde felt as though she just kept repeating herself.

Trevor sighed and then pointed to a set of buildings in the distance. "Insurance. We couldn't evacuate the whole of Mississauga and Toronto is less than half an hour away. We had to make sure that we had a plan in the event that our target managed to evade or overpower our forces."

"Like he has before?" Katie asked as she recalled the comment he made shortly after she landed.

The smile Trevor offered was brief and dismissive. "It's been a long mission, Ms. Cattrell. I pray that we aren't in need of your involvement."

He wasn't the only one. Katie had had her fill of facing super-powered crazies. "How is he able to do everything that he's doing?"

"I can only tell you that we don't believe he was born with these abilities. Nor did he willingly accept them."

"Why makes you say that?" Katie asked.

Trevor glanced at his men. They all stood by the car doors, backs straight and awaiting orders. It appeared they were going to need to wait a little longer. "He needs human energy to replenish his own or likely face death. Why, I do not know, but I doubt someone would volunteer for the lifestyle of a parasite."

"Then how would you keep him alive?" Katie began. "Unless you gave him someone to 'eat'?"

Trevor's face remained stoic. "That isn't necessarily our priority. And honestly, by the time we analyze his condition and find a remedy, it might already be too late..."

"And he'll die..." Katie nodded as the realization hit her. She didn't like death, for anybody.

"You can't save everyone, Ms. Cattrell."

He gave her a peculiar glance as he said that.

"What do you know about me?" she returned.

"Allons-y!" Trevor exclaimed to the three men around him. They quickly jumped into the vehicles. He opened the door and turned back to Katie. He reached out for the box she was still holding. Katie reluctantly handed it over, drawing a quick smile from him.

"In due time," he finally replied.

Surprise, surprise...

Katie folded her arms and stared in frustration at Trevor. "Do you know how to say anything else?"

"We've had plenty of conversation to this point," he quipped, pointing to an opening in the distant woods. "You wouldn't mind following on foot, would you?"

Katie didn't respond. Instead she rose off the ground and motioned for the jerk to crank the car.

Chapter 18

Unmasked Assassin

Agent Roberts' footsteps could be heard coming down the hall.

"Finally," Donnelly muttered.

"Apologies, detectives," Roberts began, shaking the phone in his hand before sliding it into his jacket pocket. "May we proceed?"

The three men turned to Morris, the balding security guard seated in front of a half dozen monitors. He took his hands off the keyboard and mouse and turned to face them. "Just finished getting the feeds in order. I'm ready when y'all are."

"Morris thinks we have a pretty good look at our shooter," Wreings added.

"Well let's see it," Roberts replied. He folded his arms and stepped next to Donnelly.

The guard nodded and double-clicked his mouse, expanding one of his open windows. "This is from the service entrance camera. It's located right above where any vehicle could enter. You'll see the timestamp at 11:25. That's when you boys arrived here and..."

"Could we get to the video that shows the shooter, please?" Roberts interrupted. "And maybe sans the commentary?"

Morris glanced back at the agent. "Sorry, I was just trying to start from the beginning for you fellas."

"It's alright Morris," Wreings assured the guard, drawing an irritated look from Agent Roberts. The detective pointed to another one of the windows open on the main screen. "Is that the garage with the elevator?"

"Yes sir," Morris nodded and tripled-click the mouse, sending four separate windows to fill each corner of the screen. "We got four cameras in this area. One you just saw at the entrance, one at the exit right here, one in front of the elevator, and one in the corner over here. This is where you can kind of see everything going on so I'll bring that one up."

"Thanks," Wreings said. "Do one of these show how he got in?"

"I don't think so, but I haven't gotten that far yet," Morris replied as he positioned the new video angle to the center of the screen. "I was just working on getting the tapes of the actual incident ready for y'all."

They continued to watch as the transport van slowly turned around in the middle of the garage. The back doors were now facing the elevator. There were two squad cars parked side-by-side a few feet away against the wall. Once the van had stopped moving, four officers stepped out of their cars.

"There's Hopkins, Carey, Estes, and McTigue," Donnelly said. The anger in his voice was loud and clear.

Agent Roberts was the next one to enter the frame from the passenger side of the van. Wreings glanced over to see an equally intense look on his face, his eyes unwavering from the screen.

"Agent Orlovski stayed in the van," Roberts said. "He wanted to check in with the others."

Detective Wreings nodded. "Any of you see where our shooter could have come in?"

"Not yet," Donnelly said. "But I'm looking."

The video continued. Roberts was now doling out instructions to the four officers. Each nodded as the agent's finger landed in front of their faces. Then Hopkins and Officer Estes walked with Roberts toward the elevator, while Officers Carey and McTigue took their ill-fated positions on either side of the van.

"How long were you upstairs?" asked Wreings.

"Ten minutes," Roberts replied. "No more."

"So it must have happened fast then," the detective said, turning back to the screen. He could feel the tension rising amongst everyone in the security room.

Suddenly, there was a small flash in the corner of the frame. "There!" Wreings shouted. "That's a gun, that's him!"

"I didn't see how he came in," Roberts chimed in.

"Wait, wait!" Donnelly said, pointing to another frame on the screen. "Can we rewind that and play it from this angle?"

Morris hit something on the keypad, reversing the playback. He then enlarged the requested angle for all of the men behind him to see.

Wreings looked closely as a figure appeared on the screen by the driver's side door. He aimed his gun inside the window, firing twice. Neither officer seemed to notice.

"Silencer," said the detective. "Carey and McTigue never even heard it."

The figure hadn't stopped and was quickly around the other side of the van. There were two more flashes, each resulting in an officer slumping to the floor. Detective Wreings cringed at the limp bodies of the fallen officers.

"That piece of shit shot them in the back," said Donnelly.

"What's he doing now I wonder?" Roberts began as the masked figure stood between the bodies. He then started pulling the body of McTigue farther away from the other officer. He appeared to glance over at the elevator and the body a few times before walking away.

Wreings shook his head as the masked figure then stepped out of frame. "I don't know. Morris, can you get us another angle?"

"You bet," the guard replied. He had another window open almost instantly. The new shot had the figure leaning his back against one of the wide columns that flanked the elevator ramp.

"Now he's waiting," Roberts said. "Fast forward to when I came back down."

"Wait a minute," Wreings cautioned. "It looks like he's got something in his hands."

"Can you get any closer?" Donnelly asked.

Morris shook his head. "Not without severely distorting the image."

"I can't make out what's in his hands," Wreings said.

"It looks like whatever it is, he's putting it under his mask and...maybe in his ear?" Morris said.

"His mask never comes off though," Roberts added. "He knows where the cameras are."

The detective agreed. Whoever this shooter was, he knew exactly what he was doing. "How long have you guys been planning this?"

Roberts shook his head. "Not long. Three days."

"Well it looks like this guy had the place well scouted," Wreings replied.

"Do you want me to fast forward still?" Morris asked.

"Yes," Roberts replied.

They sped through the video until the nine and a half minute mark. The figure still hadn't moved.

"He's very disciplined," Roberts said.

"You going to keep giving this bastard compliments?" Donnelly called out.

Roberts shrugged. "I'm giving him a profile."

"Right," Donnelly replied.

"Hey, there's the elevator," Wreings interjected.

The gurney was halfway out when it stopped abruptly. Officer Estes was the first to run out, followed by Hopkins, both with their guns drawn. Then Roberts stepped into frame and signaled for Hopkins to go back inside. Meanwhile, the shooter remained pressed against the column.

Roberts and Estes were quick to go down the ramp, each walking in the direction of the closest body to them. Wreings instantly remembered what he had seen earlier.

"He separated the bodies to separate you," Wreings said.

"At least our attention," returned Agent Roberts.

"Look what he's doing now," Donnelly pointed at the screen.

The figure appeared to tap his right ear. Suddenly, the remaining officers and Agent Roberts pressed their hands to their ears. They all began to stagger, seemingly unable to find their footing. Soon they were all on the ground.

"I've never seen anything do that before," Donnelly added.

The shooter then spun around and emerged from behind the column. He first aimed his gun at the bewildered Hopkins, before lowering it to point at the head of Oswalt. A few seconds passed before the pistol flashed once more.

Wreings sighed as if he were watching Oswalt get murdered again in real time. He already knew how this scene ended. But when he saw Hopkins push the gurney into the shooter, the detective also noticed something strange.

"Hey Morris, hold it for a sec," he said quickly. "Can you go back a few seconds to right after he shot Oswalt?"

"Yep," the guard replied.

"What's up, V?" Donnelly asked.

The detective focused on the screen for a few moments as Morris replayed the shooting. "There!" Wreings exclaimed. "Did you notice that?"

"Notice what?" his partner asked.

"Rewind it again, Morris," the detective leaned in eagerly. He pointed to the right side of the shooter's head as soon as he fired his gun. Donnelly and Roberts moved closer to the screen. "Watch right here. He taps whatever that thing is he has. Can you pause it when it happens?"

Morris paused the playback perfectly showing the shooter tapping his right ear.

"So what?" Donnelly asked.

"You remember when I was trying out that headset thing with the new phone but it didn't work?" Wreings began.

Donnelly shot back a quizzical look. "The Bluetooth? Yeah, I remember *you* not being able to work it..."

"Well, one of the things I kept doing was..." Wreings had already begun demonstrating with his hand when his partner caught on.

"Hitting it like a jackass!" Donnelly said. "Yeah, I can see that."

"Doesn't it look like he's doing the same thing?"

"I guess," Donnelly replied. "But what does that have to do with anything."

"His device may have been malfunctioning," Roberts jumped in. He turned to Wreings with a curious look. "Or perhaps he's communicating with someone?"

Wreings nodded. "My bet is the first one. Just look! Right after he taps it, Hopkins looks like she's able to see him. Look at how she turns toward him."

"Yes, I remember that sound stopping at one point," Roberts said.

"Hey, hold on!" Donnelly chimed in. Everyone turned back to the screen as Hopkins and the masked man fought. Then what looked like a blade sprang from underneath his glove and he rammed it into the shoulder of Hopkins. She fell to the ground, clutching the mask.

"The lady cop really kicks ass," Morris said before changing angles to follow the shooter. He clicked the space bar emphatically as he left the frame on a front shot of the shooter's face. "And here y'all are!"

Wreings, Donnelly, and Roberts simultaneously leaned forward. The video was a little blurry, but the detective could make out a narrow space between the shooter's eyes which sat underneath a set of thick bushy brows. He had even more hair covering his upper-lip, coming down into a thick beard along his chin. The sides of his hair were buzzed short with the top slicked over to the right.

"That's a good shot," Wreings said. "Do you have any more cameras along that tunnel?"

"Just one," Morris returned. "But..."

He pulled up a new window and the shape of the shooter could be seen fast approaching. Suddenly, there was a flash and the screen went to static.

"Christ, he's a good shot," Donnelly said.

"And very knowledgeable," added Agent Roberts. "He barely had to look to find the security camera. How does he know where he's running to?

"Maybe that's the way he came in?" Donnelly suggested.

"You catch that on the tapes, Morris?" Wreings asked.

The guard shook his head apologetically, "I was only able to go through the fifteen minutes of the incident before y'all got here..."

"It's not a problem," Wreings assured. "This is good. Can we get a copy of the tapes from today?"

Agent Roberts held up his pointer finger. "I'd like to review this entire week with my team."."

"The week?" questioned Detective Wreings.

Morris turned to face the FBI agent. "I'm sorry but we don't have anything past Sunday. The hospital..."

"Just get me everything that you have then," Roberts cut him off. "It's clear that this wasn't the first time the assassin has visited the hospital. Detectives, I will see if this man's identity can be gleamed from our database. It may take some time so I suggest you two spend yours trying to collect and classify as much physical evidence as possible."

Donnelly laughed the same way he always did before he was about to ream a wise-cracking perp, but Wreings signaled for him to keep it cool. He then turned to Agent Roberts and offered a slight nod. "You guys have a larger database, you'd probably find the identity of this guy faster than we could."

Roberts stared at Wreings for a few moments before turning toward the door. "Please have the footage ready, I will return in a few minutes."

"No way the Feds are going to get this one, V!" Donnelly said. "Those are our guys lying under sheets out there."

"They've got as much stake in this as we do, Don," Wreings returned. "One of their guys and a Federal witness was killed too. At least we're still bringing the rest of the evidence to the station."

His partner shrugged. "It starts with the tapes, V. Next thing you know we're not even riding shotgun when this piece of shit is caught!"

"I know, I know. But I have a feeling that they may already have a good idea who this guy is," Wreings replied, recalling the shooter holding the gun in his left hand. "Remember me telling you last night about what happened to the other two Majority members they had in custody?"

"Yeah. You think it's the same guy?"

"I think they do," Wreings said.

"It wouldn't surprise me one bit," Donnelly added. "I can't wait 'til these assholes leave, especially Roberts. He's a real prick!"

Wreings nodded. He had worked with federal agents before, each time with its own set of issues. Roberts was arrogant like most of them but there was something off with his comments about the detective and The Flying Girl. Wreings wasn't sure whether the agent actually knew anything or not. But it was clear that he was a little more than fixated.

"Yeah. He's a real piece of work," Wreings replied.

"He's a real piece of something," Morris chimed in, drawing a rare smile from Donnelly.

"Leave it to the Feds to bring a nutjob with them when they come to town, right?" his partner said.

"Yeah," Wreings began as he took a quick glance back at the screen, which featured the still frame of the shooter's face. "Let's just hope he's the only one."

~

It was entertaining to watch all of the people in their various uniforms. They moved around death like bees would have buzzed around a hive. She had never stayed behind long enough after an assignment to see things from inside the yellow tape.

She kept a close eye on the examiners near the transport van. The way they stepped ever so carefully around the dead bodies as if they were afraid to wake them was humorous.

"Hey."

The call sounded as though it had been directed at her. She turned to see a short man dressed as she was in the light blue shirt and plastic white gloves. She remembered them being called EMTs. This one wore a tag labeled 'Burt'.

"The others already took care of all the live ones so I think we're done here," he continued. "You okay?"

She nodded.

"It's a mess," Burt proceeded, shaking his head and moving closer to her as he spoke. It seemed to be a common American practice to intrude upon each other's space. "A real mess."

She remained vigilant, quickly noting any potential witnesses should she need to dispatch of this 'Burt'. But he stopped just a few inches away and turned to look out onto the hive. He was shaking his head as if he was still in shock by what happened. That hardly made sense considering his country and profession.

"You want a ride to the front?" he asked.

The assassin shook her head, adding a polite smile. She couldn't leave yet. She had to be sure.

Burt looked at her, seemingly deciding whether to ask more inconsequential questions. But thankfully he left her alone and hopped back into the ambulance. Soon he was navigating his way to out of the garage and her attention quickly turned back to the van.

She saw one of the examiners finally pick up the small pack of matches she had placed by the front tire. Once they had bagged it, she pulled out her phone and began typing into the keypad.

Job done.

Chapter 19

Fear the Reaper

Walking through the overgrown woods did little to ease Katie's nerves. Though it was the middle of the afternoon, the scenery seemed cut from the handful of horror movies she'd seen. It got denser the deeper they went and every time Trevor stopped their group, Katie's heart would skip.

It was a hyper-anxious person's definition of a nightmare.

"Could you please keep it quiet?" Trevor whispered harshly.

He had already told her to stop humming, but Katie *needed* something to distract her. "I can't help it."

An impatient glare was thrown back at her. Trevor then raised his hands to stop the other soldier's advancement. "You are aware of what it is we're currently doing here, aren't you?"

Katie nodded. "Look, it's how I keep from freaking out."

"Yes, and it's likely alerting anyone within earshot of our presence. No matter his likely weakened state, we cannot cede any advantage to our target," he replied, shaking his head before pointing upwards. "Perhaps some higher ground would be best from this point on?"

Katie stood still for a few moments, watching Trevor turn to lead the soldiers ahead. She glanced at the thick brush above her. The thought of lifting off the ground and into the open was tempting, but Katie knew the nerves she was dealing with now might not allow her to come back down should she be needed. The blonde closed her eyes and took a deep breath before catching up with the men in front of her.

212

She almost called out to Trevor before remembering how dumb that would have been. Instead she floated a few inches off the ground and flew closer toward him. "So he's been living out here?" she whispered.

The Frenchman's exhale had a clear trace of impatience. "Living? To the extent that he's not dead, then yes he has." He didn't look back.

"And without any people and all that," Katie continued, trying to sound less nervous than she actually was. "He is, like starving?"

"Is this really necessary right now, Ms. Cattrell?" Trevor snapped.

"I'm just asking," replied the blonde. "I have never seen him or anything so I would kind of like to know if he's still 'super' even when he's hungry."

"He's likely not at that level yet."

Something about the way Trevor said that seemed curious to Katie. "I don't understand. If you said you've had him trapped in here for a while then why wouldn't he be?"

This time, Trevor glanced back. The moment Katie saw his eyes, she knew he hadn't told the whole truth.

"Our people in the Canadian government managed to pass a temporary order barring anyone from accessing the quarantined area while the 'cleanup initiative' was underway. However..." he paused and returned his focus to the woods ahead. "You can imagine how hard this has been to keep hidden from the public. There was one unfortunate incident of an overzealous news crew who managed to enter through what once was a blind spot in our perimeter."

"What happened to them?" Katie continued.

"Well, we have yet to see them leave, if that gives you any indication." Trevor replied.

There was such a lack of emotion in his voice. Still, Katie fought to keep her resolve. "So..."

"There were only two members of the crew. It has been six days," Trevor sighed. "It's unlikely that we'll be dealing with him at full capacity."

"But if he is...?"

"That is where you come in," Trevor said quickly. "Now if you don't mind...let's save the talking for later shall we?"

Talking about human beings like they were snacks was morbid. "Why is she like that?"

"Now what are you talking about?"

"Um...your boss. She's a huge bitch," Katie replied.

Trevor sighed. "You'll find the Commander is not terribly fond of working with civilians, and with good reason."

What's that supposed to mean? "Because...?"

"We've worked with civilians in an official capacity before," Trevor began, raising his weapon slightly as he continued to look forward. "While it's typically been a dull affair, we have had one or two instances where the partnership has come back to haunt us."

"How?" Katie pushed forward her inquisition.

"You know, it will be hard to catch our target unawares if we continue to engage in this nervous chatter," Trevor said sharply.

"Well maybe if you had filled me in before putting me out here, I wouldn't have so many questions...," Katie snapped back.

"Shhhh!" Trevor said suddenly.

Katie's heart nearly stopped as she looked past Trevor at the clearing a few yards ahead. The flapping wings of a large white sheet were folded over an outstretched tree branch, forming a makeshift tent. A thin stream of smoke rose from a pile of sticks just in front of the opening. Katie couldn't see for sure, but the tent looked like it had somebody inside.

Trevor held his hand in a fist above his head, halting the movement of the rest of the soldiers around him. He quickly pointed to his left and right, and two of the soldiers moved to flank the clearing. After they signaled that they were set, Trevor then tapped the shoulder of the other soldier and pointed at the tent.

He nodded and began to slowly approach.

Trevor followed.

Katie waited.

A chill ran up her spine as she watched them maneuver to the makeshift campsite. Their guns were aimed at the entrance to the tent. The meticulous approach seemed to drag on for an agonizingly long time. None of them made a sound as they expertly moved forward, avoiding the brush and debris that littered the ground.

The soldier leading was the first to make it to the tent. He glanced at Trevor who gave him a quick nod in return. The other men lowered their stance; their guns remaining trained ahead. The leading soldier walked around the side and kicked against the sheet.

A body fell from the opening, followed swiftly by another. Everyone quickly repositioned their aim. The soldier prodded the bodies but, to Katie's relief, he let his weapon down to his side. The others followed suit, except for Trevor who still had his weapon aimed at the entrance of the tent.

"Our intruders?" he asked the soldier.

"Ay," replied the soldier, kneeling down to take something from the first body. He held it up to show Trevor. It looked like an ID fob. "This one's the cameraman, sir."

Trevor groaned in frustration. He finally lowered his gun and glanced back at Katie. She knew she probably looked mortified and didn't even try to hide it.

"Here's our reporters," he said before returning his attention to the tent. He moved toward it to take a closer look, leaving Katie to finally catch her breath.

She closed her eyes and exhaled deeply.

"Hold on," the apprehension in Trevor's voice snapped her eyes open. "These are two males. One was a…"

Suddenly, the second body sprang from the ground with a large branch in hand. He cracked it against Trevor's shoulder, knocking his gun away. The two flanking soldiers fired their weapons at him, but he already had a hold of the other soldier.

A wide hood blocked her view of his face, but Katie immediately knew who it was. She could only watch as her limbs seemed frozen with fear.

"Shoot!" commanded Trevor.

There were at least two more shots from either side of her. A pair of large darts struck the back of the attacker. His movements seemed to slow but his hands were still grappling with the downed soldier who was desperately shielding his face

Trevor scrambled for his gun. "Shoot him again!" he yelled.

But the hooded figure of the Reaper was unrelenting and before another shot could be fired, he had already ripped off one of the soldier's gloves.

"Aghhhhh!"

The desperate scream finally sprung Katie into action. She shot across the clearing and rammed into the cloaked assailant sending him hurtling into the woods. She quickly knelt down to help the soldier but was horrified by his near-shriveled appearance. His face had lost all of its color and shape, his lifeless eyes rolled back into his skull.

"Oh my god!"

"Ms. Cattrell!"

Katie spun around to see Trevor clutching his right arm. He motioned with his eyes toward the fleeing figure.

The blonde quickly refocused and shot off after him. He was definitely moving fast but not enough to get away from her. She caught up to him just outside the woods. In a flash, Katie grabbed him by the arm then slammed him into the ground.

The figured remained motionless and for a few moments, Katie was worried that she'd been too rough. But then he rolled over and slowly rose to his feet. His pale face was now unobstructed. Two dark eyes were sunken above hollow cheeks and his disheveled brown hair hung down to his shoulders.

He definitely looked like death.

"Jeez, what are you?" she said.

"What are you?" he mumbled sickly, looking over her as though he were a wild animal. Then without warning, he leapt for her.

The Reaper landed just a foot away but his hand could almost reach her face. Katie was able to avoid his initial attempts to grab her but his movements were faster now than they'd been just a few moments ago.

He's getting stronger...

Backpedaling, she tried to put distance between them but within seconds, his frigid hand had grabbed a hold of her *bare* fingers. In her frustration with Trevor, she had forgotten to put on the gloves. A sharp pain shot up her arm, causing her to lose her balance momentarily. But her instincts kicked in and with her free hand she swung her fist at the face of the Reaper. The hit landed just above the chin, knocking him off his feet and tumbling across the grass.

But the Reaper climbed back to his feet and simply opened his mouth wide and forced the bones back into place.

"Oh my God, that is so gross," said Katie.

As he came at her again, the blonde moved to defend herself. Her legs felt oddly weak and she nearly fell but recovered fast enough to get another swing at the incoming Reaper.

He easily dodged her strike.

What's happening?

It was really hard to stand now and she felt her consciousness waning. But passing out wasn't an option as the Reaper's deathly visage was glaring down at her.

She desperately swung again. But this time he caught her fist. He immediately began squeezing her knuckles.

The blonde screamed.

Her skin was constricting her insides. As she peered into the dark eyes of the man in front of her, she could see the veins bulging in his neck. Katie flung a kick at his stomach in an attempt to knock him off but fell to the ground instead.

Her eyes turned toward the bright Toronto sky. She had to get away before he attacked her again. The blonde turned over and scrambled to her feet before leaping into the air.

She seemed to hover a few feet above the ground before plummeting back down harshly.

The impact stung her right side. It was then she noticed the scratches on her hands. Her heart thumped desperately against her chest as she finally realized the horrifying truth - the Reaper had somehow taken her strength.

She was powerless and in trouble.

The pain she now felt was greater than anything she had ever experienced.

"You don't look so good," the raspy voice spit into her ear.

She saw him reaching for her again as her vision rapidly faded.

Chapter 20

Preparing For A Call

Glades was clearly fired up as she paced around her office. "To just take the video from the attack without even communicating with me...I don't give a shit if the FBI has jurisdiction!"

Wreings nodded. "I think Roberts knows more than he's letting on. About the shooter, about Oswalt, about everything."

"I can't even think about that right now," the Captain groaned in frustration. "The press have been foaming at the mouth to get more on this."

"Christ," Donnelly huffed, rubbing his face with his palm. "Can't wait for tonight's 'Hot Take'."

"For God's sake please don't mention Shay Donovan," Glades said. She leaned over her desk for a few moments before letting out a deep sigh. "I need to reach out to the widows of McTigue and Carey. We've been keeping their names out of the press while their immediate superiors made the house call. I'd also like them to hear from me before they see their husband's faces show up the evening news..."

Wreings and Donnelly nodded.

Suddenly, the Captain lashed out with her fist on her desk. "Goddammit, Goddammit, Goddammit!"

The sudden outburst from Glades caught the detectives off-guard. They stood silently as the Captain turned and rubbed her face.

"Sorry," she continued. "Carey was a good officer. A kiss-ass sometimes, but a damn good cop. And McTigue's wife, Marilyn...they're expecting their first kid in another month. Lt. Herschel was planning some kind of party for him."

"Jesus," Donnelly said.

Glades nodded solemnly. "Look, I don't care what the FBI does. You two need to find me whoever pulled the trigger."

"Yes, Captain," Wreings and Donnelly replied in unison.

Wreings left the Captain's office and slumped in his chair but noticed his partner hadn't come with him. He glanced back to see that Donnelly was still inside.

The pair looked like they were talking about something intense for a couple of moments until a hint of a smile appeared on the Captain's face. It was a strange sight as his partner's one-on-ones with Glades rarely ended pleasantly.

Donnelly left the room shortly after, closing the door behind him. But before Wreings could ask what all of that was about, Donnelly was already back on the case.

"Did we get anything else good from forensics...?"

His voice faded away as Wreings' attention shifted back to the Captain's office. He watched Captain Glades through the blinds of her office window. She was sitting on the edge of her desk, facing the door as she often did when her blood was boiling. But unlike other times, Glades wasn't about to chew someone out. Instead of her typical scowl she wore the look of someone who wished she could be anywhere else.

Wreings had sat at the same desk outside of Glades' office since he made detective over six years ago. In all that time, he couldn't remember ever being there when she had to make *the* call. It was hard to watch the visibly shaken Captain taking deep breaths as she walk back to her chair. She picked up the phone, hesitating for a few moments before finally putting the receiver to her ear.

"Reyes," she called to the tall officer walking in front of her office. "Could you get that for me, please? Thank you." The officer nodded and slowly pulled the door closed.

When Detective Wreings saw her lips begin to move he felt a tug deep in his stomach. Whether Glades had started with McTigue's or Carey's wife didn't matter. He knew their worlds had changed permanently - much like his had the day the doctors told Cass and him about Mitchell. He knew that feeling and hated that someone else had to go through...

"Hey, V!"

The detective spun his chair around to face his partner and pushed away the lingering memories of Cass, the hospital, and Mitchell, returning to the here and now.

"Yeah sorry," Wreings began. "What was that you were saying?"

"Basically, they didn't find any prints, which makes sense cause this guy was wearing gloves," Donnelly sighed. "They did find some blood in the area where we think he got out, but we won't know anything until they look at that. The sewer system splits off into three directions about a half a mile down. If we're right and he went down the drain, then the shooter could have gone either to the Upper Westside, Meridian Central Park, or even Midtown."

Wreings pressed his hand against his forehead. "That's a pretty big haystack."

"Yeah, the problem is that we've got to find this needle before it pricks us in the ass again."

"Yeah. Aside from police and FBI, Oswalt didn't have any visitors, so the logs are a bust," Wreings added.

"Unless it was an inside job," Donnelly returned.

The idea had crossed Wreings' mind, especially after Roberts took all the footage with him. But if the FBI had wanted to kill Oswalt, they were just one successful transfer away from doing it in the privacy of their own confines. "Maybe, but I don't think the Bureau are the bad guys this time, Don. What else do we have to go on?"

Donnelly shrugged holding up a baggy with a matchbook inside. "Not much aside from this. I told the guys to bring up the rest of the evidence once they finished with it. Shouldn't take too much longer."

"Right," Wreings returned as he stood up from his chair.

"Where you going?" Donnelly asked.

"Heading down to the lab," Detective Wreings glanced again at Glades through the Captain's window. The phone was still pressed tightly to her ear; her face buried into the palm of her hand.

The detective needed a change of scenery. "I need to talk to LJ and Jess, if he's there. I'll stop by and check on our evidence too."

His partner glanced at him as if he had something else to add, but turned his gaze back to his computer. "Thanks."

Wreings left the desks and made his way through the back of the station. As he walked toward the stairs, he noticed there were very few eyes looking up. There was hardly any chatter or groups talking about what happened like there had been when the President was shot the day before. But he didn't need to hear their voices to know what was going through their heads.

That could be me...

Captain could be on the phone with my wife, my husband...

There wasn't a badge on the force who hadn't thought either of those things at least a dozen times since the day after graduating academy. Most of the time it just seemed like noise, a surefire way to end up getting yourself or your partner killed. But when there's two dead cops lying on slabs just beneath your feet, that noise was nearly deafening.

It was going to take a while for things to go back to normal. Once they nabbed McTigue and Carey's killer, there would be a small feeling of satisfaction. Eventually, after the sentencing and news stories had come and gone, everybody would likely carry on as if the whole thing was just a bad dream. Some people might even forget it had ever happened. The reporters would move on to Meridian's next big tragedy.

Everyone's lives would go back to normal. Everyone except for the loved ones of the fallen. It would never feel 'like a bad dream' for them and there would never be any 'normal' for them anymore either. There would only be a vague memory of what 'normal' had felt like a long time ago.

The days that followed would be filled with disbelief. Every morning they woke up, they'd wish they hadn't. Every step they took would feel as though they were past the point of exhaustion. Even the laughs they managed to keep those closest to them from worrying would be empty. Nothing would ever fill the hollow of the human-sized void they now had in their lives.

~

Kline watched the people they passed along the road. Some kept to themselves while others spoke on the phone. There were men and woman walking by one another, unaware of their neighbors' presence. He briefly wondered what it must be like to experience their mundane existence, simple in comparison to what he had already achieved with his.

While there was likely the odd exception, the people of Meridian were truly uninspiring.

He heard his phone ringing and soon saw the number of Jameson Slater appear on his screen.

"Well this is a pleasant surprise," he greeted. "Ms. Slater, what can I do for you?"

"Good afternoon, Mr. Kline," she returned warmly. "I hope I'm not interrupting..."

"Not at all," Kline said, peering forward out the car window. He saw his destination was a few lights away. As much as he'd like a prolonged dialogue there was unfortunately work that needed to be done. "I don't have much time, however. Is there something that I can do for you?"

She seemed to hesitate for a second before continuing. "Well, I'd like to get your thoughts on that project I mentioned that Mayor Edison has been trying to get approved. I know you don't have much time but we could discuss it this evening, maybe over dinner, if you're still available?"

The prospect of a dinner with Slater was one that Kline relished, even if discussing business was the main intent.

"I'd love to," said Kline, glancing at his watch. "Though I'm not sure of the timing yet. I may be held up until seven here."

"Oh, that's not a problem at all, Mr. Kline," she replied. "Have you ever heard of a place called The Razz and Jazz? It's a nice little wine and tapas bar that features live music on Thursdays. I could get us a table at eight?"

"That would be perfect," he returned, watching as the town car pulled along the curb and slowed to a halt. "I do apologize but I need to step into my next engagement..."

"I'll see you in Bankrow later tonight."

"I look forward to it."

The door opened as Denard Kline ended the call.

"This is the seventh precinct, Mr. Kline," the driver began.

"I know," the big man exhaled as he stepped out onto the sidewalk. "Thank you."

"Not a problem, sir."

Kline smiled expectantly as he looked over the entrance of the Meridian Police Department. The two Roman columns that stood on either side of the door captured his attention immediately, much as they had when Slater had brought him here during his trip in February.

"I'm not sure I'll be able to stay parked here," the driver continued. "But I think there's a garage a block ahead..."

"That would be fine Judson," Kline replied. "I don't envision this being brief."

Chapter 21

Shared Interests

KNOCK! KNOCK! KNOCK!

"Just a second," Reagan called out as she closed her laptop and approached the door. Her hand turned the knob and she wasn't sure whether she expected or just hoped to see her sister's face on the other side. But when she opened the door, Reagan was surprised to see that it was Nancy Zorowitz looking back at her.

"Hi," Nancy greeted with a forced smile.

"Hi," Reagan returned, though it came out more as a question.

The dark-haired Nancy continued to play down the awkwardness. "I'm sorry to bother you if you were in the middle of something..."

"No," Reagan said, glancing over her shoulder to the laptop. "I...wasn't really doing anything."

An uncomfortable silence followed. The young doctor had no idea why her sister's roommate, who she had never had a one-on-one conversation with, was standing in front of her now. Her first instinct was to question whether Katie had sent her 'protector' over...

"Could I come in?" Nancy suddenly asked.

Reagan pressed her palm against her head. "I'm sorry, of course. Come in!"

Nancy stepped toward the kitchen and glanced at the counter. "Is it alright if I put this here?"

"Sure," Reagan replied. "But I do have hooks if you'd rather use those."

"Oh, I'm sorry I didn't even notice."

"No I'm sorry, that probably sounded..."

"Like a fine idea," Nancy laughed and shook her head at Reagan's attempted apology as she hung the purple bag on the wall. "I'm so used to putting my things on the counter at home. It's probably the only thing I can take being untidy."

"It must be hard living with my sister then," Reagan returned.

Nancy offered a slight smile which grew as she turned her head to the living room. She was so different from Katie, who often wore a look of caution regardless of where she was. No matter how hard she tried, Reagan couldn't picture them being best friends. Her seemingly carefree demeanor and fancy clothes made their friendship all the more bizarre.

"I really like this," Nancy began with a hint of surprise in her voice. She leaned down in front of the black bookshelf that stood to the left of the bedroom hallway. "You have a very nice apartment."

"Thank you. Can I get you anything to drink?"

"Do you have any tea?" Nancy answered. "I haven't been able to shake the craving since I got back."

"No," Reagan replied. "I actually haven't had tea in a long time. I do have water, coconut water..."

"Water would be fine."

Reagan nodded and walked into the kitchen to get a cup. "You were in France, right?"

"Yes, for a few weeks," Nancy replied. "But only for the fashion show. I spent a lot of time back in England before and after."

"It must have been pretty."

"Yeah," Nancy smiled. "You would probably really like it in Paris. Katie said that was one place that you always wanted to go when you were younger."

"I'm surprised she remembered that. I was barely ten when I caught my traveling bug."

"You would be surprised at what your sister remembers," Nancy returned.

The sudden shift in tone was enough for Reagan to know that her sister's roommate hadn't stopped by to simply say hello. "Not to sound rude but, I didn't really expect to see you here."

"I thought we could talk," Nancy replied as she followed Reagan into the living room.

"About..."

"About Katie," Nancy returned. Her smile waned. "And this thing, whatever it is that's been going on between you two."

"I see," Reagan began. "I don't know that I really care to talk about..."

"Look at this," Nancy quickly reached into the pocket of her black pants and pulled out a folded piece of paper. She slid it across the table toward Reagan.

"What is this?"

"It's a note," Nancy replied. "Katie left it for me this morning while I was at the shop. It's for me, but I thought you should see it too."

Reagan took the note and immediately began to read it...

"Hey Nance,

I hope you and your friends had a good time last night and I hope if you have a hangover that this won't make it worse. I'm not very good at writing. Actually, I'm awful. I wanted to wait until you got back, but I guess I'm bad at waiting too. Honestly, I really don't know a lot that I'm good at.

But I want to be good at something and talking to Reagan today made me really, really want to find that thing. It's just hard. This whole year has been hard. Handling both sides has been hard. Not knowing who I am is hard. It's all just been really hard for me.

I feel like I'm rambling though and you don't deserve that. I'm basically writing this to tell you that I've gone to find answers. Cross your fingers they're good ones.

I'll call you as soon as I can. Hopefully I'll be home tonight.

P.S. – Troy has your number. He's had it for a while but just in case of an emergency, since I suck with phones. So if he calls...please just cover for me.

Oh, and P.P.S. – you said something last night, you probably don't remember, but when I get back I'd like to talk more about it.

Bye – K"

Reagan slowly lowered the letter. "What's going on?"

"I don't know," Nancy began before closing her eyes. She released a heavy sigh. "Well that's not completely true. I think I at least know where she's gone off to. It's completely bonkers. But what I was hoping you could tell me was *why...*what did you say to her?"

"Wait, wait, wait!" Reagan returned. "Backup. Where did she go?"

~

She heard the voices of two people, or maybe three, or maybe it was just an echo. Either way, her brain felt as though it were vibrating with each word they said. And however many people were around her, their voices had begun to get louder and the reverberations in her head became painful.

"Then do you have a preliminary report?"

"Not quite. The samples we got..."

"Did you not get enough? Because getting a needle through her skin again isn't going to work."

I wish they would stop! They're so loud and aren't even making any sense...

The conversation was definitely happening near her, but she didn't know where that was. Her body felt distant, numb aside from the growing headache. She could have been floating in the sky for all she knew.

"It's not the quantity. We've just never seen anything like it before, Commander."

Needle? Commander?

Katie's eyes opened as she realized that she wasn't dreaming. The numbness lifted simultaneously with her eyelids and she could feel a cold metal wrapped tightly around her wrists and biceps.

She was strapped down to a table!

There was sets of restraints around her ankles, her thighs, and chest. Katie immediately tried to rip them off, but something was wrong. The straps didn't budge!

"What's happening?!" Katie yelled anxiously. A nearly forgotten sense of dread had emerged again as she heard steady footsteps drawing closer to her. "Whoever is there, please let me go!"

"So good of you to join us," the voice of the Commander accompanied a sharp ringing in Katie's ears.

She could feel her breath accelerating and her eyes moved quickly from side to side. The air in the room was getting thin, the space around her was shrinking. A panic attack was coming and it was coming fast. "Let me go! Please, let me go!"

"Is something wrong?"

Katie kept trying to break loose of the straps. "Please, you need to let me go!"

The figure of the Commander finally walked into view. She didn't respond, just looked on as the blonde shook violently on the table.

"Please!" Katie pleaded as she fought to control her breath. Sweat formed on her face. She needed a distraction – big time. But the claustrophobic fit had come too fast and she couldn't calm her mind long enough to even think. Instead she found herself only able to repeat her base desire over and over and over…

"I can't breathe. Please, I can't breathe!"

The Commander sighed before signaling to someone else in the room. "Remove the restraints."

As soon as the latches loosened, Katie pushed the restraints away from her and rolled off the table. Her body made a loud thud against the floor. Once she made it to all fours, she looked around frantically until she saw a door.

Scrambling to her feet, Katie pushed her way out of the tiny room and onto the pavement. She quickly bent over and vomited.

"Feel better?" She heard the Commander call out from the doorway. Her arms were folded across her chest and she wore an impatient frown on her face.

Katie pulled her hair back and spit the lingering bile from her mouth. She barely remembered the last time she'd thrown up but she was certain it hadn't been from an attack. Those usually ended with her in tears, huddled up in a corner. But this brief and unexpected attack had been excruciating.

She breathed in and out slowly a few times before finally glancing back at the woman by the door. "What did you do to me?"

"Anything that you're experiencing right now can be blamed on your own naivety," she replied.

Kate saw flashes of the hooded Reaper. She slowly turned her hands over and saw that the scratches on her palms were still there. It was then that the rest of the pain hit her as her back and shoulders began to throb. The ringing in her ears had stopped but the headache she'd woken with while strapped to the table had only gotten worse. She went to stand but got dizzy and had to sit back down.

"What happened?" she finally asked.

"Isn't it obvious?" the Commander replied.

"You know, you can really stop being a bitch," Katie snapped. "Any time…"

"Am I hurting your feelings?" Began the Commander as she knelt next to the blonde. "I'm sorry if I'm not sensitive enough to your emotional needs."

Katie turned away, looking over her surroundings. She was outside a different building than their outpost. It was closer to the fence line bordering the park. "What happened to the others?"

The Commander stood back up and moved toward the door. "Finally interested are you?"

"Just tell me what happened!"

"They're alive!" the Commander returned angrily. "Most of them anyway. Hopefully, this cock up only ends in one casualty."

Katie recalled the horrific sight of the soldier in the forest. "Did we catch him?"

"We?" the Commander laughed. "No *we* didn't catch him. Saved you though."

Katie looked back at her hands. "When he grabbed me, it felt like a pin running under my skin or something."

"Consider yourself fortunate," replied the Commander. "A few seconds of his touch would have been enough to kill the rest of us. It appears to only have rendered you more useless."

"What is your problem?"

"You, my dear, are my problem," the Commander returned, shooting a disgusted look Katie's way. "After you and Theodore Bishop's destructive grand entrance, the world we knew ceased to exist. You see, before people like you, it was much easier to do what we do and stay hidden from the world. We've had to go to great lengths, alter our procedures, and put more bodies in the field just to keep Gillem from killing any more people…"

"Oh whatever!" Katie cut in. "You act like I know what the hell any of this is! But in case you haven't been paying attention, no one seems to want to tell me anything! Who are you people? How do you know my name? What the hell is going on? And what the hell is a Gillem?!"

The Commander didn't move for a moment but her expression softened as if she was considering Katie's questions. Finally, and much to Katie's surprise, she offered her hand. "Get up," she said. "And come with me."

The outstretched arm gave Katie more questions than answers, but she grabbed hold and let the Commander help her up.

As she followed, Katie had to focus to keep her balance. It was as if her body had forgotten how to function without powers. "Where are we going?"

"Back to the hub."

"Is that the command center outpost thing?" Katie asked.

The Commander glanced back before nodding. "You're not what I expected."

"Sorry to disappoint you...Commander," Katie returned sarcastically.

"My men call me Commander. You may call me Elizabeth."

Wow. Okay, maybe we're getting somewhere... "Okay, Elizabeth."

"You're not trained nor are you an official part of this team or organization, so there is no need for the militaristic formality," Elizabeth continued.

"Who are you?" Katie tried to stay hopeful.

But the Commander shook her head. "I am afraid that is not for civilian ears."

"Of course..."

"Trevor has told you about my strong displeasure for enlisting civilians, no doubt," Elizabeth continued. "But there are reasons behind that."

Like…?

Katie waited for her suddenly civil companion to elaborate. The Commander finally continued as the building came into view.

"I can't tell you who we are, only that we've been operating in secret for quite some time. In the past, we used civilians on projects and missions when necessary. Deep infiltration, research, and the like sometimes required such outside assistance. Generally, the civilians chosen were heavily vetted and deemed reliable. However, there was one occasion when monitoring a tremendous potential breakthrough we loosened our standards."

Katie was very intrigued now. This was a lot more information she had gotten from Trevor earlier that day. "What happened?"

"We were led astray," Elizabeth said bluntly. "And inevitably betrayed."

"Oh," Katie replied. The two continued toward the entrance to the building in silence for a few moments before Elizabeth glanced back toward her.

"You may not find me in such a giving mood later, Ms. Cattrell."

"Gillem. You said something about something called a gillem?" Katie quickly spit out.

"Bradley Gillem," Elizabeth stopped at the door to let the soldier guarding the outside open it for them. "You've been calling him the Reaper."

Katie followed the Commander along the platform. The area below had less people working in it than earlier that afternoon.

"He was an accused murderer," the Commander continued. "Though he was never convicted, the damage to his already middling reputation was done. He lost his job, his ability to gain any meaningful employment, and eventually his accommodations. Within three years of his initial arrest, he was living on the streets of Meridian."

"What?!" Katie gasped. "When did he...how did...?"

"How did he come to be in Canada?" Elizabeth prompted. "We believe he was a victim of an underground human-trafficking operation. You may have heard about it on the news. For months there were reports of your city's homeless population disappearing."

The blonde nodded. "Yeah, I think I remember hearing about that. I don't remember if the police ever found out what happened."

"They didn't," the Commander replied as she began to descend the stairs. "But we did. We discovered that the homeless individuals were being used to conduct experiments."

Katie followed closely behind her. "Oh my God, that's awful! Who would do that?"

Elizabeth nodded. "That is the painfully unanswered question. We thought we may have had an answer earlier this year. Two people were found dead in Syracuse, both suffering from a nearly identical affliction as the other Reaper victims. But the person of interest disappeared. Unfortunately, the operation was apparently shuttered before we could gather any other significant data or trace the location of the facility. What we do know is that it was in the northeastern United States, and that the trafficked were transported via boat to a port in New York."

"So Gillem was kidnapped and then experimented on?"

"That is likely the case," Elizabeth replied. "We can't be absolute, but we've been able to make a number of inferences from analyzing his victims as well samples of his blood."

Samples? Katie suddenly felt a pain in the crease of her left arm as if the word itself had just pierced through her skin. "You took samples of my blood too, didn't you?"

The Commander sighed and joined her hands behind her back. "When we learned that we could, it was the only natural conclusion. Why waste a perfectly good opportunity?" she replied.

"You could have asked," Katie returned.

"Waiting offered no guarantee," said Elizabeth plainly. "You had already regained some of your muscle mass in the minutes it took to prep you."

Katie's ears perked up and she quickly checked at her wrist. She hadn't felt the bracelet when she had first woken up in the other room. However, Katie could now see the faint outline of it fade in and out every few seconds. "Do you think it will tell you what's happened to me?"

"Possibly," replied Elizabeth. "At the very least it might confirm a few things."

"Such as...?" pressed the blonde.

"That's classified."

Katie didn't know exactly what that meant, but she bookmarked the thought and continued with the other lingering questions. "Do you know how Gillem does it?"

"Not fully, no," began the Commander. "Part of his condition seems technology-based, while the other..."

"What do you mean?"

"That's all I can say," Elizabeth returned with a look that Katie recognized as 'next question, please'.

"Okay...Well, how did you find me?"

"We have access to equipment that no one else does," began Elizabeth. "And a power like yours leaves behind certain traces. Once we knew where to look it was only a matter of time before we found you."

"That's not creepy at all," Katie replied sarcastically. "Is that how you found the Reaper?"

"His trail was decidedly more gruesome."

Chapter 22

Near Confessions

"Hi!" LJ's smile radiated life even when surrounded by death. She waved gently before putting down the scissors and scalpel. "You look very pensive," she continued.

"It's...it's just been one of those days," Wreings replied.

Her expression shifted to a somber one. "Of course. I'm sorry for the loss of your colleagues. I don't think I ever had the pleasure meeting either one of them."

"Thanks," Wreings returned. "I didn't really know either of them but...any time this sort of thing happens it's a real shame."

"I...I understand Officer McTigue and his wife were expecting?"

The detective nodded. "Yeah, they were."

The examiner closed her eyes and lowered her head. "That poor family."

"Yeah," returned Wreings quietly. "Captain is calling the widows now. I was actually coming down here to see if there was any prints or anything we got from evidence that could help us find this guy."

"Oh, I'm not sure," began LJ. "I pulled one of the bullets for ballistics to look at, but I've otherwise had my hands full."

"Of course," Wreings returned.

"I'm sure it will be ready soon," LJ nodded. The two then stood silently for a few moments while forensic techs walked by the room. Finally, LJ glanced at the occupied slabs around her. "I have a few autopsies..."

"Oh, yeah, yeah, I'll get out of your..." Wreings hastily began.

"No please," LJ quickly returned. "With everything that's happened and it seeming so chaotic down here, it would be nice to have some company...for however long you can spare it. If you don't mind me working while we talk?"

Wreings couldn't keep the smile from drifting onto his face. "Sure." He said timidly as he stepped closer to the examination table.

"So you've been busy, today?" asked the detective.

LJ glanced over her shoulder at the rows of steel cabinet doors behind her. "I've already completed two autopsies and the preliminary x-rays for this young man. Though one of those only called for an external examination."`

"So you didn't have to cut him open?" Wreings asked. "That must have been nice."

"Not really," LJ replied as she picked up a chart. It was only after she glance at Wreings' confused face that she must have realized how her answer sounded. "Oh, I hope you don't think I meant that in any morbid way."

"Well..." he began, deepening his look of confusion.

"No, no," the examiner said flustered. "I only meant..."

"Relax LJ," the detective returned with a grin. "I got what you meant...sort of."

LJ wagged her finger at Detective Wreings, but accompanied the motion with a smile. She put down the clipboard and returned to the half covered body.

"You're a hard one to read, Detective," she said.

Wreings thought he knew what she meant as an image of her leaning in for a kiss flashed across his eyes. "How are you doing?" he asked.

Her glance toward him was patient. "This morning was a more difficult one than I typically experience. However...I think it'd be premature to declare that my alcohol consumption was completely to blame."

Now he was sure.

"Look um, about last night..."

"No, I'm sorry," the examiner quickly intervened. "I should be the one apologizing for my behavior last night. I suspect you were right about the error of my calculations. I was embarrassingly intoxicated and acted very, very poorly. I know you must have been uncomfortable with...I am the one who should apologize."

"No," Wreings wished he could simply nod along to LJ's version of events. While her impaired state would have accounted for him backing away from her affections on a normal day, it had been flashes of his son's grave that really ended the night before it had even began. Hearing the regret in LJ's voice sent guilt through to his core.

Wreings rubbed his forehead and sighed deeply. "It wasn't like that...I, um...the thing is...the thing is that I just couldn't. Not last night and...I don't know."

"Why?" LJ replied softly. "Was something wrong? Did I..."

"No, LJ that's what I'm saying. It wasn't you. Not then, not ever."

The examiner looked at Wreings for a moment before turning her attention back to the body. "On some occasions, we're able to discern what happened just by examining the superficial wounds..." she began, taking a quick glance at the detective before pointing at the body in front of her. "...of a victim. But it's never just a simple gunshot to the head, or the heart, is it? Only a full examination uncovers the mystery of how they ended up where they did."

"What if..." Wreings returned hesitantly. "What if it's hard, harder than that?"

LJ looked back up at the detective. Her smile was much more muted than it usually was. "Harder than not having a clue where to even look?"

Detective Wreings let his eyes wander into LJ's. She deserved to know, but she also didn't deserve the burden, the one he'd been carrying for the past twelve years. "I meant what if what you find isn't all that inspiring? The uh...the dead don't always have that great of stories..."

By the time he had finished, LJ had taken off her gloves and come just inches away from him, similar to the night before. However, this time she wasn't looking at him with an amorous gaze. Her expression was a mix of concern and possible reassurance. Both he and the brilliant woman in front of him knew what they were talking about.

Wreings couldn't tell how much time had actually passed, but what was likely a few seconds felt like ages as he stood staring at LJ. He felt her softly brush the back of his hand with her fingers. Then, for a few moments, their hands were intertwined.

"I know there's dangers of searching in dark corners, Detective." her words trailed off and she let her hand slip away. "That doesn't diminish my desire...my *need* to know."

LJ walked back toward the slab and examined the clipboard before separating a fresh pair of autopsy gloves. Before Wreings knew how to respond, LJ was already reaching for a scalpel.

"I wish you good luck in your search, Detective," she said. "I hope you bring this villain to justice."

"Yeah..." Wreings replied. He wanted to say something else, anything else. But as LJ began to dive into her autopsy the detective thought it'd just be better to leave her be. He offered her a smile that he knew she wouldn't see and turned out of the room. He closed the door between them and took a deep breath.

"What am I doing?" he muttered.

"Are you alright, Detective?"

Wreings looked down the hall to see Officer Hopkins approaching. She had an orange t-shirt on now, but you could see the bandages on her shoulder peeking from under the wide neckline.

"Yeah, good as I'll be," he quickly replied. "How are you feeling? I thought Glades would have sent you home by now."

"I think she's going to but she's still on the phone," the young officer returned before pointing to her shoulder. "But the forensic guys wanted to check out my stab wound to see if they could find a potential match."

"Yeah, that's a good idea," the detective replied. "Sounds like it'll be painful though."

Hopkins made a knowing face as she nodded. "Yes it does. But hey, maybe it can help put a face to whoever did this."

Wreings smiled and shook his head. "You're one hell of a cop."

"Thank you sir. That means a lot coming from you," she replied shyly. "Though I'd rather you not be around when they start poking at me in the lab. I'll probably be screaming like a baby."

The detective laughed. "You kidding? There's not a cop in this building that wouldn't do the same. You've never seen the look on Don's face when someone comes at him with a bandaid."

Hopkins smiled. "I'd love to see that. Oh and speaking of Detective Donnelly, he needs you back upstairs. He's got some guy wanting to talk to y'all, said he's big time."

"Big time?"

"That's what he said," Hopkins replied. "They're using one of the witness rooms."

The detective, still unsure of what his partner had meant, started for the stairs. "Oh!" he called back to Hopkins. "I came down for the evidence from this afternoon. If you see Jess or..."

Lennox McCaskill

"I'll bring it back up with me," the officer returned.

Wreings nodded and quickly went up the stairs and back onto the main floor. His growing curiosity sped him through the desks toward interrogation. When he finally got there, Donnelly had just stepped out of a room and was pulling the door closed behind him.

"There you are," he began as Wreings approached.

"Yeah, I ran into Hopkins and..."

Wreings trailed off as his eyes met those of the well-dressed man sitting patiently on the other side of the glass. When his partner had said someone big time had come into the station, he wasn't exaggerating.

"Denard Kline?" the detective muttered.

"Yep," Donnelly returned. "Thousand dollar suit and all. Came in here and asked to speak to whoever was 'presiding over the unfortunate tragedy he saw on the news' or some shit."

"What's he want?" asked Wreings, who had yet to take his eyes from Kline.

"Don't know. I'd normally brush off these big shots but he said he knows who's responsible."

"What?"

Donnelly shrugged. "Don't know. But get this, when I finally told him he could talk to me, he remembered that you were my partner and asked that you 'be present' too."

The detective gave him a quizzical look, which Donnelly quickly returned.

249

"I guess I'm chump change compared to 'Mr. Meridian'," his partner added. He then opened the door back and insisted Wreings enter first.

"Detective Wreings, is it?" Kline said. He stood up and offered his hand. The detective tried not to hesitate and returned the gesture.

"Mr. Kline," he began. "I'm surprised you remember me."

"Still humble I see," the big man returned. "Your heroics at the Phoenix Gala weren't exactly forgettable."

"Thanks," Wreings returned with a courteous smile. He continued to stand in front of Kline while Donnelly moved to the other side of the table. Kline's demeanor instantly struck him as strange. He didn't seem nervous or worried, something he was used to seeing in suspects and witnesses alike. Wreings actually thought that the big man seemed...excited, like a kid who was trying really hard to hold in a secret. "So what brings you to the station?"

"I saw the news today," began Kline. "It's unfortunate what happened. If there is anything myself or Klymacks can do for those poor officers' families. Perhaps a college tuition fund for their children..."

"That's really nice of you sir," Wreings cut in. "I'm sure they would appreciate that. But...you told my partner you know who's behind this?"

"Yes, I do," Kline answered simply.

Donnelly leaned over the table. "So you have a name?"

Wreings wasn't sure whether it had to do with the way he felt about Kline but he could have sworn that the big man was holding in a laugh or something. He was brimming, but Donnelly didn't seem to notice.

~

If he had been unaware before, he was almost certain now. Detective Wreings was suspicious of him. He tried to contain it as best he could, but the realization had ignited a feeling of exhilaration that he had experienced only one other time.

Ironically, it had been the only other time he had made the detective's acquaintance, after he had planted a Thumpers' casino token in the wallet of Judge Richards. That was the moment he had played his opposition into check, a move that eventually disposed a number of troublesome players and cleared a path for him to continue the game.

Now, as the questioning eyes of the detective were on him, he realized that fate had given him a truly difficult task. They were undoubtedly no match for the skill of Mr. Tilte, especially with him still armed with the frequency manipulator. But having only one need left for the mercenary, Kline had to somehow find a way to give these detectives enough to advance his game while continuing to stay beyond the periphery of their suspicions.

The thrill of the game had truly picked up.

"Not exactly," Kline replied. He cleared his throat and adjusted himself in the chair. "But I think I know what the sound weapon is he used."

Detective Wreings looked at his partner.

"There was a weapon like that used, wasn't there?" Kline continued. "They reported it on the news. A number of doctors and patients at the hospital complained about disorientation after hearing a 'ringing in their ears' I believe was the phrase?"

"Yeah," Detective Donnelly replied. "Didn't realize that was already on TV."

"Yes," Kline returned. "And I thought the press in New York were ravenous."

"So what do you know then?" Detective Wreings rang in. "About the weapon."

"One of yours?" The detective's partner quipped.

The big man stared at him for a moment before returning a polite smile. "The device was meant to function as a replacement for the ear," he returned proudly. "An advanced hearing aid that would allow a deaf individual to hear *everything.* But...there was a miscalculation with a few of the components. Instead, the malfunctioning device effectively weaponized sound."

"You serious?" blurted Detective Donnelly.

Kline nodded. "Unfortunately, the elder Kline had his eyes on other things pertaining to our company's merger so the issues were never addressed. It was stolen from a truck carrying some of Kline Tech's legacy projects earlier this morning. I was hoping to fix it, as well as other unsuccessful projects."

He looked over toward Detective Wreings. He appeared skeptical as he folded his arms across his chest.

"I can imagine how this revelation sounds," Kline continued. "Especially given some of the accusations leveled against Kline Technologies, and later Klymacks. However, I can assure you that we weren't, nor will we ever be, in the weapons creation business."

"With all due respect, Mr. Kline," began the detective. "You created a weapon that was used in part to kill two police officers, a federal agent, and a suspect in a federal investigation."

"But that wasn't the purpose. No matter how much they wanted it to be..."

"Who is 'they'?" asked Detective Wreings.

Kline glanced at the reflection in the glass across from him. For a moment he could see Gregor's face expressing his approval.

"Well played, Mr. Kline."

Chapter 23

Lectures in Vulnerability

"How are you feeling?"

Katie looked up from the table to see the familiar face of Trevor standing just inside of the doorway. His right arm was in a sling and he had a large square bandage just above his cheek.

"I don't feel like complete crap anymore," the blonde replied. She took another bite from the banana in her hand and watched as Trevor approached the chair across from her.

"How are you?" Katie returned.

He maneuvered himself into the chair before replying. "I'll manage," he began, "I see you've quite the appetite."

Katie glanced down at the cluttered space in front of her. She had been too anxious to eat when she'd first arrived and found herself famished shortly after the encounter with the Reaper. Aside from the mound of wrappers from the gummy snacks and protein bars she had brought with her, there were three apple cores, the peel of her current snack, whatever was in the squeegee pack she had first demolished upon sitting down, and an empty bowl that had twice been full of oatmeal.

She took another bite of the banana before attempting to emulate the dry expression she had grown accustomed to seeing. "If that conclusion suits you. Yes."

Trevor sighed. "And there's the delightful wit."

The blonde shook her head. "Look, I really needed to eat and one of your soldiers pointed me here and said I could have anything in this box." She eyed the box sitting at the end of the table. "No one put a cap on the amount so...don't be judgey."

Trevor nodded. "It was merely an observation. With the likely level of exertion from your flight over and your run in with our target, I imagine it must take an impressive amount of sustenance to replenish your fuel."

Impressive? "Yeah," Katie returned. "I turn into a fat kid sometimes. Thanks for noticing."

"But you don't seem to show it," Trevor continued. "Your metabolism must be very advanced..."

"You should have led with that," Katie quipped. The way his eyes seemed to be examining her as if she were an exhibit in a museum made her uneasy. "Could we maybe not talk about this?"

"Of course."

"I've been thinking about the bodies in the tent," Katie began. "The reporters...there was one missing, wasn't there?"

"Obviously." There was hardly any change in Trevor's face. If he were taking any pain medication, it was doing little to loosen his emotions.

Katie wasn't terribly surprised either and quickly moved the conversation along. "Well, what happened to the other one?"

"Probably the same thing that happened to her coworker," Trevor replied.

"But you don't know," Katie returned. "In fact, how do you even know how long Gillem could survive after just one...feeding?"

Trevor leaned his uninjured arm on the table. "As I told you when you arrived Ms. Cattrell, we've been monitoring our target for some time."

"But short of him falling over and dying, you wouldn't really know for sure exactly how long he can last," the blonde returned. "I mean, that makes sense right? You guys only know what, the average time between each attack?"

Finally, the man at the other end of the table seemed to understand what Katie was getting at. "Interesting. You think he's stored food for later?"

"You mean *people*, and yes, I do," Katie replied. "I'm saying regular people can go days without actual food. They may feel bad, but it's not like they will just fall over and die from starvation until what, like a week?"

"Closer to three weeks," Trevor replied. "Before we contained him, the feedings had started to spread out more than they were in the very beginning..."

"See! If Gillem is this super-human after each attack, then what's stopping him from being able to go longer?" Katie asked, turning her eyes back down at what was left of her various snacks. "Like I did."

"An interesting perspective, certainly," Trevor replied. "But an appetite such as his would undoubtedly be harder to ignore. The fact that he'd go through multiple feedings a week at the risk of drawing even more attention to himself says as much."

The blonde shrugged. "That doesn't mean he can't ignore it, especially if he knows you guys have him trapped."

Trevor was about to say something else when he narrowed his eyes at Katie. "Why did you bring up the reporters?"

She looked him in the eyes. "Because what if the other one...what if she is still alive?"

"Are you suggesting that we form a search party?"

"Well...?" Katie shrugged.

Trevor stood from his seat and walked around the table. He grabbed the last apple from the box Katie had been eating out of. Without as much as a warning he flung it at the blonde, who bobbled it before eventually reeling it in between her palms.

What the hell?

"Can you crush that apple?" He asked plainly.

"What?"

Trevor moved until he stood next to her chair. "Can you crush it?" he demonstrated with the hand that was in the sling. "Can you squeeze the apple with your bare hands until it flattens?"

Katie almost wanted to do it, just to prove Trevor wrong. However, she wasn't sure if she could, not yet anyway. The scratches on her hand had mostly healed, but they were still there, as was the nagging pain in her shoulders, neck, and back. She placed the apple on the table.

"I take it that's a no then," Trevor began.

"Who cares about the apple? There could be someone out there who could still be alive," Katie snapped.

"With all due respect Ms. Cattrell, we sought you out because of what you *could* do to that apple," Trevor returned. "Counting what happened to Sergei, whose rations you just happen to be eating, we have lost four men. Five, if you count me, since I'd be useless in the field with one arm. And the five darts we shot into Gillem today should have flattened him, yet I can still see him running into the forest as if we had just pumped him with adrenaline. You may have survived your encounter with him but that encounter also made him a much different animal to catch. Had you worn the gloves I gave you..."

"I'm sorry, okay?!" Katie yelled. "I'm sorry about Sergei, not wearing the gloves. Sure, blame it on me. Considering you didn't tell me anything!"

"For heaven's sake it's not about blame. It's about understanding your limitations," Trevor said incredulously as he shook his head. "From the acquisition of your powers until now, I presume you've been able to cope with nearly everything thrown at you simply by using your brute strength. You likely thought you were in less danger than the rest of us when we were out there today because of your powers. Ms. Cattrell, I hope you realize the fallacy of that line of thinking. You see we – me, the Commander, this entire unit – in many ways we are actually much better off than you in these instances because we are still very familiar with our own human fragility."

He paused for a moment and took a few breaths. This was as emotional as Katie had ever seen Trevor. His eyes had widened and his mouth almost resembled a snarl as he continued.

"The fact that you've forgotten is very much a weakness, one that someone clever, or desperate in the case of our target, can easily exploit." Trevor's eyes slowly turned toward the apple, still whole as it sat next to Katie. "Because of that and your...untimely frailty, I'd say our chances against this enhanced version of 'The Reaper' would be minimal and we have to devise a different approach. Not wander aimlessly in search of an individual who appears as reckless as you."

With that, the Frenchman quietly exited the room, leaving Katie at the table to stew in her own emotions – not that she even knew how to feel about what he'd said. Trevor's blatant shaming had her heated. But what made her angrier was the inescapable feeling that he might actually be right. As she recalled her confrontation with the Reaper, she realized that she could have avoided him siphoning her

Why didn't I put on those stupid gloves?!

But where the Frenchman was incorrect was what really grinded Katie. If she hadn't grasped the reality in Gillem's powers, it was because she had only known about them for an hour before. The lack of information was as much a weakness as her supposed forgotten humanness.

In many ways, how Trevor had talked to her reminded Katie all too much of the uncompromising sister she had flown cross-country to prove wrong.

~

"I'm sorry," Reagan interrupted. "I'm really having trouble wrapping my head around this. What's in Canada and why is my sister there?"

"Someone or maybe something" Nancy began. "Anyway, there is this monster that's apparently been terrorizing parts of Toronto. There are people trying to catch it and they asked her for help. It return, they said they may be able to help her find out where her powers came from."

Reagan shook her head and took a couple of deep breaths.

"I assume Katie told you about them," Nancy continued. "If you didn't already know before..."

"Well it certainly isn't every day you see your sister fling someone through a wall," snapped Reagan. She buried her face in her palms. "I can't believe this is happening. Why...how did she even get there?"

"Well that part should be obvious shouldn't it?"

"This isn't a joke Nancy," Reagan came back. "If she's not careful she could really get herself and a lot of other people hurt. Besides, she's never been so far away before, not without supervision."

"Supervision?" Nancy began, shaking her head. "I don't have to imagine the sort of conversation you two had this morning. She's an adult, not a child. And she can look after herself pretty well."

"Are you kidding?" Reagan returned. "You know the things she's capable of now? Do you also remember that she's claustrophobic and likely agoraphobic as well? If she has any kind of episode..."

"She's doing better..."

"But there's a pretty significant difference between doing better and being better!" Reagan replied. "Have you ever been in an elevator with her? Have you ever seen her regress? Have you ever been there for her after a blackout?"

"Look, I'm afraid too," Nancy said. "But you just have to trust her now. She's done some pretty amazing things."

"And if she…If something happens, then what? I guess it's just you and me who have to shoulder that burden then," Reagan continued. "She is just like dad was. Too much like him."

"I think it's harder for her than it is for us. It was probably the same with your father," Nancy said.

"Don't talk like you know anything about him."

"You're right, I never got a chance to know him," Nancy said in a calm voice. "But I know from the few times she's actually mentioned him that your sister thought he was the bravest person in the world."

Reagan couldn't believe what she was hearing. "Stop, just stop, okay? Katie doesn't…she didn't know him, not the person that was there after mom died. She may remember him as 'brave', but really he was just too drunk to be afraid."

"I'm sure that…"

"What exactly are you sure of?" Reagan hadn't finished. "You think that flying into burning buildings or jumping in front of trucks is something to clap for? Do you know how many careless heroes I've had to resuscitate in the ER? Do you know how many I couldn't?"

"She wants to save people too!" Nancy said. "And I don't think she's as reckless as you make her sound. She's very smart you know."

"How smart is it to chase after some unknown monster for some unknown group of people in a place she's never been to?"

"I don't feel the best about it either," Nancy's reply caught Reagan off-guard. "Honestly, I don't think it really matters where her powers came from. But if this is what she needs to help find herself, then I think *we* should be as supportive as we can. That's why I came here."

There was a time when a declaration like that would have sounded so nice to Reagan. "Katie does not need to be playing hero. She's going to hurt herself or someone else."

"Your sister isn't playing a part. She *has* helped people."

"But who's going to help her?" Reagan returned. "You're not listening to me! Do you know how bad she was after the accident? She didn't talk to anyone for three months. Literally, we could not get her to speak. We had to put her in therapy, take her out of school. She quit swimming and wouldn't leave her room! And when our father couldn't figure out anything else to do, I had to."

"I know..."

"No you don't!" Reagan snapped. "And neither does she. She's hanging on to this image of dad - this 'great, brave fireman who selflessly died doing his sworn duty' - but that wasn't real. He did his job okay, but he was an irresponsible alcoholic. And the more you or other people encourage her to be like him..." She glanced at Nancy with heated eyes. "I don't want to lose her too."

"I might not know much about your father," Nancy began. "But I know a lot about Katie. Her heart is so big, Reagan. She'll follow it...use it to do the right thing. We just need to trust her."

"You're romanticizing *my* sister's life like it's some movie. It'll be your fault if something happens to her," Reagan returned.

"Excuse me?"

Reagan had tried her best to keep her feelings about Nancy out of this conversation. But the things she kept hearing come out of her mouth were just too ridiculous.

"I knew you were going to be an issue for her the moment she told me about you," started the young doctor.

"Is that right?"

Reagan held her stare for a moment before turning away from Nancy's growing displeasure. "Never mind."

"No," Nancy scooted forward on the chair. "Do tell. I'm listening."

"You're nothing like her," Reagan finally returned.

"And you are?" Nancy shot back.

"At least I can understand what she's been through."

Nancy's laugh was incredulous. "I don't think we've ever had a conversation one-on-one until now. Forgive me but, what in the bloody hell makes you think I don't understand Katie?"

"Oh I'm sorry, I forgot that you bonded during you *court imposed community service*. What was yours for again? Shoplifting or whatever it is you spoiled rich princesses do to get attention?"

"Is that who I am?"

"Oh yeah," Reagan nodded emphatically. "I didn't have to hear a word from you to know exactly who you are. I've seen plenty of people like you. If you're not tormenting girls like my sister, you're latching onto them. Whether it's because they look up to you or it's having someone weaker around to prop yourself up, I don't know. But I do know that you...people like you, have this power over them to make them do stupid things. Most of the time for your own entertainment. Only, unlike you, who has mommy's money to bail out your whims, the money that we got after...that money won't last forever."

Reagan took a second to catch her breath as her anger continued to grow. "So that 'big-hearted' Katie? I grew up calling her Margaret. *Margaret Katherine Cattrell*. And you know what *Margaret* has to do? She has to finish school – which is harder for someone who can barely sit in a crowded room without anti-anxiety medication. *Margaret* has to get a job – which is harder for someone with her mental issues. And *Margaret* has to be able to have a normal life – which is Goddamn near impossible for someone who watched their own mother die! She is *my* sister! And I don't care if I sound selfish, I don't care if I'm being mean, I only care about her! She's fragile, and as hard as I've been on her, it's always been to keep her from breaking because that's what you do when you really love somebody. You don't cheer them into danger. You don't try to confuse them with all of this other nonsense, you keep them focused, and you keep them grounded. Katie isn't a toy...*Margaret* isn't a toy, or whatever it is you're using her for."

Reagan opened her mouth to speak again, but it was Nancy whose words came quickly. "If you took one breathe of your adult life with your head out of your ass, you'd see just how wrong you are about me...and more importantly, about Katie," she began. "You would know that the fragile little Margaret isn't there anymore. Of course, Katie still gets scared. Of course she still has her moments, but it wasn't me that caused your sister to change – it was her! Did you know she rode in an elevator…?"

"What?"

Nancy quickly wagged her finger to silence any further reply from Reagan. "No, I've listened to you drag your sister's name around like it was her who has so many issues. But really it's you and I think it's time for you to understand the damage you're doing! Your sister means a lot more to me than you give me credit for. When she met me, I wasn't this little princess you're so convinced I was. Now you're right, I did try to get attention. But not because I was bored but because I wanted someone to help me…I needed someone…"

Tears began forming under Nancy's eyes and she slowly slid back down into the chair.

"Ramona was gone a lot. It wasn't always an issue when we lived with my father, but after they got divorced and she started dating…" she continued. "Most of them were okay, but never Ramona material. But then there was one, she really liked him. And to this day, I think he really liked her. But…he also really liked me."

Reagan's mouth dropped open. "Oh my God."

Nancy's mouth started to tremble. "I was twelve when it started. I hated him so, so much. But he said things like 'your mother would be heartbroken if she knew'. So the most I could ever say to her was that I didn't like him, never with any reason. I just couldn't dream of hurting her."

Her words became harder to understand as she broke down.

"Six years. I was alone, trapped for six years, and I didn't know the right thing to do," she continued. "So I did the wrong things. Many of them. Eventually, that man left me alone and then left Ramona too. I was relieved at first but then she was so upset when he left. I wanted to tell her then, about him. I wanted to tell her how vile he truly was, how repugnant. But she was already so hurt and part of me thought it was my fault. So even when it was over, I still felt...the feeling, it just...I didn't want to live with it anymore."

Guilt stirred inside of Reagan. "Nancy, I..." The words that she had spoken moments earlier echoed cruelly in her head. Her sister's friend wiped under her eyes and tried her best to smile. The expression suddenly took on a different meaning for Reagan. It was no longer pretentious or two-faced as she had long assumed. It became the mark of a struggle she had seen in the countless abused women who were brought into the MMC, and she had let her prejudice for Nancy blind her from it. "I had no idea. I'm sorry. I'm so sorry."

"So that weak, fragile girl you spoke of," Nancy slowly continued. "The one who needed supervision and needed to focus – that was me. By the time I met your sister, I didn't think much of myself...or my life. The other girls I had to work with during my service, they didn't think much of me either. And they were the ones who tormented your sister. But you know what? I'm glad they did! Because if they hadn't been so mean to Katie, I would have never asked her to sit with me for lunch...and I don't think she would have accepted. We wouldn't have become friends. I needed a friend, Reagan. I really needed someone then and I can honestly say that I probably wouldn't be here today without your sister. She saved me long before she had any powers."

Reagan just stared ahead, still in shock by what she had just heard.

"I can't believe I just told you that. You of all people," Nancy sniffled. She wiped away her tears as she took a breath. "No offense."

"By all means, offend away," Reagan returned.

Nancy finally released what was truly genuine laughter. "Being around your sister, seeing her strive to overcome those 'disabilities' you and others kept reminding her of…it made me realize how little I was doing with my own life. She inspired me to be better, at least in my everyday life. Especially recently."

She paused for a moment and then pulled up her shirt slightly, showing a purplish bruise above her waist before embarrassingly sliding her shirt back down.

Reagan's hand flew over her mouth. Nancy looked away as she continued. "I let myself be treated like I was nothing for a long time. Even believed it at times. But your sister *and* The Flying Girl – they helped me realize that I was letting my past define me and that I deserved better."

"Does Katie know?" Reagan asked. Nancy shook her head.

"Katie always thought Jimmy was a creep, but I think after last night she probably knows it now," Nancy returned. "As for me being…as for what happened to me as a child, no. Only he and I knew for ten years. It was so hard to talk about it all that I just didn't. I finally told Ramona this summer…It's funny, because for the first time I think we might understand one another. But as for your sister, I...I'd like to tell her. One day."

"I won't say anything," Reagan said. "Not that she'll probably ever talk to me again."

"Please," Nancy said, returning to her feet. "If you haven't been able to shun her with your unabashed criticism for her life choices by now, I doubt another squabble would do it."

Reagan didn't share Nancy's optimism. "Everyone has a limit."

Her sister's friend walked toward her purse, took out a tissue and wiped away the rest of her tears. "I know that you love Katie. But your way of showing it...it just doesn't work for her. Be her friend, Reagan. Be her sister. Be anything else than what you have been."

"I want to," Reagan replied. She picked up her cane and walked toward the door to join her sister's friend. "I just don't think I really know how."

The only trace of the earlier sadness on Nancy was the light pink swell around her eyes. But even that was soon concealed when she slid on a pair of sunglasses from her purse.

"You know, if you're having trouble and..." Reagan began.

"What?"

Reagan cleared her throat in the least awkward way she knew how. She was sure she had failed. "I'm sure Katie would be there for you if and when you decide to tell her the things you just shared with me. But if for some reason you're having trouble and wanted, or needed, to talk to someone..."

"I have you?"

"Yeah, something like that," finished Reagan.

Nancy smiled politely. "Thank you," she said as she stepped closer to Reagan. "But you're not my doctor and you're not my friend. To be honest, I think there are a few things you need to work out for yourself. And while I appreciate you offering what is admittedly a much needed therapy outlet for my past, I didn't come over here for that. I came here because Katie means a lot to me. Get better or please just get out of you sister's life."

Chapter 24

Prime Suspect

Kline stepped into the dusk that had settled outside the seventh precinct. He breathed in deeply and as he exhaled he remembered the look on the detectives' faces when he made his admission...

"Are you sure?" Detective Wreings had asked.

"As sure as I can be. It was over ten years ago and I barely had much to do with the actual business side of the company," he had said. "But the name, Billet Chaud, stuck out because my father had trouble saying it. He was awful at other languages. Is that significant?"

The bewilderment of Detective Wreings at that moment had been priceless.

"What's up, V?"

"Billet Chaud. That's the company that owned Thumpers," the detective's reply had been so muted, Kline could barely hear him utter those most important words. "That's Gol's company."

Kline finally allowed himself a laugh as he searched for his town car. He eventually spotted its headlights approaching from the opposite direction. He waited as it pulled up to the curb before walking toward it.

The big man took a parting glance at the police station as the driver opened his door.

"Could you take the quickest way home, Judson?" he began. "Now that the day's work is done, I'm eager for this evening's festivities."

~

"That seem weird to you?" Wreings began as he followed his partner to their desks.

"Kind of," Donnelly replied. "But the guy is a complete kook and probably the whitest black guy I've ever seen."

"No, I meant all of that," the detective returned. "I mean, this guy is part owner of this huge company and he actually walks into this station instead of calling or something."

His partner shrugged. "Probably wanted to make sure no one overheard his little bit about accidentally making weapons. I mean, I thought that shit was supposed to be a rumor."

"No Don, the thing was supposedly *selling* the tech to make weapons to international terrorists," Wreings returned. "But the way he tells it, our government put that rumor in play to pressure them to sell to the US military."

"Yeah, I wouldn't be surprised," Donnelly said. "But apparently they weren't the only ones interested..."

Wreings nodded as his partner turned his focus to his computer. "Didn't think we'd have Gol's name turn up again."

"Hey, the search came back and I think we've got something!" Donnelly exclaimed, pointing to the screen.

"What?" Wreings walked behind his partner's desk. Donnelly picked up the red, yellow, and blue striped matchbook.

"Turns out we were both right," Donnelly continued, scooting his chair over so Wreings could see the screen. "I couldn't find any hotel that still offered them. Couldn't find any restaurant or bar either."

The detective took the matchbook from Donnelly. "So that's where you were right…"

"I'm getting to you, Einstein," Donnelly continued. "When you said it looked like a European flag, I remembered that Alex from Narcotics was from Austria or something."

"Armenia," Wreings corrected.

"Yeah sure," Donnelly continued. "Anyway, he agreed and knew exactly which one: Romanian. And not only that, he says that a couple of Euro clubs in Midtown give out stupid favors like this during festivals and what not."

Anytime someone combined Europe with Midtown, Wreings automatically had to ask. "Clubs like Thumpers?"

Donnelly grinned but shook his head. "Funny, I thought the same thing. But no, I actually think it's this restaurant that turns into a nightclub inside a hotel a few blocks down on East Anderson. I was just looking it up and it turns out that the two guys who currently run it are Romanian. But…"

His partner scrolled down the page and pointed to an area marked "Owner". Detective Wreings sighed wearily, lowering his head after he read the name.

"It had to be him, didn't it?" he began. "Son of a bitch, why am I even surprised?"

"He's apparently owned it for the past five years," Donnelly continued. "So you want to go check it out?"

Wreings nodded and stepped back to let his partner stand up. "Good work, Don."

"Thanks," Donnelly replied, pointing out the set of folders on Wreings' desk. "Hey, did we get anything else on the van?"

"Actually..." Wreings turned but a figure walking through the station entrance caught his attention. It was Agent Roberts. He had cleaned up, wearing another black suit and the pretentious smirk that had been present on his face every time the detective had seen him. He held a dark brown folder by his side.

"Detective Wreings. Detective Donnelly," he began. "I didn't expect to see you here so late."

Donnelly scoffed as he put on his suit jacket. "We're cops asshole. It ain't like working a nine-to-five."

Roberts seemed somewhat amused by Donnelly's harsh return but didn't bother replying to it. Instead he turned his attention to Wreings. "Have you any updates on the evidence?"

"Maybe one or two," Wreings replied cautiously. "You got an ID on our shooter in there?"

Roberts teased the folder at both men before turning his gaze in the direction of the Captain's office. "Perhaps we should speak in a more private setting?"

"After you," Donnelly replied. Wreings followed Roberts and his partner as they walked into Glades' office.

"Captain Glades," Roberts began. "Thank you for..."

"I've got a very low tolerance for bullshit right now, Agent Roberts," Glades shot out. "I wanted an update, you said you had something, so get to the point."

It looked as though the lack of respect he had gotten from Donnelly *and* Glades in succession had done enough to sour his pretense. He opened the folder and pulled out a still from the surveillance video they had seen that afternoon.

"This is the man who is responsible for today's ambush," he stated as he handed the photo to the Captain. He waited a moment before producing another photo and handing it to Wreings. The same man was in this photo, only this one wasn't a still from the security cameras in the garage. Instead, he was standing behind a suited man at a craps table.

"I've seen this place," Wreings said, leaning to his left to show his partner.

"That's the casino at Thumpers," Donnelly said.

"This is from Gol's tapes," Wreings added. He felt like he'd said that name too many times in the last few minutes. "The ones we were *supposed* to see before..."

"Before his activities became of interest to the FBI," Roberts cut in. He pulled out another set of photos and handed one to them.

"Who is he?" the Captain asked.

Roberts looked knowingly at them before replying. "He's used a number of aliases, but we believe his latest name to be Ezra Tilte."

"A hitman?" Wreings asked.

Roberts rotated his hand slightly. "So to speak."

"What the hell does that mean?" Donnelly jumped in.

"He was utilized by a number of organizations and political factions as an operative who could 'influence' certain outcomes," Roberts replied. "Regime changes, wars, diversions, etc. We often call men like him *hands of fate*. Their assassinations are almost impossible to attribute."

Donnelly shrugged. "So he was some government's hitman?"

"Yes, but again, not your run-of-the-mill hitman. Tilte was a highly-skilled infiltration specialist and covert assassin," Roberts returned. "There were dozens of agencies besides the FBI who have at one time or another attempted tracking him. He's suspected in over one hundred international murders and assassinations, however there are only two that we can confirm were done by him. Ironically, those deaths resulted in his supposed demise in 2002."

"So why's this guy showing up now?" Donnelly asked. "And why the hell do all this just to kill some low-life terrorist?"

"And kill him in front of a bunch of cops?" Wreings added.

Roberts glanced at everyone in the room once more, only this time his expression was far more serious. That immediately got Wreings' undivided attention.

"What I am about to say," the agent spoke steadily. "Cannot leave this room."

Everyone nodded.

"We have strong reason to believe the murders of the surviving Majority members, including the two supposed suicides of Quinton and Nelson, were part of our more wide-ranging investigation," Roberts finally began. "Into an operation that we have been tracking for well over two years now. The illegal production, selling, and transporting of arms domestically and overseas."

"You mean the one you guys busted last year?" Donnelly returned.

"I thought that investigation was over?" Glades added.

Roberts shook his head. "That is our public stance on the matter. We had identified Zander Maxwell - 'Bullet' - as a key figure on the domestic side and had been monitoring him for months before Theodore Bishop came along. His unsolicited killing of Maxwell threw a wrench into all our work."

"You had to move in..." Wreings muttered. "You couldn't risk losing anyone else."

"Especially with someone as powerful and equally unpredictable as The Flying Girl still in Meridian," Roberts added with a glance toward the detective. "So all the potential we had of taking down the entire operation went up in flames before we could identify the broker or the manufacturer, or *manufacturers*."

"You think there was more than just one group making the weapons?" Glades asked.

"We have a theory about that," Roberts began. "But we were unsure how deep the operation really went."

"Well back up then," Glades pressed. "How does The Majority fit into all of this?"

"When I told you that the FBI learned practically nothing from the terrorists Quinton and Nelson, that was more of an oversimplification...at least as it pertained to Nelson's interview," replied Agent Roberts.

"What did he say?" Wreings asked with obvious anticipation.

"He said he didn't think the attack on the Wiesenberg Hotel had originally been part of their plans," Roberts returned. "Apparently, he overheard Eric Bronson and Alexa Luger referring to it as a 'paying gig from the enemy'."

"The enemy?" Donnelly began. "What does that mean? Like someone rich?"

"And crooked," Wreings added.

Glades stood up from her desk and rubbed her face. "Okay, did he say anything else?"

"Well, he also claimed that he overheard Bronson talking again some other time. Only this was with Nathaniel Byers himself, and another man...with an accent," Roberts began.

"Ezra Tilte," Wreings recalled Hopkins' description. Roberts nodded.

"Did he hear what they were discussing?" Glades asked.

Roberts again rotated his hand. "Only a little, he mostly heard times and someone referred to as the target," he replied.

"Who?" pressed Donnelly.

"Mr. Leonard Franks," Roberts replied confidently. "You see, we highly suspect that his death that night at the Gala wasn't coincidence. Especially since we had begun to suspect his involvement in our case."

"So you're saying The Majority was hired as hitmen…by another hitman?" Glades asked. "Why?"

Suddenly the words of Cameron Kelley, one of the pick-up boys for the Russian mob he and Donnelly tracked down in February, rang in his ears.

"I hear things out here, things about someone maybe looking for people who know something they don't need to know."

"Because someone wanted him and anyone else involved in the Meridian operation eliminated," Wreings threw out before Roberts could reply. The detective could almost see the fear in the troubled kid's eyes as if he were again standing across from him in that alley. It had been the last time he'd seen him alive and the boy's death had never sat well with him. The police report had chalked it up to street violence. But it appeared his last words were more prophetic than he had realized at the time.

The agent gave Wreings a seemingly appreciatory nod before turning his attention back to Glades. "That was one of our theories. Shortly after we made our arrest in November, many of the other key figures we were tracking either disappeared or were found dead."

"Like someone was clearing house," Donnelly said, giving an 'I can't believe you were right about this shit' look to Wreings.

Glades passed a subtle look to the detective as well before sitting back down at her desk. She seemed more agreeable now that Roberts had finally disclosed his findings. "Does the FBI have any idea who is calling the shots?"

"Yes, we do…"

Everyone's eyes were now fixed on Roberts who let his pause linger for a few moments. As it had the first time Wreings had met him, the Captain's office seemed to be just a stage to him. He tucked one hand in his pocket while slowly using his other hand to point to the casino photo on Glades' desk.

"Yannick Gol," was the name that exited his mouth.

"Gol?" Glades returned. "You mean the asshole you guys have in a holding cell somewhere?"

Roberts nodded confidently as he picked up one of the photos. "He was running more than his fair share of illicit activities in that casino. This picture here is the key."

Glades looked over the casino picture again before shaking her head in amazement. She turned it around for Wreings and Donnelly, who both stepped closer to view. "Recognize anyone else?" she asked.

Wreings' eyes first gravitated toward Tilte standing by the craps table in the foreground. But as he scanned the background, it was immediately apparent who Glades was talking about as he recognized another man sitting with two others at a table.

"That's Franks!" Wreings said, before taking the picture from the Captain. "And that looks like…is that Gol next to him?"

Roberts nodded. "And the man sitting across from him, the one with part of a gun exposed...that is the infamous gold-plated gun of Zander Maxwell, attached to the waist of 'Bullet' himself."

"Christ," Donnelly said. "He couldn't have been a bigger asshole..."

"We believe that he is, or at least was the broker," Roberts added. "But this picture alone proves nothing except his casino being well visited by the underbelly of Meridian. We have far more hard evidence into his other crimes than this one. That being said...potential testimony from Ezra Tilte could be what helps us finally close this investigation. Unfortunately, we were not fully prepared for him this morning and..."

"Wait, wait, wait," Glades cut in. "You said that like you knew he was coming?"

Roberts' smile was one of someone who had said too much. "The potential was high. That's why I made the..." he hesitated, throwing another quick glance at Wreings before finally continuing. "...Particular requests I did yesterday."

"Let's just find this Tilte before he skips town," Glades said after a frustrated breath.

"I think we might have a place to look," Donnelly said. "The matches found on the scene belong to this hotel on East Anderson. Guess which piece of Euro-trash owns it?"

"Gol," Glades replied. "I will be so glad if that's the last time I hear his name."

"Sorry Captain," Wreings began. "But it looks like you'll be hearing it one more time. Denard Kline, that guy from Klymacks, left the station about five minutes ago. Apparently, that sound thing that took out our guys was built by him ten years ago. It was supposed to be some kind of high-tech hearing aid but it apparently just messed you up instead. Guess who not only knew about it, but also tried to purchase the designs from Garrison Kline..."

Glades looked ready to explode. "I'll get a SWAT team..."

"No, we need to be discrete," Roberts interjected. "Tilte has proven to be a very formidable tactician. The longer we wait and grow our forces, the more likely we'll only increase the casualties on our side. Especially with him in possession of whatever this balance-altering weapon is."

"So three people?" laughed Donnelly. "Against some fated hand bullshit?"

KNOCK! KNOCK! KNOCK!

Everyone looked toward the front of the office as Hopkins stuck her head in. She immediately recoiled. "Sorry, I..."

"No please," Roberts reached out. "You may be of help."

"Officer Hopkins is off-duty, Agent Roberts," Glades said. "And I'd prefer not to put her through another ordeal like this morning."

Hopkins stepped into the office. "If I may, Captain," she began timidly. "I've been itching for another chance at bringing this guy down."

"Your shoulder?" Wreings asked.

The officer wound her right arm like a pitcher. There was a slight grimace but she did well to mask any other pain she might've been carrying. "I'm good to go."

"Well get some body armor and send a call out to the patrol units in that area," Glades said. "It might not be SWAT but at least you'll have some cover if things do escalate."

Roberts reluctantly nodded and turned toward Wreings and Donnelly. "My car is parked out front."

With that, he was out of the office. Donnelly shook his head but followed the agent outside.

"Something wrong Detective?" Glades asked.

Wreings thought for a moment before turning a confused look to the Captain. "Yeah, it's just, Gol?"

"What about it?"

"I mean, the guy is a scumbag and he probably was involved but...remember what we said about Denton Jones' apartment?" Wreings began. "The whole thing just felt staged, like *someone* wanted us to find those tokens for the casino."

"But those murders weren't connected to the arms dealing," Glades replied. "Honestly, Gol had his hand in so many pots that there is no way to iron out a motive without asking the asshole himself."

The detective slowly nodded. "Yeah, I guess you're right about that."

"Don't focus on the why right now," Glades added, giving Wreings a concerned look. "Just focus. I'm in no hurry to make any more phone calls. Do you understand?"

"Got it, Captain."

"Good," Glades said. "Now get this hitman off my streets."

Wreings nodded and turned toward the door, trying to shake the feeling that something just didn't feel right.

Chapter 25

A Night To Remember

Katie looked down over the railing at the small group standing by the computer hub. Amongst them was Trevor, who was pointing out something to a woman wearing a lab coat next to a screen. The blonde's eyes scanned the rest of the crowd in search of Elizabeth, but the Commander was nowhere in sight. Her eyes then strayed over to the display everyone seemed focused on. It looked like some sort of tracking system and when she saw a bright red dot flashing in the top right corner of the screen, she realized what they were looking at.

"That's him, isn't it?"

Her question caught everyone's attention. She hurried down the stairs and was quick to approach the crowd.

"Ms. Cattrell," Trevor said, stepping to his right to block her view of the screen. "I take it you're finally satiated?"

"No, not really," Katie shot back. Her glare bounced around from person to person until it fell back defiantly on Trevor. "You people might not think that reporter's life matters, but I do."

Trevor sighed and wiped his brow. "This is precisely why you should stay here. Heroism might read nice in a comic book, but in the real world, *this world*, it takes more than some costumed crusader rushing in to save the day. It takes tactics, strategy, and sacrifice...and the willingness to execute upon the parameters if need be."

Trevor's dry delivery made Katie think of a heartless robot.

"You don't have to come with me," she returned. "In fact, it'd probably be safer if you and your little gang stayed here."

She moved to sidestep Trevor, but he stuck out his arm to stop her. Katie grabbed hold of his bicep and squeezed lightly, which was still enough to bring a painful grimace to the Frenchman's face.

"Agh!" he yelled. Their audience quickly backed away.

"Good thing that wasn't an apple, huh?" she said before letting his arm go. Though she didn't feel at full strength, she was strong enough to not get bullied around again. Katie pushed past Trevor and returned her attention to the screen but the radar display was gone.

"You don't know what you're doing," Trevor replied, shaking away the pain from his good arm.

"Well I'm a quick learner," Katie returned. She glanced at the woman next to the screen. The reflection of the radar display was on her glasses. Katie could see her eyes through them, and she didn't nearly look as stone-faced as Trevor, or the soldiers that had just appeared next to him. Her hands were visibly shaking as they held onto the tablet.

"Could you please put it back on the other screen?" Katie asked politely. She felt her point had already been made but the woman glanced at Trevor.

"It's alright," he said. The woman nodded before returning the radar back onscreen.

Katie leaned over the desk and pointed at the flashing red dot. "Is that him? Is that the Reaper?"

"Such a ridiculous name to go on using!"

Katie turned quickly to see Elizabeth staring at her from the platform above the stairs.

"It fits," returned the blonde.

"Well, it's clear that you don't," Elizabeth returned. The scowling Commander slowly made her way down the stairs. "You're not equipped for this...*Flying Girl*."

It appeared that Elizabeth's five minutes of civility had gone. Katie had had just about enough of the way she'd been treated otherwise. "That's not my name," replied the blonde.

"Really? Yet you've let yourself be identified as that for almost a year," returned the Commander as she approached the hub. "So even your denouncement serves more as an indictment of your lack of fortitude. Not that we..." she paused and passed a quick glance to Trevor. "...Or at least I, needed the example. You see we've been watching you for some time. The fairly well-executed rescue at the Wiesenburg, presumably under the guidance of the Meridian detective, had made some consider you a worthy civilian asset. But you are childish, impetuous, and hardly as in control of your abilities as we had hoped."

It's like she only knows how to be a complete bitch...

"Whatever lady, say what you want about me. I don't care!" Katie shot back. "And I don't care if I'm the only person in this room that gives a damn about that reporter's life. What if she...what if she has children? A family?"

"Ah yes," Elizabeth shook her head. "Another reason I knew you wouldn't be able to handle this mission. The scars of your past have rendered you completely incapable of doing what's required."

"What's that supposed to mean?"

"It means that if we needed you to kill the target, you couldn't," replied the Commander coldly. "At least not until you knew whether he was without someone to mourn over his loss. You're simply not in the habit of making a necessary orphan."

Katie absolutely hated that word. No matter when it was used, it always had the same ugly connotation to her.

"Whatever," returned the blonde as she tried to keep her mind on the reporter. "Everyone deserves someone to care about them."

"How sweet," the Commander began. "How loathsomely witless. It's a shame that caring isn't a real superpower."

"Just stay out of my way," Katie returned sharply, taking note of the dot's position on the screen. She started toward the stairs only for the Commander to cut off her path.

"Move," Katie warned. When Elizabeth refused, Katie shrugged and reached for the woman's left elbow only to get a right hook thrown in her face.

The stinging blow caught Katie off balance and she fell to one knee.

"I'm not an apple either," the Commander said.

"I asked nicely," Katie said as she leapt to her feet. She quickly grabbed hold of the Commander but was again floored after a heavy knee to her stomach.

The pain was much worse this time, but she noticed Elizabeth's leg came back slightly slower like the blow had hurt her as well.

"Why are you doing this?" Katie asked.

"Because this is my command," she replied. "And in your current state you're more of a risk. Gillem is not going to wait for you to charge him, he is going to come at you. You're the unlimited buffet he's been searching for."

"I'm stronger!"

The Commander scoffed. "But clearly not strong enough, not to mention that I doubt you could handle getting in a scrap with someone you can't touch...you can hardly handle someone you can."

Katie glared at Elizabeth who seemed to have stabilized after the last hit. The rest of the people in the room had formed a circle around them, a few of the soldiers were holding their weapons. What she hoped was going to be a show of strength had degenerated into the sort of fight she'd had in high school. Only this time, the bully standing across from her wasn't prissy Tina Aldridge.

She considered trying to fly but was worried that she still couldn't. So she tried again to muscle past the Commander, only to get flipped on her back.

But Katie was quicker to respond, grabbing Elizabeth's ankles and pulling them out from under her. The Commander fell but flipped herself back up in seemingly one motion. She swiftly lashed out with a kick to the blonde's ear.

"Ow!" Katie screamed.

Lennox McCaskill

Okay, I'm through being nice.

The blonde rushed at the Commander and tackled her to the ground.

"Ugh!" her adversary groaned as her back hit the floor. Katie naturally let up when she heard the pained cry which was just enough to be tossed to the ground by the Commander's unexpected counter.

"Jesus lady! I don't want to hurt you," Katie shouted.

Elizabeth spun around to all fours. "But I *will* hurt you to protect this mission."

"You're crazy..." the blonde said, taking a few steps back before offering a wave. "And on the wrong side of the room."

The blonde quickly made a dash for the stairs but only made it a few steps up before she felt arms wrap around her neck.

"Determined is the word you're looking for," the Commander spit into her ear.

Katie tried to shake the woman from her back but only felt the hold tighten.

"Let me go!" Katie said, feeling a tingling heat rise up from her arm. She glanced down to see the outline of the bracelet wavering in and out around her wrist again. Suddenly, her skin felt like an oven. In an instant, all the noise around her faded away, giving rise to the sound of crackling fire.

She quickly looked around. There was no facility, no crowd, and no Elizabeth. A blinding blue light flashed in her eyes. When it disappeared, Katie found herself staring into a raging fire.

289

"Aghhhh!" she heard a familiar male voice cry. Katie tried to peer past the flames but they seemed to move as she did. The voice cried out again and the blonde realized that someone was trapped inside the fire.

She reached for her phone but soon realized that it wasn't there. She watched as two ends of a bracelet slowly crawled toward one another until they met around her wrist. A searing pain shot through her body. Katie quickly realized what moment she was reliving.

"What's happening?!" Katie heard her voice but it sounded more like an echo in her head rather than something she said.

The glow of the bracelet soon engulfed most of her hand. Once it spread to her fingers it arced up and over until she was holding an orb of energy the size of a bowling ball.

It felt as though Katie were standing in the fire, but she realized that it was her own skin that was scorching hot. As smoke rose from beneath her feet, the blonde quickly saw that she was burning through her clothes.

The orb started sparking and looked like it was going to burst at any moment.

"Don't hold it in, Margaret..."

Katie turned toward the voice she'd heard. "Mom?"

"Let it out, baby girl. Let it out!"

Without another word, Katie threw her arm forward, releasing the orb into the woods. The crackling stopped, the burning feeling went away, and the vision disappeared with the hurling ball of energy. Katie soon found herself looking out at a silent audience atop the steps of the platform. The Commander had released her. Compared to the others, her face was not one of complete shock, but the expression she wore was much less cold than it had been during Katie's stay. It sort of looked as though she were impressed.

What's going on?"

Katie's eyes continued to move around the room, peering at each stunned face that was pointed to hers. Her eyes widened as she finally noticed a dark hole in the wall. Steam rose from the edges of the perfectly round opening. Katie turned her attention to her hands as the last remnants of the memory flickered in her mind before fading away, along with the sight of her bracelet.

"Aren't you full of surprises," Elizabeth began, pulling herself back up to a standing position on the steps. She turned her attention to the hole in the wall and quickly went over to inspect it.

"What happened?" asked Katie.

"You tell me," returned Elizabeth.

Trevor left the crowd to join the Commander at the wall. Katie followed suit. As she approached, the circle of people around her parted.

"That was some blast," Trevor said.

"Yes it was. I hate to imagine what would have come of me had I not dodged it. She may not be a complete lost cause after all," Elizabeth said. She signaled to one of the non-soldiers back at the computers. "Get a reading of this, now."

"A reading on what?" Katie was almost at the wall when the Commander stopped her.

"There may be a way to get what we both want," she began. "Can you do that again?"

"Right now?" Katie asked.

Elizabeth rolled her eyes. "Of course not now. I don't need to turn this facility into Swiss cheese. I meant could you replicate a similar blast from long range?"

The blonde looked past the narrowing eyes of Elizabeth to the hole. *I have no clue...*

"If I had to," she replied. "I guess."

There was a moment of hesitation from the dark-haired Elizabeth, almost as if she could see through Katie's pretense. However, she soon nodded and turned toward the Frenchman in the sling. "Get a rollout group ready."

"Yes, Commander."

"Keep it small," Elizabeth added. "And show her how to use the cuffs before you move out."

"Wait," Katie cut in. "You're going to help me?"

"*You're* going to help us take down the target," returned the Commander. "And if the reporter is still alive then you will have saved her as a byproduct."

Katie smiled slightly as solders passed her.

"Oh, and another thing."

Katie turned to face the Commander.

"In the field it will be just you, my men, and him," the woman continued. "Don't mess this one up."

Chapter 26

Our Own Devices

Something was off. Kline hadn't left the balcony door open, yet the faint addition of white noise inside his usually serene suite was unmistakable.

Denard Kline restarted the knotting process for the yellow tie he'd chosen and left the bathroom, continuing out into the main room. It was dark but there was light from outside. His eyes moved from the mantle of the fireplace to the round table by the kitchen area, before settling on the balcony.

There was no one standing outside and it didn't appear that there was anyone in his suite either. He soon realized that with his attention elsewhere, he'd done his tie incorrectly. With a sigh, he undid it, confirmed that the balcony was sealed, and closed the curtains.

As he began to head back toward the bathroom mirror, he stopped and let his hands fall to the side. He looked over his shoulders at the large red curtains covering the outside view of Meridian.

"I prefer to keep my privacy," he said, glancing toward the shrouded corner of his suite. "Especially amongst the clouds."

From out of the darkness emerged the figure of a woman wearing an equally shadowy toned outfit. Her jet black hair partially covered the eye patch she wore. Had she not had such a pale complexion, it would have been a struggle to even see her face.

"I see you're already dressed, Ms. Paklovic," Kline continued. "I wish I could say the same. But I can't seem to complete this knot. I don't suppose you've tied one of these before?"

She didn't respond to his sarcasm. Instead, she walked toward his bed and ran her hand along the embroidered headboard. Each step Paklovic took was deliberate as the heel of her boots whispered against the floor.

Kline wasn't sure what her intention was, as he remembered Tilte's warning about the mercurial assassin. But while he didn't want to bring out any of her violent tendencies, he also didn't want such worries to allow any lapses. "And not to be rude," he began. "But the less evidence that exists of you actually being in here..."

Paklovic looked over her hands before pulling a pair of gloves from the thin pouch on her hip. As she slid them on, Kline backed away toward the bathroom, careful to keep the woman in his periphery.

"Thank you," he muttered. He turned on the faucet and brought handfuls of water to his face. He spoke over the water as he continued. "Now, you've had some time to get better acquainted with the city I presume?"

~

It amazed her how talkative this man was. It was almost as if he was more afraid of the silence than her. She stepped into view of his mirror and pulled one of the knives from her leg strap. The action drew a mild look of concern from the big man, though he tried to hide it. But his eyes betrayed him when they followed the blade as she tossed it from hand to hand.

She watched as he turned off the water and dried his face delicately with a towel. His attention then strayed to the other side of the mirror. "Yes, I'm sure," he said, though for the first time it seemed as though he wasn't addressing her. She stepped to see if there were someone else in the bathroom with him, but there was no one. Who was he talking to?

Kline then returned his gaze to her. He seemed to hesitate for a moment before turning to walk past her and back into the hallway. He made it as far as the table before pulling out a chair and motioning for her to come over.

How strange.

"I do have a dinner engagement I need to get to," he began, glancing at his watch. "So let's attend to our business, shall we?"

The assassin raised a brow before walking over to join him. She declined his invitation to sit.

Kline offered a curious smirk before seating himself at the adjacent chair. There was a computer on the table and when he opened it a dull green light shot out from the tiny hole at the top. It flickered a line across his eyes before producing a gentle chime.

"Retina scan complete, welcome back Mr. Kline."

A computer that speaks? How interesting.

"She's broken from her normal patterns," he said excitedly, attending to his tie as the machine in front of him loaded. "And though I can assure you that she will not be there, I don't know with any certainty for how long."

He pointed to the screen and glanced toward her, as if it were some unspoken cue for her to come look. She bored easily with technical buildup. The only thing she needed to know was where to be, when to be there, and which weapon to use. She had already done the man one favor and that was out of character. Whatever this unexpected task was he was going on about now made it sound as though she were about to make that two.

"The indicator...*here*," Kline said, putting an emphasis on the word denoting the placement of his finger. He glanced at her questioningly. Paklovic finally walked behind him and turned her eye to the screen. The screen was broken into a grid with a small blue dot in the middle. It had a glowing aura around it, but otherwise was unexciting.

~

"Thank you," continued Kline, unsure why this assassin was struggling to obey his commands. "This indicator hasn't moved since I found this particular energy signature last February."

Kline then typed in something on the keyboard that expanded the grid, showing the outline of the United States. The woman immediately pointed the tip of her knife to a set of separate flashing dots just beyond the top of the map. They were almost right on top of one another. Kline expanded it one more time to show the connected outline of Canada.

"Yes, this is what I was saying," he continued. "One of these two indicators belongs to The Flying Girl. The other..." Kline paused and narrowed his eyes at the other dot. He groaned in frustration. "The other is an unfortunate leftover from another project. But that's a problem for another time. The important thing is that her behavior marks a far departure from her normal."

The woman behind him released a breath. Kline was mindful of the open blade in such close proximity, but kept his focus on explaining his goal.

"You may have more time on your hands than I originally accounted for," he continued. "But I want to be sure. So for now we will stick to the original time we discussed previously. 10 PM."

Paklovic tapped the side of the knife against the chair before stepping back and wandering toward the fireplace. Kline watched her, somewhat impatient with her lack of understanding and urgency. It was a far cry from Tilte's professionalism, at least when it came to business. But the way things had played out, he needed the versatility of another queen.

The assassin had gotten close in proximity to the Zeus statue on the mantle. It was clear that it had her attention. Soon she was just an arm's length away and Kline could see a curious expression on her face.

"Believe me, Ms. Paklovic!" his exclamation thankfully distracted her before she could follow through on her curiosity. "I understand your frustrations. The wait for this moment has driven me crazy as well..."

The woman's mired stare made it clear she had been unhappy with his choice of words.

"Figuratively, of course," Kline continued, gifting a smile that he hoped would serve as a placating gesture. He hardly had the time or desire to increase his stress levels with another disgruntled associate. "But even so, I've been tracking her energy signature for months and tonight might be the only night that she's gone long enough and far enough away to finally get it! So this plan has to be carried out with extreme precision and caution. There are no contingencies. I prefer not to have anyone, or even The Flying Girl herself, walking in on you as you search for it."

~

Search? The more this man spoke the more Paklovic wanted to slit his throat. He must have sensed as much as he made another adjustment to his tie.

"I also meant search figuratively," added Kline as he stood up from the table and walked back to his bedroom. She followed closely, knife still drawn.

"There's a small box in the side pocket of that suitcase," he pointed in the direction of the closet before stepping into the bathroom. She walked past him as he continued to speak. "In it, you'll find a black device that is programmed to alert you when you're near the energy signature."

Paklovic eyed the suitcase for a moment before retrieving the small circular device.

"Once activated, it will vibrate intermittently when you're within one hundred feet. With each additional ten feet, the vibrations will become more sustained."

The assassin rotated the device in her hand until she saw the outline of a button. Naturally she pushed it, prompting the tiny device to tremble every few seconds in her palm. The vibration was hardly audible and the small green light to indicate the device was active wasn't too obtrusive. It would be useful, so long as it worked.

When she stepped out of the closet, the time between the vibrations shortened. Paklovic stared at it in confusion before taking another step forward. The vibrations came faster still. By the time she was back at the bathroom the device wouldn't stop shaking, though a red light had appeared in place of the green one from earlier.

She glanced up to see Kline looking at it from the bathroom mirror.

"That light means that while a similar signature is...very close, it's not an exact match to the one I calibrated the tracker with," he began. "The light would be flashing green otherwise."

He turned around to face her and offered to take the device. After a moment of hesitation, she placed it into his open palm. Kline held down the button until the device appeared inactive again.

"Trust me," he began. "It works."

~

"Trust?" Katie laughed. "I think I remember you saying something like trust wasn't required?"

"Touché," he replied as he walked through the door. "But at the very least, you understand that there is no margin for error here?"

"Yeah, I got it," returned the blonde. She zipped up her jacket as she stepped outside. The night was much colder than in

Meridian and her thoughts turned toward Troy and Nancy. She checked her phone but there was still no service.

"Are you ready then, Ms. Cattrell?" Trevor asked.

Katie nodded and lifted the green briefcase at her feet off the ground and onto the back of the nearest truck. She unlatched it and stepped back, letting Trevor open it the rest of the way. He signaled one of the soldiers nearby to do it instead.

Katie noticed him grimace as he moved. "How's your arm?"

"Which one?"

The blonde shrugged. "I asked you to get out of my way."

"Indeed," returned the Frenchman. "But it is important for us to hold our resolve, even in the face of a disproportionate contest. Which reminds me, how are you feeling?"

"On a scale from one to ten..." Katie paused and tried to feel a connection to the force of the bracelet. After a few moments she thought she could feel it rolling from her wrist up her body and back down her torso. It found its way through her legs and to her feet, before gently pushing her off the ground. She held herself in the air for as long as she could before dropping back to solid footing.

Her calves felt strained and she wasn't sure if she could do that again at the moment. But Katie hoped that the brief display of control would help ease the minds of the men around her.

"Pretty close to an eleven," she finally said confidently, hiding the fact that she was drawing extra breaths.

Trevor nodded in approval and signaled to the rest of the men to finish packing. "Very good, but that could mean that we'll be catching a very hungry target."

Katie glanced behind Trevor at the other soldiers. "Maybe you should all stay here," she said. "If you just tell me where he is..."

"This mission still requires strategy, Ms. Cattrell," Trevor cut in. "And while your foray with the Commander may have somewhat proven us wrong about your capacity to develop raw tactics, the experience of myself and these men could well be the difference."

"I don't want anyone else to get hurt," Katie returned.

Trevor glanced at her momentarily before motioning the blonde to return her focus to the briefcase. "Take a look at these."

The interior of the case revealed what looked like two large metal mittens in a cushioned space. "I take it these are the cuffs Elizabeth was talking about."

"Yes, and they're how we intend to neutralize Gillem," he returned. "The inside of these are designed to mold around his hands."

"Like a glove?"

Trevor nodded. "And once activated, they become magnetized, binding his hands together like handcuffs. He would also be injected with a sedative on each of his fingertips by the small needles we've placed inside."

"Ow," Katie shuddered at the thought.

"Ideally, the higher concentrated dose we installed will have him unconscious before his brain can even register that he's been stuck," Trevor finished.

"Wait, if he's not getting the sedative until after he's cuffed, how exactly are we planning to get these on him?" Katie asked Trevor, who returned the cuffs to their place in the case before responding.

"These were designed some months ago, when we thought it may be possible to apprehend him while he was hungry," he began. "We adapted when the need to modify our approach bore its head, hence why we created rounds of sedative as munition."

"But I thought the sedative didn't work on him?" the blonde quickly countered.

Trevor nodded. "Yes, but we've increased the potency. Just one prick to any finger inside of these devices would almost kill a regular human, and that's a tenth of what we plan to inject him with. Even then whatever the effects of the sedative are secondary to containing his primary source of attack."

"I get it," Katie looked toward her hands and nodded in realization. "So you want me to take him out with a blast first, then slap these on to keep him contained?"

"Precisely."

Katie clenched her fists as she continued to nod. "I still think you should keep your men as far away as possible. I don't want anyone getting hurt on accident, you know?"

"My men will form a perimeter around you and will only engage if necessary," the Frenchman replied, reaching into his pocket to pull out a crescent-shaped earpiece. "I will trail the party in the truck. I'll communicate with this. You simply need to tap the small button on the back to respond."

Katie fit the rubbery device onto her ear. She was about to test it out when she saw one of the soldiers carrying the remote control looking thing she'd been greeted with.

"Elizabeth said you could track me by the energy I put off," she pointed to the device the soldier was carrying. "And you said the same thing about the Reaper."

The Frenchman glanced in the direction she was pointing, but he quickly turned back toward his vehicle.

"I promise Ms. Cattrell, once we've contained our target we'll have all the time in the world to talk."

Chapter 27

Numbing the Pain

Reagan didn't want to talk. Instead she sat as patiently as she could on the couch as she waited for her aunt to return. The flashes of light she saw out the window weren't yet accompanied by the boom of thunder, but the storm was definitely on its way.

She hoped Laine would make it back before the rain picked up any further. Her aunt had a tendency to pull over and wait out bad weather rather than drive through it. With her hysterical sister crying in the next room, Reagan preferred not to be there any longer than she had to. The falling rain did its best to drown out the sobs, but whenever there was a let up, they came through loud and clear.

"Margaret?" Reagan called. "Margaret, would you turn on some music or something? You're giving me a headache."

"Screw you!" her sister screamed back.

Reagan sighed, again glancing at her phone to check the time. She noticed a missed call and message from Laine and quickly checked her voicemail. It didn't take long into the message for any hope she had of leaving soon to disappear. The torrential downpour had already made it to the other side of town and her aunt had decided to stop at the store to get groceries and wait it out. Of course.

"Great," Reagan muttered in frustration. The doctor slid her phone back into her scrubs. She hung her head and clasped the back of her neck with both hands. "Thanks Laine."

The forecast for the evening looked bleak – on many levels. The worst of the storm was supposed to hit within the next half hour. That meant her aunt probably wouldn't be home any time soon to take over the 'babysitting'. Reagan had hoped to enjoy the rare night off studying but Laine's ridiculous proclivity for caution left her stuck.

"Everyone in this family is crazy," she said. Reagan breathed in and attempted to keep herself from getting too worked up.

The young doctor closed her eyes and let the stormy sounds from outside be her therapy. Soon the wind stopped pelting the rain into the window and for a few moments there was peace. But of course it didn't last as Reagan's ears easily picked out her sister's whimpers. She shook her head before finally leaving the couch and walking down the hallway.

"Margaret?" she began, nudging the door to her sister's room. She hadn't been in it for over a year, but through the small opening she could see the bed had been moved to fit into the corner by the window. Her sister had her head buried and her arms were wrapped tightly around her knees. Her hideous brown satchel and its contents had been strewn in front of the dresser; the black converses flung to the foot of the bed.

Reagan pushed the door open the rest of the way but didn't move from underneath its frame.

"You can't let it get to you," she began. "I mean them, people. All you're doing is putting a bigger target on your back."

"Go away."

Reagan shrugged as she reached for the door knob. But before she could close the door all the way she saw a familiar photo taped onto the mirror next to the dresser.

It was the four of them from one Christmas morning. She had to have been about eight when it was taken and doing her best not to smile while her mother tickled her sides.

"You *will* smile for this one you little curmudgeon!" her mother had teased.

"I will not!" Reagan remembered saying in between her adolescent cackles.

Margaret hadn't needed the incitement, she had always smiled for the camera. The little blonde stood in her Snoopy pajamas, a huge smile on her face and her wiry arms wrapped tightly around their father's neck.

"I think I got it working this time," he assured. It had been his third attempt at using the timer of the camera. "Everyone say cheese!"

"CHEESE!"

The camera snapped. The photo was taken. A carefree moment was sealed into the confines of a photograph that would serve as a reminder of a time when happiness still existed.

Reagan stared at the picture a little longer before taking a deep breath and entering the room. She took a seat on the bed just in front of her sister's shoes.

"Can I see your hand?" she asked gently.

Margaret's blonde strands shook from side-to-side, "Leave me alone."

"I will," Reagan returned. "Once you show me your hand. I want to make sure you didn't break anything."

Her sister finally lifted her head. Her face was bright pink, especially underneath her eyes. "It's not like I hit her that hard."

"You hit her hard enough to knock her out…"

"I did not!" Margaret shot back. "Tina was fine! I made her nose bleed and that was it! The other girls made up all that other stuff because they hate me!"

"Alright, alright, just let me see your hand," Reagan asked again. This time her sister stuck out her arm and laid her hand into Reagan's palm. The spot between her middle and pointer fingers was already turning purple. "Wow that's going to be a pretty bad bruise. Does it hurt when I…"

"OW!"

Reagan let go of the spot. "…touch it. Okay, let me get you some ice. Hold on."

She hurried to the freezer and picked up the first bag of frozen veggies she could find before coming back to the room.

"Here, hold this on the bruise," Reagan said. Her sister huffed once but followed the instructions. "This should help a little."

"Thanks…"

Reagan let go of her sister's hand and looked her over. "Laine doesn't want to drive in the storm. Do you need something to eat?"

Margaret shook her head and leaned back into the corner.

"Have you even eaten today?" Reagan asked, receiving what seemed like an uncertain nod in return.

A few seconds of silence passed before Margaret exhaled and tossed the vegetable medley on the bed and went back to holding the position Reagan had found her in.

"Margaret, you can't..." Reagan began in frustration before pausing again to keep herself from getting overly angry. Sitting with her sister was like being with a trauma patient. She needed to be careful not to push her too far. "...I know it's been hard for you since you moved here, but you have to do better to fit in."

"I'll never fit in," her sister returned.

"That's not true."

"That *is* true!" Maraget snapped. "And I don't need a lecture. I'm sure I'll get an earful whenever Laine gets home."

"Well you need one," replied Reagan. "Because you can't go around hitting every single person who calls you names or pokes fun at your claustrophobia."

Margaret shook her head. "That's not what happened! I told you that's not what..."

"I don't care what happened, Margaret!" Reagan shot back. "You have to be smart..."

"Stupid orphan."

Reagan immediately glared into her sister's watery eyes. "What did you say?"

Margaret sniffled as she stared ahead. Her lips trembled and her face looked as though she had the taste of something sour in her mouth.

"Tina asked if she could have my invitations," she began. "For graduation. She wanted more people to be there to cheer for her. She'd never talked to me before. We had three classes together but not one word…until today. That's why I said, 'Why are you asking me?' And she smiled…she actually smiled like she was going to say something super nice. But she said that I didn't need them, because 'how many people could a stupid orphan invite anyway'…"

The tears started pouring again and soon Margaret had dug her face into her knees again.

Reagan was left in somewhat of a shock. Two or three minutes may have passed before she finally knew what she needed to say.

"Lashing out isn't going to bring them back, Margaret," she replied.

Her sister picked her tear-stained face up to glare back at Reagan. "Do you even miss them?!"

BOOM!

The sudden rip of thunder startled Reagan awake and she shot up on the couch. She quickly looked around for her sister only to realize that she wasn't at Laine's but in her own apartment. She didn't remember falling asleep, but she must have been out for a while. The room was completely dark now, save the open laptop beside her on the coffee table.

She yawned as she picked it up. Part of her wanted to keep reading, but she figured she had a pretty good handle for how to diagnose PTSD.

Thunder sounded overhead again. She propped her elbows on her knees and wrapped her hands around the back of her neck. As she breathed in, she felt a stray tear land on her cheek. She figured it must have been a remnant from the dream she'd had.

She hated the memory of that night. Even more so lately because it constantly found its way into her subconscious, along with seemingly every bad memory from the past year. Part of her felt like she deserved the torment. After all, when faced with one of her sister's many weak moments, Reagan put on the brave face she had perfected over the years and basically told her sister that '*she didn't have time*' to miss their parents. It had been a response that elicited more crying from her sister back then and more guilt in Reagan now.

"I do," she said shakenly as she looked around her apartment. "I do miss them...and I miss you..."

She knew the words she was muttering now were words she should have said years ago. She also knew that Katie may never be patient enough with her again to listen.

Her sister was gone, with no one to look after her. She could be hurt herself or accidently hurt someone, and all because Reagan did what she always seemed to do.

Reagan braced herself on the couch as she stood up slowly. Her legs were still slightly sore but the pain in her back felt as bad as it ever had during the entire recovery. Each muscle seemed to scream out as she stretched to straighten it. Reagan held in a scream as she reached for the cane that was leaning against the table. She had almost gotten her fingers to it when pain whipped up her spine.

"Agh!" she said as she toppled to the carpet.

Reagan lay motionless as the sound of the rain trickled in from outside and the various images of her sister's tear-stained face rippled inside of her head. She began to feel the warm pressure on her face and soon, she was crying into the coarse fibers of the floor.

She wasn't sure how long she stayed there, only that the storm worsened by the time she made it to her knees.

Using the cane to stand, Reagan slowly limped into the kitchen, grimacing with every step. She opened the cabinet by the fridge and reached for the closest cup she could get and filled it with water. Her eyes quickly turned to the shadow of the pill bottle on the stand by the couch.

As pain reverberated inside her, Reagan knew that she had to be numb again.

Chapter 28

Tipsy Encounters

Kline clasped the stem of the glass and swirled the wine as he contemplated taking a sip. Slater, on the other hand, was blissfully coming to the end of her second glass.

She wore a green dress, this one closer to the curve hugging variety that had first enticed him at the Gala. But the key differences were the embellishments she had decided on taking that evening. Her hair was down, straightened in a way that seemed to denote a lengthy preparation. It fell just over the dress straps on her otherwise bare shoulders, which like the rest of her skin appeared more sun-kissed than the previous day.

"I'm so glad to hear that you're on board," she added, her glass midway to her mouth. "I'll send you the draft proposals first thing in the morning."

"Thank you," Kline returned. "I've always thought about giving back to the city I grew up in, on a personal level. I think this project of yours will help me do just that."

Slater smiled and placed her glass down on the bar. "I appreciate you being a good sport about all of this. I know you're probably tired from talking about business all day."

"On the contrary, Ms. Slater," Kline returned as he raised his glass, finally bringing the edge to his lips and slowly tilting it up. He analyzed the taste as the ruby red liquid washed over his tongue. The sample was too fruity at first, but the hint of cinnamon toward the end made it palatable. Kline took another, more prolonged sip. "I look forward to our conversations, regardless of the subject matter."

"You're quite the charmer, Mr. Kline," she replied.

"It's funny, you're the only one who tells me that."

"I call it like I see it," she laughed. "I was looking forward to talking with you tonight too, and not just about the project."

It was a candid admission, and though it caught him off-guard, Slater's words satisfied Kline. He smiled in reply, cautiously hoping that she would continue.

Slater maintained her smile, though now she looked to be somewhat embarrassed. "I admit, I had only done cursory research on you, Ms. Lymacks, and your company before we first met," Slater's voice was tickled with what sounded like playful guilt. "But it mostly centered around your bio and the unbreakable metal. It wasn't until after we spoke that I became more and more intrigued with some of the things y'all used to do. I never really got into computers or that sort of thing so it's all so fascinating to me. So, I do have an ulterior motive for asking you here tonight."

"Do you?"

She nodded and was about to continue, but the hostess who had sat them at the bar stepped in beside them.

"I apologize for the mix-up," she began. "Your table is just about ready ma'am."

"That'll be fine. Don't worry about it. We've been enjoying the bar..." Slater glanced at Kline's mostly full glass. "...at least I have."

The big man smiled and took another sip of the wine. "I've learned to take my time."

"Well again, I do apologize, Ms. Slater. Someone will be right with you to show you to your seats."

"Thank you!" replied Jameson Slater.

As the hostess walked away, Kline returned his glass to the wooden counter. "So what is it that really brought us here, Ms. Slater?"

"Right," she began. "How does it work?"

"How does what work?"

She pushed her now-empty glass to the side. "How do y'all make that unbreakable metal?"

"You won't give up will you?" Kline laughed. He'd known the question hadn't been far away. She'd asked at least once every time they had met with one another. "The details would bore you."

"But see, that's the thing - I love those details," Slater returned excitedly. "Honestly, I think it's because I could never think of these sorts of things myself."

"We've gone to great lengths to keep our process a secret," Kline replied.

Slater pressed her lips together before pulling an invisible zipper across. Kline's smile grew. Something about the interest Jameson Slater had in his work was gratifying to him. For so long he had simply been a hidden figure, rarely having opportunities to explain the intricacies of his innovations. Small minds like those of the detectives could only focus on the tasks at hand while the unappreciative ones like Lymacks could hardly be bothered with the means that filled their pockets.

As he stared at Slater, there was a genuine look of wonder in her eyes. The kind of look he used to get from Gregor, whenever Kline would tinker in the confines of his suite at Ivory Towers. It was a look that he desperately missed and one that excited him. So much so that he decided to go against the repeated thought in his head.

"Nanotechnology," he replied.

"What's that?"

"It's basically like utilizing tiny, microscopic computers, millions of them. We can construct and program nano-components to complete simple tasks or design them to take on certain elements and their properties, like carbon or hydrogen."

"That certainly doesn't sound boring at all," Slater returned. "But how do you get it so it makes a piece of steel unbreakable?"

"We have a process which introduces nanites to change the composition of the steel into something much more durable without altering its basic function," Kline replied.

Jameson Slater leaned forward like an eager pupil. "That is so interesting! I don't know that I've even heard of something like that."

"Well the use of nanotechnology is far from widespread in most industries," he replied. "But it's becoming more common now in the medical industry. Which is where Kline Technologies primarily was before the merger."

"Oh that's right! Y'all used to make medical equipment."

"Indeed we did, though the official line back then was that we made 'advanced medical solutions' for the common man," he said. "Heart monitoring equipment, x-ray devices, pacemakers, even hearing aids - all reimagined and redesigned with advanced technology."

"If you don't mind me asking," Slater began. "What happened? Just about everything I have read about the merger between your father's company and Lymacks Incorporated was light on the details."

"And you love the details," Kline said.

"I didn't mean to seem nosy..."

"No, no I am sorry for that," he replied quickly. The thought of Garrison Kline always agitated him, especially when it came to the days of the merger. Kline could almost hear the voice of his so-called father as he finalized the deal with Benjamin Lymacks over the phone, compounding his treachery.

"I'm sorry Denard, but business is business."

Kline shook away the memory and offered an apologetic smile to the confused Jameson Slater.

"It was an astute business decision, but one that I didn't particularly care for," he added. "Kline Technologies made revolutionary, wondrous things that, unfortunately, regular consumers could not afford and most investors didn't trust. Lymacks Incorporated was a declining company lacking in innovation and had only managed to stay afloat because of their cunning business acumen."

Kline waved his hand in the air as though he had finished some elaborate magic trick. Slater's eyes showed that she was listening intently. "So Klymacks was born! But like most arranged marriages, the relationship was hardly a warm one. Our products, my inventions...my work - the programs were quickly dismantled."

Slater seemed even more confused. Kline attributed it to an understandable ignorance on the subject. "Did you ever hear of the Kline Tech Remote Defibrillation System?" he asked.

"No, but defibrillation is that thing," she replied, demonstrating with both hands. "With the paddles?"

"Yes," Kline nodded. "The typical device was restricted in mobility, but I thought there might be a way to minimize the obtrusiveness of the device without losing its function." He wiggled his fingers. "In the end our engineers created an exoskeleton that fit like a glove around the fingers and palm. It had a power cell that was five percent stronger than the standard lithium battery and had the ability to generate an even stronger pulse to revive the heart."

"Oh wow," Slater replied.

"Seeing it finished would have been like watching a dream become a reality," Kline continued. "But it never made it past the testing phase. My father let Ben Lymacks strip it down and market the power cell and the pulse generator - both of which we secured patents for - separately. The same became true for everything except for our nanotechnology development. That was too valuable to sell..."

Kline suddenly realized how aggressive he was sounding and let out a light laugh to gloss over his mood. "The technology needed to be refined and implemented elsewhere to save lives, not become just another item at a grocery store."

Slater seemed to have already sensed Kline's frustration. She reached over and placed her hand on his arm. "But selling the ingredients is sometimes just as important as cooking the meal, isn't it?"

"Only if the meal is prepared for the same purpose," Kline returned. "The medical field no longer had exclusivity to our technology. The real money came from selling to independent contractors or companies who didn't always have the betterment of mankind in mind with their newly-acquired products."

"Oh."

"Those absurd rumors about weapons manufacturing grew from that." Kline stopped himself from going any further. "I'm sorry, my frustration is probably inappropriate."

"Mr. Kline, believe me it's perfectly fine," Slater replied. "There's things in every job that will leave a bad taste in your mouth. I don't always agree with the decisions that sometimes get pushed through city council. It's nice to talk about it sometimes. My mother hears me vent all the time but...I know it must be hard for you."

Kline nodded. "Yes, unfortunately my father wasn't one to listen to many grievances. The only person I ever felt I could talk to...well, he's dead now."

"I'm so sorry."

"Don't be," Kline returned to his glass and after another sip, let his expression revert to a pleasant one. "You've been a very nice relief for me this evening. I didn't even know it was possible to feel so relaxed."

Slater nodded. "They say talking is the best kind of medicine."

"Yes, well like you Ms. Slater," Kline said. "I have a project or two that also helps with my therapy."

~

Wreings didn't need Cass' therapy right now. However, he sighed and began texting his reply to her repeated messages.

"I'm not blowing you off again. Promise. Now really isn't a good time."

The detective hit send and tried to return his focus to the plan but he couldn't help but notice the time on his phone.

8:33. His eyes froze on the screen. He pictured the green hue of a heart monitor climb. And climb. And climb once more. Each peak was shorter than the one before it. The trend continued for another minute. It had felt more like an eternal agony back then.

But then 8:34 came around and the line bottomed out...

"Hey, are you all right?" Donnelly's question halted Wreings' mind from wandering further. The detective nodded and slipped his phone back into his pocket.

"Yeah, I'm fine just tired of waiting," he replied.

"You and me both," quipped Donnelly.

"Do you think Roberts..." Wreings suddenly felt his phone vibrating again. He sighed and retrieved his phone once more to turn it off but was surprised to see the number for the lab in the caller ID. "Wreings here," he answered.

"Detective," began LJ. "I stopped by your desk but..."

"Hey, they're finally coming back," Donnelly cut in. It was pouring rain but Wreings thought he saw Hopkins and Roberts coming back from the hotel.

"Hey LJ," the detective returned. "Sorry, we are about to be in the middle of something but I didn't catch that last part."

"Oh, of course. I only wanted to tell you that I've found something very interesting when analyzing the wound left on Officer Hopkins," she began. "I compared it to another similar wound I'd seen this year, ironically one of your previous cases."

"Which one?"

"The murder of Wheeler Hix," LJ replied excitedly. "The weapon used was a thin, longer blade."

"Like for fencing," Wreings returned. "A foil or something, right? Was it the same kind of weapon?"

"No," the examiner said emphatically. "It was the *exact* same weapon."

The detective stared forward as the car doors opened. Roberts and Hopkins slid inside the vehicle.

"We still can't go in there?" Donnelly immediately asked.

Roberts held up one finger and then turned his attention to Wreings. "Who is that?"

"Thanks, LJ," Wreings began. "I'm kind of in the middle of something right now. Do you mind if I call you back?"

"Of course," she said. "Have a good night."

"Yeah, you too."

Wreings closed his phone and fit it back into his pocket. He didn't know how to react to the news LJ had just given him. It made sense, especially if Tilte had been working for Gol, but for some reason the detective wasn't sold entirely on that idea.

"Some news?" Roberts asked.

The detective glanced over at the waiting agent only to shake his head. "Nothing really. What's the deal with the staff?"

"No one inside has seen him, so they say," Roberts returned. "But according to housekeeping, there is one resident that requested to do their own cleaning."

"And has been staying there for over a month," Hopkins added.

Roberts nodded. "Room 409, registered to a Sam Moonson."

Donnelly shrugged. "Sounds suspicious as hell to me. We going to get him or what?"

"If this Moonson is not really Ezra Tilte, then we may have lost our chance to find him by alerting the entire hotel to our presence," replied Roberts.

Wreings glanced over what he could see of the building. "We got another way in besides the front door?"

"We've got access to the service elevator," said Hopkins. "It's right behind the restaurant area in the hotel."

The detective nodded, but thought of the matchbook. "Should we check there first?"

"We already have," Roberts said. "The restaurant is closed for the day and the nightclub portion won't be opening for another half hour."

Wreings sighed. "Upstairs it is then."

The four of them agreed and quickly stepped out of the car. Roberts opened the trunk and handed a bullet proof vest to everyone. Wreings strapped himself in. Donnelly helped Hopkins, who was struggling to lift her wounded shoulder.

Roberts eyed her before adjusting his firearm in its holster. He shut the trunk and signaled for everyone to follow him around the back of the hotel. As they made their way past the restaurant, the agent slowed his pace to walk level with Wreings, letting Donnelly and Hopkins lead in front.

"Detective," he began. "If you recall my proposal from yesterday, now would be a good time to confirm my suspicions."

Wreings almost laughed. "You're a real piece of work."

"Still..." Roberts returned.

Detective Wreings really considered sending the blonde a text right then and there, but remembered his words of warning to her from the night before. "I wish I could tell you something different. Hell, I wish I could call in SWAT right now. But like you told Glades, it's less risky for these people if we're on our own in here."

Roberts looked skeptical for a moment before returning his focus ahead. Once they made it inside, the agent led them down a corridor to a large open elevator.

"This is our way up," Agent Roberts began. "And around the corner is a utility entrance to the kitchen of the restaurant. Officer Hopkins, it may be good of you to be stationed there while the three of us continue upstairs. You can easily access the lobby or the back staircase in the event the target eludes us."

Hopkins looked annoyed but still nodded. "Copy that, sir."

Roberts waited until Wreings and Donnelly had joined him in the elevator to tap the "4" button on the pad.

"Ezra Tilte may be a valuable asset to us and our case against Gol," the agent began as he fell back against the wall. "We need to take every necessary measure to ensure that he is taken alive."

"Is that why you put a bullet through the wall instead of his head back in the garage?" Donnelly shot out.

Roberts smile carried more than a hint of frustration. "The agent killed today had been my partner for six years. I can promise you, if I had been able to see straight at that moment in time, we would not be in this elevator."

"Good to know," his partner replied. "Hard to trust."

"As is your attitude..."

"Alright guys," Wreings cut in. "Let's play nice for a little bit, or at least until we catch this guy."

"I just want to make sure we *all* have each other's backs," Donnelly returned to Wreings. "Cause if I see this bastard pointing a gun at your head..." he paused and passed a glance to Roberts. "*Either* of your heads, I ain't going to be trying to miss."

Roberts glared at Donnelly and pulled his gun from the holster at his belt. He disengaged the safety, almost as if for show, before placing it back at his side. The three remained silent until the doors opened.

"Fourth floor. Be ready," Roberts said as he walked out into the hallway. Wreings was next to follow. He shook his head at his partner before trailing the agent. Donnelly didn't stray too far behind as the three men walked carefully down the long corridor.

"So what exactly is the plan here?" the detective whispered to Roberts. "We might outnumber him but as long as he can use that sound thing I'm not exactly feeling our chances."

The agent nodded and quickly reached inside his suit pocket. He pulled out three small packages, each with two orange rubber buds.

"Ear plugs?" the detective returned. "You think that's going to work?"

"If sound is his weapon then we need to prevent his 'shots' from hitting us directly, no?" Roberts replied. "Like a bullet proof vest for the ear."

Wreings looked over one set of plugs before tossing another back to Donnelly. "Yeah but if these don't work..."

"There's no time, Detective," Roberts whispered, pointing to the door at the end of the corridor. "Room 409 is right there. Go ahead and put your earplugs in."

Wreings quickly ripped his pouch open as did his partner. He was about to place them in his ear when a sound behind them gave him pause. He hurriedly waved at Roberts and pointed down the hallway. "Someone's coming," he whispered.

Roberts already had one plug in his ear but he took out his gun before putting the other one in. Wreings watched as the shadow of a figure took shape on the floor in front of them before the person it belonged to abruptly stopped. Each second that passed only increased Wreings' focus. The detective toggled his eyes between the shadow and the edge of the corridor before slowly stepping toward it. When he was a few feet away, he began shifting toward the left side of the hallway to get a better angle.

Glancing back, he saw that Roberts had moved to the opposite wall while Donnelly was knelt down with his gun trained on the corner. They all traded eye contact and slight nods of readiness. Wreings returned his attention ahead and continued moving toward the corner. When the arm of the shadow moved, the detective quickly drew his gun.

"MPD! You, in the hall, don't move!" he warned.

Suddenly, Wreings heard a screeching howl in his ears. He yelled his warning again but could barely hear his words as the disabling sound cut through the earplugs. The hallway felt as though it were leaning heavily toward the right now. Wreings knew he was seeing double as he helplessly watched seemingly two identical men step from around the corner. Wreings tried to aim but couldn't steady his gun. It eventually slipped from his hand and hit the floor.

As the detective tried to find it, he lost his balance and fell on his side. When he looked up, the room was almost upside down. The gun of the figure remained unchanged. It was aimed directly at him.

BANG! BANG!

The detective shut his eyes as the shots rang out but was surprised that he didn't feel a bullet burn through his body. The howling sound had grown fainter and when Wreings reopened his eyes he thought he saw a few drops of red on the light fabric of the hallway carpet in front of him. He covered his ears and shook his head. A few seconds later, his eyes reoriented themselves and he could now tell the distinctive red as spots of blood.

"V?!" Donnelly yelled.

"I'm okay, Don," Wreings attempted to stand but was still off balance. He turned to see his partner was also on the ground. Agent Roberts on the other hand was leaning heavily against the wall, his gun wavering in the direction of their assailant.

He was breathing deeply. "I remember what it was like the last time. I may have hit his shoulder, maybe his arm, I couldn't tell. It was like aiming at a moving target…"

"Well, it was a hell of a shot," Wreings said, finally able to stand.

"Yeah," Donnelly chimed in, almost having to crawl to his feet. "Good shot, Roberts."

The agent nodded. "Unfortunately, now is not the time for plaudits. Our target is on the move."

Chapter 29

Facing a Stampede

"Stop!"

Katie held her breath as she waited for Trevor's voice to buzz in her ear again.

"The readings show he's somewhere between thirty and fifty meters in front of you," he continued. "There is some structure ahead, correct?"

Katie could faintly make out the outline of what looked like a water tower. "Yeah, I think so."

"The radiation is off the charts," Trevor continued. "If he's not in there now then he's likely been frequenting this spot."

"Like a lair?"

"In this case, that's likely a possibility," Trevor replied.

"Then the reporter might be in there too!" Katie said.

"Also a possibility, though again we must only focus on Gillem," Trevor returned. "Once he has been incapacitated, we can address the reporter. Understand?"

Katie nodded as if the Frenchmen were in front of her. "Sure. So what do you want me to do?"

"We need to draw him out of the tower. The Delta team is moving into their positions. They won't engage unless it's necessary, but you will have cover once he's in the open," Trevor said reassuringly.

"Okay," Katie breathed in deeply. "So what, I just knock?"

"More or less. But remember, we don't know what kind of condition he is in. He could still be quite formidable," Trevor said. "You have to be ready."

Katie closed her eyes for a moment and thought about the reporter, putting various faces of those she cared about on the body of the unseen woman. "Yeah, I'm as ready as I..."

The blonde trailed off as a strange sound suddenly pounded into her ears. She cringed as it grew louder and louder, like the sound of a fleet of horses trampling nearby.

What is that?

"Hello?" Trevor buzzed in her ear. "Cattrell, are you still there? You didn't..."

Katie pulled off the earpiece and looked around. The park was calm, much calmer than the sound she heard. She slowly approached the tower and the noise grew even louder. It was then she realized she wasn't hearing a singular sound. She managed to separate five distinct patterns. That's when she recognized that they weren't just patterns, they were the sound of heartbeats other than her own.

"Shut up!" Katie said as the realization took hold.

She focused harder and soon was able to trace the beats back in the direction they were emanating from. Four of the steady beats surrounded her, almost at equal distances. Those had to belong to the soldiers. But the fifth beat that was bludgeoning her ears had to be someone else. She wasn't sure why she felt it but for some reason the frantic thumping made her think of her own heart beating when she was afraid.

"Hey, Trevor," Katie said as she quickly put the earpiece back on. "Trevor."

"Report. My men told me you took off your headset?" he returned. "What is going...?"

"I don't think he's here!"

"What?" Trevor asked.

Katie shifted her eyes around the dark space before returning them back to the water tower. "I don't think it's him that's in the tower."

"What do you mean? Be clear!"

"I can hear someone in there but I don't think it's him," the blonde replied. "I think you're right about this being his lair, but I think someone else is inside."

There was silence on the other end for a few moments. Then, with a skeptical tone, Trevor asked. "How do you know that?"

Katie again listened to the pace of the heartbeat coming from inside the tower.

Because they're scared...

"I just have a feeling. Gillem isn't in there."

"Well then fall back," Trevor said. "We need to locate the target..."

"No!" Katie snapped. "If that's the reporter, we need to make sure she is okay in there first."

"We will do *no* such thing. Our priority is to capture Bradley Gillem," Trevor returned. "We must meet this objective before any others come into consideration."

Katie scoffed. "We can't just leave her!"

"You being the exception Ms. Cattrell, 'The Reaper' has lived up to the moniker with those he comes into contact with" began the Frenchman irritably. "If she's not dead then she has likely been untouched. But the last thing this mission needs is another civilian to keep account of while this beast is loose! Now the trail behind you is clear, so fall back and reconvene with the Delta Team."

The blonde didn't take her eyes off of the tower as she shook her head in disgust. "No..."

"That is an order, Ms. Cattrell."

"I'm not a soldier, remember?" she quickly shot back before shoving the earpiece into her jacket pocket. "I don't fight for you."

Katie quickly bent at the knees and catapulted herself above the roof of the water tower, hanging in the air for a few moments before landing on top. The blonde sighed in relief as it appeared she had regained her normal power and possibly added a few new ones too.

From where she stood now the racing heartbeat was almost deafening.

"It's okay! I'm going to get you out of there," she said over the noisy barrage.

She stepped to the center of the tower and dug her fingers through the rusted top. Gripping tightly, the blonde pulled back a section of the covering until it looked large enough to comfortably fit her body through. She could only see darkness inside the deep hole, but Katie heard the muffled whimpers of a woman underneath the heart beating. She immediately thought to drop into the shadows but an all too familiar feeling held her back.

SCREEEEEEECH!

The blonde jumped back as the sound of braking tires pulled at her nerves. She could suddenly feel herself spinning like she were once again tumbling down into the woods, strapped to a seat in her mother's Volvo.

"No! Not now, not now!"

The continued pleas from inside the water tower served as a torturous chorus for Katie's sudden paralysis. She stared anxiously at the opening, knowing that each second that passed was precious time wasted. Trevor might have had a cold view but he was right about one thing, as long as the Reaper was loose, everyone was in danger. But the dark space inside the water tower seemed a hell she wasn't prepared for.

She tried to start humming the Colossal Cleaners jingle but could barely hear it as every other sound around her rose with her voice. The cries, wind, the heartbeats...

Wait!

Katie closed her eyes and pressed her hands against her ears. It surprisingly dulled some of the intensity from the sounds enough for her to concentrate. She focused on the separate heartbeats and gasped as she realized that there were now *six*!

"Shit!" she said, pulling the earpiece out of her jacket. "Trevor! Trevor!"

"What are you doing up...?!"

"Not now!" Katie warned. "Get your men out of here, the Reaper is coming back!"

"Yes, I know!" Trevor returned. "His signature just popped back on my map. He's not very far away so if you want to be a hero you need to hurry up!"

Katie glanced back at the hole.

"Did you hear me? Ms. Cattrell? Katie...!"

She put the earpiece back in her pocket and pushed out a desperate breath. Closing her eyes again, she slowly retraced her steps until she knew she was standing at the edge of the hole. "C-O-L-O-S-S-A-L, C-O-L-O..."

And then she let herself fall in.

It immediately felt as though she had been dropped into a coffin buried beneath the earth. It was dark and there was a dank, moist smell that filled the air. She quickly lost track of the tune and almost let the claustrophobia take her again. But the crying coming from just a few feet away gave her some much needed resolve.

"It's okay! I'm here to help you," she said trying to make out the shape of the person in front of her. Katie thought back to the night she was trapped underneath the Emerson building after her fight with Bishop. She had somehow used the light from her bracelet then, now she just needed to get it to work again. Holding her hand forward, Katie concentrated until she saw the blue flicker of light. After a few seconds, her wrist illuminated her view. It had worked!

But the excitement was short-lived.

"Oh my God!" Katie gasped as the sight she had now was much worse than that of the dark.

Along the sides of the tower were four dead bodies, their skin shriveled and their expressions warped disgustingly. Their heads had been twisted, some flattened as though every ounce of fluid had been squeezed out.

She clasped her mouth and shut her eyes, but the images of the corpses were already burned into her brain.

Come on, Katie! You have to get through this!

The blonde snapped her eyes open and zeroed in on the bound woman across from her.

"Hold on!" said Katie as she approached. She ripped the ties from the woman's hands and feet and untied the gag. The woman screamed but Katie quickly tried to calm her.

"No, no, shhh!" she began, placing her hands on her shoulders. "It's okay. I'm here to save you."

The woman was trembling and her skin felt frigid. She smelled as though she had been sitting in vomit and urine, but Katie held her close until the woman reciprocated.

"Please help me," she said.

"Definitely! Hold on!"

Turning her tunnel vision toward the stars outside, the blonde levitated them up and back through the hole she'd made in the top of the tower. The woman seemed to be chugging the fresh air as Katie continued floating them away until she lowered them back to the ground.

The woman collapsed and cried as soon as her feet touched the ground.

"He…he…kills people!" she said in between sobs. "Just by touching…it was…"

Katie rubbed the woman's back as she imagined Nancy would have rubbed hers. "I know, I know. But it's okay. You're safe…" she paused as she remembered that wasn't actually the case.

The heartbeats had moved. The soldiers sounded like they were grouped together now. Their rhythms were slightly more elevated than before, but all four were still alive. She focused to block out theirs and the crying woman's and again find the excited beat of the Reaper.

It didn't take long. It was coming straight at her.

"Don't move," Katie said as she turned. It was dark and a slight fog had set in, but she didn't need to see him. The fury of his heart sounded like loud footsteps in her ears.

"Oh no, oh no," the woman began hysterically. "Please don't let him…!"

"I won't," returned the blonde confidently. She put the earpiece back. "How close is he?"

"You cannot just..." Trevor's angry voice began.

"Later Trevor!" Katie cut him off. "Just tell me how goddamn far away he is."

"Close to a hundred meters, but he's moving fast."

Katie nodded. "Yeah, I know."

She opened her hands and concentrated. The past two times she had managed to shoot out the energy orb, she had Bishop or the Commander's arm around her neck. That couldn't be the case this time. Katie imagined that she was standing at the park with Nancy again and tried to locate the power she knew was inside the bracelet...

"What are you doing?" Trevor's voice cut back in. "Are you just standing there? Do you have a visual?"

"Quiet..." Katie said softly as she felt her skin begin to heat up.

"He's less than fifty meters..."

"Quiet," the blonde said again. She glanced at her wrist. The outline of the bracelet had begun to appear. "I can do this..."

"For heaven's sake, Ms. Cattrell!" Trevor yelled. "He's..."

"Shut-up!" Katie yelled as the light from the bracelet cascaded into a bristling ball of energy in her hand.

The woman behind her screamed and Katie quickly looked up to see the hooded Reaper's outstretched arms just a foot away from her face.

This time that was as close as he came to touching her. Katie shot the power into the chest of the monster, knocking him back into the shadows.

Everything went silent. Her hand lingered in the air for a few moments. She listened. Soon the slowed beat of the Reaper's heart could be heard again. If he wasn't dead, he certainly sounded close to it. "I got him. He's still breathing though."

A couple of seconds passed before Katie heard the sound of a motor approaching. She glanced behind her to see headlights pulling up the trail in between the four soldiers.

As they neared, Katie's ear buzzed again. "We're bringing the containment unit and cuffs to you," Trevor said calmly.

Katie exhaled and returned to the shaking woman sitting beside her. "You're okay now," she began. "These are the good…"

The blonde's words halted as she remembered what she had seen inside of the water tower.

Why were there more bodies? I thought they had closed the park?

Before Katie could think about it anymore, the truck pulled up beside them. One of the soldiers quickly pulled the briefcase from the truck bed.

"Ms. Cattrell," Trevor's voice called out from the vehicle. He stepped out of the passenger side and watched one of the soldiers remove the cuffs from the case. "Would you mind getting these on our friend while he's agreeable? The Delta team will provide you with cover."

As the soldier offered the device to her, Katie hesitated. Something didn't feel right, but the Reaper couldn't be allowed to get away again. She took the cuffs and bounded several yards through the air and landed just a few feet away from the sunken figure of Gillem. He was definitely out.

CLICK! CLICK!

Katie snapped the cuffs closed and stepped back, watching as they suddenly came together under a dull hum.

"Cuffs are locked and active," she heard someone call out from behind her. She turned to see the four soldiers quickly approaching. Two were heavily armed while the other two were holding a long steel rod.

"What's that for?" Katie asked.

Neither one of them answered. Instead, they just hovered the rod over the Reaper's hands until the magnetic pull forced the cuffs to latch onto it. Soon the soldiers were dragging him toward the approaching truck, the armed two following closely behind with their guns trained on the fallen target. Katie watched as they worked fast to load him into the large steel crate in the back of the truck. It was almost like they'd done it before.

"Secure!" one of them yelled, closing the back of the bed. With that confirmation, the truck sped around the other side of the water tower and back down the trail.

Trevor was now kneeling by the woman. Two more soldiers were setting up lights around the tower. Katie glanced at it and then the lights before finally settling her eyes on Trevor.

"There's more inside," she said.

"Pardon?"

The blonde pointed to the tower. "There's four more bodies inside there. Who are they?"

The lights flipped on and Katie could now clearly see a rare look of amusement on the Frenchman's face. "Are you sure?"

"Come on," she returned. "You guys have been watching this whole place right? How did you not know that four more people came into the park?"

Suddenly, Katie heard the sound of another engine approaching on the trail. She gazed suspiciously at Trevor.

"Well we couldn't have our new friend here riding along with her captor could we?" he said, smiling at the woman.

"That doesn't answer my question," Katie returned. "Did you know about those other people?"

"It's complicated," he said as the truck stopped behind them. A couple of soldiers jumped out of the truck bed and ran over to the tower, one was carrying some kind of saw. "Bring the bodies back to the lab for examination," Trevor ordered. "When you're finished, burn it down."

Katie shook her head. "Is this where the cover up starts?"

Trevor laughed. "Would you rather incite a panic?"

"I'd rather the families of whoever they are not spend the rest of their lives wondering what happened to their son, daughter, father, whoever they were," Katie said.

"You're very noble, Ms. Cattrell," began Trevor. "And very naive."

The blonde was about to press on when one of the back passenger doors opened and out stepped the Commander. She turned her back toward the light, almost as if to keep her face shrouded in darkness. But Katie didn't need to actually see her callous expression to know that it was there.

Great! Just who I wanted to see...

"Lieutenant," Elizabeth began, aiming her gaze toward the cowering woman. "Could you please escort the journalist back to headquarters?"

"No!" the woman yelled and latched on to Katie who stood firmly opposite Elizabeth and Trevor. "I'd like...to go with her, please."

"It's okay my dear," Trevor returned, offering his hand and a hint of a smile. "You're still in shock but we're not going to hurt you. How would you like food and some new clothes?"

"Why aren't I coming with you?" Katie asked pointedly.

"Because," Elizabeth began. "You and I need to talk."

Chapter 30

Knight takes Queen

Thunder struck in tandem with the flashes overhead. The Meridian skies had really opened up now and Wreings hoped the storm wouldn't get any more severe than this. The street lamps and neon bright marquees lit up pockets of rain all down East Anderson but there was one section that remained in darkness.

Thumpers, or at least that's what it was called when Gol was running it, was more like the black eye of Midtown's club and bar scene now.

Two sets of headlights were already outside the two story building when Roberts pulled up to the curb.

When they got out, they were met by a short, stubby police officer Wreings had seen around the station from time to time. He wore their police issue rain jackets with the hood drawn over his head. "Evening detectives, Hopkins, and...?"

"Roberts. I'm with the Federal Bureau of Investigation."

The officer nodded. "Right. How you been, Mick?" he turned to greet Donnelly.

"I've been better. This is my partner Wreings."

The officer reached for the detective's hand. "Sergeant Shawn Larrabee. Wish we could have met under different circumstances."

Wreings shook the man's hand and quickly turned his eyes to the hollow letters on the building in front of them. For the first time ever, the detective wished the pink, dayglow lights of Thumpers were shining. "Did he take any hostages?"

Larrabee shook his head. "The place has been shut down since they found the casino. I don't even think the bums want to go near this place, even with weather like this."

Wreings noticed blue and red swirling lights approaching. "We call an ambulance out here?"

"There was an accident right before we got here," Larrabee returned. "Three cars just spun out and ran into one another. Don't know if it was the rain or that damned noise. Gave me a headache as soon as I pulled up."

"Consider yourself fortunate," Roberts said.

"It sounds like his little toy is getting weaker," Wreings added.

"Yes, so it's curious why he chose not to take his chance to escape," Roberts returned.

"Maybe he doesn't know," Hopkins chimed in.

"Well, it doesn't matter now either way, we need to make sure he doesn't get out the back," Wreings continued.

"Already got a unit back there to seal it off," the sergeant replied.

Donnelly nodded to Roberts. "Hey, you got any more of those earplugs?" he asked.

Roberts reached in his pocket and pulled out two more sets. "This is it."

"Let's get those to the guys in the back," Wreings said. "Sergeant Larrabee, get this block sealed off. The perp's got this weapon that can make whoever's in earshot feel like they're falling. We can't let anyone else near this building until we know for sure that it's not working the same way anymore."

"We don't have much time," Donnelly said. "The clubs are already lit and should be opening in the next ten minutes. East Anderson will be flooded in fifteen."

"Then we can't waste any time," Larrabee replied. "I'll get it done."

~

Kline rolled back his sleeve to check the face of his watch. The words "In Use" were still flashing on and off as they had for the past half hour. He casually took the final sip from his second glass of wine and leaned across the table, into to the ear of the toe-tapping Jameson Slater. She had become even friendlier since the fourth glass of wine and seemed to be oblivious to anything except for the music.

"I need to step away for a moment," he spoke over what was an electrifying jazz ensemble. "I shouldn't be long but feel free to eat without me if the food arrives."

"I'll do no such thing," she replied, rubbing his hand.

Kline smiled and slipped his hand away before turning toward the bathroom hallway. He continued to walk until he came to a set of glass doors that led outside. After a moment of consideration, he pulled out his phone and held down the call button while pressing down on the watch face.

There was only a brief dial tone before he heard the other line connect. Kline listened for a few moments and smiled when he realized the sound he heard was that of very heavy breathing.

"You sound tired," he greeted.

"What? Who's..." began Ezra Tilte. "Kline? What the bloody hell...?"

"I apologize for not telling you before, Mr. Tilte," Kline continued. "But there is a limited range communication system in the frequency manipulator."

"Is that why this piece of shit won't work the way it's supposed to?" replied Ezra Tilte.

Kline smiled knowingly. "Are you sure it's not just user error?"

"I'm serious!" Tilte snapped. "They tracked me to the hotel somehow. One of those tossers was able to shoot me after I'd already switched it on. Bloody shh...shh...shot me!"

Kline's smile widened as the man on the other end began to struggle to get out his words. "Where are you?"

"Gol's place," Tilte replied. "Was hoping the cops hadn't found his safe, but it's already been cleared out. Look mate, I...I...need you to get me out of here. Is this th...th...what the hell is happening?!"

"You're at Thumpers?"

"What the hell is the matter with you?" Tilte returned. "I just said that. Can you fix this thing remotely or not? I know every one of your goddamn toys is wired up to your computer..."

Denard Kline glanced at his watch which had started flashing a different warning. Finally. This had been the one he'd been waiting for. "I'm afraid it's not that simple, Mr. Tilte."

~

"You ever miss the days when things were simple?" Donnelly began as he followed closely behind the detective.

"What do you mean?" Wreings shined his flashlight against the wall. He continued to scan the vacant tables and stages around them.

"You know, back when we didn't have to chase super-powered psychos or dirt-bags with jacked up weapons," his partner added.

"Those were the days..." Wreings trailed off as he led the way through the club, cautious at every turn. His partner remained silent as they secured the area by the main stage before opening the back door to let in two armored officers, Hopkins, and Roberts.

"All clear around the bar. You three check the rooms down here," called out the detective. "We can check out the upstairs."

Roberts didn't look like a fan of taking orders, but followed the detective's without a fuss. He instead turned to Hopkins and motioned for her to follow him.

Wreings noticed the supreme focus on the Hopkin's face. "How you feeling?"

"Like Christmas came early."

~

"This truly came earlier than expected," Kline began. "I suppose it's a testament to the determination and ingenuity of the Meridian Police Department and the FBI."

"Wha...what are you going on about?"

He could barely hear the mercenary's reply over the noise in the background. "You're moving? Where are you going?" Kline quickly asked, glancing back at his watch.

After a few seconds, the commotion on the other end ceased, save the heavy breathing of Ezra Tilte. "Gol's secret room above the loft. I doubt they would have found this during their sweep. There's got to be an...another...a bloody gun up here."

"Careful not to show too many of that villain's secrets," muttered Denard Kline. "We wouldn't want the FBI to think you two are in cahoots or something."

"What are you on about? You had me watching..."

The mercenary's voice trailed off. For all his gruff and inappropriate babble, Tilte was a very smart man, which made his realization of his circumstances all the more satisfying for Denard Kline.

"You double-crossing bastard..." Tilte's now-incredulous voice continued. "I wondered how they knew where to find me. You're set...setting me up."

"*Set*, Mr. Tilte," Kline corrected. "And I must thank you for helping put the final nail in Gol's coffin. Now if I were you, I'd save your last few breaths, it sounds as though you need them."

A heavy sigh on the other end flowed into a laugh. "Oh no, mate you...you've got it all wrong there. I've put up with your prima donna bullshit for too long to be robbed of putting a bullet in your head..."

Kline cut off the man with his own laughter.

"You can laugh now," Tilte continued angrily. "But what about when I...I...I...slit your pretty little bitch's throat, eh?"

Kline's laughter quickly died. It would prove to be an empty threat, but it still enraged him to hear it. "You know it's your own arrogance that has led you to where you are now," he began. "Have you forgotten why I hired you? I don't need loose ends, Mr. Tilte. It was only a matter of time before you became one yourself."

"Piss off, mate!"

"And your constant barbaric witticisms..." Kline continued. "It was refreshing at first, but the more I heard you speak the more you sounded like a belligerent pirate. How could you ever think you had ingratiated yourself with me to the point where you thought your fate was avoidable?"

"I cleaned up your messes!" Tilte snapped back. "I wiped up your shhh...shit for years and...You know what? Maybe I'll just let the coppers take me in? That'd put a wrench in your precious plan now would...wouldn't it?"

"I think I might just enjoy hearing your final breaths," Kline replied.

"Only in...your dreams."

"Then the Sandman has come early tonight, Mr. Tilte," Kline returned coldly after another look at his watch. There couldn't be much longer now. "It appears I learned more about you during our business arrangement than you did me. In the years you've worked for me, do you really think I'd leave your fate up to chance?"

Kline listened to Tilte's breath grow more rapid. "God...goddammit you cocky bastard! Stop shitting in circles!"

~

Wreings paused on the stairs and held up his hand to Donnelly and the officer behind him. "You hear that?" he whispered.

His partner nodded. "Sounds like someone's yelling."

"Yeah, but the room is right here," the detective returned. "It almost sounds like it's coming from above us."

"Nah, there's only two floors to this place, V," Donnelly returned. His partner walked up the stairs to join him. "The Feds swept this place from top to bottom."

Wreings lowered his gun. "I'm not sure the Bureau is doing the best to find *all* the evidence."

"What are you talking about?"

"Nothing," Wreings returned. "The Gol theory just doesn't make sense."

"You don't think Gol is behind all this?" Donnelly continued to press. "The guy who ran an illegal casino in a strip joint to launder money from his mob friends? The guy who had a sitting judge on his payroll...?"

"Shhh!" The detective tried to keep his partner's voice contained. "Look, I know it sounds crazy but now is not the time."

His partner shrugged. "V, you know where we are standing right now...?"

"Don, who the hell planted those coins on Hix and Jones?" Wreings started. "Remember, the FBI had nothing on him, not until after they were killed"

"It was probably this prick!" Donnelly returned.

"Okay, well then why use The Majority if you have a hitman like Tilte? How is Bishop involved...?" Wreings began. "Hell, we still don't even know the ID of the woman found dead at Bishop's house..."

"Why can't it be as simple as Gol had his hands in everything? I mean just about everything points back to him," Donnelly reasoned.

"It does now," Wreings returned.

"Hey!" his partner warned, pointing his gun up to an opening in the ceiling of the loft.

Wreings quickly aimed his barrel also, returning his focus back to the matter at hand.

"There's a third level to this place," he turned to the trailing officer on the stairs. "Run down and get the others."

~

"You're already dead, Mr. Tilte," Kline said bluntly. "The moment you activated the manipulator in the garage, your life was no longer in your control."

"What do you mean?"

"That counter frequency I told you would keep you safe from the effects of the device?" Kline continued. "Well, sound is truly a miraculous weapon. While it does keep you safe from the vertigo-like effects, the device had a fatal flaw that we never got to address before the merger. You see, after prolonged exposure to the counter frequency, your brain began transmitting very detrimental signals to other parts of your nervous system. That stammering you keep doing is just one of the symptoms. That heavy breathing is your lungs naturally trying to hold onto the air that your brain is telling them isn't necessary. You'll likely suffocate in less than a few minutes."

"You...I'm going to kill...kill you!"

Kline felt a wave of excitement in hearing the weakness in Tilte's voice. His watch was flashing red now, with bold black letters looping over and over.

Danger! Danger! Danger!

The big man shook his head. Tilte had been exposed to the frequency long enough to guarantee imminent nervous system collapse. "Contrary to some of my comments, this was never personal. I actually should thank you..." Tilte's retort was unintelligible. Denard Kline laughed briskly before continuing. "Let's see, what's that pirate adage? That's right: *dead men tell no...*"

"Drop the gun!"

"MPD!"

"Drop the gun!"

A bombardment of loud gun shots rang out on the other end. Kline couldn't tell which side was shooting but he covered the receiver of his phone as a member of the kitchen staff strode by.

He held his breath for a moment before bringing the phone back to his ear. There was only silence.

He knew that sound could only mean one thing. He waited a few more seconds just to be sure before ending the call. A small drop of blood fell from his nose onto the screen.

~

Wreings' eyes moved from the barrel of his gun over to Officer Hopkins. She had knelt down on the other side of the crate they'd both taken cover behind. Her gun was still aimed straight ahead, as was her unwavering focus.

"I think we got him," he said, pulling himself to his feet.

Hopkins let out the deep breath she'd been holding for the past few seconds. Wreings patted her arm again and she finally lowered her weapon, breaking the trance.

"Are you hit?" she asked.

"No, I think most of his shots hit the wall. He was really all over the..." Wreings quickly left his statement behind as he saw the foot of Ezra Tilte twitching. The detective quickly moved toward him, drawing his gun once again. He kicked aside the long barreled gun at the hitman's feet and looked him over.

He was decorated with six bullet wounds, almost all were on his chest, but one had sprung a leak from the left side of his neck. Detective Wreings quickly undid his tie and pressed it against the wound to stop the flow, but he doubted it would save him.

"Who hired you?" Wreings asked.

Ezra Tilte's lips started moving and the rest of his body began to twitch. "Ka…Ka…" he began to spit out.

"Detective…" Wreings heard Roberts call out.

"Wait a second, he's saying something!" he replied, his eyes focused on the mouth of the dying Tilte.

"Kla…Kli…" this time the hitman spit up blood, "Nnnuhh."

"Detective Wreings, you should…" Roberts again called out.

"Hold on!" the detective shot back only to see Tilte's lips had stopped quivering. Wreings dropped his head. "Shit!"

"Sir!"

The graveness of Hopkins' voice sent a sharp pain racing to his heart. He quickly spun away from the hitman's body to see Roberts and the two officers standing behind Hopkins, grim-faced and on her knees by a set of outstretched legs.

Hopkins made way as the detective ran over to see his partner's back against the crates, a growing pool of blood beneath him.

"I told you the only vests worth a damn were at the Pen," Donnelly choked.

"Yeah, yeah, you were right, Mick!" Wreings began frantically. As his partner's eyes began to close, the detective patted his partner's face.

"Huh?" Donnelly muttered as he began to lean to one side.

"Stay awake, Don!" Wreings pressed. "Come on buddy, stay with me."

353

Donnelly nodded his head and made eye contact with Wreings. He smiled. "I miss the days when things were...were..."

"Simple, right?" Wreings finished as his partner's eyes closed. "Don? Come on, buddy just...come on!"

He glanced behind him at Roberts and a mortified Hopkins.

"CALL IT IN!" he yelled.

Hopkins finally seemed to snap out of her trance and reached for the radio on her shoulder.

"This is Officer Hopkins, I got a ten double zero at East Anderson and 8th! I repeat, ten double zero, officer down! Send a med team pronto. Officer down, I repeat. Officer down!"

Chapter 31

Underneath the Surface

Her eyes drifted from her computer screen to the vibrating phone on the floor beneath it. Reagan tapped the space bar to pause the movie and then balanced against the table as she picked up the phone.

"Hi Peter," she greeted slowly. "You got my message...messages?"

"Cat, I'm standing outside your door," he replied.

She sat up on the couch quickly before shuffling over to the door. She slid it open to see Dr. Sava standing with a drenched lightweight coat draped over his arm. He was holding an Arby's bag.

"Are you okay?" he asked.

"Oh yeah," Reagan replied. "Why didn't you knock?"

"I did...for like five minutes."

Reagan glanced back toward her laptop on the coffee table and would have stumbled had she not been holding onto the door. "I was...into the movie I guess. I'm sorry."

Dr. Sava raised his eyebrows. As he walked into the kitchen he seemed to keep his eyes on her. Reagan stood by the open door for a few moments, unsure of what she had done to elicit Sava's strange reaction.

"Can I help you with something?" she finally asked.

"Can you help me?"

This was getting frustrating. "That sounds a lot like an echo."

"Yeah," Sava's expression dipped. He lowered his gaze to the fast food bag on the counter before turning a concerned look toward Reagan. "You don't drink."

"I don't..." The conversation was really confusing Reagan. "Is that a problem?"

"That in itself isn't," he continued. "But what it does mean is that you're taking something. Something that you probably shouldn't if it spaces you out like this."

Reagan's smile was shaky. "What um, what makes you say that?"

"Oh wow," he continued as if she had actually answered his question. "You really are on something. Holy shit, Cat! Holy shit..."

"Stop it, Peter," Reagan returned. "I'm not taking anything except my pain medication..."

"*Let me see it.*"

Reagan wagged her finger. "No."

"Cat, this is the second time you've gone zombie on me," Sava returned. "Whatever they prescribed you is way too strong or something.

"I'm fine!" the young doctor argued.

Her friend began searching the kitchen cabinets. "Where's the bottle?"

"The bottle of what?" Reagan asked innocently.

"The prescription!" he returned.

"It's by the couch," she began. "But Peter will you stop for a second, I need to talk to you."

Dr. Sava was already on the way to the living room. "About what?"

Reagan trudged back to the couch she had vacated and slumped down. "About being the worst."

Sava smiled and took the seat next to her. "What are you talking about?"

"It's me Peter."

"What is?"

"Katie...it's..." Reagan could feel her eyes watering and quickly turned away from her friend. "It's my fault she stole Laine's car..."

"Wait, wait, wait...are you talking about your sister, Katie?" Sava began. "Like Katie-who-can't-drive, that Katie? Jesus, do you know where she is?"

"Yes..." Reagan began. "Actually no, I don't know where she is anymore...but it's my fault."

Sava ran quickly around the coffee table and into the kitchen.

"Cat, if your sister's out there driving right now..."

Reagan shook her head. "Oh no, Peter. This was years ago."

"Oh," Sava said. "Okay, that's good I guess. Did she say something to you?"

"Yes," she replied, more tears falling as she quickly dove her face into her hands. "I mean no. But I know it's true. It's because of me."

"Cat..."

"No Peter!" Reagan said as she finally turned her pathetic face toward Sava. "It always has been, I've just been too stubborn to see it. The way I treated her after the accident...I was so cold. I thought it would make things easier for her."

Sava slid closer to Reagan and put his arm around her shoulder.

"Mom was so good at comforting her," Reagan sobbed as she continued. She cuddled into her friend, not minding that his shirt was still a little damp. "All I ever did was make things worse. When people made fun of her, I just told her to get over it or grow up. I said she would never be anything so many times that she would do things, stupid things to prove me wrong. It's my fault she stole Laine's car...I told her she would never drive if she was always so afraid. Everything I've ever said to her, everything I've ever done...I pushed her away so many times, Peter. And now I don't think I will ever be able to get her back."

"Hey, hey, hey," Sava began, bringing his other arm around her and rubbing her shoulders gently. "You're sisters. You guys are going to fight, that's pretty much a law, you know. But at the end of the day, you two love each other."

"I don't think she does," Reagan spat out.

"It'd be hard not to love you, Cat," Sava returned.

Reagan laughed for the first time all night. "You're full of shit, Dr. Sava."

He returned with a smile. "I'd like to have a second opinion, Dr. Catt..."

The thought of kissing him had been there long before she'd texted him to come over, but this moment seemed right to finally act on it. Reagan held his cheeks and fell farther into his arms. For a brief moment, she ignored the faint pain that had begun pushing against her skull. She ignored the memories of her sister and Nancy's condemnations. She ignored the realization that she could probably never be a doctor again. The only thing floating around in the jumbled mess of her mind was that her lips felt right against his.

But the feeling was brief. Dr. Sava had his hands on her shoulders, holding her away. The surprised look on his face pierced Reagan's heart.

"That was not where I was expecting that to go..." Sava began.

Reagan was mortified. She quickly wiped her face and shot up from the couch. She almost fell but managed to catch herself on the coffee table. "I...I...oh my God, Peter, I'm so sorry! I must look like a complete idiot to..."

"Wait, Cat no!" he quickly returned. "It's not that...look, you're kind of out of it. It wouldn't be...I..."

The pounding in her head had gotten worse. It felt like the whole room was moving, her balance continued to waver. Her stomach churned as she swayed back and forth. "Oh," she managed to cough out. "Yeah, that makes...that makes...Oh, I'm really dizzy right now."

Sava reached for her arm but she shooed him away.

"I'm fine," she said.

"Are you?" Sava replied. His voice was full of doubt, his eyes filled with concern. Her friend quickly turned to the medicine bottle on the side table. His eyes widened as he looked at it. "Holy shit, Cat! You've been taking this?"

Reagan reached for the bottle but fell back onto the couch. "It's for pain."

"No, it's basically a tranquilizer," Sava replied. "This is three times the strength you should be taking and dangerous as hell. How many days in a row have you taken this?"

Reagan closed her eyes but that only seemed to make things worse. The floor beneath her started spinning and she could feel her brain pounding against her skull.

"I know what I'm doing. I need to sit up," she replied.

"Okay," Sava helped her up and steadied her on the couch. "Tell me what's going on. Do you feel like you're going to throw up, Reagan?"

"You never call me that," she began. The spinning had gained momentum. She couldn't see Sava anymore.

"Because this isn't funny, it's not a joke," he said, his voice sounded distant. "You could really mess yourself up or get addicted to..."

"I'm not addicted," she began in her delirium.

"Hey, hey, hey!" Sava's words came in loudly but then his voice began drifting away from her ears. "I think you're having some kind of reaction."

"I just wanted the pain to go away…"

"What?!" her friend's voice was that of a fading echo now. Soon Reagan's body felt disconnected from her brain and everything around her fell into darkness.

~

Once Trevor and the reporter were out of sight, the Commander seemed to be ready for their talk. "I was listening to the transmission," she began. "You've more gumption than I gave you credit for."

"I'm glad you're impressed," scoffed the blonde.

"I didn't say that," returned the Commander. "But I admit that I was surprised by how quickly you disposed of Gillem. The power that flows inside of you is staggering."

Katie glanced back at the tower as the soldier sawing the side of it stopped. He climbed into the newly cut hole while another soldier laid a long tarp over the ground. Soon he was back at the truck tossing out four long bags from the bed.

With Elizabeth being even more tight-lipped than Trevor, chances were slim that Katie would get any answer on who the four dead people were. Instead, she pushed forward with the conversation. "You said we needed to talk? Talk."

"You may not agree with the way we do things…" began the Commander.

"No kidding!" mumbled the blonde as she crossed her arms underneath her chest. Katie offered a blatantly sarcastic smile and waved for Elizabeth to continue. "I'm sorry, I didn't mean to say that out loud."

The Commander shook her head. "So much power...inside of a child."

"A *child* you needed a lot of help from," Katie returned. "Look, if all you're going to do is talk down to me, then I think we're done here. I can find my own way back to the base."

There was no response.

Katie shot an icy glare at Elizabeth before brushing past her toward the trail.

"So you don't want your answers then?" The Commander called out.

Katie stopped in her tracks but didn't turn around. She wanted nothing to do with these people's mind games but the events of the night had only added to the questions she'd had. Still, she felt like this – the soldiers, Canada, the Reaper...the entire quest hadn't been the least bit fulfilling.

But as she glanced at the stars above, she thought of Troy and what he was doing without her tonight. She wondered what Nancy thought about the note she had left. She even wondered if her words to Reagan had done anything to change her sister. Suddenly, all of those other questions Katie had seemed much less important than the ones she had about the people she cared about. Maybe Nancy had been right all along.

"You know, I'm not sure I really care anymore," the blonde confidently replied. She gave herself a smile as she started walking away.

"You don't care to know about your powers?" Elizabeth yelled out. "I'd thought you'd at least want to know about that *thing* around your wrist?"

How does she...?! "What are you talking about?" Katie tried not to show her surprise but she almost fell over at the mention of the bracelet.

"I know that to the unattached, it can't be detected with the naked eye," Elizabeth continued. "But the energy the harness emits is unmistakable."

"Harness?" Katie said under her breath, trying not to glance at her wrist.

The Commander nodded. "I know that you have it...or does it have you? You certainly seem more damaged than the typical twenty-two year old American girl."

Katie finally turned and rushed back to stand face-to-face with the smiling Elizabeth. "Yeah, well that has *nothing* to do with a 'harness' or whatever, okay? So if you have something less-offensive to say..."

"I have plenty," Elizabeth returned. "You might not call it a harness and, though it's unlikely, you may not even be aware of its existence. But we've been tracking you for some time Flying Girl and we know that it has attached itself to you. Have you ever felt a strange sensation, warmth perhaps, just beneath your palm? It could also be in your chest or neck, generally anywhere you would normally detect a pulse. The wrist was just a guess..."

"How do you know that?"

Elizabeth looked straight into Katie's eyes. "Because we helped design them."

Katie wanted to ask a dozen more questions but she stood speechless. Soon there was one word reverberating in her head: *them*. She immediately thought of Theodore Bishop and hoped that his was the only other one. His bracelet, which 'unattached' itself from him after all the power from the Bankrow substation struck him down.

"I can see that I've finally regained your interest," the Commander continued. "I'd like to submit to you that the feeling is mutual. You see, that harness was always meant to give the holder enhanced abilities, but you...we never imagined you."

"How does it give a person powers?" Katie asked cautiously. After waiting for almost a year to know, she had never been more uncertain of whether she actually wanted the answer.

"Olympium."

"What?"

"Olympium," she repeated. "It's a naturally occurring element whose radiation has varied effects on those who come into contact with it. Improved eye sight, quicker healing, better agility and durability; these are just some of the things tied to Olympium exposure. That's why it's been so sought after."

"I've never heard of it," Katie returned. "Like, ever."

"Maybe not by name. It's been called so many things throughout history," Elizabeth replied. "It was only after the start of the twentieth century that we made sure it became a very poorly disseminated myth. All records of its discovery have been purged from every database, there is no current nor planned introduction of the element to the periodic table, and there are decidedly few alive who know of its existence. And even fewer that know where the remaining Olympium deposits are located."

Katie couldn't believe what she was hearing. "So wait, then why did you make the bracelet...err, harness? If you didn't want people to know about this stuff then why not leave it alone?"

"That is classified."

"Are you kidding me?" Katie groaned and followed Elizabeth as she began walking back toward the truck.

"Just understand that my job, and the job of our organization, is to ensure that the world remains balanced as it is," replied the Commander. "It's an imperfect balance, but it's one that must be kept to ensure the safety of every man, woman, and child around the world."

"Is that why you made me? Is that why you made Bishop?"

The Commander glanced back. "We didn't make you nor did we make Bishop, at least not intentionally. When I said that we oversaw the design of them, I meant the original design. The version of the harness that you have is well beyond our scope."

"So somebody else made this?" Katie held up her wrist.

"Yes."

"Who?"

"Classified," returned Elizabeth, much to the mounting frustration of the blonde.

"Right...Hey! You said the Reaper had an energy trail or something." Katie began. "Is he...?"

Elizabeth shook her head. "No. But you and Gillem do share a few similarities. For instance, there's a synthetic product running through his veins that does indeed contain traces of Olympium, only in much smaller quantities and in a more volatile state. Our analysts believe whatever experiment that produced him was likely meant to produce some sort of vaccine, likely a cure."

"For what?" Katie asked. "Oh...is that classified too?"

"No," replied Elizabeth. "As I said, Olympium exposure can help heal. For those afflicted with a currently incurable disease, the temptation to experiment with the element would be irresistible – even if they knew how dangerous it was. We've encountered this scenario a few times before, but they've never been successful...or produced an animal like Gillem."

One of the soldiers moved a body bag into Katie's line of sight and she quickly narrowed her eyes at Elizabeth. "So what about them? They sure didn't end up on the safe side of your program."

Elizabeth glanced at the bodies before turning back to Katie with a curious look. "Do you actually want the truth?"

"That would be a nice change," the blonde returned.

"One of those bodies belongs to Tyler Milbane, convicted of serial rape in 2001 in Wyoming," began Elizabeth. "Another is

Anton Virgil, convicted of a half dozen murders in Virginia spanning from 1997 to 2000."

"They're criminals?"

"Yes," she returned.

Katie wasn't sure what to say next. She stared at the bodies for a few moments more before turning her attention to the stoic woman in front of her. "How did they wind up in Canada?"

"Really? I thought that would have been obvious," the Commander returned. "We brought them here."

"What?" Katie said.

"I'm afraid that we haven't been completely honest with you. You see, we've had Gillem trapped in this area for more than just a week," the Commander continued. "It's been closer to a month actually."

"What?!" Katie shot back.

Elizabeth pointed to the tower. "Do you really think that we wouldn't have been able to track Gillem to this place? We've known about his lair for quite a while, even left him 'nibbles' on his doorstep when necessary."

"Oh my God, why?" Katie returned. "They may have been bad people but still!"

"We needed to evaluate him. Learn more about his abilities, patterns, and weaknesses," returned Elizabeth. "We needed to understand Olympium better and as long as he was contained and monitored, keeping him alive posed no threat to the surrounding residents. This park was closed, along with several other points along the shore..."

"Except to the innocent reporters who...wait, was she a criminal too?" Katie asked.

"No," returned the Commander. "They were actually a pair of nosy reports who managed to breach our perimeter. Hopefully the journalist will be willing to tell us exactly how that happened so we can address any weakness."

Katie didn't like the sound of that. Not at all. "You better not hurt her or...AGGGGGGHHHH!"

The blonde fell to the ground screaming as electric currents ripped through her body. She had been caught so off-guard by the revelations that she hadn't seen her remove the metal disk that was now on Katie's stomach, sending electric pulses throughout her body.

"Our tech team calls it a shock block," the Commander said. "We identified electricity as a possible weakness to the harnesses after your fight with Bishop."

Katie couldn't do anything but convulse on the ground. The bracelet began flashing as if an alarm had been sounded in her body. Elizabeth knelt down beside her, offering the slightest look of satisfaction before turning toward another truck that was approaching from the trail.

"We can't have people like you and Gillem loose amongst the public."

Chapter 32

Discoveries

She carefully slipped the blade between the window and seal, inching it from right to left in search of the weak point...

CLICK!

That was easy. She hoped finding Kline's toy would be so simple.

Paklovic slowly raised the window and surveyed the dark room. Empty. She reached in the small bag at her waist and slipped on the plastic sleeves to cover her rain soaked boots before sliding the bottom half of her body through the opening. Unlatching the hook from her belt, she released the bungee and quickly grabbed the inside of the window to pull herself the rest of the way in. She bounded past the bed, silently landing in a squat on the floor.

A musical beat seeped through the walls. The dark-haired female she had seen earlier through the balcony window was still awake. This would need to be done quickly.

Paklovic removed the tracking device and pushed in the button at its center. The vibration began immediately and held no matter which direction she...

Suddenly, she stopped turning. Paklovic took a step forward, then another, and another until the device was moving so fast that it nearly fell from her hands. She halted just short of a dresser and turned off the beacon. If it did what Kline said, then his trophy was likely sitting in the piece of furniture in front of her.

She slid the device back into her pouch and began carefully opening the drawers, beginning with the bottom. There was nothing there but shorts and tanktops. The middle drawer was equally disappointing. But when she opened the top drawer Paklovic's ears popped as though she were sitting on a rising plane. She moved closer to the open drawer and as she did she felt a mounting pressure against her face. She ignored the strange feeling and began searching through the soft underwear until her fingers ran against something warm and firm. Paklovic pushed everything in the drawer aside until she pulled out a rectangular box.

For a moment, she wondered whether to open it or not. After all, the 'harness' Kline had described was apparently of tremendous power. But surely this small trinket couldn't house anything like that. Could it? There was no lock or keyhole, so if she wanted to see for herself, she certainly could.

She ran her hands over the top of the box gently as if caressing it would satiate her curiosity. It didn't.

Paklovic placed the item on top of the dresser and removed the latch. As she slowly opened it, she lost track of where she was. The room suddenly felt distant to her, as though she were peeking in through the windows again. Her feet no longer felt the solidity of the ground. Her mind had floated her body away into some surreal hallucination.

But Paklovic had no desire to detour. She maneuvered her almost numb hands to where she knew the box lid was and shut it back, ending the peculiar episode.

Her senses quickly readjusted. It was quiet now. Where was the music? She realized that she was no longer alone in the room.

She went for the blade but was stopped as she felt an electric jolt plunge into her side.

~

"The suspect allegedly responsible for killing two police officers and a federal agent earlier today has finally been brought down inside of Meridian's Midtown district. Police have sectioned off..."

"We are still gathering information but initial reports say that the officer who was shot has been rushed to Meridian Medical Center for emergency surgery..."

~

He'd been waiting on surgery to finish for what felt like hours. There was a small part of Detective Wreings that refused to accept where he was. It was hard to focus on anything but the eerie feeling of déjà vu. Every sound reverberated in his ears. He couldn't tell whether he was actually hearing them or if they were the remnants from the day Mitchell died.

"Tobias, what's happening?"

Wreings closed his eyes as the memory of Cass' desperate cry pierced his ears.

"Tobias, is Mick okay?"

The detective suddenly realized that it wasn't his mind torturing him again. He turned to see a frightened Nadine Avery calling from down the hall. She hadn't yet pulled closed her umbrella and left a trail of water behind her.

"Nadine!" he replied as he shot up from the chair. He took a deep breath. No matter what was going on inside his head, he wasn't the one whose boyfriend just got shot through the vest. "I'm sorry, I guess I was in my own little...Hey, sit down. Let me get you a blanket or something..."

"I'm fine," she said. There was a laser-like focus in her eyes as she stared back at Wreings. He knew that look, he'd worn that look. Nadine had probably spent the time it took her to get to the hospital telling herself that everything was going to be okay. For her sake, Wreings hoped things worked out better for her. "Where is he?"

Wreings pointed at the operating room two doors down from where they stood. "They've got him in surgery right now."

Nadine nodded. She was struggling to hold back tears.

"What happened?" were the only words she managed to get out before getting choked up. The nurse quickly swallowed it back and tried to put on a brave face.

Wreings rubbed her shoulder before bringing her into his arms.

"I want to know what happened," Nadine continued firmly. "I don't want to hear about it on TV."

"Yeah, I get that. At least sit down," Wreings began, waiting for the nurse to take the chair before continuing. "We tracked down the guy who shot up the hospital garage this morning. He trapped himself inside Thumpers and when we cornered him he started shooting. A stray bullet hit Don through the vest."

Nadine's finger trembled as it pointed to different places on her upper body. Wreings knew exactly what she was asking. He sighed and hesitantly pointed to a spot on the left of his chest. The nurse closed her eyes and pressed her hand against her heart. "Oh dear Lord, please…"

Wreings wanted to say something comforting but the truth was that he was struggling himself. He watched as she hid her face with her hands. After a few moments of listening to Nadine's heavy sobs Wreings finally sat down in the chair next to her and rubbed her back. She quickly embraced him.

"I'm so glad that you're here," she said. "Mick would really appreciate that."

"Well, I'll tell him he owes me one once he's out," Wreings returned with a hopeful smile.

Nadine glanced up at the detective, showing a glimpse of appreciation through the tears. "Thank you."

Wreings nodded. "You don't need to thank me Nadine."

"Is the man who shot him…is he dead?"

The detective again nodded.

"Then *thank you* for that," returned the nurse.

Before Wreings could respond, he felt something vibrating between them. He checked his phone but it was Nadine who answered hers.

"Hi Laniella," she greeted. "Thank you. I'm…I'm just waiting I guess. No, Tobias is here with me. No, all the doctors are in surgery, I think…Thank you, we'll take all the prayers we can get. Thank you."

As Nadine hung up the phone Wreings looked over the notifications that had mounted while everything was going down. There were messages from Cass, LJ, his mom, and the Captain. He hated the days he was popular.

"That was LJ," the nurse began.

Wreings nodded. "Yeah, I..." He saw the door to the operating room open. Wreings immediately stood up when he saw a doctor emerge.

"Excuse me," the clean shaven man began. "Are any of you the family of Mr. Donnelly?"

"I'm his partner," Wreings replied stepping forward.

The doctor looked slightly embarrassed. "Oh, that works too..."

"No, not like that," returned Wreings.

"I'm Mick's girlfriend," Nadine managed to get out after clearing her throat. "His mother lives in Connecticut. That's the only biological family he's got."

The doctor hesitated for a moment and glanced down the hall. "His condition is stable."

Nadine finally breathed. "He's going to be okay then?"

"The bullet missed all the major organs and lodged in his shoulder. He did lose a lot of blood," the doctor continued. "He will likely have limited mobility in that shoulder, and some numbness until the nerves rebuild."

"But he's going to be okay?" Nadine asked again.

"Yes ma'am," replied the doctor.

Nadine smiled and fell back into the chair. "Thank you."

The doctor gave a courteous smile to both of them before disappearing down the hall. Wreings stood silently for a few moments, as if the doctor's assurances hadn't yet hit him. But when he saw the relief on Nadine's face he finally seemed to understand what he had just been told.

"Don's going to be okay," he muttered.

The nurse in front of him began nodding. She kept nodding as she leaned back in the chair.

"We're going to be okay," she said softly, rubbing her stomach with both hands.

Wreings immediately recognized the action. "Wait, Nadine, are you...?"

"Detective!"

He stopped his question short and again looked down the hall. Agent Roberts was waiting by the entryway.

"They said you were here. Do you have a moment?" he asked.

Wreings held up his finger to the agent and returned his attention to a still-nodding Nadine. He opened his mouth but didn't get the rest of the question out before the nurse waved it away.

"Go to work. My sister is already on her way," she said, adding a slight smile. "And yes, we are."

Wreings couldn't help but smile at the confirmation. "Jesus Christ," he replied before sharing a laugh with her. He shook his head as he thought about all the weird moments between him and his partner from the past few days. "I...wow!"

"I should kill him for not telling you," joked Nadine. "Now go. Get to work, Detective."

"Yeah," said Wreings distractedly. He looked back at Roberts, who had his arms crossed, leaning against the wall. "Call me if you need anything, okay?"

"I will."

Wreings left the nurse and headed toward the waiting FBI agent. Roberts greeted him with the look he had grown used to.

"How is your partner?"

Wreings sighed, still in disbelief from what Nadine had just said. "Looks like he's going to make it."

"Excellent, that is fortunate," Roberts returned.

"Tilte?" Wreings asked knowingly.

"He was not so fortunate," Roberts returned. "He was long dead before the ambulance arrived. But his death wasn't wasted."

"How's that?" Wreings asked.

"Aside from helping us find the secret room, the crates inside were from the shipping yards," continued Roberts. "With Tilte dead, we would have been back to square one. But now we have the physical evidence to link Gol to Franks. Though they were empty, we are taking it all back to our lab for closer inspection. If we can find any traces of the weapons we've already confiscated..."

"You'll finally put Gol down for good," Wreings finished.

Roberts nodded. "He and all of his associates will never see the outside of a federal prison."

"Great," replied Wreings. For some reason, more news of Gol's guilt didn't really move him. He looked back down the hall at the operating room and Nadine before turning back to Roberts. "So you guys are done?"

Agent Roberts stepped away from the wall with an uncertain look. "For the moment, it appears so."

The way he answered struck the detective as odd. "Is there something else?"

"What did he say to you?"

"Who?"

"Ezra Tilte," Roberts returned. "You were standing next to him and said he was trying to speak. Could you understand anything?"

Wreings thought back to that moment when he realized that Donnelly had been shot. His heart had been pounding, his limbs barely working, but his ears were still alert enough to pick up the final noises of the dying hitman.

Ka-kla-kli. That was how it sounded. "He was just spitting up blood," Wreings replied.

"Are you sure?" Roberts asked again, staring straight into the detective's eyes.

Wreings played the scene in his head one more time. "Look, I told you I..."

He stopped as the sound of Tilte's last breath reverberated in his ears.

Nnnuhhh. Maybe that wasn't a breath. The detective's mind worked quickly to put the two utterances together.

Kli-nnuhh. Kli-nuh. Kline?

"Detective?"

Wreings realized that Roberts was still waiting. He offered the agent a shrug. "Couldn't understand him."

Chapter 33

The Box

She'd only been conscious for five minutes, but the strain of screaming had left her breathless. Even though she was exhausted, Katie couldn't stop trying to get out of the nightmare she'd been thrown into. She slowly picked herself back up and drove her shoulder into the wall of the containment unit.

ZAP!

"Agh! Let me out!" she cried the moment she made contact. She felt the current of the electrified wall sting her side. Setting herself for another lunge, she hurled her fists at the wall, managing to leave two imprints in the steel before the shock struck her back once more.

The jolt sent Katie to the floor of the closet-like containment unit. She tried to stand back up but could only make it onto all fours. The blonde panted desperately.

"Let me out..." Katie said each word in between quick breaths and kept her eyes to the ground. She tried to ignore the feeling of the walls caving in on her. "Please, I just want to go home."

"That won't be possible."

Katie immediately pointed a glare upward. She could barely see anything but a few slivers of dark skin through the thin slits in the wall, but the harsh voice of the Commander was unmistakable.

"Why are you doing this?!" Katie demanded.

"I believe I've already told you," Elizabeth replied.

"I'm not a monster!" screamed the blonde angrily "Let me out!"

"No."

The Commander's tone didn't change. Even though Katie knew it was unlikely, she didn't stop trying to appeal to whatever humanity was there. "You don't understand. I can't be in here, please!"

"You're claustrophobic," Elizabeth began bluntly. "We're aware. This unit is only temporary until we can transport you to one of our facilities."

"Let me out!" Katie swung at the slits but was again knocked on her back.

"I just increased the deterrent by fifty percent," Elizabeth said over a series of loud beeps. "Seventy-five percent, now. Does it hurt?"

Katie didn't reply, she simply pointed her eyes back to the floor and began humming her tune.

"I promise, we have no intention of torturing you for some sadistic purpose, that's why we allowed your confinement to be outside. You've actually been an interesting study," Elizabeth continued.

"Why are you doing this?"

"Olympium is not one of the most dangerous substances on the planet - it *is* the most dangerous," Elizabeth returned. "There is no comparison. Just a trace amount of the substance has the potential to destroy an entire city if mixed with the right materials, a handful could destroy one of your largest states.

And your body is currently full of it. So you can understand why we need to take precautions."

"I didn't ask for these powers," Katie said. "I never wanted to be this, any of it! Even if what you're saying is true, you can't just lock me up because of it. I'm not a bomb!"

"Not yet. Olympium exposure doesn't just change you physically, it changes you mentally as well. Everyone who has come in contact with large quantities of pure Olympium - and survived - has also lost their hold on reality," said Elizabeth. "You've known a few cases yourself. Theodore Bishop, Bradley Gillem..."

"That's not fair!" Katie screamed.

"You of all people should know by now that life isn't fair," the Commander laughed.

"You don't know anything about me..."

"I actually know quite a bit, Ms. Cattrell. I know that you've spent more than half your life making appointments with therapists and grief counselors stemming from the death of Claire Elizabeth Cattrell, and later, Jonathan Nicholas Cattrell. You've also been diagnosed with a variety of anxiety disorders and have a history of incidents that more than confirm the potential for mental instability."

Katie couldn't hold back her rage. She punched the wall repeatedly, ignoring the counters of pain. "They were my parents! They were my parents! THEY WERE MY PARENTS!"

On the final strike, the blonde felt a greater electrical push back. She fell to the ground, gasping for air.

"One-hundred percent is not the maximum we can raise the deterrent," Elizabeth stated as she stepped back.

The blonde took a deep breath and picked herself up. She peered through the slits. The Commander was far enough back that she could see the dark scar that ran up her neck. To Katie's surprise, the look in Elizabeth's eyes wasn't as cold as she expected. Instead, there was a noticeable amount of fear on display.

"If I am so dangerous, why did you even ask me for help?" Katie said between breaths.

"Haven't you figured it out? I would have thought the clear evidence of preparation with the shock box would have made it obvious."

"You just wanted to capture me..." Katie gritted her teeth at the realization. She had been tricked. "You brought me here just to lock me away."

"When we first neutralized Gillem we realized that we not only needed to learn more about him, but he would also be an invaluable asset for your capture. The challenge was in keeping him active, but contained, until your arrival."

"So you fed him people?"

"*Convicted felons,*" Elizabeth returned, stepping closer to the box.

"And innocent people," Katie shot back.

"Oh, I didn't lie to you about the reporters," began Elizabeth. "As unfortunate as it was, their presence did give us more time."

"And more death..."

"Coming from a walking, talking weapon," Elizabeth's voice was incredulous. "A power like yours, unchecked or manipulated, could destroy us all, or at the very least, it could destroy you. It may not look like it now Ms. Cattrell, but you need us just as much as we need to understand you, Olympium, and the harness. In time you'll see that this arrangement will benefit all of us."

"Go to hell..."

There was a patch of static and Katie heard Elizabeth step away from the box.

"Report," she stated.

"Commander, we need your help at the filtration building," the voice of Trevor came through. "We may have a problem with the reporter."

"Handle it, Lieutenant," Elizabeth replied.

"I'm sorry sir, but I think you need to have a look at what's going on for yourself."

Elizabeth sighed. "I'm on my way. I'm starting to wish Gillem had taken her life too."

"If you hurt her..." Katie began fiercely.

"Senseless murder is not something we do. Besides, you're in no position to exact the threat of your words."

"Let me out of here!" cried the blonde. She waited for a reply but the Commander was already walking away. It didn't take long for Katie's mind to fall back into the slender spaces of her dark confines.

A few excruciating minutes passed until Katie heard the sounds of footsteps drawing closer. Katie wanted to scream for help, but her muscles felt paralyzed and weak.

"Is this it?"

At first, Katie thought it was her imagination, but she soon realized the voice belonged to the reporter.

"Yes."

That voice was definitely Trevor's.

"Open it…"

"Ms. Hajar, don't be foolish. This won't…"

"Stop talking and just open it!"

Suddenly, the dull electrical hum overhead stopped. She hesitated momentarily before pressing her hand against the wall in front of her. To her relief, it opened like a door.

She stumbled out onto the gravel.

Thank you!

Katie glanced to her left to see the sling-wearing Trevor. His good arm was in the air, and the holster at his side was empty. The trembling hands of the reporter had it aimed at the back of the Frenchman.

It took a moment to process the scene. She collected a much needed deep breath before turning toward the clearly frightened woman.

"Thank you," said Katie.

"You're her, aren't you?" the reporter questioned. "The one they call The Flying Girl?"

Katie nodded slowly.

"Thank you!" the reporter's face quickly cracked. She lowered the gun and shrank away from Trevor. "I don't know who these other people are, but I just want to get out of here," she said, looking back up at Katie through teary eyes. As the woman began to cry, the blonde realized that she could not only save her, but she was probably the only one that could. "Please help me."

It felt like all of her strength was rushing back into her body. For the first time since little Melody Riker refused to let her go, Katie didn't feel like a monster.

"It's okay," Katie replied, reaching out for the gun. "I just want to get out of here too. Here, let me have that."

The reporter nodded and handed it over as the blonde turned her attention to Trevor. He slowly retreated as Katie advanced toward him, but she stopped just short. Holding up the gun in front of his face, she ripped it apart and tossed it to the ground.

"I don't need this," she said menacingly, looking the Frenchman square in the eyes. Whatever fear he may have had when he saw the blonde carrying the gun toward him had already vanished and he was back to his usual, emotionless gaze. She wanted to tell him off more but knew it wasn't worth it.

She and the reporter needed to leave as quickly as possible. Katie turned her gaze toward the sky.

"Do you expect to just fly out of here?" Trevor said in that annoyingly cocky tone Katie had gotten so tired of.

That's the idea...

"Are you afraid of heights?" the blonde asked, turning to the reporter.

"No."

"Good, because we're going to..."

ZAP!

Whatever hit her felt worse than any of the shocks she'd taken from the box. The blonde was thrown back abruptly, skidding past gravel and concrete until she came to a painful stop against another building. She clenched her teeth as she writhed on the ground for the next few seconds.

What the hell was that?

"It would have been much less agonizing in the cage."

Katie looked up to see Elizabeth standing beyond the reporter and Trevor. In her hands was a large weapon that looked more like a cannon than it did a gun. She had it aimed directly at the blonde.

"We've had time to prepare for you," the Commander said before firing again, sending a softball-sized pulse of electrical energy hurtling toward Katie.

The blonde held her hands up instinctively but could only take the devastating hit again. Her bracelet began to light up. The shine seemed different however, almost reminiscent of how

Bishop's bracelet looked as he took the full power of the substation.

"You're crazy! Stop it!" the reporter said as she rushed over to Katie.

Elizabeth signaled something to Trevor, who gave a parting glare at Katie before hobbling away.

"I assure you Ms. Hajar," she began. "I am neither crazy nor interested in the continuation of this unchecked *thing* wandering free in the general populous. Now I wonder how much electricity would be required to neutralize that harness of yours..."

"Stop!" the reporter pleaded, acting as a shield in front of Katie.

"Move."

"Please, just stop..."

Elizabeth lowered the weapon for a moment before quickly aiming it at the reporter. "We have no plans to harm innocents. But containing the threat that lies behind you is our current number one priority and thus takes precedent over procedure. Now move..."

The reporter shook her head vehemently. "No!"

"Move!"

The reporter flinched, but she didn't budge.

The blonde caught her breath again and reached for the reporter's hand. "Lady, she's going to shoot you!"

"You saved my life," the woman returned. "And I'm pretty sure they want to kill me anyway. Whatever this is, they won't want anyone knowing about it."

That was a good point, but part of Katie felt like Elizabeth's words might be genuine. In some backwards way, the scarred woman wielding the weapon just a few yards away appeared to believe she was a good guy.

Under the flood lights of the complex, the shadow of the Commander stopped just feet away from them. She looked like someone who was frustrated but resigned to the decision she had made.

"So be it," she said. There was another loud zap before a round of energy surged toward them.

Katie pulled the reporter down with one hand and shot out an unexpected ball of energy from the other. It swallowed Elizabeth's shot and kept sprinting forward. The woman dived out of the way and then watched Katie's blast blow through the fence and surrounding trees.

"Whoa!" Katie muttered.

But Elizabeth was quick to her feet and several soldiers appeared from around the buildings. They needed to get out of there.

"Hold on," the blonde said as she picked up the reporter and leaped into the sky. The facility was soon a distant nightmare beyond the trees and the Toronto city lights.

They flew across dark waters and several tall buildings before she felt the reporter tapping her shoulder.

"Can we stop, please?"

Katie could barely hear the reporter's voice with how fast they were going. She slowed down and looked for a place to land. She eventually landed on the tallest in a grouping of buildings.

"Are you hurt?" she quickly asked as she let the reporter down. "I didn't mean to hold you so..."

"No, no it wasn't you!" the reporter replied. She rubbed the back of her neck and passed a grateful look toward the blonde. "I just needed a minute to breathe."

Breathing doesn't sound like a bad idea...

Katie turned away from the reporter to peer off the edge of the roof. Whatever city they were in reminded her a lot of Meridian. She saw bright towers off in the distance and roads that were lit on every corner. Only it didn't have any cranes or marks of the ongoing construction that she could readily see back home. And everything looked like it fit into grids.

"Where are we?" the reporter asked.

"I don't know," Katie shrugged.

The woman wandered over to join her on the ledge. "It's beautiful, wherever it is."

"Yeah."

The blonde reached into her pocket and realized that she didn't have her phone. Elizabeth had also taken her goggles and jacket.

"Who are they?" the reporter asked.

"I don't know," Katie answered somberly. "And I really don't know if I want to."

"Do you think they'll find us?"

"Maybe not you," Katie replied, glancing knowingly at her wrist.

"That man," the reporter continued. Her hands shook as she spoke. "The one who...the one who killed all those people. I thought there was something strange going on when they closed off the parks but I never..." She couldn't finish her words as she covered her tears with her hands. "And poor Dillon. He was only there because of me. I just wanted a better camera and now he's...he's dead because of me!"

Katie hesitated before rubbing the woman's back. "You didn't do anything wrong."

It surprised her to hear that sentence exit her mouth.

No matter how often Dr. Mack or others said it to her, Katie always felt that she was partly to blame for her parents' deaths, especially her father's. Katie had fallen apart after her mom died, leaving her father to mourn the loss of two of the three women in his life. That was as good a need to drink as any.

The reporter's sobs got weaker as she leaned into Katie. "I'd be dead too if it wasn't for you."

"I could say the same thing," the blonde quickly returned. "I don't know how long I could have lasted in that box."

The reporter nodded. "I saw the truck walking back with Trevor," she began. "When I asked him what was happening he said that everything was going to be okay. I didn't know what that meant. He took me to this building...it looked like an interrogation room of some kind. I took his gun as soon as he got close enough."

"Why didn't you just run?" Katie asked.

"I thought about it, but I was so scared," the woman replied. "Nothing around me made any sense. I thought that was a waste water facility but it looked like there was nothing but soldiers there and...the only thing I recognized was you."

"Really?"

"Yes, we've run stories about The Flying Girl of Meridian on CTV," the reporter began. "Not all of them have been good ones though..."

Katie sighed but smiled. "It's okay."

"I'm sorry!"

"No really, it's okay," Katie returned. "I guess I should just be stoked that I'm on TV in Canada."

"*Everyone* has heard about you. Anything you do, even if it's just a story about someone spotting you eating a chocolate bar on the corner of a roof," the reporter continued. "Gets bumped up to the front."

"Oh wow," Katie said with disbelief. "That's amazing...and terrifying. Actually, it's just terrifying."

The two shared a laugh for the first time that night.

"Tonya Hajar," the reporter said, offering her hand. "I've heard a few different names but I have to ask, do you actually go by The Flying Girl?"

Katie shook her head. "Someone came up with it, but it wasn't me."

"So what can I call you?" asked Tonya.

"A friend," Katie replied, shaking the hand of the reporter. "A lost one actually. I don't know if I'll be able to get you back to where you want to go…"

"I think I'm going to stay," said Tonya suddenly. She glanced at Katie with a somewhat unsure look. "Those people, whoever they are, they knew who I was. They probably know everything about me. I don't think I can go home."

"But you don't even know where you are," Katie returned.

"And neither do they."

The blonde couldn't find any fault in the logic.

"It's okay," Tonya continued. "A city with this kind of view can't be that bad, right?"

Chapter 34

Conclusions

The night had provided a natural high for Denard Kline. He entered his quarters with a jubilance he rarely enjoyed outside the confines of his own mind. Dinner with Slater had been an unbridled success. Any question about whether there might be an avenue to pursue with her was answered when she offered a warm embrace and the slightest touch of her lips to his cheek before she departed into the taxi.

Indeed, she seemed to be drawn in by his intellect and accomplishments as much as he was with her adoration. Whether she actually comprehended most of what he'd said was irrelevant. The jovial setting and conversation were the perfect way to celebrate a triumphant evening for Kline and a reminder of a life he had thus far not experienced.

He removed his suit jacket and laid it across the foot of the bed. There was a point in time when Kline had been worried that he wouldn't have the chance to realize his vision, especially after Theodore Bishop's presence had accelerated his plans. But fate had truly been on his side all along as The Flying Girl's energy signature had confirmed the harnesses had not been lost in the house fire.

"This will always be a game that favors the patient."

Kline looked behind him to see Gregor resetting the chess board on the small stand by his bed.

"It never matters how long you must play," the old man continued, periodically glancing at a young, bed-ridden boy. "Only that you are not defeated."

"What if I can't keep going?" the boy asked weakly.

"You have to keep going," he replied. "You understand that don't you, Mr. Kline?"

"Of course," Kline returned as the old man and the boy faded back into his past.

To think, he was once that crippled and scared boy, completely reliant on the likes of Garrison Kline and Dr. Krouse for his survival. Twelve years and now he was on the precipice of being an unchallenged king. The money from the weapons gambit had more than paid for the continued research into ending the fatal fragility of his condition. Perhaps the best part was that now there was no one that could prove that he was a part of it.

As he walked over to the balcony window, he recalled hearing Tilte's body hit the floor. His death completed the game. Now, the responsibility for the operation would end at the feet of Yannick Gol, whose unforgiveable trespass so many years ago made him the only scapegoat worthy of the trouble.

As he peered out into the rainy sky of Meridian, Kline's mind closed the chapter on what had been and drifted into the blank pages of what was surely to come.

He saw the enticing figure of Slater walking toward him in the reflection. Her bare feet whispered delicately on the wooden floor, her nightgown swaying with the movement of her hips. He waited patiently for her arms to wrap around his waist and her head to slide onto his back.

"Come to bed, Denard," she said.

But a flash of lightning killed the pleasant vision, leaving only himself and one other in the reflection of the glass. It took a few moments to realize that the figure behind him was real and Kline quickly turned to see a waiting Paklovic standing by the table.

"Did you find it?" Kline asked.

The assassin sighed before sliding a small rusted box onto the table. She took out the tracker, turned it on and placed it beside the box. The device nearly vibrated off the table. Kline was now brimming with delight. Nothing else mattered more than what resided inside.

He was about to remove the latch when he noticed how wary Paklovic was. He laughed at the uncharacteristically timid display. "You should never be so afraid of power, my..."

His words trailed off as he noticed a cut below Paklovic's eyepatch. As he took a step closer he realized that the cut was actually a scratch from someone's *fingernail*.

"What have you done?"

~

Katie didn't like flying during storms but she was ready to be home again. While it had been a short hop to Canada, the trip back to Meridian had turned into a much longer quest. The adrenaline had long worn off and weariness had begun to creep back in. Worse, she was starting to feel the cramping in her stomach, her signal she'd been exerting too much power.

The blonde thought she could see the signature oval lights of the Glasgow building through the curtain of rain. It was much harder to see without her goggles or hood to keep the wet hair back. But as Katie passed more familiar lights, she was happy to discover that she'd been right.

"Almost home," she said slowing down as she tried to gain her bearings. A crash of thunder helped her refocus and soon she was jetting off in the direction of her apartment.

It wasn't long until she felt the firm embrace of her roof again. She bent over and took several deep breaths in succession. Her lungs were burning as though she had just finished a relay. She hadn't flown straight for that long since the very first night she'd discovered her powers. A smile briefly danced across her face as she remembered shooting out the balcony window that night.

So much had changed since then.

Katie straightened her back and looked to the sky, letting the rain trickle over her weary face. She closed her eyes and listened. The rain was all she could hear at first but then she thought she heard the faint sound of a plane braving the weather. She looked around for a few seconds before spotting it over the interstate. She followed it with her eyes and concentrated. Her ears popped and soon the once faint engine was purring in her ears, completely drowning out the pattering of the rain against the roof.

It appeared that even more things were still changing for her.

Lightning lashed out in the sky prompting Katie to finally make her way down the stairwell. The first step she took echoed aggressively in her ears. She grimaced, covering them before taking the next step with caution. This time, the noise wasn't nearly as loud.

I'll get the hang of that one day.

"Laser beams and super-hearing, Nancy's going to flip…"

The blonde continued down the stairs until she finally reached her floor. After opening the door to the hall slowly, she trudged the rest of the way to her room.

"Shit!" she said as she realized that she didn't have her key either. With those soldiers still out there, they were definitely going to need to do more than just change the lock. But that was a problem for the future. Right now she needed food and a bed. She bent over gingerly to pick up the key they had taped to the bottom of the welcome mat.

Katie tried to open the door quietly. Hopefully Nancy had long gone to bed. The only light in the apartment came from the glow of Meridian outside the balcony. She navigated around the kitchen slowly, picking up a handful of snacks as she walked softly toward her room.

She'd passed the couches before she realized something felt strange. The feeling went almost unnoticed behind the fatigue and cramping, but it grew with each successive step she took. Something was wrong. Something was…

The other bracelet!

Katie dropped the food and quickly ran to her door. She never left the door open, but tonight she could see straight into her room. Her first thought turned toward the Commander and Trevor until her eyes fell to the horror that lay at her feet.

The motionless figure of Nancy was strewn on the floor. A stray light from the window highlighted a stab wound on her chest.

Katie took another step forward, her lips quivering. Her foot brushed against the Taser her friend kept in her purse.

"Nancy? Nancy, no..." she whispered and shook her head, hoping a denial would end the cruel nightmare. But the nagging feeling of an impending truth brought Katie to her knees.

She cradled Nancy, resting her friend's head on her shoulder.

"Nancy?" Katie spoke louder as if she were trying to wake her best friend from a cruel slumber. "Please Nancy, say something..."

But there was no reply. No hint of movement. Nothing. A lone tear fell from Katie's eye. More soon followed.

"Say something," Katie pleaded through her sobs. "Nancy, please, please, please...!"

Katie rocked back and forth, desperate to hear anything that would prove that this was all some mistake. She closed her eyes and listened for even the slightest hint of a breath. As a barrage of sounds flooded her ears, she was left with a pain greater than anything she'd ever felt before. After a few moments, the shaking blonde couldn't contain herself anymore.

Nancy was dead and Katie opened her mouth to release her sorrow. The only thing she heard as she wailed was the lonely beating of her broken heart.

To Be Concluded...

Identity

Detective Wreings didn't move from the doorway. He kept his eyes on the FBI agent that paced around his hotel room.

"You still haven't answered my question," said Wreings. "What are you doing *here*?"

"We thought this would be the best place to talk," Roberts replied.

The detective shook his head. "It's not."

Agent Roberts smiled slightly before pointing his eyes at the gun Wreings was holding. "I think it would help if we were both truthful to one another."

"What makes you think more than one of us has been lying?"

"Very good, Detective," Roberts returned. "But I know you were lying that night in the hospital. I could see it in your eyes. Ezra Tilte said something to you, a name perhaps?"

"Maybe," Wreings began. "But it's not like anything I could give you will change the case the Bureau already has against Gol."

Roberts shook his head. "Correct, but..." he paused with a knowing smile. "I'm not asking on behalf of the FBI."

Wreings clutched his gun tighter. "Who are you asking for then?"

"We don't have a name, not officially," Roberts returned. "But I can tell you that we want to make sure that those who would bring destruction to us all, be it intentionally or unintentionally, are locked away where they can do no harm. The man you're after, the one whose name I suspect slipped out of Tilte's mouth, is in possession of something very, very dangerous."

"And what is this thing?" Wreings asked.

"The power of The Flying Girl."

Roberts' answer was not what the detective expected. His grip on the gun loosened as he stared quizzically at the agent. "What are you talking about?"

"In due time," Roberts returned. "Once we…"

"You make it sound like we're already working together," Wreings cut off. "Who did you say you work for again?"

For the first time, Roberts' eyes left Wreings and turned toward the corner. The detective realized that in his suspicion of Roberts, he hadn't checked the parts of the room he couldn't see. He followed Roberts' gaze to find a woman in a black suit standing quietly in the shadows, her arms folded behind her back.

"Who the hell are you?" Wreings demanded as he pivoted his aim between her and Roberts.

She sighed and took a step into the light. She immediately reminded him of a soldier with her battle hardened expression. Her hair was cut military style and there was a deep scar spanning the length of her neck.

"You may call me Elizabeth," she replied plainly. "Put the gun down, Detective. I think we can help each other."

~~~~~~~~

Thank you for reading! If you enjoyed *Fallen*, please share your experience and help others enjoy this book too by:

Reviewing it on the site you purchased it on, your preferred book site, or your blog.

Recommending it to other readers on Goodreads, book clubs, book stores, etc. If you think a friend or someone you know would really like this story, *Fallen* is **lending-enabled** so feel free to share it with them.

If you're interested in learning more about Lennox McCaskill then connect online at:

Website: www.lennoxmccaskill.com

Facebook: https://www.facebook.com/lennoxmccaskill/

Twitter: https://twitter.com/LennoxMcCaskill

Instagram: lennoxmccaskill

Email: lennoxmccaskill@gmail.com